THE ABSOLVER

A MICHAEL THOMAS THRILLER

GAVIN REESE

LIQUID MIND PUBLISHING

Liquid Mind Publishing
This is a work of fiction. All characters, names, places and events are the product of the author's imagination or used fictitiously.

Although based on some portions of true events, this is a work of creative fiction. The characters and their names, along with the events, plots, and motives are the product of the author's imagination or are used fictionally. Any resemblance to actual persons, living or dead, business establishments, or locales is entirely coincidental.

Gavin Reese donates a portion of all his sales to non-profit organizations that benefit law enforcement professionals and veterans, their families, and the heirs, survivors, and memories of our Fallen Heroes. A portion of *The Debt Collectors* proceeds helps fund law enforcement organizations that counter narcoterrorism. A portion *The Misery Merchant* proceeds benefits organizations that improve the rescue, rehab, and recovery of sex trafficking victims. A portion of proceeds from *The Kizazi Murders* goes to help cold case homicide investigations in the Baltimore, Maryland, area.

More information is at gavinreese.com

ACCLAIM FOR GAVIN REESE_

The Absolver
By Gavin Reese

"'The Confession' is a short, jabbing novella that hits you like a throat punch. It will leave you thinking about the hard realities of the temporal and the eternal, and that's the best kind of fiction there is."
— Mike Maden, international bestselling author of the Drone Series and Tom Clancy's Jack Ryan, Jr., novels

"Written with a rare authenticity, Gavin Reese's 'The Absolver' hits hard and leaves an impression on both gut and heart. These pages also hold the promise of much more to come from this author. I know I'll be first in line to see where this story and character goes next."
—James Rollins, New York Times and international bestseller of the Sigma Force series

"Hums like a live wire with action, authenticity, and suspense to spare."
– NYT & USA Today Bestseller Michael Lister

MICHAEL THOMAS SERIES_

The Absolver
The Trafficker
The Bombmaker

For Mo Anam Cara, my mom, and everyone who believed in me.

INTRODUCTION_

The Absolver is the first book in my *Absolver Thriller Series.* Set in the same universe and timeline as the *Alex Landon Crime Series*, readers will eventually find some common ground between them.

Common themes. Common struggles. Common characters.

As with all my published works, this book is written to be read and understood as a stand-alone fiction. While readers will certainly pick up on details shared between my publications, it is not necessary to start reading from Book One.

This series uses fictional characters and events to explore questions that have plagued mankind since Cain and Abel: Does moral violence exist? To what limits? Who is entitled to vengeance, and when does God use man as an instrument to exact His own? When is it moral to take a human life, and when is our entitlement to dignity eclipsed by our detraction to the dignity of others?

More simply asked, what constitutes a *murder*, and what's a just and deserved *killing?*

Although this is a work of fiction, I used extensive research, facts, and real-life events to make this story seem *possible.* I hope the following chapters blur the lines between *fiction,* the *possible,* and the *probable.*

OATH OF THE ABSOLVER_

I, Michael Andrew Thomas, swear my allegiance to Almighty God with eternal faith in His Church and Holy Scriptures.

I obligate myself to equally care for the eternal welfare of all God's children.

I affirm that men infected with certain evils are bound for Hell without Final Absolution, which I willingly offer them as an act of eternal mercy.

I vow to offer Final Absolution to only those souls that may not be rehabilitated by any other means and only after establishing irrefutable knowledge of their grave mortal sins.

I vow to offer Final Absolution to only those who God identifies through His faithful servants placed over me, and to offer each Confession, Absolution, and Anointment.

I vow to endeavor to send God only souls fully absolved of their sins, prepared for His judgement and eternal entry into the Kingdom of Heaven.

I vow to willingly forfeit my mortal life or earthly freedom to vigorously protect the identity, actions, and purpose of myself and my fellow Absolvers.

I vow never, under any circumstance or duress, to betray this oath, my fellow Absolvers, or those God has appointed over me.

I acknowledge that my betrayal would scandalously support and defend the very evils I've vowed to defeat.

I swear these vows to Almighty God of my own free will, upon my mortal body, and with my eternal soul. Per Dominum nostrum (Through our Lord)...

PROLOGUE_

SUNDAY, 6:57 PM. THREE MONTHS AGO.
NEW YORK CITY.

"CAN we *trust* him with this burden?" Inside an expansive and dimly lit private office on the building's 20th floor, an aging Italian American sat in a plush leather chair and slowly wrung anxiety from his hands. He looked across his oversized mahogany desk and examined his subordinate's reaction. "This man you've found, can he *keep* our secrets, *and* do all we require of him? This isn't just some errand boy or street ruffian we're looking for." Even in the solitude of his secure office, he kept his voice down to protect their privacy. The bureaucrat expected his enemies and their spies could be found anywhere.

His subordinate exuded a relaxed confidence from one of two matching, brown leather armchairs placed across the desk. Briefly gazing out the large window to his left, the employee looked over the East River as though searching for careful and precise words. A sheer white fabric covered the windows, and although it muted the exterior view, the fabric prevented anyone from watching or photographing their interaction inside the office.

When he spoke, the subordinate's concerns revealed his relative lack of years and lesser ambitions. "He's devout, Opus Dai, in fact, just not the maniacal kind. He's a rather, *impersonal* man who doesn't enjoy human frivolities, so I'm confident he cannot be bought or bribed, even ignoring his ideology. His background is perfect for this kind of work, and I'm certain he will train our personnel in every facet of their appointed tasks." The employee nodded to reiterate his assertions. "There is no man better for our task, and I believe he stands without equal."

The mentor leaned forward in his chair and allowed a calculated exasperation to permeate his voice. "Yes, but can he be *trusted*? We can find dozens, maybe even *hundreds* of qualified men for the posting, but we must have someone we can trust *completely*. We're not just asking that he create and manage a clandestine training program. Even if he doesn't understand the full scope of our objectives, he will covertly help us change the world, the very composition of the human race for all the *rest of time*." His point made, he leaned back in his chair and tented his hands in front of his face. "So, we must first address this singular, paramount requirement: *can he...be trusted*?"

His subordinate nodded, glanced back to the East River, and again searched for conviction. After an appropriate contemplative pause, he met his mentor's gaze and finally provided reassurance. "I firmly believe so, *yes*. We *can* trust this man completely, even if we *don't* tell him everything we have planned for his recruits and graduates."

Leaning back in his chair, the aging mentor paused and stared at the ceiling. "We've thought that before, and we've been proven wrong. Even with your support and confidence in this man, our operations must remain compartmentalized. Give him no more detail than necessary, and certainly no more than we've discussed. Let him believe what he wants. He undoubtedly possesses a bright and deductive mind, so we must ensure he never knows what we *ultimately* intend his graduates to accomplish. He needs to remain ever-focused on the condition of the *trees*, rather than taking qualitative notice of the *forest* as a whole."

"Of course."

"You will also ensure he has no moral quandary with what he knows of our covert efforts. Our greatest danger will always be an insider. A self-avowed moralist who undergoes a change of heart can do far more damage than any external threat. Make sure to have that conversation with him, without *actually* having it."

"I've already taken care of that, sir. He's been training such men for decades to serve a secular purpose, but he's committed to *his* understanding of our course of action and to growing a cadre of men willing to serve a divine purpose. In his mind, his students will be employed in the Division of Intelligence and Counter-Espionage."

"Excellent," the aging bureaucrat chuckled. "He's not wrong, but he's not exactly right, now, is he? When will he be operational?"

The subordinate straightened his left jacket sleeve. "He assures me he requires no more than two months as he already had a property in mind for just this purpose. It would seem he's been just as divinely inspired as you, Your Eminence, and at almost the same exact time."

The older man smiled at the notion. "Then he may be just the man God intended us to find, and the perfect match you've proclaimed him to be. We must next finalize the first roster of recruits."

"That's nearing completion as we speak, sir."

"Very good, very good." The elder relaxed and stopped wringing his hands. "We'll soon have a dedicated force to go out into the world and truly do God's work. I only wish we'd come to understand His meaning much sooner. We could be so much further along by now."

His subordinate smiled and nodded. "This first class will have to make up for lost time, sir."

"*Centuries*," he countered. "They'll have to make up for lost centuries, Harold. Almost twenty of them, actually."

MONDAY, 11:30 AM. THREE MONTHS AGO_

BARRIO CIUDAD BOLIVAR. BOGOTÁ, COLUMBIA.

A COACH's whistle sounded from just down the hillside, and everyone working nearby sprang to life and hurried toward an austere outdoor kitchen. Michael Thomas wiped his hands across his brow and through his mop of mid-length, light brown hair. As the others hurried to receive their small share of the donated midday meal, he stole a few moments' rest and adjusted his black, short-sleeved shirt and its contrasting, starch-white *collarino.* The clerical tab that identified Roman Catholic priests worldwide had soaked through hours ago as he shuttled hundreds of donated cases of bottled water from a delivery truck to secure Red Cross shipping containers.

Michael's stomach growled, but there wasn't enough food to satisfy all the other stomachs present. Unlike his parishioners and the rest of the neighborhood, his pantry held a few days' rations. The recent heat wave had disrupted an already unstable power grid and crushing poverty had done its worst. Five of Michael's parishioners had lost their lives so far, and the local authorities did not know when the grid would resume consistent operation. Until the heat wave subsided and granted reprieve to the community's infrastructure, Michael expected to divide his time between aid work, grief counseling, and funeral services.

Alone for the moment, he sighed in quiet, perpetual frustration and looked back to the undisturbed pallets. Half the day had disappeared, but most of the work remained. *Back to it.* Michael moved back to the semi-trailer and up its makeshift plywood ramp. The expected sound of foot-falls crunching over the nearby gravel path wafted uphill after him. Ignoring the recurring and imminent pleading for another few moments, he entered the stifling trailer.

"Father Michael," a beautiful, familiar voice called out. Her French accent made mundane conversation interesting. "It's time for lunch! You've hauled enough water for one morning, don't you agree?"

"Not yet, Doctor, there's still too much work to be done," Michael yelled over his shoulder as he grabbed another plastic-wrapped case and heaved it up onto his shoulder. He turned back toward the trailer's open double doors and saw Doctor Merci Renard waited near the bottom of the shoddy ramp in baggy linen pants, a light denim work shirt, and a floppy white sun hat, all of which showed she, too, had been working hard in the day's heat. She held out a bottle of the same donated water Michael now labored to move.

"There is only so much one man can do, and you have already surpassed your quota for the day."

Although Michael suspected her olive skin and tall, striking figure transfixed most men, he most admired her inquisitive mind and philanthropic heart. His humanity, however, compelled him to tacitly acknowledge the beauty of her sincere, slightly lopsided smile and runner's physique. *As helpful as she is, I'm grateful she'll go back to France in another few months.* The ramp flexed beneath his descent, and Michael smiled and accepted the bottle as he stepped past her. "Thank you, Doctor, you're too kind."

"You've earned a bite or two, Father."

Michael nodded and deflected her compassion. "Do they need help passing out the rations?"

"Of course not, they have enough help, just as they do every day." She followed him to the container but stayed outside as he entered. "You'll soon become one of my patients if you don't come sit in the shade, eat some nourishment, and rehydrate. You may not believe me, but I am *not* known in my village for a compassionate bedside manner."

Michael stacked the case and stepped back outside. Doctor Renard walked beside him toward the makeshift kitchen and shaded eating area, but she maintained a respectful distance from him. After confirming everyone had been served, Michael accepted a food box comprised of a donated MRE. He followed the doctor to an empty picnic table. "Are there any new critical cases among your patients, Doctor Renard?"

"Please, Father, call me Merci."

"As soon as you call me Michael."

"I cannot do that," she scoffed as she sat across the table from him. "You're a *priest!* I'm only a medical doctor! My position proves little about my character, but yours says that you have dedicated your life in service to God and His children. That *deserves* the respect afforded by your title."

"I dunno," Michael replied off-handedly, "pretty sure I'm just an ordinary masochist." Michael crossed himself and quietly offered his gratitude before opening the food packaging. He glanced around and saw that most all the local refugees had already eaten and retreated back to cooler environs, which afforded them a semi-private meal together. "What inspired you to become a doctor?"

Merci shrugged as she picked through her own MRE. "My parents are both doctors, so it was always kind of expected. Even in France's socialized system, they have done well enough that I can work for half the year and volunteer in places like this for the other half."

"That's an incredible blessing, both for you and for those you help."

"I'll never equal the good this work gives to me. Here, I am relegated to first-aid, minor infections, and wound treatment, which isn't much. Even though I can only do a little thing for these people, what they do for me is *so much greater*." She settled on a package of crackers and peanut butter. "Until I began international relief work, I never knew intrinsic fulfillment, Father. I had felt 'accomplishment,' such as when I graduated medical school. I thought they were the same, but that is not true.

"There is no feeling," she continued, "no *emotion* like volunteering. I spend half the year helping people who can do *nothing* for me, and it feels, like, *magic*." Merci scrunched her shoulders and face, just for a moment, before drinking from a donated water bottle. "I imagine that's how you feel most all the time, yes? I mean, who can do *anything* for a priest, a man of God who has no Earthly needs, correct?"

"I don't think it's quite as glamorous or saintly as that." Michael eyed the contents of a package the MRE manufacturer claimed was beef stew.

He hoped stirring and Tabasco might improve it. "I'm just a man, and I have all the same issues as everyone else. I just don't have a mortgage and credit card payments, so I suppose that makes things easier, actually."

Merci rested her elbows on the table and shook her head. "No, I've met a lot of priests and clergy in my travels, and you're not like the others."

"How so?" Michael hoped for a protracted answer that would allow him to eat.

"You're much more, what's the word, *fiery*? Most of the ones I've met who are your age, they are not as, *passionate*. They've mellowed by then, I suppose." She chuckled at her backhanded compliment. "You know what I mean, Father, you must see it, too! You're out here with the younger men, while most of your peers have chosen to stay indoors and *manage* the efforts of those *working* in the trenches, yes?"

"I got into this work a little later in life than most," Michael conceded. "I still hope that one man can really make a difference, really *change* a community. A community changes a province. A province changes a nation. Maybe even the world." He risked a big sporkful of the mystery stew. *Nope, not beef. Maybe rat.*

"Some of your parishioners spoke about your efforts to build new infrastructure in the community. New wells and cisterns, with or without the help and financing from the Columbian government or the Church. That's a tall order, even for a Superman like you."

Michael blushed at the community's confidence, ignored her compliment, and chewed on the mystery meat for a moment. *I should feel guilty about being so attracted to her, but there's an ocean of difference between recognizing my humanity and degrading myself in sin. She could have altered the course of my life in years past, it's too late for that now.*

"The people can't wait for the government's permission and funding for essential services," Michael offered, "and I think there are some unique, uh, *opportunities* for the Church to work with corporate and philanthropic partners to improve things here, so, I want to pursue it. It's the right thing to do, and it's *unjust* for everyone with enough men and guns to control the water wells and resources. They shouldn't get to decide who's worthy of a drink and who goes thirsty."

"See?" She pointed at him with a peanut butter cracker. "Fiery, like I said."

Michael chuckled and shook his head. "Maybe the other priests are a bit more realistic about what they can influence and achieve."

"You're a dreamer *and* a man of action, Father Michael, the kind of man legends and folk songs are written about."

Michael laughed. "I've been pragmatic, and it only helped the status quo. I might be a dreamer, but I try to keep a solid base in reality."

"Do you really think the companies will support these projects if the government isn't forcing them to do so?"

"Companies need employees and customers, so they have a vested interest in the community's safety and security." Michael spread his arms to his sides to bring attention to their present environment. "You're here from a private aid organization, and I'm here from a faith-based organization. With corporate funding for this project, we could act much faster and reach much further."

Merci grimaced. "I don't trust companies to show that much compassion for strangers unless the government forces them, but I'm French, so I'm *always* a little cynical and untrusting, no?!" A self-deprecating smile spread across her face before she nibbled at another cracker. "What about the men we hired to guard water bottles with guns?"

"Predators will always hide among our neighbors, and I believe God allows moral violence, such as self-defense," Michael explained. "Modern governments concern me because they want a *monopoly* on violence by limiting how people can protect themselves. They alone want to decide *who* and *what* are worthy of defense."

Merci coyly smiled, cocked her head, and spoke between her remaining cracker nibbles. "That doesn't sound very much like '*turn the other cheek*,' Father. Are you a real priest?"

Michael grinned at her question. "Or, I'm the world's best and poorest actor."

"So, what does a priest who advocates personal sacrifice and 'moral violence' do for fun? When you're not constructing cisterns, I mean."

Michael smirked at the reaction he expected to elicit. "I teach martial arts for free at a neighborhood dojo."

"You take your 'moral violence' seriously, Father Michael! You are a veritable onion, a man with unexpected and endless layers! And, if I may add without agenda, a handsome one at that. There must've been a line of young matrons pursuing you with wedding veils in their back pockets!"

Michael blushed again. "In my former life, I devoted myself to police work and living my faith. I was almost married once," he off-handedly explained, suddenly unsure why he brought it up, "but I felt a much stronger commitment to God."

"You were a police officer? An American police officer with lots of guns, and a police uniform, and you *still* managed to avoid marriage?"

"Yes, but they only gave us a couple guns." Michael smiled at her assessment and avoided her latter question. *There's no reason to try explaining Catherine to her.* "American cops are nothing like what you see on international news networks. I went to college in a small town, and I became a cop there after I graduated."

"Did you go out, drive fast in your big police car, and arrest every indecency you found?" She ate another piece of cracker and peanut butter and smiled at her own joke.

"No, thankfully, I mostly got to help people, and I was training to become a detective when I resigned. I think they're called 'inspectors' in France."

"That's impressive! What is training like for inspectors in the U-S?"

"Some of it's predictable, like interviewing suspects, victims, and witnesses, and extra training on the laws. A lot of it, though, is stuff you wouldn't expect, at least, I didn't."

"Such as," Merci prodded between nibbles.

"Picking locks. Surveillance work. Following suspects to see where they go, what they do, who they meet. Using a team of detectives and their cars to trap a suspect inside theirs. Searching for hidden weapons and drugs in cars."

She again cocked her head to the side and eyed him suspiciously. "Were you training to be a spy?"

"No," Michael laughed, "spies have to be *good* at those things! I drove a police car, so everyone knew who I was and where to find me. I would have been the worst spy ever!"

"Well, with all that authority and weapons, you must have done something bad in your work as a police, yes? There must be something, Father Michael, for *you* to confess to *me*."

"Actually, yes, there is." He leaned close and spoke just above a whisper despite their relative privacy. "I *swear,* like, *a lot.* I might be addicted to the word 'fuck,' but I can still quit whenever I want!"

Merci snorted and spit a piece of cracker onto the table, so she slapped a hand over her mouth and laughed harder. Michael immediately grew self-conscious that they might have made a spectacle of themselves for the few volunteers around them. *People rightly expect different behavior from me.* He looked down at the table and sat a little farther back on the bench.

"Thank you for that, Father, I love laughing like that, even at my own expense!" She wiped tears and sweat from her face and smiled back at him. "So, in *all fucking seriousness,*" she quietly teased, "why did you leave the police and enter the priesthood?"

Michael adopted a less jovial tone. "I wanted to do more to help people, to improve the quality of life in my town, but, as a cop, I was kind of a Band-Aid."

"How do you mean that?"

"My friends and I would show up, intervene in the biggest problem we found, and then go intervene in someone else's problem without ever really fixing anything. We rushed off to the next problem, the next call, the next victim. Most people I met needed counsel and guidance to ease their long-term suffering. As a priest, I hoped to offer more permanent solutions." Their dialogue and obvious, mutual admiration reminded him of Catherine and revived his long-suppressed guilt. *If I'd ever married, it should have been her. I'm lucky to have loved her, and I wish things had turned out differently in her life. I'm happily married to the Church and to God, and I've got no interest in divorcing them. Not for Catherine, or Merci.*

"You've lived an incredible life already, Father, one that *my* father would say is destined for even greater things, for national service in political office, perhaps. Do you think you will rise through the Church to become *Pope* Michael, or maybe the American *President*?"

Michael shook his head. "No, we need someone better in those positions. I read a story once about Abraham Lincoln, the President during our Civil War. At a big dinner the night before an important battle, a Protestant pastor offered a blessing and asked God to be on 'our side' in battle. Lincoln didn't give the expected 'Amen,' so the pastor asked him about it later, why the *President* of the United States, the *Commander-in-Chief* of the Union Army, didn't want *God* on their side in such a clearly defined war with evil. Lincoln said he was fallible and would not always be just, so he preferred to pray that *he* found himself on *God's side.* That's the kind of men we need in political office, not dreamers and has-been cops like me."

Merci watched him for a long moment as though gazing deep into his soul. "I understand that your President Lincoln was also a man of great humility, Father. You might have more in common with him than you appreciate."

TUESDAY, 8:32 AM. THREE WEEKS AGO_

LA IGLESIA DE SAN FRANCISCO. BOGOTÁ, COLUMBIA.

INSIDE HIS PRIVATE, spartan living quarters, Michael reverently knelt on the stone floor with his eyes closed and his hands clasped just beneath his bowed head. To better organize his thoughts and emotions, he first allowed them to run amok, quieted their chaos, and then came to God in prayer. He expected to address the same topic he had wrestled with for months now: vengeance.

Michael often compared his past life as a cop to his present service as a priest. While working as a cop, he and his partners had been capable of swift and decisive action. They swooped in to aid victims, detain the accused, investigate allegations, make arrests, and deliver the aggressors to jail. *No longer,* he thought. *I wanted to provide long-term guidance, and I didn't realize how good I had it. With rare exception, I can no longer intervene to stop cruelty and malice, and I have to keep more secrets than a mob lawyer.*

Michael sighed and squeezed his eyes shut tighter. He pleaded for a quiet mind, but it wouldn't rest.

Instead of a Batman tool belt with gear to use against the aggressors, I now carry compassion, sympathy, and blind faith to offer victims, and, in fairness, the aggressors, as well. I understand that God hears our prayers and will take up vengeance in His own time and in His own way. Regardless of what I hear during confessionals, no matter how heinous, I cannot break that seal and tell the authorities what's happened, or who's responsible for it. And the victim can never expect to know or understand God's timing or reasoning for whatever does, or doesn't, happen. Oh, yeah, and 'everything happens for a reason,' which we mortals aren't capable of understanding, either.

Michael shook his head a little without realizing it.

It's no wonder people are leaving organized religions in droves; they can't accept the old arguments for blind faith. Contradictions throughout the Bible would suggest man is meant to enjoy righteous retribution and vengeance now and then. David didn't pray for Goliath to undergo an intrinsic, moral schism, he picked up a damned rock and killed the man for assaulting David and his people! Why is the modern era so afraid of just violence? Have the Church and the Holy See begun endorsing the U-N's mantra of monopolized, state-sponsored violence committed against its people?

Michael paused, inhaled a deep breath, and begged his mind to be still. *I'll have to get knee replacements if I don't pray soon...*

God, dear Heavenly Father, please settle my mind and give me spiritual guidance on this. I can't see how to support the Church teachings on revenge and justice when I can't even reconcile them myself with Your Holy Scriptures. I—

A light knock on the door interrupted him, and Michael opened his eyes but didn't rise. "Come in." Monsignor Medina, his typically unflappable supervisor, hurried inside. The concern on *his* face concerned Michael.

"Sorry to interrupt, Michael, pardon me," the man offered in Michael's native English. "Jesus Salinas wishes to see you. I explained you were busy and offered to help, but he's very distraught and only wants to talk to you. What shall I tell him?"

Michael rose and brushed off his knees. "Wait, which Jesus Salinas? Montes or Escobedo?"

"Escobedo. Montes won't darken our door until Christmas Mass. I suspect it has something to do with Escobedo's daughter."

"Of course, I can make time for him now."

Medina glanced down at the floor where Michael had knelt and frowned. "*Ay Dios mio!* What's this," his mentor asked with displeasure, almost betrayal, evident in his voice.

Following his mentor's gaze to the thick foam kneepads he used for private prayer, Michael shrugged. "Kneepads. God did a lot of great work, but he didn't design kneecaps to survive stone floors."

"Blasphemy," the man facetiously surmised. "You'll be lucky if they don't excommunicate you for easing your suffering."

Michael smirked at the monsignor's jest. "They've had far better reasons all along, so I don't think this will be the straw that does it."

"We'll see about that, right after *you* see what Jesus needs." His superior's tone reverted back to its normal, caring inflection as they entered the hallway together. "Please let me know if I may help either of you."

Michael nodded and walked ahead of the monsignor. He soon entered the back of the church and found his distraught parishioner seated alone in a small side chapel. Fluent in Spanish, he spoke the parishioner's native tongue. "Sir, how can I help you today?"

"Father Michael, I need your help," Jesus responded in Spanish. "I need your guidance, your counsel, and God's forgiveness." He wiped tears from his cheeks and dried them on his pants leg. "I want to do something, something *horrible,* and I had to come here first."

"Would you like to speak in the booth, or someplace more private?"

"I'd prefer to speak in here. If anyone from the neighborhood sees me walking into the confessional booth in tears, they'll think I've gone back to my old ways. I'm too proud, Father, but the old hens around here peck and squawk too much. They'll assume I've done something wrong again, and then my wife and mother will hear about it before I can even walk home.

"I used to do terrible things, Father," Jesus continued, "but that was a long time ago and I'm not that man anymore. I've been faithful to my wife for many years now, but the memories in this neighborhood are much longer. I hope you understand."

"Of course. How can I help you?"

"I have hate in my heart." His bottom lip quivered, and fresh tears fell on his cheeks. "My youngest daughter, Marta, she went out last night for the first time since her husband died. I heard her tell my wife that she just wanted to dance and feel like a woman again, that it'd been so long since she felt like anything but a widow and a mother."

Jesus paused a moment, slowed and deepened his breathing, and held back his emotions. "She went to a club not far from where we live, met a boy, well, I would have to admit a 'man,' if not for what he did. She sat in my kitchen this morning, *in tears*, Father, and told my wife about how *this animal*, how he drugged her and had his way with her. She woke up on the street, Father, on the *goddamned* street, like a *dog*, and she knew what he had done to her."

Michael leaned forward and placed a sympathetic hand on the man's shoulder, which approached the cultural limits on physical compassion unrelated men could show one another there. "I'm very sorry, Jesus, for what's happened to your baby girl. Take all the time you need, and I'll help however I can."

"She knows who he is, Father, and, because she doesn't know I overheard everything, *I* know who he is, too. I want to kill him, I really, really do. I want to make him hurt worse than he ever hurt anyone in his whole life, and I'd do it in a *second* if it could take my baby's pain away!"

"You have nothing to be sorry for, Jesus, you're feeling the way any father, any parent, would. The fact that you came *here* to talk to *me* instead of going out *there* to look for *him*, that tells me everything about the purity of your heart."

"It'd be so easy, Father, so quick. He stays just up the alley from the dojo where you teach at night. I could have killed him and been home before my wife even missed me. We might be poor, but I'm a very principled and resourceful man, Father. It would've been so, so easy..."

Michael paused and spoke in a more official capacity. "Romans 12:19 tells us that vengeance is best left to God. The unjust aggressor will answer for his sins, for the pain he caused your daughter and your family. We can be certain of that. We may not get to see it or even know that it's happened, but, *please*, take this to heart: God will make him answer for what he's done, for the misery and suffering left in his wake." *Please make my counsel feel more sincere and helpful to Jesus. It rings so hollow with me right now...*

The aging parishioner breathed in a deep breath and sighed. "I knew coming here might help keep me out of prison and, maybe, out of Hell. I hope this hatred subsides a bit, Father, *before* I see this man walking out on the streets."

Michael appreciated the man's candor, despite his insincerity in counseling him. "Thank you, Jesus, for trusting me, and for giving me the honor of helping you and your family through this difficult time." He paused, and Michael couldn't prevent his swelling outrage from taking advantage of his humanity. "Forgive me if I've already forgotten, but what did you say this *animal's* name was, again? The one who lives by my dojo?"

TUESDAY, 11:47 AM. THREE WEEKS AGO_

LA IGLESIA DE SAN FRANCISCO. BOGOTÁ, COLUMBIA.

WHEN HE FINISHED SPEAKING with Jesus Salinas Escobedo, Michael desperately needed his own spiritual guidance. *Maybe even a confession. I've got the same raw, vengeful emotions welling up inside me that sent Jesus here in the first place! All we accomplished was transferring his rage onto me.*

Within a few minutes, he learned that Monsignor Medina would be tied up on an errand outside the chapel for several hours. *I could do it. Escobedo, being the girl's father, he might not get away with it, but no one would think I had motive to target this monster. How many other people has he harmed over his life, and how many more will be victimized so long as he walks the Earth? He might even offer to harm me, which allows my self-defense, something that justifies using force against him. If I can find him, the hardest part will be convincing him that I'm a weak target and that I want to be left alone. Predators are great at reading people, that's how they survive. If he suspected I was ready for him, he'd move on to an easier target.*

Michael breathed deep and pushed back against his emotions.

In all fairness, all I've heard is what he's alleged *to have done. Most people leave that part out of the revenge business: a just actor would need evidence to corroborate the allegations and prove the crime and the aggres-*

sor's intent. With that in hand, though, I could make a very satisfying field trip into the barrio.

Michael considered a deliberate and unsafe detour back home from his dojo that night, and his planning inspired a call for help. Not in the form of backup and better weapons that he wanted but, instead, help from a reliable sounding board and devout moral compass. He strode back to the small office he shared with Monsignor Medina and retrieved his international calling card from the belly drawer of a simple desk. Michael pulled a chair over so that he could see out into the chapel through the open office doorway. He needed to both keep watch for parishioners in-need and avoid having them overhear his conversation. *People tend not to react well to the reality that priests need counselors and guidance. Turns out we're people, too, just like everyone else.*

He dialed the international code, entered his parent's home telephone number, and sat forward in the chair. His elbows rested on his knees, and Michael held the desk phone's receiver up to his ear. The call picked up on the second ring.

"Harry's Roadkill Café, home of The Hundred-and-One Uses for a Dead Cat Buffet."

Michael chuckled. "Hey, Pop, it's me. You need caller-ID if you're gonna keep that up. What if the bishop calls to check up on mom?"

"There's two kinds of people in the world, Michael, those that have fun and those that hate them for it. Besides, Sam would laugh at that joke, it's one of his favorites."

"Mom's not home, is she?"

"No, she's out with your Aunt Jacqui. Good to hear from you, son! They got a statue built in your honor yet?"

"No, I don't think they've broken ground on the project, but I'll keep you posted."

His father's inflection changed in response to Michael's. "Everything alright down there? Do you need something?"

"I need an ear, and you're about the best man for the job."

"The well musta run pretty damned dry if that's true. What's troubling you, son?"

Michael spent the next fifteen minutes running through a brief synopsis of what he'd learned that morning, excluding, of course, any victim or confessor identification that would have violated the Seal of the Confessional. "So, that's where I'm at, dad. How am I supposed to guide him when I struggle with the same questions? I don't know how to reconcile that, pop, not when I want to leave class tonight and go back to hunting monsters in dark and lonely places."

His father sighed, and Michael feared that he had transferred his heavy heart. "Son, you're asking tough questions that humanity has wrestled with for all time. The bad news is that there's no new information. All we have for guidance are the *old ways*, and anyone that says otherwise wants you to buy something. Vengeance is *not* justice, no matter how much lipstick you put on that pig. What you're talking about, what your parishioner is talking about, is just that: vengeance. I'm sure you're guiding him the right way, regardless of your personal feelings, but that remains the righteous answer. He needs to convince his daughter to go to the police before *all* the evidence is lost, which, I suspect, is the same thing that Michael the Cop would have recommended. You called it right, these are allegations. Anyone who wants to take up the reciprocity business had damned well better think twice about it. Mankind's corruptible systems of justice are themselves flawed, and they fall well short of God's *perfect* system of judgment, right? So, if it's wrong in The People's Court, you can rest assured it's gonna be damned wrong in God's Court. Have faith and know that God will work this out in His time and His way."

Michael sighed at the redundant counsel. *There's gotta be a reasonable middle ground here somewhere.* He forced a smile and hoped his father heard it in his voice. "Thanks for listening, Pop. Things are a little different down here, so they probably won't go to the cops. I'll see what I can do."

"I'll pray that it works out for all of you." His father's voice warmed Michael's heart. "It won't be easy to make it, but I'm cooking green chili chicken stew if you want to stop in for supper tonight."

Michael smiled and leaned back in the chair. "I'll charter the first plane outta here, but feel free to start without me."

"The leftovers are always better, anyway. I'll let your mother know you called. For five bucks, I'll tell her you're having the time of your life in the land of milk and honey. She worries, you know."

Michael glanced up and saw several folks seated in pews around the chapel. "Put it on my tab. Looks like I've got some folks waiting."

"We pray for you every day, son, and I'll keep your concerns close to my heart. Be safe back there, and don't do anything I wouldn't do. We love you, Michael."

"Thanks, pop. Tell mom I'm thinking about her. I love you all, too."

Michael hung up the receiver and stood. He stuffed his problems back down into their proverbial box and set them aside for another time, perhaps another day. His parishioners needed him, and he had to be at his best to serve them. *At the end of the day, I'm just a visitor here. These folks are born and buried within a few blocks of this church. I owe them everything I can muster for the little time that I'm here.*

TUESDAY, 7:27 PM. THREE WEEKS AGO_

LA IGLESIA DE SAN FRANCISCO. BOGOTÁ, COLUMBIA.

Monsignor Medina returned from his appointed rounds and errands out in the neighborhood, but Michael couldn't secure a private audience with him until they met for their evening meal. They kept with the Columbian practice of a small supper, and the clerics shared buttered arepas and hot chocolate that night. Michael's troubles remained in his heart, however, and not in his stomach. *As my superior, I should discuss this with Medina, but I've only been here for six months, and I've never sought such personal counsel from him before.*

"We haven't spoken since this morning, Father Michael. Are there any special needs among our parishioners?"

Perfect. He's gonna break the ice for me. "Well, actually, that's something I need to discuss with you, Monsignor. I'm struggling with what's happened, but I don't want to risk breaking the Seal of the Confessional."

"Let's start by taking all the identities out of our discussion. Never mind *who* told you *what,* just discuss with me what's troubling *you.* That should maintain your strict confidence."

Michael hesitated and considered the best and most careful explanation. *I prefer him to assume that Jesus Salinas is struggling with these ideas for now.* "My trouble, Monsignor, is that I'm wrestling with the concept of vengeance and the morality of violence."

"Go on."

"I've offered counsel to a parishioner that they are to avoid vengeance at all costs, and that God has demanded that we leave the revenge business up to Him alone, while we are incapable of understanding how, when, where, and why God chooses to act or not to act against those who wrong us."

His mentor buttered another arepa and waved his hand for Michael to continue.

"But, there are numerous examples of God's favored people, the blessed and anointed personalities throughout the scriptures who took vengeance into their own hands. They turned their righteous indignation into violence, and God rewarded them for it."

"Such as David and Goliath?"

"Yes, for starters."

"Michael, these are basic questions directly answered by the Catechisms, specifically in dealing with the Fifth Commandment, 'You shall not kill.' How is it that you're troubled by such a simple topic?"

"I mean the contrary examples throughout the holy scriptures that suggest otherwise. 'O Lord, God of vengeance, O God of vengeance, shine forth!'" Michael had prepared for a possible showdown with Medina.

Medina swallowed a bit of arepa. "'You shall not take vengeance or bear a grudge against the sons of your own people, but you shall *love your neighbor* as yourself. *I am the Lord*.'"

"'Since God *indeed* considers it just to *repay with affliction those who afflict you*.'"

Medina now set down his arepa and frowned. "'Beloved, never avenge yourselves, but leave it to the wrath of God, for it is written, 'Vengeance is mine, I will repay, *says the Lord*.'" The monsignor emphasized his last phrase by pointing down at the table several times at its keywords.

He thinks his quotation from Romans should have ended this, Michael realized, but pressed his point further. "God was with Jehoshaphat, Monsignor, while he placed forces in all the fortified garrisons in the land of Judah, and He honored him with great riches for his faithfulness! Did God bless him for building those garrisons and filling them with *cheek-turning meekness*, or for filling them with *sword-wielding warriors?*"

"We are *commanded*, by the *scriptures* and by the *Church*, to *set aside our wrath*!"

"And what of David," Michael continued. "When the Philistines deprived the Israelites of blacksmiths to prevent them from possessing weapons, they sharpened their plows, axes, and sickles, and then followed David into battle against those who'd wronged them!"

"*God* led them and He used David and the Israelites as a tool to execute *His own* intent!"

"And when Moses said, 'Arm your men for war, that they may go against Midian to execute the Lord's vengeance,' what of that? Must we have the word of a prophet before acting?"

"Father Michael, I—"

"And Psalm 58:10, Monsignor! 'The righteous will rejoice when he sees the vengeance; he will bathe his feet in the blood of the wicked! Men will say surely there is a reward for the righteous!' How do you reconcile that?! It's counter to the teachings, I'll give you that, but it's not ambiguous at all!"

Medina leaned forward in his chair and drew himself closer to Michael. "Your rhetoric borders on heresy, Father Michael! You *know* what the Church teaches, what the Catechism says on this! The scriptures have been misinterpreted and maliciously used for *centuries* by those who wish to substantiate and promote their own cause! That is *not* the way of God, and it *will not* be the way we counsel His children in my chapel!"

Casting his eyes down to the floor, Michael sighed and shook his head. He'd hoped his intended dialogue would not have devolved into a shouting match of juxtaposed and entrenched ideology. "I'm sorry, Monsignor, if I've somehow been unclear. I *didn't* counsel him to take revenge. I'm asking, *for me*, how to reconcile the difference between the Catechism and the scriptures themselves."

Medina's eyes reduced to angry slivers, and disdain dripped from his voice when he spoke. *"Father Michael Andrew Thomas, just who the hell do you think you are?* Who are you to question the teachings of God, and of His beloved Church, of the Pope, God's appointed representative on this Earth and the divine successor to Saint Peter?" The man stood, shook his head, and looked away from Michael in disgust. "Now would be a good time for you to devote yourself to study and prayer. If we both pray hard enough, maybe we can figure out what God wants done with you."

TUESDAY, 11:32 PM. THREE WEEKS AGO_

LA IGLESIA DE SAN FRANCISCO. BOGOTÁ, COLUMBIA.

AFTER COMPLETING HIS NIGHTLY PRAYERS, known to Catholics worldwide as the *Compline*, Michael stepped from the small stone and stucco chapel and strode into the darkness of the surrounding barrio. *Tonight's the first time I've recited Saint Michael's prayer since I turned in my badge and quit being a cop. I'll have to keep it in the rotation if I make a habit of doing cop-ish stuff again.* Michael's Krav Maga class ended between eight and eight-thirty twice a week, so it wasn't unusual for him to be out late at night. His parishioners seldom needed his help at night, so it was odd that he walked *away* from the relative safety of his chapel. Despite the familiarity with his neighborhood "patrol," Michael required only a few dozen steps into the nearest alleyway to re-evaluate his vulnerability. *The last time I did this, I had two guns, a vest, a radio, friends, and all the cop tools. Tonight, I've got a collarino and a cassock.* He smiled when a realization buoyed his confidence. *For the fights that really matter, this clerical garb is far superior weaponry. Besides, what's the point of spending fifteen years in martial arts training if I can't quietly watch over the defenseless?* Although he had a general idea where to find his specific target, Michael didn't have an exact location. Addresses and mail service didn't exist there, and the barrio looked different at night, even the area he knew reasonably well near the dojo.

One half of Michael hoped to find the urchin responsible for the woman's suffering, and the other half prayed his overnight exploits would dissuade him from making this a habit. *If I could intervene like as a cop, just without their special arrest authority, then I could deal with these problems without violating my oath to protect the Seal of the Confessional. Or I might just drive myself mad trying to manifest solutions that can't exist.* Each passing block steeled his resolve that he could safely navigate the neighborhood at night. At minimum, he could act as a roving patrol and make himself available to help anyone who needed it. *If someone really wants to push the issue, I can work on changing the priorities of anyone trolling for victims in here at night.*

Michael stopped at the intersection of two alleys, each equally dark and foreboding. He held a deep breath, closed his eyes, and listened for movement worth investigating. His past cop life had taught him that desperation never slept, and few did while living in his grasp. Despite the hour, Michael estimated half the local population was still awake, and those asleep now wouldn't be so for long. No one else braved the dark and dangerous world outside their shanties, and Michael considered the insanity of refuting their example. *What if I did find this kid, what then? He probably won't talk to me about what he's done or been accused of doing, and I can't drag him by his ear to the police station to confess his crimes like some Dennis the Menace character. What the hell* am *I doing?*

Unguided by suspicious noise among the relative, late-night din, Michael opened his eyes and searched what he could see of the shadows in every direction. He had never personally encountered a poorer neighborhood. The local inhabitants had used all available space and materials to erect tenement shelters, but nothing here constituted a traditional "house." He'd been told the local construction materials succumbed to the wind, rain, and repeated burglaries several times each year, and anything as sturdy as tin siding often migrated from one shanty to another whenever opportunity allowed its theft and relocation.

Movement drew Michael's attention deep into the alley to his left. Someone, probably a man, stepped into the glow of a warming fire and then disappeared back into darkness. A light *splash* echoed down the alley. He was far enough away that Michael couldn't determine if the man drew closer or was walking away.

With nothing else to interest him, Michael moved off in that direction.

He stole periodic glimpses through the nooks and crannies as he stalked past the shanties, and the extreme poverty comforted him. *If any baddie in the barrio got their hands on a firearm, they'd rob markets and people with money, not their neighbors' small share of nothing. The most dangerous things will be knives, maybe a pipe or a bat, but, mostly, it'll be numbers. Two opponents are easy enough to defeat with the right spacing and surprise, but three gets tough. I have to run from four, at least far enough to spread them out and pick them off. If it comes to that, I'll make quick examples of the first two to make sure their friends want no part of it.*

Michael stopped and tucked himself back into the darkness near where he thought the man had crossed in front of a small fire. This stretch of alley was little wider than Michael's arm span, but its shadows and anonymity compelled him to pay attention to the surroundings. A sense of claustrophobia unusually welled up in his chest and throat, and he took in a slow, deep breath to suppress it. *If I survive the consequences of my own actions tonight, I can credit my confidence and awareness. If I fail, I'll blame my arrogance.* His fear reminded him that frogs cooked in similar fashion. *Small changes alter your perspective until it's too late. If the danger around me increases slowly enough, I'll never appreciate the intensity of my problems.*

THURSDAY, 8:57 PM. TWO WEEKS AGO_

BARRIO CIUDAD BOLIVAR. BOGOTÁ, COLUMBIA.

Just inside the entrance to the abandoned building he used as a dojo, Michael stuffed his gear and training equipment into a large duffel bag. He slung it over his left shoulder and followed the last of his Krav Maga students out the open entrance. They politely parted ways, and Michael strolled along the main road for several blocks. Once all his students were out of sight, he backtracked toward the dojo and turned right to walk through a narrow, darkened alleyway. He repositioned the duffel bag so it rode on his back with its strap over one shoulder and across his chest. *If anyone recognizes me out here, it'd be easy enough to claim I'm out visiting a sick parishioner.*

Michael had made nightly treks out into the neighborhood, which had helped define what he hoped to accomplish. He first intended to merely intervene and help anyone who needed it but now, after about a dozen such back-alley forays, Michael hoped to take the victims' place. He wanted the predators and local thugs to find him instead of his parishioners. *Predators go to work just like everyone else, and I can be the kind of victim that inspires a new career path.*

That first quiet night had helped familiarize him with the barrio and where he might find trouble. Although several men approached him over the following nights, Michael's awareness and confidence had prevented any conflict. Just as other mammalian predators recognize each other, all three potential adversaries had melted into the background once they drew close enough to interact with him. Just the difference in his posture identified him as a threat, and they could have assumed he had a gun or weapon by the way he carried himself. In response, Michael altered his behavior patterns, slouched his shoulders, took smaller, more cautious steps, and tried to present the persona that local criminals sought. A slight limp helped sell the image of a reasonably feeble target.

Each footfall away from his makeshift dojo allowed Michael to transition further into his "victim" character. Before he had taken more than a few dozen measured steps into the isolated alley, Monsignor Medina emerged from a doorway just ahead and to his left. He saw his supervisor first, but Michael had nowhere to hide and couldn't avoid interaction. Surprise swept over Medina's face when they made eye contact.

"Father Michael, what are you doing out here? It isn't safe out here, especially for an obvious foreigner. Some of the people walking these alleys won't care that you're a priest if they want something you have."

"I just need to clear my head," Michael weakly offered. "Class wasn't very productive tonight, and I thought a walk might be good."

"Then I should join you on your way." Medina fell beside him, and the pair took up most of the alley's width. "It hasn't been so long since you were a police officer. You should understand the dangers this place poses after sunset."

Michael nodded his unavoidable agreement. "If it's safe enough for our parishioners to live here, we should feel compelled to walk here just as they do."

"That's very romantic and idealistic, Michael, but look around. We're the only ones foolish enough to be out alone after dark. All the sheep are inside with the safety of friends and family, and all the wolves are waiting to prey on the stragglers. You understand all this, so I presume some specific purpose drives your conduct."

Michael avoided his monsignor's gaze as they walked, and their silence ground on his conscience. *He's waiting for me to respond, which is a great interrogation technique against people who don't appreciate it.* "I just wanted to clear my head, Monsignor, but I don't mind if the evils in here felt some of the intimidation they wield against everyone else."

"So, what happens after you're beaten and stabbed with a rusty screwdriver, or worse? Have you thought that through? By what just and holy plan do you intend to convince the aspiring murderers to turn their life over to God? Good men have struggled with this since the dawn of time, but, if you have the answer, you should share it with the world."

Michael swallowed his righteous indignation and questioned how much to reveal. *The man's nearly a pacifist, so he'll never understand inviting danger to stop it.* "The criminals and thugs have been running this *barrio* for generations, *Jefe*." He kept his voice down despite the emotion coursing through his veins. "All the care, compassion, and prayers of our predecessors have done nothing to change that! Can we allow the mere threat of *potential* violence to keep us indoors, leaving the worst parts of society unchallenged and free to prey upon victims? I don't believe God calls us to stay safe and protected while wolves stalk our flock."

"You're not a policeman anymore, Michael. You gave up the badge and the gun, and it's come time to abandon the mindset, as well. Police *can't* be priests, and *priests* can't be *police*. You've got only a *collarino* and *big balls* to protect you." He reached over and unzipped the very top of Michael's thin athletic jacket and exposed his starch-white collar tab. "I see you've chosen to keep all three of them hidden. Now, must I remind you the people you wish to intimidate are *also* God's children whom we're called to serve equally?"

Michael ignored the Sunday school lecture. "The local police refuse to patrol these alleyways and streets, and our flock is left to fend for themselves every night." He stopped and turned to Medina, who responded in kind. The narrow alleyway seemed even tighter now. "It's like you're a visitor in your own city, and you've turned the streets over to the worst criminals imaginable!"

Medina inhaled and stepped even closer to Michael. He spoke with the hushed anger of a father forced to discipline his child in public. "Your arrogance is typical of an American tourist. *You* know what's best, you're the *only* brave one out here sacrificing for the people, and you're *too willing* to tell the rest of us *everything* we've been doing wrong all these years. You can leave and go home when it finally gets *too dangerous*, when your life is *finally* jeopardized, or when the lives of your *family* are finally threatened. Oh, wait, that's right, you don't *have* any family in danger here, do you? The thugs that run this neighborhood can't get to your mother, your sister, your father. They can only get to *you*, and I envy the freedom in that. Your actions here won't cost the lives, or *safety*, or *dignity* of anyone you care about, but you don't understand that. You look down on the rest of us who *do* have something to lose here."

"Monsignor, I meant no—"

"*Shut up!* I got my first death threat while you were still shitting your pants, so I won't allow you to criticize me based on your reckless fantasies!" He stepped a half-step back and lowered his voice. "The difference between us is that I refuse to allow my loved ones to answer for my part in this fight."

Michael nodded his understanding. *He's right that I'm risking myself, but we're not alike.*

The elder cleric softened his tone but stayed close to Michael. "The fact that you're here alone, in such a dismal and desperate part of God's Earth, that's a blessing *and* a curse. Don't think, not even for a second, that I don't know *exactly* what you're doing out here, or that I haven't done the very same thing for the very same reasons." He held Michael's gaze and nodded just slightly. "A decade ago, I would've joined you out here, and I still might today if the consequences weren't so terrible. As it is, with what my sister and her children have to lose in this *barrio*, I can't do anything but pray for you from inside the chapel, both for your safety and that God changes your heart."

Medina briefly pointed a finger at Michael's exposed clerical collar as he continued. "Don't bother hiding your collarino because you think it will dissuade them. The men you're after will offer no quarter or mercy because you're a priest. If anything, you might incite their wrath. Many blame God for their lot in this life and, by extension, *you*. You're not the first man of God to enter this slum to avenge those we care about. You also won't be the last of us to pray for God's forgiveness, Michael. Vengeance is His alone, but you already know that, and you're out here in spite of it."

Michael merely nodded. *No point in denying any of it.*

Medina stepped back and offered a more conversational tone. "Be safe, Father Michael, and remember there's never just one of them. In my experience, the second one you see is usually the one to worry about." He took a few steps toward the chapel, stopped, and turned back to Michael once more. "I'll wait up because I want to know that you're safe, even if you don't care for your own welfare. I'll wait until dawn to call the police and the *enterrador* to help find you."

"I'll do my best to disappoint you, Monsignor."

Medina nodded and stepped off into the darkness. "That's what concerns me, Michael."

FRIDAY, 12:46 AM. TWO WEEKS AGO_

LA IGLESIA DE SAN FRANCISCO. BOGOTÁ, COLUMBIA.

Michael snuck through the Saint Francis chapel and to his shared living quarters behind it. Light leaked out around the aging door, and his stomach dropped a little as though he'd again broken his high school curfew. He scanned the room as he stepped inside, and a single floor lamp dimly lit the space. As promised, Medina sat on a simple wood rocking chair next to a mismatched wood table. The monsignor held a half-empty glass of lager in his hand, which he placed on the table as Michael pulled the door shut and joined him inside the quaint living room.

Medina made a show of looking at his watch and letting relief visibly wash over his face. "I'll tell the police *and* the undertaker they'll have to wait to meet you another night."

"Perhaps," Michael sheepishly replied while approaching his mentor. *I really have no idea how this is gonna go.* He sat on a rickety wooden chair across the small table from Medina. "I'm sorry for not putting more faith and trust in you, Monsignor, and I should've—"

"You've said too much already," Medina waved away the apology. "I forgave you while I was still shouting."

"Good, well, *thank you,* and good night." Michael started toward his private room.

"Where do you think you're going? Just because I forgave you, that doesn't mean we're finished dealing with this." Medina downed a gulp of his beer, wiped his chin, and returned the glass to on the small table. "What happened back there in the alleys populated with predators, prey, and a priest?"

"Nothing. I didn't find anyone that needed help. Didn't hear anyone calling out."

"And, presumably, you didn't find the man you thought you were looking for?"

"No," Michael quickly replied, "I did not."

"Many things might keep a man like that away. Jail, prison, unexpected death." The elder cleric smirked. "Perhaps he heard a *vigilante priest* wished to offer his last rites, and he fled the country to change his ways."

Michael clearly understood his message. *He isn't trying to stop me, but he won't do anything to stick his neck out for me on this, either.* "I think he's probably landed himself in jail or someone else killed him."

Medina leaned back in the rocking chair and crossed his arms over his chest. "Interesting choice of words: someone *else...killed* him. Has He already told you how this will end?" Michael's superior pointed up to the heavens just to clarify who "He" was.

"That's not what I meant, but, in my experience, the end is usually up to *him*. The bad man, not God."

"On behalf of God Himself, I am compelled to remind you that He can intervene in anything He chooses to."

"I agree, but my experience has shown me that God does not often make that choice, at least not that I can directly point to, and certainly not as much as our parishioners deserve His direct help."

"You're lucky I don't wish to turn you in to the archdiocese, Michael. Some areas of your faith require serious examination. The small miracles mean the most, and you're focused on the big, life-altering examples. Evil will always walk among us, and the devil will always get a say in human events. If you demand absolute proof of His power, mercy, and love, I fear you'll soon find yourself in a position in which you need them all *very badly*."

"I don't doubt any of that, Monsignor, I only doubt that He actively works all the time. I think God spends more time watching what we do with the circumstances we create, and the ones He puts before us, and then judges how we react to them. He can do anything He wants, but I believe He focuses more on our exercise of free will and how we live our lives."

"You're lucky I like you, Michael," Medina announced and finished his beer. "It wasn't that long ago that the Church burned people at the stake for less heresy. However, your secret's safe with me. For now."

Michael started off toward his private bedroom. "Peace be with you."

"And with your spirit." The monsignor's suspicious gaze didn't match his tone. "I'll keep the undertaker on stand-by. Lucky for you, the *enterrador's* a patient man. He'll wait."

WEDNESDAY, 11:51 PM.
PRESENT DAY_

BARRIO CIUDAD BOLIVAR. BOGOTÁ,
COLUMBIA.

MICHAEL AGAIN WANDERED the darkened streets and narrow alleys in one of Bogotá's most prolific slums. A clerical shirt and collar hid beneath a black nylon athletic jacket and black pants. His worn-out running shoes couldn't protect him from hidden puddles, but he expected to need their traction and stability at any moment. He carefully picked his way through meandering, rutted dirt alleys to avoid mysterious, pooled liquids and piled feces, both canine and human. Even at this late hour, he heard hushed conversations on every block, as well as domestic arguments, and the occasional, muffled cries of hungry and unhappy children. Watchful, distrusting eyes periodically stared back at him from behind the tin and cardboard walls that passed as housing construction in this part of the city. *Every night that I hunt increases the odds that I'll find what I'm looking for.* The specific object of his efforts hadn't yet shown himself, so Michael had settled on manifesting an equitable substitute.

He stopped at the next intersection and searched for recognizable landmarks. *Hell, I can't make anything out, and I have no idea where I am. That's dangerous in Beverly Hills and far worse here. Just one reference point and I can be on my way.* Michael glanced down all four available routes and found each of them equally dark, narrow, and uphill. *I'm standing near the rough center of a trough, a 'kill box.' They're called that for a reason...*

Michael turned right and strode uphill to the nearest high ground to orient himself back to the chapel. As he reached the midpoint between intersections, Michael's fight-or-flight response kicked in. He reflexively slowed and paid greater attention to his surroundings. *Someone's nearby.* Michael stuck to the center of the tight footpath to ensure he had equal reaction time to threats from either side, but the encroaching shanties complicated his effort. A glance behind him confirmed no one was following. *Not yet anyway. These guys almost always work in pairs. They're better off splitting more frequent profits, and not many victims fight back if they're outnumbered.*

Threat right! Michael saw the man just before he spoke because his clothing was darker than the shadows that concealed him. Adrenaline dumped into Michael's veins, and he fought to conceal the reaction.

"Alto," the shadow gruffly commanded. *Stop.*

Michael quickly glanced to his left to ensure he didn't step into a second, unseen adversary while backing away from this one. Most humans are right-handed, so the man should've hidden on Michael's weaker left side if he were alone. *He's got a partner somewhere close, or he wouldn't have given up that advantage!*

Michael swallowed hard against the lump in his throat. *"Puedo ayudarle, señor?" Can I help you, sir?*

The man materialized from a shadow and stepped forward into the dim moonlight. He looked rough and no more than a few years younger than Michael. *He doesn't show any fear or apprehension. He's confident that he knows what he's doing and how this will go. Where's the partner hiding?!*

"Dame todo, ahora." The well-practiced words fell easily off his tongue. *Give me everything, now.*

"Espera, dejame ayudarte," Michael replied with both hands up in front of his chest, just about shoulder height. He knew most people would misunderstand his posture as a "surrender position." Those well-versed in the technology of empty hand combat knew better.

"¡Dame, todo, ahora!" He took another step forward, and Michael pressed his back against a corrugated metal shanty. Movement from the aggressor's right pocket confirmed Michael's assumption that he was

armed. He withdrew a large, hidden blade and recklessly displayed it before pressing closer to his target.

Just as he'd practiced thousands of times in training, Michael thrust his left hand out to block and control the man's right forearm and simultaneously landed a devastating throat punch with his right fist. The shock of overwhelming and unexpected force stunted the robber's advance. Without pausing, Michael controlled the man's knife hand, broke his wrist, and turned the blade in on his attacker; in that same fraction of a second, he stepped back and loaded his right leg, which Michael used to deliver a knee strike into their mass of hands and plunge the blade deep into his opponent's abdomen. The knife stopped when its oversized hilt prevented further penetration. The crippling blow thrust the robber up off his feet before gravity yanked him down into a heap on the hardpacked dirt alley.

hhuuuurrrhhhhhh

Michael released his grip, stepped a dozen feet away, and stayed back long enough to ensure he stayed down. The entire confrontation lasted single-digit seconds, and enough adrenaline coursed through Michael that he tasted metal in mouth and checked to see if he was hurt. Moonlight reflected off the knife's handle as it protruded out from the felled attacker. The wound audibly gurgled around the handle. Michael expected the man to scream, but he suspected the long blade may have punctured a lung. *Can't yell without positive pressure in your chest. Can't breathe either.* Michael forced his eyes open wider and glanced around to break up the tunnel vision that naturally formed during critical incidents. With no other threats around them, he focused back on his would-be mugger. *Nothing, no one. This asshole was* really *alone.*

A large, dark pool emanated out from beneath the man, and the knife trembled with the man's labored, futile breathing. He laid back on the alley dirt and lightly touched the handle with his right hand.

"No hagas eso," Michael warned, *"te desangrarás." Don't do that, you'll bleed out.*

He dropped his hand, and Michael knew he didn't have much time. *He will die soon, even if this had happened in a fully staffed operating room. Paramedics don't respond to this neighborhood. Instead, the government sends in clean-up crews and evidence collection after the fact. He's D-R-T, even if he doesn't know it yet. "No tiene mucho tiempo.* Do you believe in God?" He asked the question in English and hoped to use his native language. He didn't respond and his face showed no comprehension. *Yep, he's for-sure Dead-Right-There. There's only one thing I can do to help him now.* "*¿Crees en Dios?*"

"*Sí,*" the dying man uttered and nodded his head.

Michael unzipped the top of his black athletic jacket to reveal his starch-white collarino. "*Soy un clerigo. ¿Me dejaras ayudarte ahora?" I'm a priest. Will you let me help you now?* The downed man answered with a simple nod and closed his eyes for a moment. Moonlight glinted off tears that fell down the sides of his face. "*¿Me permitirás orar por ti? ¿Puedo pedirle a Dios que te perdone por tus pecados?" Will you allow me to pray for you? Can I ask God to forgive your sins?*

The man nodded again; this time much weaker than the last. Beneath the light of a full, late-summer moon and surrounded by the fetid stench of the desperate Ciudad Bolivar slum and its shanties, Father Michael Thomas crouched in an anonymous alley over an equally anonymous and dying man. He held the man's hands, both as an act of comfort and to keep him from taking the weapon back. *He's too weak to fulfill the full sacrament of confession, contrition, and absolution, but we have time for to ask God to forgive his sins and absolve his soul.*

Michael finished the hurried prayers as his assailant's soul irretrievably slipped from its mortal shell. He looked at the man's body, closed its eyelids, and crossed its arms over the chest. His hands began trembling as he stood up and looked around. One life had just been threatened and another taken, and not another soul had bothered to investigate. *My corpse could be laying there just as easily as his is now.* Michael briefly considered his lack of animosity for the man. *I hope God forgives his trespasses and spares him the eternal damnation we all deserve. This may be the very pinnacle of my service to God in this lifetime.* He stood there for a long moment and waited for something to happen.

Once it became clear that no one else had called for help, Michael inhaled a deep, calming breath to counter the remaining adrenaline and walked away to go call the cops on himself. *God may have put me here in that exact moment to call my assailant home and ensure that he never victimized anyone else again. I really hope He doesn't make a habit out of this.*

SATURDAY, 6:34 PM_

Inbound Approach to Runway 26, Sunport International Airport. Albuquerque, New Mexico.

MICHAEL LOOKED out a small window of the Learjet 36A as it descended toward Albuquerque's international airport. The official diplomatic transport had been configured to the Vatican's specifications with seats for seven passengers, excluding the two-man flight crew in the separate and secured cockpit. Despite the capacity, Michael shared the opulent cabin with only his luggage and his thoughts.

The past two nights had offered little sleep and no real rest, but not for the reasons Michael had expected. His adversary's attempt to stab and rob Michael defined him as the suspect in their encounter, especially to the *Semper Cop* portion of Michael's brain. *I don't feel guilty about killing him, or even about allowing myself to be attacked. That's no different than when I walked foot patrol through dark alleys in Silver City. He got what he deserved, I know that rationally, but I feel guilty for* not *feeling guilty. I took a man's life. I should be wrought with sorrow and regret. What kind of monster am I?*

As the plane approached its assigned runway, Michael replayed segments of that night. Despite the late hour, he'd walked to the nearest police station and reported the man's passing. The cops had recognized and respected Michael's collarino, so they allowed him to return to the scene without the indignity of handcuffs. They hadn't even called out a detective. Michael gave his statement to the uniformed lieutenant, who claimed to know the dead man on sight as a dangerous lifelong criminal. *A recidivist. When I pushed the black-and-white bumper around Silver City, I only knew the pastors, the neighborhood watch captains, and the problems. Mostly the problems, they were the ones I spent most of my time with.*

Within an hour, the police had taken him back to his chapel, where Monsignor Medina had again waited up for him. His mentor had shown no surprise when Michael and the cops revealed the killing to him. In fact, he showed no emotion at all. *I had expected some sort of anger at the attention it would bring to the chapel. At least an 'I told you so,' or some indication that his fear and apprehension about my actions had been justified. He hasn't offered two unnecessary words to me since, not even after the Church granted his emergency reassignment request to send me back home to my family's chapel.*

Michael also thought about Merci, Doctor Renard, just as the jet's back wheels struck the asphalt runway.

THUMP

I didn't get to explain any of this in person, Michael thought as the plane rapidly slowed. *I won't know if the other Red Cross volunteers delivered my letter unless Merci's willing to contact me. If not, I'll just have to accept that God didn't want it to happen. I'd like to tell her my side before she makes a judgment call from whatever she hears in the barrio. I shouldn't care so much about what she thinks.* He sighed and watched the environment slow outside his window. *Any esteem she holds for me is so heavily rooted in my calling that she'd never have the same interest in Michael the Husband that she does in Father Michael the Priest.*

The pilot's heavy, northern-Italian accent projected through the cabin's speakers as the plane began taxiing. "Welcome to Albuquerque, Father Michael, and welcome home. We hope you enjoyed the flight and our short layover in Mexico City for fuel. One of the charter aviation companies here has graciously allowed us to make use of their hangar, so we won't have to go through the hustle and bustle of the larger terminals to your right. We'll stop in the private hangar in a moment, and a Customs official will meet us there to go over our paperwork and belongings as necessary. On behalf of the co-pilot and myself, we wish you safe travels and a blessed stay in the Land of Enchantment. Peace be with you."

"And with your spirit," Michael replied toward the closed cockpit doors, even though the pilot could not hear him. "I'll be much more at peace once I know what's to become of me," he uttered to himself. "No one gets whisked back home on a diplomatic jet for awards and commendations. This whole thing feels like consequences are coming."

Michael unfastened his seat belt for the first time since leaving Mexico City and again looked out the window as the jet slowly rolled into the private hangar. A uniformed *Immigration & Customs Enforcement* official stood alongside a beloved old friend, an aging overweight Hispanic man. Relief washed over Michael's heart. *He still looks like Jerry Garcia's Halloween costume!*

Although he didn't intend to suppress his wide smile, Michael's innate cynicism quickly drove it from his face as he questioned the man's foreshadowing presence. Monsignor Eduardo Hernandez, "H," had been a part of Michael's entire life since birth and baptism. Even if the end of his clerical service and employment would soon follow, Hernandez's presence inspired a fleeting moment of happiness. *Monsignor Medina didn't tell me what to expect from all this, he just gave me the written travel orders. H gave my first communion and convinced me to go into the priesthood. If the archdiocese wants me to spill my guts, he's the perfect man to run the interrogation.* Michael sighed. *I'm looking forward to finding out what everyone else has planned for me.*

The plane softly stopped, and its engines shut down as the pilot emerged from the cockpit. He smiled at Michael and opened the outer hatch, but Michael remained seated until he'd finished. The interior cabin was too short for him to fully stand, even though he measured but 5'11". *There are a few times I'm grateful to have never been 6'2".* A conversation between the pilot and a Customs official wafted into the cabin, so he rose, retrieved his two duffel bags from a small compartment near the hatch, and stepped down out of the plane. Hernandez smiled at him, but it was the greeting of a tired and worried friend, not the unreserved joy he'd always known from his lifelong mentor. The ICE official gave his declarations manifest a cursory examination. He asked no questions and didn't open his passport. "Thank you, Father, and welcome home." The man reached out his hand, which Michael accepted and shook.

"Thank you, and thank you for your service. Peace be with you."

"And with your spirit, Father." The official crisply turned around and strode away from them, so Michael dropped his bags and embraced Hernandez.

His mentor sighed. "Welcome home, Michael," Hernandez uttered while they hugged. "I'm so very sorry for the circumstances, but I'm also so grateful to God that you're safe and well."

The men released one another, and Michael retrieved his luggage. "As long as I have to answer to a monsignor, H, I'm glad it's gonna be you for a while." Three days of unanswered questions sprang to the front of Michael's mind, and he glanced around to make sure no one would overhear their conversation. "I've been in some kind of communication time-out. My monsignor in Bogotá even forbade me from speaking with anyone else about what's happened! Has anyone talked to my family? Do they know anything about what happened, or that I'm even back in the U-S? What the hell am I doing back here, anyway, if the Columbian authorities had no interest in pursuing charges against me? All I got was a written order that I was reassigned to San Miguel and leaving on the next flight home!"

"Well, one thing at a time," H offered as they walked toward the hangar's parking lot. "No, no one's talked to your family, at least as far as I know, and I think I would be their *first* phone call if they heard the news. As far as what you're doing here, I'm not sure *anyone's* sure. At least not yet. This whole thing is new for everyone involved, so we're all sorting out what needs to be done, and, also, what can be overlooked and forgotten."

"I think I'm owed at least some sort of explanation about what they're thinking. I'm not sure if I'm being saved or executed here, H."

"Well, let's not go getting ahead of ourselves, Michael," he abruptly remarked as they exited the hangar. "Nothing like that's happening here, and I'm not so sure there's any concern about negative consequence or repercussions from this. I mean, all men, even those of the cloth, have the right to defend themselves from violence and harm."

"Then why does it feel like I'm being scolded? It's like my monsignor in Bogotá told me to wait until my father gets home, and then sent me to you for a good, proper lashing. I didn't even know the Vatican had aircraft."

"They don't, publicly, anyway," Hernandez explained. "The pope always makes a show of flying commercial on Alitalia and such, but, when they need people and things moved about quietly, they have a small fleet that goes far and fast. Don't forget that the Vatican is overseen by the Holy See. Just like every other nation, they've got ambassadors, diplomatic pouches, documents, and people that get legal protections under the Geneva Convention. You wouldn't want to put state secrets in the overhead bin on a commercial flight, would you?"

"Of course not, I guess I'd just never considered the need."

"How was it," H asked through a broad, Cheshire Cat smile. "The plane, I mean?"

"It was pretty great," Michael reluctantly acknowledged. "A real table, soft leather seats, and actual legroom. And no layover in weird airports I'd never choose to stop in. If I could skip the suspicious circumstances, I'd be happy to fly like that again."

"If you start killing people every time you want to go somewhere, you'll have much bigger problems than just worrying about your job!"

Michael and his mentor both laughed at the gallows humor. Even as a teen, he'd enjoyed H's dark comedy. H had served in the Army just after high school, but he'd rarely spoken of it. When Michael became a cop, he saw that same jaded humor in all his coworkers and realized Hernandez had likely developed it over time and trauma. *Just like the rest of us faced with the repeated choice to laugh or cry. Laugh now, cry later. Preferably into a tall glass of whiskey.*

"Come on, Michael, let's get you back to Santa Fe for some well-deserved rest," Hernandez offered as they approached a beige, aging sedan that had been assigned to their beloved San Miguel Chapel for the past two decades.

"I haven't talked to my folks for almost a week, how are they doing?"

"Your mother, well, she's pretty much the same from what I can tell. Not getting too much worse, just not getting any better. Your father, ever the caretaker, refuses to admit she won't make a complete recovery someday. I think he'll accept nothing less, and, quite frankly, I worry about how he'll react when God calls your mother home."

"So, nothing's really changed?"

"No," Hernandez replied, "not really." He opened the trunk, and Michael dropped his duffels inside. "You wanna stop at *Sadies, El Pinto,* or *what*? What've you missed the most?"

"I need to see my parents, H. They need to hear this from me, not from someone in the archdiocese grapevine." Michael gently closed the trunk and heavily pressed down to overcome the car's familiar resistance. "They know too many people for this to stay quiet. So, how about the *Gordo's* drive-through on the way home. I'll buy."

"*Oooo,* excellent choice, best stuffed sopapillas in the world! Green chili and family, no better New Mexico than that."

MONDAY, 0803 HOURS_

ARCHDIOCESE OF SANTA FE.
ALBUQUERQUE, NM

MICHAEL FOLLOWED HIS MENTOR, Monsignor Hernandez, through a dimly lit hallway on the second, less-public floor of the Archdiocese of Santa Fe. Sconces high on the dark brown walls directed soft light upward to the coffered, light cream ceiling. The long, tacit hallway seemed to glow from above, which had likely been the decorator's intent. *This hallway's always had a distinct, rich aroma, but I've never been able to place it.* Michael breathed in deep through his nose as he walked. *It smells like tradition. And history.* His steps noticeably sank into the plush Berber carpeting and kept even their purposeful strides silent. Michael expected this allowed the daily efforts of the Archdiocese to politely go on without disturbing the influential few who worked nearby.

Even if he hadn't been urgently summoned there, Michael would have been wearing his black cassock and collarino. *My assignment to a prestigious and historic church like San Miguel Chapel demands the traditional clerical garb.* He now dutifully followed Hernandez to whatever fate awaited him and didn't want to be dismissed in something as irreverent as a black button-down shirt.

"This way, Michael." The aging monsignor checked his wristwatch and lightly shook it as though he hoped the watch was broken. "We're almost there, and almost on time, I think." The back of the taller man's black tunic lightly took flight in his ample wake, while his legs mercilessly mushed the front of the garment onward. Staying up with Hernandez required effort from the shorter man, even though Michael stood nearly six feet tall.

If my fate's already been decided, there's nothing I can do to positively change it, Michael told himself. *Hell, I'll be lucky if they even let me stay Catholic after everything that's happened.* He shook his head at his own melodrama. *They won't actually deprive me of the sacraments over this. The Holy See and the Vatican don't excommunicate people for killings, not even for murders. I just need to believe my imminent dismissal isn't the worst thing they can do to me, but, for them, it's probably just a run-of-the-mill 'loss of clerical status.'*

They strode past a small group of older men, who each looked at them with a mix of curiosity and concern. *There are few Catholic emergencies worth our rush, after all.* Michael self-consciously avoided their eye contact. Toward the end of the hallway, Hernandez stopped in front of a heavy solid wood door and firmly rapped on it twice.

"Enter," an unfamiliar voice called out from the other side.

Hernandez pulled the heavy door open and stepped aside.

Michael nodded at his beloved mentor and strode into the room. *This finally resembles the consequence it feels like.* Four old men in black cassocks sat in a line of matching dark leather chairs on the other side of a long, heavy wood table. Their clerical robes matched his own and gave Michael no indication of their position in the Church hierarchy. No one smiled at him or directed Michael to sit in the lone empty chair opposite them. Presuming its intent, he approached and reverently stood next to the chair and waited for their permission.

"Please, sit," the man to his far left offered, and Michael realized he'd been the one who had granted them admittance to the room.

Michael sat, but deliberately maintained a stoic, upright posture. *I've nothing to be ashamed of, and I won't leave here with a sad heart and hanging head.*

"You understand why you're here today, Father Michael?" The same man spoke while the others remained silent and stared at him as though attempting to examine his very soul.

"Not explicitly," he replied, "but I assume it's because of the recent events in Bogotá."

"Yes," Far Left confirmed. "We hoped you would openly discuss that with us."

"To what end," Michael inquired. "What is it that you hope to accomplish by doing that, sir? I'm sorry, I don't even know your name."

"Peter."

"Peter...?"

"Yes. Just, Peter."

"And what is it you do for the church," Michael asked. "I don't believe we've met before."

"I do, well, whatever's necessary, Father Michael, and today," he raised his hands just above the table, palms up, and motioned toward Michael, "well, today, I'm here to speak with you."

"And, if I may, Father Peter, who are your colleagues?"

A second, elderly man, seated next to the apparent leader, raised his hand. "I'm Father Peter."

The third merely smiled and nodded at Michael. "I, too, am Father Peter."

"So, I suppose that means," Michael waved his right hand toward the fourth man, a middle-aged Latino also dressed in a black cassock, "that, you're also—"

"Father Pedro," he dryly replied.

Michael chuckled. "Of course, it is, my apologies." *The very rocks upon which the Church is built.*

"And we're here to help, Michael," Pedro continued.

"I'm sure you feel that way, sir." *I bet. A backroom inquisition by four anonymous church elders. Historically, these things have never gone so well for men on this side of the table. Maybe the new Vatican's becoming so politically correct that I'll be excommunicated, after all.* Michael smiled and sought to play nice for as long as possible.

"Father Michael," Far Left asked, "can you tell us about what led you to the cloth?"

"It's a long story, sir, and I'm sure—"

"We may not have many years left, Father," Far Left interrupted, "but we *do* have time for details. If you don't mind, of course."

So, they wanna drag this out and assure themselves they're making the right choice. So be it. "Well, I was born into a devout family in 1980, so, I suppose it started there, unless you wanna go back to my parents' upbringing in the church that assured mine." Far Left smirked and nodded as though Michael should continue. "My birthday's November first, so, All Saint's Day, a Holy Day of Obligation. Even though the local bishop long ago waived that requirement, my family always attended mass whether the holiday fell on a Sunday or not."

"Tell us about your family," Pedro interrupted and emotionlessly demanded. "What was your upbringing like?"

Michael inhaled and briefly pondered how to answer such a broad and complicated question. *How do I sum up decades of love and trust, and the memories and experiences that they created?* "I'll do my best to give you a short answer. I grew up on my family's ranch surrounded by cows, alfalfa, and the Roman Catholic church, at least until the water crisis worsened and we moved into town. My family's been part of San Miguel Chapel for more than eighty years, ever since my great-grandparents moved their families into the area."

"Can you tell us more about your family life, your development and growth in the Church," Far Left patiently asked.

Michael nodded and tried to offer what he believed were the relevant highlights. "My parents and I walked an annual pilgrimage to San Miguel. Growing up, they were so confident in my Catholicism that we freely discussed other religions and faith systems. For example," Michael continued when Far Left motioned for more detail, "they explained the days around my birthday were important to so many different peoples that they must have inherent value and significance for all God's children.

"Mom taught me that All Saints' Day falls just after the pagan holiday *Samhain*, secular Halloween, overlaps with *Día de los Muertos* in Mexico, and immediately precedes the Islamic month of *Muharram*.

"My dad," Michael further explained, "he loves Halloween, but made sure I knew and appreciated the Roman Catholic history of my birthday and its celebration of all the faithful departed. He taught me about Pope Boniface IV cementing All Saint's Day in our dogma in the 7th-century about three-hundred years after the holiday began. Pope Gregory declared it a Holy Day of Obligation and moved the celebration to November 1st in the 8th-century. My folks believe my birthday was a divine indication that I would always live a pleasing life of service to God. The Church and the scriptures have been so much a part of my life that unless someone was contagious, we never went more than four days without stepping into San Miguel Chapel."

Pedro maintained a dispassionate poker face and deeply inhaled when Michael paused and waited for the next question. "What about your education?"

"I graduated high school in 1998, went to U-N-M to study theology. The ultra-liberal environment there felt oppressive, very... *antagonistic*... to my beliefs and my faith. I transferred to Western New Mexico State and finished degrees in Spanish and Theology in 2002."

"Was it actually *antagonistic*, as you say, or just *unfriendly* to our faith and dogma?" Pedro seemed put-off by Michael's wording.

"I think 'antagonistic' is a fair assessment," Michael responded. "Just a few weeks into the fall semester, I walked to the SUB, sorry, the *Student Union Building*, to meet friends for lunch. A woman walking past me saw my shirt, which was from a youth church retreat I'd worked the previous summer, and spit phlegm on me without even asking what I thought or believed. So, yes, I think antagonistic is accurate."

"So, Daniel was cast into a pit of lions for his faith, but you had to endure being spit on by an angry woman?" Pedro's disapproving gaze assured Michael he had no support from this anonymous Church elder. "That must have been *very* difficult for you."

"Is that when you entered the seminary? After college?" Number Three's immediate questions deterred Michael from responding to Father Pedro.

"No, sir, I worked as a student intern with the Silver City Police Department for three years and I grew pretty enamored with law enforcement. I thought it would be a great way for me to serve both God and His people."

"Was it?"

"Yes, sir, it was, for a time. I started the police academy right after graduation and worked there for five more years. I lost patience with the limited role that police officers and the criminal justice system play in helping the needy."

"You lost faith," Number Two cautiously asked, "in the police force?"

"No, not in the Silver City Police Department, or even in cops as a whole," Michael explained. "When I became a cop, I imagined taking the fight directly to the evil that victimizes the weak, the defenseless, and the vulnerable. I thought I would really make a difference, really have something to show at the end of each day for what I'd done to improve the quality of life around me."

"And that wasn't what happened?" Pedro had softened his tone, but his skepticism remained apparent.

"No, it wasn't." Memories of similar conversations with his SCPD peers, bosses, and mentors quickly flashed across his mind. "As a patrol officer, I was just a cog. Actually, a *very small* cog in a much larger and complicated criminal justice machine that seemed unable and, maybe, *unwilling,* to do what's necessary to address the difficulties encountered by the least among us. It was more of a meat grinder, I suppose, and it didn't care who went in or how they fared going through to the other side."

"You didn't like the work of a sausage maker," Far Left snickered and asked.

"No, I suppose I didn't," Michael grinned at the man's dark, familiar humor. *Funny, that's something a cop'd say.* "The tougher realization was that the system itself prevented me from caring about what happened to anyone I sent in. Once I made and processed the arrest, I was powerless to further affect any outcome, but I didn't understand that yet. I tried to stay involved with the victims and witnesses, even the suspects, sometimes. I wanted to serve everyone involved and help make all their lives better. It took me about three years to become overwhelmed and realize I was trying to do a different job. I entered the seminary about two years after that. The last six years have been clerical assignments in South America."

"Sounds to me like you tried to balance the work of a priest and a cop. Maybe, more accurately, you were a priest *masquerading* as a cop," Far Left offered, along with a sympathetic smile. "I've always found the two positions incompatible."

"Tell us about Columbia," Pedro interrupted and politely demanded, "about Bogotá, specifically."

Michael paused and took a deep breath. *They already know the answers I'm gonna give, just like any decent investigators would. Never sat on this side of an interrogation before.* He calmly exhaled. "By the time I started work in Columbia, I had already descended into a pretty low, dark place. I didn't have effective systems to deal with all the burdens of my role there. I heard dozens of confessions every day, and the people are suffering, so badly, that many of them had endured or committed terrible acts just to survive."

"You became angry, disillusioned, maybe," Number Three offered, "unable to help?"

"Yes, that's a fair summation," Michael conceded. "I couldn't involve myself, couldn't break the Seal of the Confessional and tell the authorities what was happening. All I could do was—"

"Motivate, counsel, and pray," Far Left finished his thought.

"Yes."

"I was asking about a more specific event," Pedro explained, "about *that* night, and how you feel about it now."

Michael shifted in his chair and wondered how much Hernandez had already passed along. *I think my actions deserve some context.* "As I mentioned, I struggled with hearing so much suffering and predatory behavior in confession. I didn't have a close, trusted mentor there to offer spiritual direction. I dealt with the burden of my work through physical exertion, through martial arts. I took whatever classes I could and frequently taught others. I became a black belt in Brazilian Jiu-Jitsu, and an advanced instructor in Krav Maga and Muay Thai kickboxing. Some Silat Melayu, but it's hard to find advanced classes in Malaysian knife fighting in the South American jungles." Michael saw three of the four men chuckled with him.

"And, back to the night in Bogotá," Pedro directed.

Michael didn't want to answer the question yet, not before he'd explained the background, the justification, for what had happened. *I deserve for them to understand that I didn't just murder a man and take off before the cops showed up.* "Right. Not long after I arrived in Bogotá, the workouts no longer helped. I started imaging I was sparring with the predators that victimized my parishioners. Then, when that no longer helped, I started upping the ante." Michael took a deep, calming breath, well aware of what he had to tell these four nameless strangers. "I started seeking out danger. Not for retaliation or retribution, but I started putting myself in bad situations. I think I was offering myself up as a victim, hoping that one of the predators might try to attack me. Unlike the victims they usually encountered, I thought I might be able to do something about it.

"I took the long way home at night. Routed myself through dark alleys, down streets no one should ever walk alone in daylight, much less after nightfall. I wanted bad men to come out of dark places in search of low hanging fruit and find nothing but remorse and immediate consequence for their troubles."

"You wanted swift justice," Far Left summarized. "Wanted to protect your flock from the dangers of their surroundings. Sounds to me like you reversed roles and had become a *cop* masquerading as a *priest*."

"Let Father Michael tell us," Pedro impatiently commanded with both his hands raised just off the table, "in *his* own words."

All four inquisitors turned their attention back to Michael. Another deep breath. "Yes, I believe that's generally accurate," he replied. "I wanted the monsters and predators to find *me*, to have to deal with *me*, instead of the weak and vulnerable. I wanted to give them what they deserved, to be the righteous consequence their conduct demanded. I hoped to motivate a few to turn from their evil ways, but, especially after my work as a cop, I knew the majority wouldn't change, at least not from what little, *uh, encouragement,* I could provide.

"So, that last night in Bogotá, I had done exactly that," Michael explained and paused briefly. "I again took the long way home, stayed out almost four hours after I should have been indoors, and found myself in a dark, narrow dirt alley with a desperate man. He demanded everything I had. I offered to help him, but, instead, he produced a knife and stepped in close, whether to stab or convince me, I don't know.

"He didn't bother trying to hide the knife at all," Michael continued. "He wanted to terrify me, to exert malicious control and force his will on me. When I saw the glint off his blade, I reacted on instinct, on my training. By the time I remember consciously recognizing that he'd pulled a knife on me, the handle was already sticking out of his side, in the exact place I've trained to insert it." Michael looked among the four silent men and tried to assess their response.

"And, what happened, *after* that," Pedro slowly asked.

"I knew what his injury meant and that no emergency services could save him, even if they'd been on-scene when it happened. He slowly collapsed to his knees, and then, quickly, onto his back. The knife protruded from his wound and trembled with his breathing, but I stopped him from removing it. He'd have just died sooner. I think it caught him so off-guard that he didn't ever have a chance to process what I'd done to him.

"I knew I couldn't save his life, but I hoped I might have a chance to save his soul. I identified myself as a priest and asked permission to pray over him, and to ask God for forgiveness for his sins. He nodded his head, and I knew he wouldn't live long enough to me to hear his confession and contrition, much less to anoint him and absolve his soul. I only had time to pray over him and make sure he wasn't alone when he died."

"And what about the police?"

"There was no one else around, in the alley where it happened. I called out, but no one responded. I walked to the police station, reported the man's death, and told them what happened. I took them to the body and walked their supervisor through the scene."

"So, after this man *threatened* you, tried to *rob* you, and then attacked you with a *deadly weapon*," Far Left summarized, "you, of your own volition, fulfilled your avowed, moral obligation to offer him some portion of his Last Rites? Did the police identify your involvement because of your own voluntary admission to them?"

Michael momentarily pondered the complicated question to ensure he answered accurately. "Yes, I think, to both. I don't know if they ever found any objective evidence of my involvement, but I don't believe so."

"Did the police arrest or interrogate you?" Number Three appeared bored with the protracted story.

"No, they did not. They took my word, as a man of God. I'm not sure they even interviewed the neighbors to confirm what I'd told them."

"Did you know the man who assaulted you," Far Left asked.

"No, I'd never seen him, I don't think. I certainly didn't recognize him."

"According to local police records," Number Two explained, "he was addicted to illegal street drugs, mostly methamphetamine and its derivatives, and had been victimizing that neighborhood for *years* before his death. The police didn't investigate because they didn't care *who* had killed him, or how. Their concern stopped with his death, like they were satisfied he wouldn't prey upon anyone else. They never told you that?"

"No, sir, they neglected to pass along that bit of news."

"How did you feel," Pedro inquired, his eyebrows raised, "*after* the Bogotá incident?"

That's a complicated answer, Michael thought. *Where to start?* "In the moments, hours, and days after taking that man's life, I've experienced every possible human emotion. Rage, guilt, sadness, regret, everything. Mostly, though, guilt."

"Over his death," Number Two quizzically inquired.

"Oh, no, *not at all,*" Michael hastily retorted. *If they're gonna make me go into this kind of detail before seeing me out, they're gonna get the full Monty.* "I feel guilty for *not* feeling guilty. I was sad that I could take a life without remorse, even if that life had preyed upon those around it. I felt anger that I could so easily protect myself by destroying one of God's most precious creations. I felt deep, devastating regret that everything I thought I knew about myself was probably a lie. I couldn't reconcile that I'd sworn my life to serve God and His children, but then had no intrinsic upheaval after taking the life of one of them, regardless of his actions that precipitated the event. Killing him was easy, and leaving his body there, in that trash-strewn alley, was even easier. None of that should've been true, but it was. I suspect it still would be today."

"How are you dealing with all that," Far Left asked, "all these caustic emotions waging war on your psyche and spirit?"

"I normally don't spend much time thinking about it, sir," Michael lied. *I still dream about it.* "And, as the archdiocese there accommodated my monsignor's request for a swift transfer home, almost no one knows about it. Except for my family and Monsignor Hernandez, this is the first time anyone has asked me about it, actually."

"So, if you had to sum up your feelings, your emotions about Bogotá, in just one sentence," Pedro proposed, "how would you do that?"

"Even though I keep praying that God has forgiven him, he got what he deserved, I don't regret it, and I'd do the same thing all over again if I had to." Michael had quickly blurted out the statement without first thinking about it. All four men initially bristled and looked at each other. They promptly nodded as though they'd all reached some sort of tacit, collective conclusion. *Here it comes, the loss of my clerical status. Termina-*

tion from the cloth. All for being human. At least they can't excommunicate me for this. Well, the Church hasn't traditionally done so, anyway.

"We appreciate your honesty, Father Michael," Far Left offered. "Candor and self-awareness are essential in our daily lives, and in our service to God and the Church, but are even more significant in matters such as these. As you might expect, you're not the first among us to grapple with these circumstances, or with the emotional aftermath. With your particular background, training, and, *um,* rather *unusual* paradigm for a fellow man of the cloth," he stopped as though searching for his words. "We couldn't agree more with your sentiments, and thought you might be interested in an *alternative,* assignment."

Michael blinked hard at the unexpected statement. "Away from San Miguel?"

"Yes, it's a fair assumption that you might never be assigned to the Chapel again," Far Right responded. "Or, really, to any chapel, again."

"I don't, know, what do you mean? Where will you send me?" Michael paused a moment and tried to understand the possible reality emerging before him. "What, exactly, do you mean by 'alternative?'"

"Ever been to rural Wyoming, Father Michael?" Far Left leaned back in his chair after asking the question, a knowing, mischievous grin spreading across his face. "I think you'll like it up there. They've got just the sorts of programs and, um, *activities,* that should interest a priest like you."

MONDAY, 1:47 PM_

NEW YORK CITY.

When the private phone line expectedly rang atop his opulent Italian mahogany desk, the aging bureaucrat urgently rose and closed the door to his reception area. His personal assistant had grown accustomed to his frequent need for privacy and took no offense. Not that he would've cared, anyway.

Hurriedly returning to his desk and the still-ringing phone, he picked up the receiver and answered it without sitting down. He'd been waiting for this call for several hours now and anticipated good news from his subordinate. "Yes?"

"The Disciples are all in place."

"Even Andrew?"

"Yes, we've just had a last-minute addition from an archdiocese out West. He came very highly recommended. A former police officer, they said. It turns out that he's recently taken such matters *into his own hands,* as it were."

He briefly pondered what Harold meant by that, but he'd have to wait until they met in-person to hear the details. Beyond the typical duties of his office and position in New York, he held a supplemental assignment as an Assistant Deputy Ambassador for the Holy See's diplomatic mission to the United States. This, of course, was merely a facade to more easily facilitate his *actual* appointment in the small nation's clandestine intelligence service. Along with his public roles as a Cardinal and ADA, Paul Dylan worked to serve the covert intelligence collection and counter-espionage needs of the tiny nation-state and its theocratic Vatican City hierarchy. "I know he hasn't yet met them, but does he at least have their files and approve of the chosen candidates?"

"Yes. Very paranoid, that one. Insisted on destroying everything as soon as he finished reading them. I really didn't care for how he chose to express his, uh, *displeasure*, for having sent him written documents. Some paperwork is just naturally unavoidable."

"One man's paranoia is another's reasonable caution, Harold. Just because someone's paranoid doesn't make them wrong."

"I know he means well, Your Eminence, and he's a very knowledgeable and useful ally in this project. I find it best to cut a wide swath around him, and to expect to forgive several transgressions every time I must interact with him."

"You're confident he's up to the task, and to keeping the confidentiality of it all?"

"You have nothing to fear. Not from John, anyway, we can trust him completely. I'm certain, in fact, that he wakes each morning *hoping* that someone tries to force secrets from him that day. The Disciples have no idea what they're in for, and he asserts that's part of his value to us. He can help determine their individual effectiveness and 'operational capacity,' as he called it, before we ever have to entrust them with the knowledge of their actual tasking."

Paul's increasing back pain forced him to sit down, even though his excitement encouraged him to do otherwise. "What are the logistics going forward?"

"All the candidates are flying commercial airlines into Denver. One of John's associates will pick them up at the airport in a dilapidated school bus and take them north. John claims it's best they meet him while they're already sore and sleep-deprived."

"Do you have concerns about our security? We've involved almost twice the support personnel that you and I originally discussed."

"I have no security concerns at this point," Harold replied. "Even the men who interviewed and recommended the Disciples believe we were looking for suitable candidates to withstand the rigors and danger of assignment to our prison missions around the world. They only evaluated each candidate's apparent capacity and comfort with violence, their moral philosophy on vengeance and self-defense, and if they could be trusted to follow orders that reshaped their own beliefs."

"That's a convenient cover story, and I'm still grateful you thought of it." Paul massaged his lower back against a tennis ball that helped relieve his sciatica pain. "Given all the uproar among the conservative and traditional Catholics about the recent death-penalty declaration, I wish we could advertise our future openings. It seems the young priests would line up around the block to work for us."

Harold chuckled at his rare humor. "It is *rather difficult* to volunteer to serve in a clandestine unit that only a few people know exists."

Paul smiled at Harold's ignorance. *And only* two *of us understand the real play at hand.* As he leaned back in his plush chair and set his heels atop his desk, the cardinal felt confident in their eventual success.

"I'm certain," Harold continued, "that no one from the interview panels will ever realize what they've helped create. I do expect to have more viable candidates to expand the interview process in the future. All the conservative young priests that're part of the current, unprecedented groundswell are potential candidates for us. The more they oppose and rebel against the aging liberal population much further up the Church hierarchy, the more useful I expect them to be to us. I've never seen or heard of conservative youth fighting the ideology of a liberal establishment. It's like we're watching history being made, Your Eminence."

Paul scoffed at his subordinate's naive assertion. "Don't sell yourself short. The current revolution in our ranks is just one aspect of God's plan. Once we help Him put our men into place and turn them loose, we'll have facilitated *altering* and *shaping* the course of human history, Harold, not merely watching it like hapless bystanders."

WEDNESDAY, 6:04 AM_

RURAL COUNTY ROAD. NIOBRARA COUNTY,
WYOMING.

MICHAEL AWOKE SUDDENLY in the early morning darkness, jarred back to consciousness as the school bus left the asphalt highway surface and jolted down a rutted-out dirt road faster than he thought reasonable or necessary. The aging metal tube-on-wheels creaked, thumped, and squealed in protest. From his position behind the obese driver and near the middle of the bus, he grabbed onto the back of the green vinyl seat in front of him for stability. Glancing around quickly, Michael saw most of the other twelve occupants had reacted similarly. The driver looked up into his rearview mirror just long enough to smirk at his passengers. Hearing the engine accelerate, Michael frowned at the back of the driver's head. *What an asshole.*

Reassured that no crisis existed, Michael wished he could have fallen back to sleep, but the rough conditions made that impossible. *Even if I didn't already ache from the awkward sleeping position in this seat, this drive's rough enough to wake the dead.* Michael intermittently tried to work the stiffness and tension from his neck and shoulders while assessing his new, unknown environment. From what little he could see outside the bus, they drove past grasslands, lightly snow-covered fields, and sporadic farm structures and windmills. *And the rough dirt road we're on.*

Even though the sun hadn't yet risen, Michael identified the brightest part of the horizon and determined it was roughly positioned to his 1:30.

He checked his watch. *6:16am. Generally headed northeast. Last I knew for sure, we were northbound on I-25 toward Cheyenne. No idea what road we're on, or what road we just abandoned.* He rechecked his phone and saw he still had no reception. *Not a* weak *signal, no signal. This thing's the smartest paperweight in the world without a network and data exchange.*

With seemingly no more intel to gather about their location and destination, Michael began his customary morning ritual. *I always feel more centered and peaceful after Laud, anyway.* He crossed himself, bowed his head, and offered his morning dedication to God. After expressing gratitude for his Blessings and asking for guidance, clarity, and trust in God's chosen path for him, Michael opened his eyes and saw the eastern horizon had brightened just enough to be noticeable. *About twenty minutes should've passed. Getting to be time for a bathroom, coffee, and breakfast.*

Michael's thoughts never strayed far from the events of the past few days, and they now lingered on the inquisition panel that had apparently sent him here. *Instead of punishing me for my beliefs and conduct, this feels like it could be some kinda reward, like the Church and I would both benefit from this assignment. I'm apparently not secretly joining a boat squad for BUDS at Coronado Island, but maybe this is some kinda selection process for some higher-speed appointments, at least relative to the typical parish work. I'm sure the Vatican and Holy See have something like the Secret Service to protect their ambassadors and dignitaries as they travel around the world. They've gotta get their recruits from somewhere, and the Swiss Army has all the security work in Vatican City under wraps, so that's definitely not an option for me.* Michael grimaced as he realized the greater possibility that an opposing reality awaited him. *Considering that no one gave any explanation of where I'm going or what I'm doing, I'm probably gonna spend some time in the Catholic equivalent of Siberia for a 'clerical time-out.' No one goes to dignitary protection training by surprise.*

Michael sighed at his unknown future. Even though all the bus windows were raised against the exterior cold, the gusting wind audibly howled as it helped the rutted dirt road sway the top-heavy bus. He looked around the bus's interior and his fellow, anonymous passengers. *This almost seems like the lead-in for some Monty Python skit, a bunch of silent strangers dressed in neckties and dress clothes take an overnight ride in an old school bus. Something poking fun at insane corporate team building exercises, probably.* Because they'd been explicitly prohibited from speaking with each other when they boarded, Michael had made up names and backgrounds for his anonymous travel companions based on their appearance and apparent demeanor. *Looks like Ice, Big Red, The Irishman, and Southern Comfort are all awake and curiously attentive. Everyone else's still ducked down in their seat or trying to rest. That's a damned losing battle right now.* He made a passing glance to the very back row and saw precisely what he expected. *Sergio's up. He still wears his hair high-and-tight like he never left the Marine Corps.* As soon as their eyes met, Michael nonchalantly averted his gaze back toward the distant front windows. *Interested to see how this is gonna go. Someone doesn't want us to know anything about each other, but I know Sergio better than most of my own family right now. Spending six months traipsing through the jungle together has that effect on people.*

Michael thought about their work at *La Capilla de San Benedicto* in rural Ecuador. *Wonder how Serge ended up here.* Michael couldn't precisely recall if three or four years had passed since they'd last seen one another. *What's his last name? Guzman, I think, yeah, just like the cartel asshole. I think he was a Marine priest for six years, maybe seven? Long enough to have seen some things. Even priests and chaplains in the Corps have to pass rifle and fitness quals, so the kid's never been a slouch. Looks like he can still handle himself pretty well today.* Michael considered whether Sergio's presence helped assure him this new assignment wasn't a punishment for Bogotá.

"*Wakey, wakey,*" the bus driver yelled over the ruckus. "Time to look alive, gentlemen, the Welcome Wagon approaches!" The few remaining passengers that feigned sleep sat up and looked at the environment around them.

Guess my questions are about to get answered, Michael told himself as he risked another glance at the last row. Sergio clearly recognized him and seemed just as interested in avoiding interaction. As he turned back forward, the rutted road grew even rougher. The driver comically bounced up and down, and Michael realized he had an air-cushioned seat. Despite that, the road had finally forced him to slow down. *Maybe he doesn't grasp how miserable this is for the rest of us. Or he doesn't care.*

The bus suddenly slowed and made a hard left turn onto a private road, which forced Michael to hang tight to the back of the next seat to stay in his own. Two large, orange-painted signs stood on each side of the dirt driveway. *No Trespassing. Trespassers Shot on Sight.* Michael chuckled at the professed absolutism. *What about the Girl Scouts? They gonna snipe the Thin Mint sellers, too?* The private drive had been far better maintained than the access road, so the driver accelerated to again navigate the bus at the far end of "reasonable and prudent."

After climbing a long and low, rolling hill, a compound came into view ahead of the bus. *Large building, probably the house, surrounded by a horseshoe of adjacent buildings and structures.* In the center of the structures, an American flag flew beside a square, yellow-and-white flag with a large, black image in the center of the white side. *Holy shit, that's the flag of the Holy See! This still might be clerical Siberia, but at least it's not some kinda priest prison camp. Probably...*

As they drew closer to the buildings, the curiosity and tension among the silent occupants became palpable. Michael realized how obvious and purpose-built some of the other features and structures were. *Concrete parade deck and flagpoles. That's gonna double as a 'grinder' where the physical torment and calisthenics take place. Sandpit for fighting and defensive tactics training. Confidence course. Shaded bench rests oriented toward distant berms for long-range rifle training. Meandering trails that wandered off into the distant hills. They get enough foot traffic to keep the grass from growing back. Whole thing's gotta be two or three miles off the rutted access road. Nobody'll ever hear you scream out here.* Just like when he arrived for his first day at the police academy, a pit formed in Michael's stomach and forced him to question if he really wanted to volunteer for what was probably about to happen. *What the hell is this place? What'd I get signed up for?* Another quick glance to the back row confirmed Sergio had his own reservations.

As the bus turned to approach the main house, a tall figure emerged from the front door and walked out onto the covered, wraparound wood-railed porch with a large mug. *Gotta be coffee, and I doubt there's any for us.* He wore a tan American flag ballcap, dark aviator sunglasses, a large mustache, dark brown barn coat, jeans, and hiking boots. *The sun isn't even above the horizon yet.* The attire concealed much of his face, even as he walked out to meet the slowing school bus. His commanding presence permeated the distance between them and settled as a pit in Michael's stomach. *He's Tom Selleck, if Tom Selleck were even more foreboding.*

As though to stay consistent with the rest of his vehicle operations, the driver waited until the last moment and pressed hard on the air brakes to stop the bus door directly in front of "Tom." Michael enjoyed one final thrust into the seatback in front of him. After cutting the engine and turning on the interior lights, the overweight driver rose from his seat, faced his twelve passengers, and paused. Gusting winds noticeably shifted the bus and leaked through its aging windows.

The driver looked at each of the passengers, and they apprehensively looked back at him as though waiting for an explanation. "Best of luck," the driver hesitantly offered. "I'll pray for you." The portly man nodded at the group and pulled the control lever to open the bus doors. A cold breeze cut through the bus, and Michael appreciated the momentary reduction in the locker room stink that surrounded him. The bus shifted slightly as the driver descended the steps and walked toward the porch.

"Tom" placed his coffee mug on the porch's wood railing and stepped forward to shake hands with the driver, who disappeared into the house. "Tom" stepped up into the bus as another gust howled behind him. Stopping at the center of the front aisle, he closed the doors and turned to face his captive audience. Still wearing his ballcap and sunglasses, he crossed his arms over his chest and silently scanned the group scattered among the green vinyl bench seats before him. A long moment passed while they formed their first impressions of one another.

"I'm John," he finally offered in a gruff, impatient baritone. Michael imagined he'd once been a smoker and suspected he might still be today. "Not *Johnny*, not *Mister John*. Just, fucking, John. I'm in charge of this training facility and the program that utilizes it. We share the same faith, religion, and employer, but we might see a couple of the details differently. I'm rough around the edges, I chew tobacco, and I swear a shitload. As far as you're concerned, though, I answer to no one but God. *I've* been sent here to offer you boys a once-in-a-lifetime opportunity to serve Him, His church, and His children by more directly identifying, deterring, and engaging the forces of evil that plague mankind in the worst and most horrific ways. *You've* been sent here because your diocese believes you have the mindset and capability to successfully negotiate my training program. They think you got what it takes to come out the other side with the skillsets required to immediately and effectively fill the postings awarded to the hard and just few who graduate.

"If all your minders kept to their marchin' orders while gettin' you here," John continued, his arms still crossed and his eyes still hidden, "then you should have no other idea about what you're doing here, where you are, and what you'll be doin' if you complete my training program. I appreciate how vague and ambiguous all of this must feel, but I assure you that all of my protocols are the product of necessary and dire security measures. I'm responsible for doin' everything possible to protect our instructors, students, and anyone who *may* or *may not* be actively working in such assignments and postings at this very moment anywhere in the world God might have called them. Nothing we do here, no matter how seemingly insignificant or unimportant is driven by gameplay. There are no shenanigans, not a single goddamned reindeer game. Everything my instructors and I do, we do with a specific and necessary purpose in mind. It's important to me that you understand and trust that, and that you're willing to trust us to act in your best interests, in the best interests of this program, and for everyone involved or associated with it. Most of all this generally falls under what we call *operational security.* If you've never heard that term before, for now, just understand it's the collection of procedures and protocols for how we keep our people, operations, and information secure.

"From a logistics perspective, some aspects of your time with me will feel like seminary. I got no idea *what* you've been doing *wherever* you've been doing it, but this is the way we're gonna do things *here.* We'll pray Laud every morning, None every afternoon, Vespers every evening, and Compline before every nighty-night. While you may experience occasional curiosity and uncertainty about what we're doing here, you should always feel like this is where you're supposed to be and what you're supposed to be doing right now. If that changes and you don't feel divinely inspired and called to be here, please lemme know and we'll get you back to what you need to be doing with your God-given time and strength."

John glanced down at his wristwatch before he continued. "You're already a half-hour late, so, quite frankly, we don't have the time this morning for a prolonged diatribe or philosophical discussion about the present state of morality among mankind, but I'll give you a few minutes to say your piece, if you got one. Questions? Comments? Concerns?"

"Where are we, exactly," asked a bald, wiry black man seated near the front door. Michael hadn't heard him speak before and thought he had a French accent. He immediately and momentarily thought of Merci.

John looked down at the man, who sat just to his left. "If you can't manage to keep track o' your own whereabouts, it sure as shit ain't my job to do it for you, son. You're right where your bosses want you to be, until I say you can't be here anymore."

"I'm sorry, John," a mid-twenty-something blonde man who sat mid-bus across from Michael hesitantly apologized, "but, who are you and how do you fit into the Church?"

"That's an excellent question, son, in fact, that's *two* excellent questions, neither of which I'm gonna answer right now. You'll get to hear both of 'em if you stay out here long enough."

After a few seconds of silence, a man of east-Asian descent seated several rows in front of Michael raised his hand. "I feel like you're not gonna address this one, either, John, but I'll throw it out there, anyway." Michael had guessed the man looked about his age. *Early thirties, but Asian ethnicities age better than whites, so, maybe he's older than me.* "What are you training us to do?"

"Probably the most important question of all, followed closely by 'how long are we gonna be out here?'" John paused to allow a particularly stout wind gust to pass. "Tell you what, son, I'm gonna disappoint you a little bit and respond to that one." John shifted his hands down onto his hips and again briefly scanned around the interior of the bus as he spoke, almost as though hoping to elicit some sort of reaction from the group. "There's a few different opportunities available to priests who successfully negotiate my program, and they're known only to those who succeed. I will *only* tell you that the work you'd be doing, regardless of the actual posting, is of vital service to the Church, the Pope, and to God. There are a minimal number of men in the world who get this training and these postings, and far fewer who get to work these assignments on behalf of God. Everyone else in the world doing similar work are in the employ of secular governments, dictators, and various other forms of corruption and evil.

"If you resign," John continued, "if you quit, or if you wash out, you don't ever have to worry about knowing what you missed out on. My program and its rules are designed to ensure that only the winners know what happens next. So, if you fail to meet my standards, or you decide the mystery of this work just isn't for you, you can head on back to your archdiocese and get your next assignment. No harm, no foul, no hard feelings. And, to help protect the *operational security* of those you leave behind, you'll have nothing you can actually report to the world about what we do out here, *whatever* it is we do, and *wherever* it is that we are."

A few moments of silence passed as John looked ready to parry the next question.

"So," a pale man with Celtic features and longish, auburn hair asked, "does that mean you won't even give us a general idea about what we're training for?"

"No, that's easy, son. You're training to do God's work, just like you been doing your whole life, probably. I do, however, promise to spill that secret to every asshole in here that does navigate my course with sufficient precision and accuracy to move on from here. All that matters right now is that your respective archbishops, for whatever reason, assigned you to me and my associates. Any more burning questions that I'm probably gonna refuse to answer here at Minute One?"

Michael followed John's glance around the eleven other trainees. *Everyone but Sergio looks as apprehensive as I feel. This is a damned 'blue pill or red pill' moment...*

"Just in case you're skeptical or afraid of what happens next," John offered, "y'all should understand you *ain't* gotta get off the god-damned bus. Nobody's gonna come through that little back door and shove you out at gunpoint. If you gotta be pushed, I want you to stay right where you are. Do *not* step onto my property if you feel forced to do it. Everyone *has* to be here by choice, and you can leave whenever you want, including right now. You got concerns about what's going on, about what you already saw o' my place? Think you know what we do here, and you just realized you wanna go do somethin' else? I ain't got no problem with that, hell, I *appreciate* and respect a man that knows his boundaries. It's best for everyone, though, if you admit that right now and stay on the bus."

Michael again glanced around and saw most of the others doing the same, as though they all waited for someone to speak or react.

"Well, then. Let's get your summer camp started a few months early, gentlemen," John continued. "You can think of this as a *vacation Bible study*, just for grown-ass men of action, integrity, and the intestinal fortitude to do the hard things that no one else is willing or capable of doing." Although he uncrossed his arms and moved his hands back down onto his hips, John dominated no less of the bus's interior. "You, man in the back," he called out and nodded at Sergio with his chin. "You remember the standing order everyone got when you boarded the bus in Denver last night?"

"Me, sir?" Sergio hesitantly asked.

"You're the only *sum-bitch* in the back row of my beautiful bus, ain't ya?"

"Yes, sir," he quickly replied, "I do remember the order."

"Anybody break it?"

"No, sir, not one."

"I said 'John,' not 'sir.' I *work* for a living, and you look like you oughta already understand that. I can smell the military comin' off you, Back Seat. You really want me to believe thirteen men rode a bus together, all night, and not one of you said one goddamned word to each other?"

"Not that I saw or heard, su, *err,* John."

"Guess I gotta take you at your word then, unless someone wants to come clean now. Integrity means everything to me and my folks, so, if you need to get somethin' off your chest, gentlemen, now's the time."

A second pale, red-haired twenty-something seated between Michael and John raised his hand high above his head like they were in grade school. Michael thought he looked like he'd grown up playing football in Nebraska and had assigned him the nickname, 'Big Red.' "Uhh, John," he asked, "I'm pretty sure we're all priests here, so, I think we oughta come with a little credibility in that regard."

"The Objector," John surmised through a smirk. "There's one of you in every group, like some kinda virus that can't get killed off until you get here. Well, Objector, we got a program for that. You get off my bus, and it could be the worst mistake of your professional life. Just because you got through seminary, that don't hold a cup of water with me. All I know for sure is you're all people, and in my experience, most people can be total pieces of shit, given the opportunity to be so. There's a reason all my friends got four legs. You bipods are despicable, and that's why I can't trust any of you until you earn it. You, Objector, you stay seated. Do not get off my bus. We clear?"

"Well, I—"

"*I apologize, Objector,*" John forcefully interrupted, "I must've *stuttered* in there somewhere to lead you to believe this was a negotiation." Even through the hat, sunglasses, and mustache, Michael understood the man's adamant intent. "*Do not, get off, this bus.* Even if the engine starts on fire, even if it overturns on the way out to the road. *Do not, touch,* my facility, under *any* circumstance."

Michael watched Big Red sink into the green vinyl bench seat, saved from whatever awaited the rest of them. *And then, there were eleven.*

"I imagine nobody else has a thought they wish to share with the group? Alright, then. Back to you, *Back Seat,*" John continued and again nodded at Sergio. "You had your own, specific instruction that came with that seat assignment. Which one of them knows someone else on the bus?"

Michael kept his focus on John while the pit in his stomach intensified. He struggled to keep his apprehension from being visible on his face. *This man knows how to read people, and I wanna stay, just long enough to see if this place's what I hope it is. Come on, Serge, don't mess this up!*

"None, John, not that I've seen," Sergio answered without any discernible deviation in his voice.

"We'll see," John sneered and replied. "Like I said, integrity is *everything* to me and my folks. Men that're unwillin' to be honest with themselves can't *ever* be trusted to be honest with me, and certainly, they'll never be honest with God, neither. Can't abide that kinda man here. Not once, not ever. So, if you got a partner on this bus, a friend from an old job posting, maybe from your former life, that's alright. You didn't know before you got on the bus. Nothing against you, you just can't be here. If that's the case, you don't even have to be honest with me, but at least be honest with yourself. Stay on the bus. Let your buddy go forth and fulfill his purpose, his true calling in this life. You can sacrifice yourself, but you'd best do it now, before your feet hit my *terra firma.* There's consequence out there. Only thing in here's another long bus ride that nobody else'll ever know about. Anyone wanna come clean? Last chance."

The lengthy monologue served as another reminder of Michael's police academy experience. *The instructors created circumstances to test our integrity. Extra money in the vending machine return slot. Random sodas on the dining hall counters. They always knew the answers to everything they asked, and this might be no different. What if he knows? What if they put Serge and I on here together as a test to see how we'd handle it?* Michael breathed, deep, quiet, and calm, to maintain a blank external expression while his innards roiled. John shifted his gaze among the occupants in search of deceit. *Fuck it. If they already know, the worst thing that happens is they send both of us home, it's not like they're gonna put us in front of a firing squad. I mean, this is, somehow, gotta still be part of the Church, right?*

"Time's wastin', then, gentlemen," John finally announced. "Everybody but The Objector dismount. Do it fast, do it orderly, but do it now. Get up on the porch, double-time, go!" John opened the bus doors into yet another gust and ambled down the steps.

Michael momentarily lost sight of John as he and the ten remaining men hustled up from their seats, grabbed their backpacks or duffel bags, and moved forward to crowd the narrow aisle. Although apprehensive about what might be required of him to succeed here, Michael suspected that tremendous opportunities could await him on the other side of John's program. *First step is just getting past the doorway.* The bus shifted beneath his feet as eleven motivated men shuffled down its steps and outside.

Through the passenger-side bus windows, Michael saw the front door of the house cracked open. Someone concealed inside stuck their arm out and passed John an upside-down, black felt cowboy hat. He accepted it without a word, and the door immediately closed. *Why'd they need to stay hidden? Lots of secrets in this place already.* Michael glanced down at Big Red the Objector as he passed. They made eye contact and exchanged nods before he descended the steps into the dim predawn light. *John's terra firma.* A subconscious glance up confirmed a lack of overhead threats. *I didn't feel this nervous walking around the slums in Bogotá!* A cold, stiff gust greeted Michael as he stepped just beyond the doorway.

"Everybody up here on the porch, quick," John called out to the group. "Line up facing the house, eyes forward, do it now. *Dress right*, if you have any idea what the hell that means."

Michael rushed along with the others to comply, despite the strange, irrational directive. He placed himself in the middle of the group and hoped Sergio, as the last man off the bus, wouldn't end up near him. A quick glance to his right assured Michael he was in line. Moving his eyes to the house, he picked a small, eye-level anomaly on the wall in front of him and stared at it, just as John had instructed. *Not in so many words, but I'm sure this's what he meant.* Michael realized he'd subconsciously positioned himself at-attention. *Bet money Serge did the same.* He felt odd holding his duffel bags at-attention and dropped them in front of his feet.

"Stand fast, gentlemen," John directed. The bus door closed behind them, and the engine turned over. Michael heard its transmission shift, immediately followed by the strain of acceleration as the bus pulled forward and turned to leave. "Nobody moves until that sum-bitch is outta my sight. If I can still see him, he can still see us."

Michael stood still while the racket from the departing bus grew more distant. The wood porch creaked beneath John's shifting weight as he slowly and deliberately moved among the eleven trainees. *Driver must be going slower takin' off, seems like he brought us here a helluva lot faster than he's leaving.*

"The Objector might be the first to leave my property," John announced while walking behind the trainees, "but he damned sure won't be the last. We're gonna see how many's left at the end of the day, but, my personal goal, anyway, is always to drop one more. Sending two home on Day One always makes me feel like we still run a tight ship out here, even if it does have to sail on a sea of windswept grass and misery."

Michael sensed the man's presence just before he realized John had stopped immediately behind him. He could no longer hear the outbound jalopy.

"Now," John exclaimed, so close that his breath warmed the right side of Michael's neck, "let's have us another word about what the *fuck* I meant by 'integrity.'"

WEDNESDAY, 6:44 AM_

RURAL PLAINS. NIOBRARA COUNTY, WYOMING.

"LIKE I SAID BEFORE, back on the bus," John exclaimed in Michael's right ear, loud enough for everyone to hear. "Integrity is *everything* to me and my people."

Michael still stood at attention, even though their apparent new boss hadn't ever specifically ordered that. *This would feel like getting dressed down at the police academy, except I wasn't hiding anything from the R-T-Os there. How long before we're pushing on The Grinder?* Michael breathed the cold air in through his nose, and his sinuses soon ached from the temperature difference.

John paused before stepping away from Michael and moving down the line to intimidate another trainee. "If you can't trust the people that swore the same oath, well, then you're pretty well screwed." He shouted to be heard and not out of anger. "You're a dead man walkin'. I will not excuse, pardon, cover-up, or ignore even the slightest hint of deceit. I cannot abide a liar, and I won't abide any of you if you rub me the wrong way."

John moved in front of their line. He spread his arms and motioned for the few distant men to step in closer. "Alright, that first asshole's gone. Bring it in and breathe for a minute, but pay attention to what the hell I'm tellin' you." His breath formed visible, short-lived vapor in the cold air as he spoke.

"First things first," he continued. "I'm not your daddy, not your uncle, and I'm *damned sure* not your friend. My only purpose in your life is to train you all to do things you've never done before, and make sure you shitheads all survive to serve God another day. I don't care if you don't like me, but I care greatly that you trust and respect me. We can't put our lives in each other's hands otherwise. You can understand, very accurately, that I'm an asshole and we can carry on just fine. But, if you think I've harmed or betrayed you in some way, that's gonna make it hard to get along, and we certainly won't get any meaningful work done together.

"There's some rules that y'all gotta be made aware of," John explained. "No phone, no email, no Yahoo, no twitterpated, insta-hooey bullshit out here. No outside comms of any kind. You get your phones for one hour a week. Make all the calls you want in that time, but we'll make sure you can't get messages to the outside world about what we're doing here. You can let mommy and her new husband know that you're doin' great at summer camp and makin' all kinds-a new friends. I can't have you end up on the back of a goddamned milk carton, but you're not gonna threaten my training program, either. You mighta noticed you didn't have cell service on the way out?" He let the rhetorical question hang for only a moment before continuing. "Yep, not an accident or a coincidence. I'll let you imagine the details. In the meantime, everything you got with a circuit goes in this box." He held up what looked like a clear plastic box, about one cubic foot in size, with an exterior metal frame at each juncture of the plastic sides. "Any of you boys smart enough to know what this is?"

Michael waited several seconds to see if John actually wanted an answer this time. "It's a Faraday box," he offered when it seemed John wouldn't proceed without a response.

"That's right, whiz kid, and what does a Faraday box do?"

"Prevents all electronic signal from reaching or leaving devices inside it."

"Right again, you get a gold star. Now, all of you, line up here. Dump all your electronics inside the box, step aside, and one of my nameless associates will then search you to ensure you've not forgotten to include anything. Sorry, I neglected to make those introductions," John apologized and stepped back to the wall of the house behind him. He tapped on a nearby window and then stepped forward just as the front door opened. A white female and four men emerged. Two of the men were white, one was Hispanic, and the last one black. Everyone but the black man dressed similarly to John, each with Carhart-style jackets, jeans, and button-down shirts in different colors and patterns of plaid.

The black guy dared to wear khakis, Michael thought. *I bet the Canadian Tux Committee makes fun of him for that.*

"These folks are my nameless associates," John explained. "You can call them 'John,' or 'Jane' as may be as appropriate, if you have to call 'em somethin', but they're here to help. By that, I mean they're here to help *me* decide how soon each of *you* gets to go home. So, like I said, drop your shit in the box, step aside, and they'll make sure you're clean. If any of you boys've ever been down to your local county jail, this'll be a familiar experience for you. In the next few minutes, we'll know for sure if you're a Jew or a Gentile. Line up, and ready to get real well-known."

Michael fell into line as instructed and again worked to avoid eye contact and proximity with Sergio. *Best if we don't share much of the same space for a few days, at least, maybe a few weeks.* While moving closer to the Faraday box, he took the time to both put his phone in airplane mode and shut it off. It didn't protect the contents entirely, but at least now John and his team would need access to state-of-the-art decryption software if they tried to get past his security code and peek inside the device without his consent. *If cops can get into locked phones, then I'm sure John's got spook buddies that can do the same. I just don't wanna make it easy for them if that's their* M-O. Within another minute, he'd dropped the phone and submitted to a very detailed search of his person and clothing. Even without specific instructions to do so, all eleven of them lined back up in their original order.

"Next thing to address is *your* identity," John explained. "I'll explain our op-sec later, but, for now, none of you gets to know anything about each other. Includin' whatever name your momma, or the court-appointed guardian, or both dads named you. The only way to trust *everyone* is *not* to trust *anyone*. So, how do I make sure I can trust all of you assholes not to give my name out to people I don't want knowin' it? By not givin' you my actual name in the first place. If anyone discloses their real name, you're out on your ear, and you can rest assured that I'll always know *who* and *where* you are, but the opposite won't ever be true.

Please ponder that reality should you ever think you've got the drop on ole John."

He retrieved the black felt cowboy hat his associates had brought out from the house, which, at some point in his wandering monologue, had ended up on the wood porch near the home's front door. John looked inside the hat, shuffled some pieces of paper around its interior, and then scanned the group. He briefly made eye contact with Michael, and it seemed that some sort of recognition momentarily flashed across his face. "Alright." He continued looking back and forth among the men but strode in Michael's general direction.

A nervous pit again anchored itself in Michael's stomach. His objective at the police academy had been to fly under the radar as long as possible. *It wasn't hard to hide among fifty-six trainees, no way I can do the same among eleven.*

John stopped directly in front of Michael and stared straight into his eyes. "Let's start with you." He reached into the hat, reshuffled the papers, and withdrew one. "You're Andrew. Hope you like it, doesn't matter if you don't." Moving along the line, John granted each of them a pseudonym and stepped to the next man while drawing his new name. "You're 'Simon the Zealot,' and I'd give serious consideration to a nickname other than 'Zealot.'

"You're 'James the Greater,'" he announced to the smallest man among them. "A-K-A 'James Zebedee.' I'd consider 'Zeb,' if I were in your shoes." John stepped to the next man.

"Matthias.

"John the Baptist, that's another great name, but I'd think about 'The Baptist' just so you're sure that your classmates are cussin' me and not you.

"Phillip.

"Bartholomew.

"Matthew," he named the Asian male.

"Thomas.

"'James the Lesser,'" he announced to the lone black student. "A-K-A 'James Alpheus,' good luck with that one.

"And," John now finally stood in front of Sergio, "by mere process of elimination, you're 'Jude.' Lucky for you, they wouldn't let me name one of you 'Judas,' even though I'm damned sure there's a Judas somewhere in this group. There always is." John turned slightly to address the whole group.

"I know there's a Judas among us, and you should expect that, as well! One of you, as you stand here on my porch, in the hospitality of my company and breathe in my fine, unpolluted air, is gonna work *real goddamned hard* to betray us! I told 'em, when they asked me to look after you worthless fucks, I warned 'em! I knew they were gonna send me at least one Judas, and I'll have the proof soon enough! One of you assholes thinks you're smarter than me, better than me, and I can assure you that you're not gonna get away with it. I don't know who you are yet, but *you* sure as hell do! You know the darkness in your soul, the larceny and betrayal in your own heart. When I find it, *boy howdy*, you're gonna wish you'd made better decisions by the time I'm done with you! The Vatican won't even have a chance to intervene on your behalf! If you're smart, you'd accept your fate, make your presence known, and let us help you get on with your resignation and atonement. The longer you wait, and the more shit that you leave behind for me to clean up, the worse it's gonna get for you. Anyone wanna admit they already know what they're capable of? Anyone? *Nobody, eh?* Okay. We've got a program for that.

"In the meantime," John continued, "you rest assured you're not the first, and you definitely won't be the last. You think the time-value of money is a powerful thing? Try the time value of *betrayal*, Judas, whoever you are. Know this: when I find you, I will definitely, *fuck, you, up*."

The unexpected tirade surprised Michael, and he noticed a bit of unknown fear creeping into his conscience. *Where the hell did the Church get this guy??*

John exhaled and shook out his arms, as though momentarily relieving his own stress. "Now that you've got your new names, get used to 'em. They may as well be your real ones, because they're all that you'll ever use here. We're gonna cover a boatload more on operational security later, but, for now, this is the important piece: you *will not* share any true personal information about yourself with anyone here, including me and my associates. No names, no past schools, no education, no former jobs, no former postings at chapels, churches, cathedrals, catacombs, or convents. You will not divulge any detail, no matter how small, that could become a puzzle piece for anyone here to identify, locate, and manipulate you or your family. The best way to trust *everyone* is to trust *no one*.

"Additionally, you will not tolerate, hide, conceal, abet, or allow anyone else to remain in my presence who's shared such information, even if by accident. I've gone to great lengths to assure my associates and superiors of the security and confidentiality of this program, and I will not have one of you compromising it. There's a real good chance one of you's a mole. Someone working against us, maybe against you, maybe against me, maybe against the Church itself. Hell, I've been known to have one of my instructors pose as a trainee just to test your compliance and let me know how y'all handle your business when you think none of us're lookin.' Because of that, you should expect that this individual will test the rules and see how many of you assholes'll go along with 'em. For that reason, you will not harbor, under any circumstance, *anyone* who breaks my rules. Do I make myself clear?"

John looked among the group, none of whom responded to the rhetorical question. "Looks to me like you're all gettin' comfortable and makin' yourselves quite at home on my porch, so we need to change that. There's a trail that starts about fifty yards north of the house here and winds a few miles through the hills. It's nice and wide, clear as daylight, and pretty well hard packed from constant traffic. We like to call it *Mother Mary* and I'll do you the favor-a lettin' you know she's five miles long. Once you find her, do not deviate from that route. It doesn't intersect any of the other trails out here, so you'd have to be an idiot to get lost. Trail runs here are just that, runs on trails, so you're not allowed to stomp my pristine grasslands by wandering where you don't belong."

John pointed off toward the trailhead for a moment. "You can't miss it, least not by accident. Before you go, drop all your shit and empty your pockets. My associates and I will go through all your bags and property in search of anything unwelcome. This program is not a team sport, gentlemen, and it doesn't matter who comes in second. Get off my porch and don't come back until that trail brings you home. Anyone that comes in last or breaks my rules will immediately regret it. As some of my best friends have long said, *it pays to be a winner*."

Just like the rest of the group, Michael wore a light winter coat, slacks, dress shoes, and a button-down shirt. Several of the men wore neckties.

Michael briefly considered asking if they could change into workout clothes but assumed John hadn't missed this fact. *He must wanna make this indoctrination process a little more uncomfortable for all of us. At least I'm not wearing jeans.*

John impatiently looked around at the group for several seconds. "*Now, go, get the hell outta here!*"

Michael and Sergio were among the first men off the wooden porch and headed out to the trail, so Michael slowed his pace and let his friend pull away from him a bit. *Can't risk John finding out I'm already breaking the rules here.* Most of the other pseudonym'ed "apostles" soon passed him by, which told Michael only a few of them had any military or law enforcement experience. *No way they're gonna keep that run pace for five miles. I'll be back in front of most of 'em before the midpoint.* He looked ahead through the pack. Sergio had settled into a similar pace and several of their colleagues now rolled past him. *I can understand not wanting us to make close ties with the other recruits, but what the hell would we ever do for the Church that demands that level of op-sec? Isn't every paramilitary operation a team sport? Unless they're training us to be spies, nobody else spends much time alone and out in the cold. Not gonna learn anything else until I get back to the house.* Michael picked up his pace just slightly, motivated both by the idea that more information awaited him beyond the finish line and that the next hilltop offered a semi-private chance to unburden his bladder.

TRAINING DAY 1, 0742 HOURS_

RURAL COMPOUND. NIOBRARA COUNTY, WYOMING.

Michael returned to the porch just over forty minutes after his departure. He'd managed to both keep up with Sergio and maintain enough distance between them to prevent any contact or communication with his friend. *Seems pretty clear that we both wanna stay and neither of us wants to risk sending the other home. It'll be good to have a teammate here, even if we have to keep up this charade.* As he stepped back up onto the wood planks behind only three other candidates, Michael saw all the luggage had been emptied and their belongings carelessly tossed into one large pile. *Gonna be a heavy and constant dose of psychological games for a while. Alright, at least I know what I'm dealing with.*

John looked down at his watch, apparently unsatisfied with their initial effort. "Get your shit, figure it out, get it done, and hustle inside. Gotta show you to your room."

Michael joined the first three runners and began sorting through the pile. They each moved with a purpose even though the bulk of the group remained scattered along the five-mile trail. Michael, however, deliberately worked slower than Sergio in gathering his possessions. After five minutes, Michael had collected everything he could identify as his, but at least one book appeared lost or appropriated. *Not so worried about theft, but I bet even a compass is contraband here. I'll find out later if the instructors grabbed it.*

As Michael started to follow the first three into the house, a pale, husky runner strode up onto the porch behind him. "*Hey*," he gasped out at Michael in a thick Carolina accent, *"what's, going on?"*

Michael thought he was supposed to call the man "Simon," but couldn't confidently remember his pseudonym. "Sort through the pile, recover your gear, and come inside."

"Thanks," he wheezed between coughs and moved to the pile.

The guy's got heart to put in that much effort. Sincerely hope he makes it. Michael stepped into the house and joined John and the others at the top of a stairwell that descended into the basement.

"Andrew, thanks for makin' time for us, asshole." John shook his head and hadn't yet removed his sunglasses. "I've already told you once today that this isn't a team sport. If that slowpoke out there isn't fast enough to get back here in time to get his instructions, that's *his* goddamned problem, and it's not up to you to fix him. We clear?"

"Yessir." Michael couldn't avoid ending up next to Sergio, so he treated the man like a stranger.

"Just 'John,' Andrew. My daddy ain't with us no more." He returned focus to the small group. "Y'all are gonna stay down in the basement. Lets me keep an eye on you, and it makes my job a damned sight easier to motivate, harass, and engage with you. I'm sure you've all played 'musical chairs' at some point while you're growing up. This is gonna be a lot like that. Sleep and rest are vital to you. They're your best and most valuable friends here, and you have to guard them selfishly. For that reason, there's not enough beds for all of you. One of you gets an old Army cot, and the other gets the floor. The bottom two performers at the end of each day will have those lesser accommodations. It pays to be a winner, and my associates and I will do everything possible to ensure you have to *fight* your way oughta last place once you get there. You four go pick the bunk you wanna start with but rest assured that you're very unlikely to stay there once we get going. All you weasels did today was prove you can outrun a wheelchair, so congratulations. Get your gear stowed. We're all gonna meet back out on the porch for the second training evolution once all the stragglers wander back in." John stepped out toward the porch, and Michael turned to follow the group downstairs.

"Get goin', fat ass!" All four of them paused and turned toward the

front door when they heard one of John's associates yell from the porch. *"You wanna tell me that's the best you got?! My dead grandma's faster than you! Move it, get up here!"*

Michael followed the other three downstairs into the basement. The room was unfinished and had no windows or insulation. *Equal parts barracks and dungeon.* Twelve evenly spaced twin beds and matching foot-lockers stood on a tan, vinyl tile floor. The walls showed the home's exposed two-by-four framing, and the ceiling had been painted dark brown. One exposed toilet and wash basin stood at each end of the room, which would force them to face the rest of the group while defecating. An open, tiled bay with six showerheads stood just beyond the far toilet.

Michael saw the Army cot and the open floor space were next to the showers. *All to make sure the two slugs are as uncomfortable as possible. No privacy here, either. I'd rather look at 'em while I pee. Wiping ass is one of the most private things I do.* Michael gravitated toward a bed near the middle of the room to get the most distance from the toilets and anyone sitting on them. Glancing back to the cot and open floor space, Michael expected they were virtually *all* assured to spend time there. *Perform or don't, I'll bet cash money that we all get a turn in the barrel. All I can do is make them find a real creative or chicken-shit reason to put me there.*

Michael turned when he heard steps overhead, followed immediately by heavy clamoring down the stairs. The fifth runner, with whom he'd spoken out on the porch, tromped down the wooden stairs. His belongings protruded from two open duffel bags that looked as though he'd packed them on his way out of a burning house. Michael figured the man stood at about 5'10" and weighed in well north of 240. Sweat streamed down his face and disheveled light grey dress shirt, and his dark brown hair was a soaked mop despite the external temps. His focused gaze presented an imposing message that countered the rest of his appearance; he conveyed an internal calm, a determination and drive that inspired camaraderie.

"What're we doing down here," he asked while glancing around the room.

Michael expected no one else would respond, given how swiftly John had rebuked him for giving the man direction out on the porch. Realizing the new arrival hadn't heard John's brief tirade, Michael saw an opportunity to quietly make a friend and teammate. "We're calling dibs on the bunks, at least for now." He stepped next to his bed, not to claim it as territory, but, rather, in hopes his colleague would choose to grab an adjacent one. Michael noticed everyone else in the room had turned their back to disavow his actions. "Whichever two of us are in the barrel get the cot and floor by the toilet and shower, but I expect we'll all get a cycle through there."

"Why's everyone else skittish?"

"I got yelled at for getting you up to speed out on the porch, so I'm sure they're just keeping their distance from whatever's about to happen to me. You're Simon, right?" Michael extended his right hand, and the man heartily took it.

"Yeah, 'Simon the Zealot.' I'mma just go by 'Z,' though, if they don't kick my teeth in for it." He released Michael's grip and tossed his sloppy duffel bags up on the adjacent bed. "Thanks for puttin' yourself out for me," he quietly offered. "Wasn't expectin' this kinda training, and I hate the fact that I'm not keepin' up yet. Gimme a week, maybe ten days, and none of y'all are gonna catch me."

"No worries," Michael offered loudly enough to be heard by everyone in the room, but not so loud as to draw attention from upstairs. "Team sport or not, we're all still brothers." *Guessing he's from North Carolina, probably did some time in the military, or maybe just played high-level sports. He pushed himself hard this morning and isn't happy with the result. If he knows his body well enough to know he only needs about a week to be at the front, he's been tested more than once.*

"Couldn't agree more," Sergio cautiously replied from across the room and looked over at Michael and Z. His brief nod reassured Michael they could count on each other for whatever lay ahead.

Muffled shouts emanated from the porch just before more overhead trampling and a barely controlled descent into the basement. The sixth man wore his duffel bag like an oversized, comedy-prop hat and clutched all his possessions to his sweat-covered dress shirt and loosened necktie. The other men allowed him only a second of lost scanning before stepping in.

"Hey, *Hat-man,*" Sergio harshly whispered and waved to get his attention. "Bring your shit over here and drop it on the bunk next to me. Get you up to speed." Sergio again briefly nodded at Michael as the newest arrival followed the directions without another thought or hesitation.

Michael sighed at the risk he had inspired them all to take together. *The police academy instructors expected us to figure out on our own that we needed to work together and do everything as a team. What's the benefit of making us isolate ourselves here? What kind of op-sec concerns can they really have?*

Even though they'd been told to choose their beds, Michael refrained from unpacking his gear. *Seems like they're gonna come down here and go ape-shit on us for having the audacity to get comfortable before anyone gives us permission to do so.* He did, however, take the liberty of sitting on the footboard of his chosen bunk.

"Y'all think they'll jump down our throats if we change outta these dress clothes," Z asked the group.

No one responded immediately. Most looked around at each other and several just shrugged.

"I'd wait until they tell us to," Sergio offered.

Another fifteen uncomfortable minutes passed while the remaining candidates descended into the basement to their chosen or mandated bunks. Anxiety returned to Michael's chest once the group had returned to full-strength. The last two men, Matthias and The Baptist, dropped their belongings on the cot and floor. Neither looked to have much fight left in them.

"On me," John shouted down the stairs. *"Get the hell up here, right now!"*

TRAINING DAY 1, 0807 HOURS_

RURAL TRAINING COMPOUND. NIOBRARA COUNTY, WYOMING.

MICHAEL and the other trainees crowded the narrow stairs and ran to comply with John's directive. They followed him back out the front door, across the small clearing in front of the house, and to a large stable about fifty yards to the north. Two large bay doors met in the center of the structure, and based on their width, Michael estimated its interior corridor would easily allow three vehicles to park side-by-side.

John walked through a pedestrian entrance just to the right of the bay doors and led Michael and his fellow trainees inside. Once through the doorway, Michael smelled straw, old leather, damp earth, and dung. *Eau de horse stable.* Its open, rectangular center had a concrete floor and was bordered by four horse stalls on the east and west, the corridor's two long sides. Near the north end, four propane space heaters stood around a collection of white, plastic banquet tables and chairs. The tables were placed in two rows, each with six matching folding chairs oriented toward the back, north wall and a long, white dry erase board that hung there. That wall, just like the south, was also comprised of two long sliding doors, but those north two were sealed shut. *Probably a futile effort to keep the wind out.* There were no animals inside, but Michael knew the stalls hadn't been empty for all that long. *The unique aroma's still too prominent.*

John turned to face the group and pointed toward the north end of the building, the apparent front of the room. "Sit."

Michael stepped toward the tables; well aware the back row would be highly sought-after real estate. As he approached, warmth from the propane heaters caressed his face. While trying not to appear selfish, he hurried to the seat nearest the back, right heater. Michael pulled that chair out from beneath the plastic banquet table and sat down. *Hope we don't spend much time in here. These cheap, flimsy chairs are the reason Protestants weddings are so short.* As he sat in the relative warmth, Michael saw Sergio had taken the far-left seat in the front row. *Couldn't get us farther apart.*

Michael further surveyed the room and noticed brand-new canvas draped over two large rectangles on the stall doors to his left. *Those could be more dry-erase boards, or large posters. Hell, they could be Transylvania mirrors for all I know right now. Lots of secrets here...probably just more psycho-babble shenanigans about what we're entitled to, what we've earned, and what we can be trusted with. This looks and feels more like the academy all the time.* Michael risked another glance at Sergio. *Wonder how the start of this thing compares to his boot camp experience? Hope I get to ask him someday.*

John walked to the front of the converted classroom space, finally took his sunglasses off, and set his coffee mug on the front banquet table.

He was actually less intimidating when I couldn't *see his eyes,* Michael thought.

"You can expect that I'll generally refer to you as 'shitheads,'" John announced. "You can take offense, if you have to, but I mean it as a term of endearment. I reserve that for my students, and despite everything you're likely to hear about our expectations and confidence in you and your skills over the next few months, I do understand that very few men ever get the chance to sit in your seats and attempt to negotiate my training course. Y'all oughta give yourselves a quick pat on the back for that, 'cause it wasn't easy gettin' here, and my primary job is to make it a damned sight harder to get the hell *oughta* here, at least to make it to graduation.

"It's easy as pie to get oughta here, though," John continued, and slowly paced about as he spoke. "If you wanna leave, all you gotta do is ask. No one's mandated to be here, and it ain't a prison sentence. I *really* don't want men who wanna be someplace else because, in my experience, there is nothin' so great as the heart of a volunteer, and nothin' so destructive as the *malice* of the *obligated.* So, if you ever decide that *whatever this is,* isn't for you, we'll get you back to your bishop and they'll take it from there, get you on to your next assignment. There won't be any hard feelings, either. I'm *happy* to do it, in fact. I'll also happily send home all the non-hackers that can't carry the water of being here. If you don't have the intestinal fortitude to admit you're a goddamned quitter, all you gotta do is fail a course or skills test. 'Failures' and 'quitters' get the same gratitude and the same ticket home. I'd rather wash *all* of you pukes than to graduate *a single one* that's not up to snuff. Sending unprepared and incapable men out into the world endangers lives. Not on my watch."

John momentarily stopped pacing and held his hands up in a 'stop' motion. "To answer the next question before y'all ask it, I *can't* tell you exactly what we're trainin' ya for. Buncha reasons for that. Like I said on the bus, there's a number of specialized postings that my graduates fill, none of which got *anything* to do with parish assignments.

"On that note," John offered and again slowly paced the front of the room, "y'all mighta noticed we're flying Old Glory right beside the Holy See out front. I like to explain the history and purpose of that, 'cause I'm sure at least one of you ain't got a clue about why.

"Just like every other official Roman Catholic site, we're flying the flag of the host nation at the same height as ours. The Holy See is the world's smallest theocracy, and the Pope is the official, elected leader of both that nation-state and the Roman Catholic Church. The Holy See came into existence on 7 June, 19-and-29, when His Holiness Pope Pius XI signed a treaty with the Italian government. The name 'Holy See' just means 'Holy Seat,' and it denotes its source of divine understanding, not some damned table chair.

"Vatican City, which is often confused with its nation-state, is located *inside* the Holy See and flies near-identical flags of both the city and the country. Each part of the Holy See flag's got significance, and you need to understand a few critical symbols in it. Unlike most, our flag's square. The half that's on the hoist side is a vertical yellow rectangle, and the outer half is white. Those colors symbolize the Pope's authority in both heaven and earth. The seal of the Holy See's in the center of the white band, and that seal is made up of a central cross, for obvious reasons. A papal tiara over the top of the cross symbolizes our confidence and faith in Saint Peter's church, as well as the spiritual and worldly power entrusted to His Holiness, who's, of course, Saint Peter's divine successor. There's a sword and an olive branch on either side of the cross because carrots and sticks just ain't that poetic. The design that encircles all the other objects is the divine Word of God, a shield that protects us and our neighbors from evil.

"And, just in case one-a y'all's from somewhere else, 'Old Glory' is one of the revered nicknames we got for the U-S flag. Fifty white stars, one for each state, on a navy-blue field that symbolizes vigilance, perseverance, and justice. Next to that, we got thirteen stripes, one for each of the original colonies. Seven red stripes honor the blood that our patriots have lost creating and defending this nation and the valor of their actions. Six white stripes honor the purity of their sacrifices.

"We try to serve both nations. If conflict arises between 'em, we're called to serve God *first* and our birth nation *second*. Thankfully, praise the Lord, I ain't seen too much of that kinda trouble in my life." John scanned the room and smirked at the men seated before him. "Speakin' of conflict, that oughta well describe your life in my training program." He paused long enough to retrieve a tin of Copenhagen chewing tobacco from his back pocket and deposit a fresh dip between his cheek and gums. He replaced the tobacco tin and spit onto the concrete floor before resuming his monologue.

"Most every day here's gonna start out the same. Rest assured that God is gonna provide us with some kinda wind. It keeps the snow off the grass, they say. You'll run every day. Sometimes for long miles and endurance, sometimes sprint work, sometimes an agility course. Most of the time, you'll be runnin' alone. We got nearly thirty miles of trails crisscrossin' the property here, and all but one of 'em connect with each other. The one exception is that five-mile trail y'all ran earlier, called 'Mother Mary.' You'll get plenty of time to know her every curve, bend, and undulation.

"Each day you're *not* runnin' Mother Mary, you'll get a personal map of the trails you *are* runnin'. We ain't got enough time to work on individual skills here, so I've gotta find creative ways to train and evaluate several at once. For that reason, every run will test your ability to read maps and navigate over land. Everyone gets their own route, so you can't rely on your partners for help. In addition to your designated path, it'll show the time you have to beat. If you fail to meet that deadline, you start over and run it until you win. If you go off-course, you start over. If, God forbid, you *lose* that map, you will run all over hell and damnation until you find it. I don't care if it blew into the next county, you don't come home empty-handed. Every workout will demand you demonstrate you got the skills and gumption to be here that day.

"After the run," John explained, "we'll usually have breakfast in the main house and then meet in here at 0-730 hours for your class work. Each day you're here, you'll be tested by the physical regimen, learn new disciplines in the classroom, and prove your mastery of each skill.

"In short, shitheads, this is a *high-speed, low-drag* course with no rest, no reprieve, and no time for bullshit. I'll weed every non-hacker from my field, even if that sacrifices the whole crop. All my instructors have extensive, personal experience in everything they train. If they tell you how to do somethin', rest assured that's what's worked for them out in the field, and probably under fire. You can also assume that *other* methods have failed them *and* their friends. We don't train to fail here.

"If I were in *your* shoes," John offered to the group, "I'd sure as hell wanna know who was standin' in *mine*. Like I said earlier, all you're ever gonna know me by is 'John.' All you get to know about me at this point is that I started workin' intelligence, antiterrorism, and counter-surveillance operations before most of you learned to use a toilet. The only detail y'all need to understand is that the folks I work for, *our bosses,* have placed me in charge of this training program. They granted me complete discretion and latitude to run it. What I say goes, and if I say, 'you go,' you'll be packed and shipped that day. No questions asked, no second chances, no appeals process. I *am* the cops, jury, and judge out here."

John shifted from a wandering amble to a purposeful pace. He strolled before the trainees like a caged predator that knew he'd soon be on the other side of the lock. "On the topic of discipline, there's lots of ways to fuck up and get yourself in trouble out here. Every one of 'em's rooted in a few infractions: failed efforts, integrity issues, operational security problems, and betrayal.

"Failed efforts might get you smoked out on the grinder, but it probably won't cost you much more'n 'at, least not the first time...

"Integrity issues will get you dismissed immediately. Can't tell you what the bishops do about it later, never gave a shit to follow-up...

"Operational security issues are a big deal. They jeopardize you and everyone involved and entrusted to your care. The punishment for givin' up secrets starts at 'severe' and gets worse from there...

"Betrayal. Only ever had this once. This will always be the one unforgivable sin in my program. If you think that hell hath no fury like the woman scorned, then you've never seen what people in my line of work do to traitors. God's *gotta* have mercy on you, cause I sure as hell won't."

John looked around the room as though to gauge their reception to his assertions, and Michael did the same. *Yep, academy 'Day One' lecture, just with greater consequence and thinly veiled threats of actual physical violence. John clearly doesn't answer to an H-R department.*

"Y'all already saw how serious I am about all this. 'The Objector' stayed on the bus this mornin' because I knew what he was and the danger he posed to all of us. The mission 'o this program is of *far* greater importance than any one of you shitheads, even more important than me. The tie does *not* go to the runner here, and I'd rather *dismiss everyone* in error than to graduate *just one* mistake. To put it another way, understand that I will burn down every last individual tree if that's what's required to protect my forest. Let that sink in." He stopped and glared at the trainees for several silent seconds.

"Now, with all that said," John explained in a softer and slightly more personal tone, "I don't enjoy being the asshole, but it don't bother me, either. I will treat every one of you with all the respect you earn through effort and demonstrated proficiency. No points for being the nice guy. Any pressing questions you gotta get out right now?"

Hearing only the silent, adult-speak for "no," he continued on.

"The next thing I gotta cover is *Operational Security,* commonly referred to as 'op-sec.' Op-sec is just a fancy, clandestine-sounding word for '*common fucking sense.*' Most o' you all grew up in homes with your own op-sec. You locked the doors at night, maybe even during the day. You looked both ways before crossin' the street, didn't talk to strangers, and never wore anything with your name on it so 'the bad man' couldn't pretend to know you. We're gonna expand on those same principles a bit.

"First, like I already made clear, no real names. That dead horse is sufficiently beat. Next, you can take all the notes you want in class, but they never leave this room. I'll supply all the notebooks you wanna fill, but it all stays in here. I'm gonna assign each of you a plastic milk crate to hold all your new school supplies. The good news is that means no homework. Once you walk out that back door, you're done for the day."

John cleared his throat. "Because of the threat that documents present, I will consider it a *betrayal* if your materials leave this room. No other reason for 'em to grow legs, shitheads. None o' you gets to keep the notes you think'll corroborate that tell-all book you wanna write in five or ten years. Try to get yourself on all the talk shows to *brag* about how *great* you are and how *lucky* everyone else is that you were there to save the day a couple times." He disdainfully spit tobacco juice on the concrete floor. "Worse yet, one of you gets heartburn about being shit-canned. Remember what I said early about fury and traitors."

John retrieved his coffee mug from the front table and heartily gulped from it. Replacing the mug, he resumed a slow, wandering pace. "Next part o' op-sec is *compartmentalization,* and it's simple. You only get intel and info that you got both a *need* and a *right* to know. You will only ever know the information that's necessary for *your* work. That's it. Not who I work for, not what I do with my time, or where in the world the men sittin' next to you at the tables are gonna be working someday. One important part of this's your clothes. Only normal civilian attire out here. Nothin' that identifies you as a priest. You'll get to shower and change in a bit, so just pack all that clerical shit away while you're in there. You won't need any of it. In short," John summarized, "mind your own goddamned business and make sure everyone else does the same."

Michael struggled to rationalize John's assertions without getting his hopes up. *I had to worry about op-sec a* little *bit as a cop, but his concerns go way beyond confidentiality and privacy rights. He's talking about the foundation of undercover, clandestine operations! What the hell* is *this place?* He scanned the room and saw that most everyone smiled and expectedly nodded along in agreement. *No one looks surprised to hear any of this! These guys all look like they know about this shit!* Cautious optimism slowly replaced the fear of looming consequence that had dominated Michael's last few hours.

The blonde-haired inquisitor from the bus raised his hand. "Doesn't the flag of the Holy See already give us away?"

Thomas, Michael remembered, *I think his name is Thomas, and he sounds like he wants to be the teacher's pet.*

"We don't *accept* visitors, Thomas," John curtly replied. He stopped near the center of the front table, crossed his arms, and stood to face his trainees. "*If you haven't figured it out by now,* we aim to turn out dangerous men to do the most demanding of God's work, and that requires us to train you all to do whatever's necessary to keep the forces of evil at bay all over the world. So, it doesn't matter how harshly I punish failures here, *reality* is a damned sight tougher than I'll ever be. Mistakes here create learning opportunities, what one of the former presidents calls 'teachable moments.' Out in the world, that shit'll take your life or physical independence. You like walkin'? Don't fuck up. Like breathin' on your own? Seein' with both eyes? Eatin' from a fork that you hold yourself? Takin' a shit that don't go into a plastic bag? *Don't, fuck, up.* The real world doesn't grant second chances, not for anyone. You mess up your op-sec out *there,* where there's for-real consequence, and you'll end up *D-R-T.* Anybody know that one?"

Michael lied and lightly shook his head. *He just lectured us about giving up personal intel. Only a few kinds of people know that acronym.*

"D-R-T," John explained, "is *dead right there,* right where you made your very *last* mistake." The domineering trainer made direct and deliberate eye contact with Michael. "Ain't that right, Andrew?"

TRAINING DAY 2, 0734 HOURS_

RURAL COMPOUND. NIOBRARA COUNTY, WYOMING.

WHILE JOHN BEGAN LEADING a morning-long theoretical discussion on moral violence, Michael slowly squirmed in his flimsy plastic chair to find the least uncomfortable position. *Every major muscle group hurts from the workouts these last two days. I can jog forever, but I haven't done much sprinting since I stopped chasing people. I'm not as fit as I thought I was, and this damned chair's driving that point home.*

"Just so you shitheads ain't too surprised later," John continued, "I'm gonna be your primary instructor for all the *combat sports*, everything that involves fightin', shootin,' and stabbin'. Those skills demand a solid base in faith and philosophical doctrine. Takin' up a sword on behalf of God or in defense of others ain't got nothin' to do with takin' a few M-M-A classes, buyin' an undersized black t-shirt, and pickin' fights all over town for shits and giggles. So, because o' that, I also teach most o' the combat mindset and warrior philosophy classes. Doesn't always work out, but I do my best."

John seems like he's been places and done things, Michael thought, *but it'd be nice to know more about the background of the guy that's gonna try to convince us his methods and mindset will save lives.*

"I wanna draw your attention to these two *panels*, for lack of a better word." John walked to the large, canvas-covered rectangles that hung from the stalls to Michael's left. With some flair and a lot of force, John pulled the canvas covers off and dropped them to the concrete floor, which revealed two massive placards. Michael saw the first one, which hung to the left, displayed verses from the Book of Matthew commonly known as "the Beatitudes" in a generic, non-descript font. *Visually plain, the beauty's in the words themselves.*

"I know y'all oughta know these by heart and most o' you probably started studyin' 'em in grade school," John explained, "but I'm gonna read 'em aloud just the same. *'Blessed are the poor, for theirs is the kingdom of heaven. Blessed are those who mourn, for they will be comforted. Blessed are the meek, for they will inherit the earth. Blessed are those who hunger and thirst for righteousness, for they will be filled. Blessed are the merciful, for they will be shown mercy. Blessed are the pure in heart, for they will see God. Blessed are the peacemakers, for they will be called sons of God. Blessed are those who are persecuted because of righteousness, for theirs is the kingdom of heaven. Matthew 5:3-10.'*"

John stepped aside to allow his trainees to read the other panel. Michael also recognized those verses, and he understood their stark contrast to the Beatitudes. *That's probably why they displayed the Proverbs in a calligraphy font,* Michael thought. *They beautified the darkness of those verses and dulled the beauty of the Beatitudes. Interesting psychology.*

"And same thing here," John announced and read the verses aloud. "*'A scoundrel and villain, who goes about with a corrupt mouth, who winks with his eye, signals with his feet and motions with his fingers, who plots evil with deceit in his heart—he always stirs up dissension. Therefore disaster will overtake him in an instant; he will suddenly be destroyed—without remedy. There are six things the Lord hates, seven that are detestable to Him: haughty eyes, a lying tongue, hands that shed innocent blood, a heart that devises wicked schemes, feet that are quick to rush into evil, a false witness who pours out lies and a man who stirs up dissension among brothers. Proverbs 6:12-19.'*"

Michael subconsciously shook his head, unsure if John understood the audience before him. *Those are two of the best-known passages in scripture, so, if we're all ordained priests, this is kinda like teaching da Vinci how to finger paint.*

John ambled away from the signs and returned to the front of the room as he spoke. "It would *behoove* you to keep those opposing lists in your thoughts and prayers. Just like a lotta things in the coming months, I expect you might find *new meaning* in what you thought you already knew."

Another round of wind gusts picked up outside and whistled through the stable's gaps.

"Those opposing verses," John continued, "are the first thing I wanted to cover with y'all today, the first *seed* I wanted to plant in your minds. That's mostly what I'm gonna try to do this mornin,' is just get the seeds planted for the bumper crop we're gonna harvest by the end 'o this thing.

"The second seed concerns the human spirit and psyche. Saint Thomas Aquinas postulated, damned near eight-hundred years ago, that they were two *distinct* and *separate* parts of our being. This is especially relevant whenever we discuss criminal psychology and mental illness. My seed is that, if they are separate, isn't there surely some interaction and relationship between 'em, considering they're both part of the same human being? Therefore, doesn't infection or trauma to one *inherently* impact the other?

"Next seed," John rhetorically pressed onward, "is the possibility of a link between criminal psychology and an evil infection of the spirit. Not talkin' about narcissism, A-D-H-D, none of those kinda things. Psychopathy. Antisocial personality disorder. Pedophilia. The kinda troubles that end up addin' the prefix 'serial' to people's rap sheets. There's gotta be a reason those people can't be fixed, right? Scientific studies provide mountains of confirmation that only a few, specific mental ailments exist that have never been rehabilitated or remedied. Is it possible, just *possible*, that evil, once rooted deep in the human spirit, has found a way to infect the human psyche? Could that be why our docs and head-shrinks are *so* unsuccessful at rehabbing these ailments, if they're tryin' to treat the psyche when the problem's rooted in the spirit? If there is a link between those two, the psyche and the spirit, then the clergy oughta be uniquely prepared and qualified to remedy these specific problems, gentlemen. If that's the case, whaddayou as priests, and we collectively as the Church, what can we do to address these afflictions that medical science has no answer to?"

Michael tried to anticipate where John was headed. *He's obviously done this before, and it's kinda like 'Public Defender 101.' The first day of law school might be spent on civil torts, but the rest of the time there is spent formulating questions that start with 'isn't it possible' and always demand an affirmative answer.*

"Next seed's a moral quandary. In the course-a your clerical duties, let's say you hear confession from a serial killer. You know *everything*. His identity, his home address, the victims and where they're buried. Let's *up* the ante and say you know he's got a victim tied up in his basement *right now*, a little nine-year-old girl, and he's gonna go back home and take her life when he leaves your booth. He admits that he's basin' that presumption on the fact that he's already killed a dozen others in similar fashion and denies havin' *any* self-control to stop from takin' another victim when he's done with the last.

"I'm not lookin' for an answer today, but what do you do? You can't break your sacred vow and violate the Seal of the Confessional. So, what can be done?"

No idea how these other guys are gonna answer, but I know what I'd do, Michael thought. *I might be able to convince that asshole to let me take him to his house to meet the cops and rescue the girl but, if he didn't agree pretty quick, I'd have no problems changing course to something less pleasant for him.*

Bartholomew responded with frustration and moral offense evident in his voice. "*We can only work within the boundaries of the sacrament of reconciliation. We* have *to care for the penitent first and foremost, so we can* only *do what they're willing to allow.*"

John frowned at the trainee and paused before he replied. "I appreciate that we might eventually get cross over issues of morality and faith, but I'm gonna *demand* you keep your goddamned tone civil. We don't know each other that well yet.

"Where was I," John asked as he scanned the other trainees. "Oh, yeah. What about your obligation to protect the human dignity of his victims, past, present, *and* future? Armed with that kinda information, doesn't that change what you might consider necessary? Are you willin' to bear the spiritual burden of having that man take another life?"

Bartholomew just shook his head and didn't respond.

John continued, with no apparent animosity over the exchange. "Is it possible that God sent the penitent into your church, into your confessional booth that day, *specifically* because He knew this man had to confess to someone strong enough to make tough choices? Couldn't that mean you've got the only opportunity God's afforded to save the lives and dignity of dozens, perhaps hundreds of His children?"

John rhetorically paused before pressing them further. "I'm sure y'all already endured similar debates in seminary, but I'm hopin' we can broaden your horizons maybe even just a bit further. So, lemme add a few things about your obligations to the penitent, the serial killer himself. You obviously have to protect his confession, but I wager you'd agree that you're called to help provide this penitent, despite his evil, the same *relief* as you would to any other child of God. The problem is that his psyche, and I assert the underlying evil in his soul, allows him to remain absolved only until his next impulse. Unlike run-of-the-mill sin, *his* temptations degrade human dignity and create new victims. Whaddaya think? Hours? Minutes? Seconds? Depends on the evil, I imagine.

"I believe," John continued, "as humans try to cast evil from our species, whether by prayer, chemical, cleaver, or scalpel, the basic reason we're compelled to do so is love. Love for our fellow man, love for God, and love for ourselves and the hope that someone would be willin' to do the same for us. So, as you sit here today, do you believe we in the Church can love such men enough, and care enough for their eternal salvation, to put in the *tough* work to absolve their sins and save their immortal souls from the *greatest* evils known to man?"

Michael followed John's gaze around the room, and he saw that everyone else seemed equally stumped. *With God, all things are surely possible, but this isn't a practical hope. He's headed toward a theoretical fantasyland.*

"I absolutely believe we can," John beamed, "*and*, that God *compels* us to do so, upon the very risk of our *own* immortal souls."

He might be all sunshine-and-rainbows on the inside right now, Michael surmised, *but his outside's still foreboding as hell.*

"I think it's important for y'all to understand somethin'," John explained. "We're talkin' about all this for a reason. I'm gonna work to get y'all prepared for special assignments in the Church and the Holy See, but that's gonna demand that you know a damned *mountain* of material about righteous warfare. Even if I can't talk about specific roles and assignments,

I believe you *gotta* know that's what we're about here. You'd best realize that early on, accept it, and be onboard with it. I hope that we're gonna challenge your hearts and your minds in how you view your service to God and mankind, but we're also gonna thicken your shields and sharpen your swords to protect and defend the same. Some of mankind's greatest goddamned problems require moral, violent, and unpleasant solutions. God's warriors are thinkin' men who prefer peace and, even when they're in the midst of violent action, always *seek* peace. I'm here to train you to be those kinda problem solvers.

"From my perspective, I propose that most all of today's topics can be tied together with just one thought. I'd like for y'all to keep this in mind, and lemme know how you think it fits in as we go along here over the days, weeks, and months ahead." He stepped to the dry erase board at the front of the room and wrote in large block letters as he spoke. "This statement was written by a Frenchman named Charles Baudelaire. He wrote a book in the 19th-century called 'Flowers of Evil.' You mighta heard this paraphrased in a movie or two, but it's gonna be a central theme to our ongoing discussions." John stepped back from the board and revealed the quote to his trainees.

THE FINEST TRICK OF THE DEVIL IS TO PERSUADE YOU HE DOES NOT EXIST.

"Like I said earlier," John reminded them, "I expect y'all oughta find new meaning in *lotsa* shit you *thought* you already knew and understood."

TRAINING DAY 2, 1629 HOURS_

RURAL TRAINING COMPOUND. NIOBRARA COUNTY.

Michael stood near his unofficially assigned seat in the classroom and awaited John's return from a short break. The instructor's philosophical questions had weighed heavily on Michael during the short lunch break, and he'd kept to himself to consider them. *How are we as priests supposed to uphold our vows of confidence and simultaneously protect humanity from evil inspiration and action? All while risking our eternal salvation to equally care for the souls of the certainly damned? I don't see it.* The dichotomy and weight of John's suppositions had kept him preoccupied through much of the afternoon sessions. *What are we really working toward here?*

As John strode through the classroom's back door at the precise appointed time, Michael sat and resumed his struggle against his flimsy chair. *Damned torture device, gotta be an international sanction against this kinda treatment.*

"I try to keep the all-classroom days to a minimum, but it just ends up being kinda necessary at the beginning of the program. Gotta get the housekeeping work outta the way near the front end-a this thing to make sure we're all on the same page."

"To that end," John continued, "we're gonna press on with some philosophy. I mentioned *Thomas Aquinas* earlier. In the interest of full disclosure, I'm an avid Aquinas man myself, got tremendous admiration for the fella. Anyone here know much about him?"

Zeb spoke up quickly. "Saint Thomas Aquinas was a friar from Italy, born in the early 1200's, and died at about fifty-years-old. His philosophy shaped much of Western Civilization and frequently focused on the earlier writings of Saint Augustine."

"Goddamned right," John happily confirmed, "he's canonized while the Church still used Devil's Advocates in that particular process to weed out all but the most worthy. Only ninety-three saints were canonized before 1983, and there's been somethin' like five hundred identified since. Speaking for myself, I like to know a little bit about the philosopher before putting too much stock in their opinions and ponderings. Just because they've been canonized doesn't necessarily mean they're the top of the pile, at least among the saints.

"Taking a secular philosopher, for example. Y'all probably heard 'o Friedrich Nietzsche, right? That ole boy's a German atheist and philosopher that wanted to know 'who's gonna watch the watchers.' 'If you stare into the abyss, the abyss stares back.' 'Those who pursue monsters should take care to ensure they do not become one.' All that pompous, anti-authority shit, along with a lot that criticized faith and organized religion." John fished a fresh dip from his Copenhagen tin and continued. "But, see, that sum-bitch lived out his years in a goddamned asylum, where he died of syphilis. So, I personally choose to seek my philosophy elsewhere. Kinda blurs the line between thought and insane, syphilitic wonderings, ya know? Maybe it's just me, but I'm kinda funny that way."

"Anyhow, I digress," John surmised. "Saint Aquinas said there were four critical components to waging a 'just war.' The very existence of the term 'just war' implicitly tells us that violence, circumstantially, is allowed and reasonable, a valid act. Anyone know what the first consideration is?"

Zeb spoke up again. "The war must be waged by those in authority. Aquinas originally identified them as 'princes,' but our understanding of the text has since expanded to include all with lawful authority over a population or nation."

Not surprised he's good with academics, Michael thought, *he looks like he spent all his time in the library and not out on the fields or a wrestling mat. He's gonna need a lotta heart to stay here, as small as he is.*

"You a history buff, Zeb?"

"Not really, but I wrote a research paper on Aquinas in seminary."

"Alright, well, put your damned feet up and let someone else answer. I know there's someone else in here that knows what Aquinas had to say. Who's got his second condition?"

"There must be a just cause for the war," Sergio answered.

Of course, he would know about 'just war,' Michael silently concluded, *he was a Marine for six years!*

"And, Jude," John asked Sergio's pseudonym, "who gets to decide, subjectively, what constitutes 'just cause' for warfare?"

"Aquinas said it could be to avenge injuries, punish wrongs, or any action ordained by God Himself."

"Still subjective, though, right?"

"Yeah, it could be, but I think he intended the underlying basis to be consistent with the scriptures."

"I can agree with that," John stated. "Anyone hung up a little bit that Aquinas identified *vengeance* as the first of his defined 'just' reasons for going to war?"

The group fell silent, and Michael mulled over the question. *This feels like my argument with Monsignor Medina, just that John seems to side with me.* "For me, there are conflicting examples in the Holy Scriptures, and even in the Catechism, that state on the one hand that vengeance is solely God's right, but then, on the other, God celebrated or rewarded violence and retaliation for unjust wrongs. It's not a hang-up for me, personally," Michael explained, "and I believe God allows and endorses conditional violence."

"I think vengeance is one of the most hotly contested topics among the faithful," John offered, "and the most-cited criticism from those that wanna punch holes in the validity and divinity of our faith. We're mostly accused of being too violent, or selectively endorsing violence against our own enemies, or what-the-hell-ever the goddamned secular hashtag is today. By the way, young-uns," John facetiously smiled at the class, "that's called a 'pound sign,' and it ain't nothin' new. Back to work. Who's got the third condition?"

"War must be waged for the right reasons," Michael answered. "We're compelled to fight either to do good or avoid evil. Effectively, we go to war to preserve or reacquire peace or justice, even beyond the initial justifications for war."

"I like that explanation," John responded. "*We go to war to preserve or reacquire peace or justice.* I'm gonna steal that, Andrew. Now, I'll give you the fourth, just because I think it's funny. Aquinas demanded that training exercises are only allowed if your soldiers don't participate in actual violence and ransacking." John chuckled and offered the first broad smile Michael had seen on the man. "That's my favorite," he explained. "You know shit was *bad* in his society when the local militia went out to train and *accidentally* pillaged the countryside. *Oops*. Talk about takin' shit too far."

Michael and several of his classmates chuckled at John's dry delivery.

"So, four considerations," John exclaimed and held up his right fist and counted them off with his fingers as he spoke. "Just authority, including God. Just cause. Just actions. And, practice-good, pillage-bad. That about sum it up?"

Michael nodded in agreement and saw most everyone else did, as well.

"So, going back to the first consideration. The head of a nation can call for war. What about a monarch, a king, can he declare a 'just war?'"

"Yes," came the near-unison student response.

"What about a president, or an elected official," John asked.

"Yes," again as a group response.

"What about a dictator, a czar? Can they declare a 'just war?'"

Silence briefly enveloped the group as they considered the question.

"Yes," Michael offered, "*I* think so. They could have still come to power through lawful means and have righteous authority over the nation they're defending."

"Good," John replied. "As long as they're the lawful authority figure over that political entity, then, in that case, I agree." John looked around the room and smirked before asking the next question. "So, what about the *pope*? Can *His Holiness* declare a 'just war?'"

The question surprised Michael, just as it seemed to do to the rest of his class. *Never considered it, but, why would he? Can he?*

"Yes," Sergio finally and confidently answered. "The pope *can* call for war."

John smiled and pointed at Sergio, but scanned the rest of the class.

"Everybody hear that? Tell us, Jude, why can the pope declare war, a 'just war' in particular."

"The pope is the head of the Holy See, a sovereign theocratic nation-state with its own jurisdiction, territory, and armed forces."

"*Facts*, gentlemen," John surmised, "*all facts*. The sitting pope *always* has the authority and the option to send the armed forces of the Holy See into combat, for both offensive and defensive purposes. Me, personally, if I were on his staff, I'd strongly advise him against a frontal assault, though, given that his small army is presently and perpetually surrounded."

"That's not where the pope has the tactical or strategic advantage, though, John," Sergio countered their instructor's half-joking assertion. "His forces are uniquely positioned inside every foreign state on Earth, ideologically driven, and would allow him a tremendous, unrivaled capacity for successful guerrilla warfare campaigns against anyone he declares to be an enemy of the state."

"Jude," John announced, "I think you and I're gonna get along just fine." He paused and scanned the other students for confirmation or dissent.

That kinda kills the debate, Michael thought. *Even if I disagree with Sergio, who the hell's gonna offer a counter argument after John makes an endorsement like that?*

John looked back to a clock that hung on the wall behind him at the front of the room and then addressed the group again. "Alright, looks like we're runnin' up on quittin' time for the day. You kiddies have a homework assignment for tonight. Starting tomorrow, I've got a new punishment and reward system to help motivate each of you to stay as ambiguous and anonymous as possible. It's a skill most people have to intentionally develop, so we're gonna motivate you the best way I know how, with both a carrot and a stick. So, as you lay on your bunks tonight staring up at the bottom of my floor, you'd best spend some time ponderin' everything you do and say that might help someone learn somethin' about you, maybe even help identify you. For example, do you speak with a specific, localized accent? Are you a big enough dumbshit to get a Texas flag tattooed on your arm before you decided to marry the Church?

"Consider all the ways that you normally give up intel on yourself and how others could use that to identify or find you. Then, change your habits and normal goddamned behaviors to stop doing that stupid shit. Once we start this little game, I'mma make sure everybody plays. You will be handsomely rewarded for correctly identifying private and personal information about your classmates, and you will be severely punished for giving up that same information on yourself. Details to follow, as I'd prefer that you have all night to get all worked up about it. Unless somebody's got anything real pressing, I'm pretty damned tired of lookin' at all-a you, so knock off for the day and be up on the porch at 0-5-45 tomorrow. Congratulations on surviving Day Two." A mischievous smile spread across his face. "Lookin' forward to seein' what you shitheads think about Day Three. Dismissed."

TRAINING DAY 2, 2056 HOURS_

RURAL COMPOUND. NIOBRARA COUNTY, WYOMING.

MICHAEL LAID on his bed and tried to immerse himself in a detective fiction, *Harbor Nocturne,* by Joseph Wambaugh. The other students similarly lounged and milled about the basement as their day drew to a close. *Glad the wind finally died down after dark, but it never really stops. At least I can't hear it down here in the basement. That's an unexpected perk.* Most of his colleagues kept to themselves and shied away from much contact or dialogue with each other. *John's gotcha-game is gonna drive us even farther apart. It's so weird to be crammed in tight quarters with like-minded men but punished for actually bonding with any of 'em.*

His need to remain "intel positive," even among his classmates, reminded Michael that his other book, *Left of Bang,* had gone missing after the instructors had searched through his property yesterday and piled it up with everyone else's. *Don't know if they confiscated it, or someone else grabbed it by mistake. Give it a couple days and see if it shows up. Ironically, I could really use the book's reminders on situational awareness and threat analysis right now.* From the corner of his eye, he saw Sergio laying back on his bunk and periodically tossing a small medicine ball toward the ceiling and catching it. His friend had done that almost every night that they lived together in Ecuador, claiming it helped strengthen his hands and calm his mind.

Movement to his left drew Michael's attention, and he saw Phillip walking cautiously toward the stairs as though he didn't want to be seen doing so. *If that guy can be trained, he'd make the perfect spy. I can't tell if he's white, Hispanic, Arabian, East Asian, or from somewhere in the Mediterranean. He's about as nonchalant as a drunk skunk, though, right now.*

After momentarily looking up, Phillip turned around and addressed the group in a hushed voice. "Hey, whaddayou guys think of the instructors?"

Michael lowered his novel and looked around the room. *Everyone's waiting for someone else to talk. Nobody trusts each other yet, probably just the way John wants it.* "In terms of what," Michael hesitantly clarified, "their competency, personalities, character?"

"All of it, I guess," Phillip replied. "They all seem pretty damned impersonal, maybe a little cold, but that one guy, the stocky brown-haired dude, I'm pretty sure he's just an asshole."

"You mean 'Double-Time,'" Sergio asked.

"Yeah," Phillip chuckled, "he says that too much."

"I think he's probably just arrogant," Sergio replied and resumed tossing his medicine ball. "Give him space if you can, and you'll be fine."

"What about 'Tex,'" Zeb asked from his spot on the floor.

"The cowboy-lookin' fella," Z clarified. "I been callin' him 'The Marlboro Man.'"

"What about the other guy? I've been using 'The Mouse,'" Matthew offered.

"'*El Raton,*'" Sergio responded and shrugged, "'cuz he's Hispanic."

"What about the African-American southerner," Z asked.

"You mean the one Southerner *other* than you," Thomas harshly injected.

"'Big Country,'" Michael replied, ignoring Thomas' confrontation.

"And the woman," Thomas asked. "Whaddayou guys been callin' her?"

"I've just been callin' her 'Jane,'" Matthias responded, "like John said yesterday."

"Yeah, sure," Thomas answered as though disappointed in the lack of creativity, "'Just Jane.'"

"I'm more worried 'bout us," Sergio offered between medicine ball tosses. "We're missing all the heavy hitters. No 'Paul.' No 'Peter.' At least they gave us John the Baptist, but I'm not sure we're gonna make it without Peter and Paul."

Michael smiled at his friend's dry humor. A moment of renewed silence passed between them all, and he returned to his novel.

"What the hell do you all think's going on here," Bartholomew asked from his bunk near the showers.

The pressing question on everyone's mind, Michael thought as he sat up.

"Introduction to the job, or jobs, whatever they are, I guess," Z offered from the bed next to Michael.

Phillip spoke up next. "I can't decide if they're training us to be security guards, criminal profilers, or," he facetiously added, "assassins. Could be anything."

"I hope it's assassins," Thomas coyly announced with a smirk, "don't have that one on my resume, yet."

"Yeah, Catholic assassins," Michael chuckled and shook his head, "pretty sure that one's been done before."

"You guys know the Vatican has its own intelligence service, right," Matthew asked. "This could be a selection program for that."

"Do they still call it 'C-I-A' and just change the acronym?" Sergio's joke elicited a few chuckles.

"Don't y'all think it's awfully coincidental that John only had eleven names in the hat yesterday," Z asked.

"Don't know," Michael offered. "Could be just that, coincidence."

"I dunno," Zeb added. "Seems questionable that the one big guy got left on the bus at the last minute, and then there's not a leftover name for him in the hat right after it happened."

"He could-a been a plant," Sergio agreed, "but, even if he was, what difference does it make? We're all here and he's not, and, either way, we all know John's serious about sending people home. If he was a plant, he had the desired effect."

"Maybe," Matthias cautiously chimed in, "one of the instructors inside the house saw what happened and just took one name out."

Bartholomew scoffed. "And they just happened to grab 'Peter,' the most critical apostle to our worldview?"

"About an eight-percent chance of grabbing any one in particular," Michael countered, "one-in-twelve, right? I mean, it had to be one of 'em." *Bartholomew's a little vocal when he thinks we're unsupervised. That makes him my leading mole candidate. He's gonna try to instigate some kinda dissent before this's over.*

"It's just fishy," Bartholomew responded. "I don't trust it."

"I think that's part of the point," Sergio counseled and continued to repeatedly toss his medicine ball in the air over his head. "This place is built on secrets, and we gotta learn to trust what we *feel* as much as what we *see* and *hear*."

"What the hell does that even mean," Bartholomew asked and shook his head in disbelief.

"It means," Sergio explained, caught his medicine ball, and sat up to more directly address Bartholomew and the rest of their group, "that as long as you *feel* in your heart that this is the *right place* for you to be, and you're here at the *right time* in your life and for the *right reasons*, then stay and carry on, even if you can't readily explain everything you see and hear. Trust your heart, *follow the path it takes you down,* and know that your head will eventually follow. In the meantime, try shuttin' the hell up and keepin' us outta trouble."

TRAINING DAY 3, 0800 HOURS_

RURAL COMPOUND. NIOBRARA COUNTY, WYOMING.

WITH HIS HEAD bowed in prayer, Michael sat in their converted classroom in the same thin, flimsy plastic chair he'd been using for the past two days. *Glad we're celebrating mass this morning, and that John's giving us time to pray the liturgy every day. It's reassuring that our focus here remains on God first and foremost, regardless of whatever else it is that we're doing.* His legs already hurt from three consecutive days of runs and sprint work, and the repeated kneeling, sitting, and standing this morning had reminded Michael he generally overestimated the quality of his physical conditioning. John had added some basic parkour exercises to their morning run and introduced them to his obstacle course. They'd finished up with a short yoga stretch routine. *I've always heard yoga is supposed to be calming and meditative, but that shit's just bodyweight strength work in disguise.*

"Amen."

Michael raised his head and looked toward the front of the repurposed stable and the aging Monsignor who delivered mass to the trainees. *He didn't introduce himself as a monsignor, but that's how he's dressed. Kinda looks like a kindly grandfather figure with an easy smile.* The plastic tables had been moved to the outside of the room for the morning mass. Michael glanced down at a folded, dark red towel just past his feet. John had provided them to soften the floor beneath their knees, but the token gesture hadn't proven especially effective.

"Let us consider the directives God has given the Church," the monsignor began his homily, "through his most beloved apostle, Saint Peter, to found His church and to shepherd His people home to him. In establishing the Church as an ecclesial ministry, the Lord our God gave her authority, mission, orientation, and goals. In order to protect and guide the People of God and to grow its numbers without end, Christ the Lord set upon the Church a variety of offices that serve the good of the whole body. The men in these offices are invested with a sacred power, a divine authority that can be traced back almost two millennia to Saint Peter himself. They are dedicated to promoting the interest of their brethren so that all the People of God may aspire and attain divine and eternal salvation through the Church and Christ our Lord.

"It is these men, Saint Peter's potential successors entrusted and tasked with the fiduciary burden of shepherding the immortal souls of all God's children, that we must place our trust, our support, and our ceaseless efforts to their appointed and specified tasks. It is behind these divinely appointed men that we must cast our lot, praying for their wisdom, humility, and complete and total submission to the word and guidance of Christ our God."

Michael listened to the rest of the monsignor's message, but his mind kept replaying the discussion among his class last night. *Today's lesson dovetails perfectly from Sergio's assertion that we must be able to trust those appointed over us here and follow our hearts, even when we don't readily know what to make of everything we see and hear. The world may provide misinformation and distractions, even deception, that our hearts should recognize and guide us through.*

"Stand fast in your own convictions," the monsignor continued, "especially in the face of criticism we know to be untrue. We are called to allow our own spiritual experience, the mysteries of our faith, to guide and deepen our personal understanding of Holy Scriptures and the Catechism. I pray that we would also expand and broaden our understanding of the human experience, even as our distractions and the noise surrounding us increase and attempt to present the false notion that the evolution of our species has outlived the Church and its divine teachings.

There is nothing new under the sun and nothing new to God. His word has provided all we require to address and solve all the struggles and difficulties that we now or will ever face and endure. Surely, the aged wisdom of His appointed leadership and His Church will see us through all that is to come before us."

After the celebration of mass concluded and the monsignor departed the classroom, John stepped back to the front. "Alright, shitheads, get the chairs cleared out of the way and go get changed again, get outta those dress clothes. Even I'm tired of all the goddamned lectures, so me and my associates are gonna teach you all to *kick the shit* out of each other instead. At some point during the day, you're each gonna get called out one-at-a-time. Hustle."

When Michael returned to the classroom dressed in athletic shorts and a t-shirt, he saw a variety of striking pads scattered around the room, along with a stacked assortment of dull training knives and simulated, solid-rubber handguns and rifles. John laid out pairs of focus mitts for well-aimed strikes, punches, and kicks, and his five associates huddled quietly in the room's far corner.

The lead instructor looked up and nodded to acknowledge Michael as he walked farther into the room. "How you feelin,' Andrew?"

"Good enough, John. Haven't pushed myself this hard in a while. It's good, though."

"I firmly believe that sweat lost in training equates to blood retained in combat," John replied and stood. "My goal here, one of 'em, anyway, is to do my best to ensure none-a you has to bleed out there, ever."

"Lofty goal," Michael surmised.

"Man's gotta have somethin' to shoot for."

Sergio walked through the back door, and John immediately began working the two of them out. After a light warm-up, they began light touch-sparring, with other students and instructors joining in as they arrived. Before long, all eleven trainees worked in pairs, with the odd-man-out going rounds with John's associates.

Over the course of the next three hours, John led Michael and his classmates through the basics of the physics, mechanics, and mindset of empty-hand-combat. He'd made time to briefly cover the very foundational principles of punches, jabs, kicks, elbows, and knees. John had just started the trainees on an introduction to ground fighting when Michael heard the back door open.

"Andrew!"

He looked out into the bright sunlight beaming in from the open doorway. Realizing The Mouse had called out his pseudonym, Michael stood and headed off to the door.

"Got an appointment," the instructor explained as Michael reached the door. "Follow me."

Michael assumed he wasn't supposed to know what the "appointment" entailed. *If they wanted me to know, they'd have told me.* The Mouse hurriedly led him to the main house and back to one of the front, upstairs bedrooms.

"In here."

Michael opened the door, stepped in, and found the monsignor from that morning's mass seated inside. The room and its furnishings had the appearance of a stereotypical psychiatrist's office, at least how Michael had seen them presented on television. *Only been in one shrink's office when the P-D wanted to make sure I was crazy enough to go to the academy.* The monsignor sat in a plain chair at one end of the room, with a loveseat and two different chairs oriented around him.

"Hello, Andrew," he greeted Michael without standing. "Go ahead and sit wherever you'd like."

And, now this *mandatory fun. The head-shrink starts evaluating my every move, from the way I walk into the room, how I respond to him, and even which chair I choose. Let the games begin.* Michael stepped directly to the elder priest, shook his hand, and sat in the chair closet to him. *Not where I want to be, but this is where I want him to see me. I wonder how he's gonna reverse my reverse-psychology.*

"We're just gonna have a short chat today, Andrew, about the training so far and your thoughts on some of the classes, in general. You can call me Father Harry."

"Nice to finally have a name to go with the face. Beautiful mass this morning, thank you."

"I do my best, son, and thank you for being here to participate in it."

"If I may ask, *Father Harry*, what is your role here, and what is the nature of *our* relationship?"

"I'm here just as a spiritual advisor, mostly to offer guidance and counsel to you and your colleagues, and, if necessary, to hear confessionals."

"So, what can I know about the confidentiality of our conversations?"

"Well, that depends, doesn't it, Andrew? I'm a member of the clergy, same as you, and I'm a clinical psychiatrist, but I'm also employed and paid by the same people that employ you. So, everything you say in here is protected from everyone but your employer, because that's who's footing the bill, and anything you tell me in the course of my duties as a member of the clergy is, of course, protected just as anyone else would be."

"Thank you for your candor and your clarification," Michael offered. *Now I know where I stand, and I know I'm not gonna tell you shit. Everything's fine, the world is a beautiful place, and I'm just excited and honored to be here, no matter what the hell happens outside your doorway.*

Michael spent the following fifty-five minutes parrying Father Harry's questions and providing what he believed to be the most benign and mentally healthy answers. *All's well, nothing to see here.* When finally released from the evaluation, Michael hustled back over to the classroom. *I'd rather trade punches than talk about why I feel what I feel.* He passed Sergio and The Mouse on their way toward the main house, and Michael did his best to ignore both men. *Must be his turn in the barrel.*

Michael stepped back into the classroom and found everyone seated on the floor in a wide semicircle around John. "Grab some concrete, Andrew. Alright, last thing before you check out for the day. We're gonna start a game called 'Guess What,' and it's gonna run the whole time you're out here. Rules are simple. Don't let anyone know shit about you, not a goddamned thing. Every day, you're all gonna get a three-by-five flashcard on the front porch before your run. You're gonna fill it out and give it back to get your map for that day's run. Write something, write nothing, I don't care. But the goal of this is to help your colleagues with their own operational security measures. If they divulge something personal to you, I wanna know about it so they can receive the remedial training necessary to avoid repeating that mistake.

"If you're the one who screwed up, there's gonna be penalties that *start* at a hundred burpees and go up from there. More penalties, more punishment. Repeated offenses, more punishment.

"If you're the snitch, I'm sorry, if you're the one that's been kind enough to help better secure your brethren, and you give me something that's *correct* about your colleague, you get half-off any burpees you're assigned. My objective here is to make you all 'intel-positive,' which means that you learn more from your environment than you give away to anyone else inside it."

Zeb half-raised his hand and spoke. "Real quick, John, how's that gonna work when the other guys find out who's been dropping paper on 'em?"

"Oh, I assure your anonymity, Zeb. The danger here, especially for those of you that go on to some kind of field work, is that giving away intel might get you hurt or killed, or someone else hurt or killed. And, you'll probably never know who did it, or why, or how you messed up. So, I don't tell anyone what they said or did, they just get punished for it. And, real quick, before someone in here quietly proposes tonight that y'all band together to not dime each other out, there will be an additional and substantial reward for the two most intel-positive in your group. At the end of the day, you're doing your classmates a favor by telling me about their mistakes. They get a little bit of inconvenient misery here for what, out there, will get 'em killed, or get you killed, or, God forbid, get the pope killed. So, for the safety and welfare of you, your partners, and all-things-holy, let the snitching begin."

TRAINING DAY 4, 0545 HOURS_

RURAL COMPOUND. NIOBRARA COUNTY, WYOMING.

DRESSED IN WARM RUNNING ATTIRE, Michael joined the other students on the front porch. *Sunrise won't be for another half hour, and it's just barely starting to break twilight. Glad when it finally starts warming up in the mornings, maybe in another month or so.*

"Good morning, shitheads," John offered as he stepped through the front doorway, his large ceramic coffee mug already in hand. "Plan for this morning is simple. Head down *Mother Mary* for a warm-up, but don't jog past the abandoned barn y'all must-a seen by now. Turn around, come back. That's about a three-mile warm-up to start with. When you get back, the sun'll be up and you can get in some uphill sprint work. I'll have more for you when I see y'all back here. It pays to be a winner!"

Michael started off toward the trail entrance with the others, most of whom still didn't pace themselves well. *They'll learn soon enough that most of this is marathon work and they'll eventually quit treating everything like a sprint.* He glanced around only enough to ensure that he and Sergio weren't near one another and worked on maintaining his own three-mile pace. Even though he wasn't very far from any of the other runners, none of them spoke out on the trail. *Hard to decide what we are. Students? Teammates? Coworkers? Rivals? Competitors? Roommates? John's prohibition on sharing all personal information does do one thing, it'll for damned sure prevent us from being 'friends.' Gotta be a reason for that.* After mulling over his own thoughts for almost a half-hour, Michael landed back on the front porch.

"Speed work, Andrew," John directed from his chair as steam rose from his full cup of fresh coffee. "Head over to the driveway with the others. Run, as far as you can sprint up toward the road, rest while you walk back to the start, and repeat that for time. We'll be out there until someone pukes or I say otherwise."

Michael complied and soon found himself with winded lungs and burning legs. By 7am, he stumbled back down the driveway toward the house and struggled for air. With his hands on his head to open the bottom of his lungs, Michael wished someone would vomit so they could stop this phase of their suffering. *I'd try taking one for the team, if I thought that would actually work.*

"Alright," John shouted from the porch, "form up around the flagpole and await further instruction." He sipped from his coffee mug and made no effort to meet them yet.

Thank God, Michael thought, *at least I think so. The devil I know is usually better than the one I don't.* As he reached the flagpoles, he bent forward with his hands on his hips and worked to slow his breathing. A glance up the hill showed the last few stragglers were coming back in. John finally stood and strolled over to meet them just as the last student arrived.

"So, here's how this is gonna work from here on out," John announced. "After the morning workout, you'll meet me here for accolades and punishments. We talked about the 'Guess What' game yesterday, so here's that news.

"Alpha," he continued, "you, Z, and The Baptist all owe me a hundred burpees for minor infractions. If you'll recall, you never get to know what you did. Just get your shit squared and stop being wrong."

"In other bad news," John said to change topics, "Zeb's on the floor tonight and Bart's on the cot. It pays to be a winner here, and you two can't pass a goddamned corpse on the trails. Get your shit moved off the bunks and over next to the shitter.

"Everyone but the three that owes me burpees can hit the showers and be back in the classroom at 0-7-30. Get buckled in tight for a couple straight days of classroom. No field trips for a while, so you ain't gotta worry about gettin' mommy and daddy to sign any permission slips just yet. You're gonna dig into some basic criminal psychology today, nothing too in-depth, just enough understanding for you to spot character traits in your adversaries that could benefit you in innumerable ways."

By 7:30am, Michael had been seated in the classroom for only about two minutes. *I hate this compressed timetable shit. Five minutes early is ten minutes late.* At the stroke of the bottom half of the hour, Father Harry, the aging, grandfatherly monsignor from yesterday's mass, entered the back of the room and strode purposefully up to the front. Michael looked around and saw that Zeb still hadn't joined them. *He'll get to pay for that later, too. That dude's never gonna get to sleep in a bed.*

"Good morning. I think I've met everyone, but, just in case, please call me Father Harry. I don't wanna be the only one without a nickname here." Father Harry smiled, and several students chuckled along with him. "I have a background in psychology, criminal manifestations, and rehabilitation therapies. I've only got the day to give you an introduction to this broad topic, so we'd best be started now."

Breaking for only a half-hour lunch, Father Harry guided a lecture and interactive discussion for the rest of the day, and they covered the most prominent topics: schizophrenia, sociopathy, psychopathy, narcissism, antisocial personality disorders, multiple personality disorder, addiction and co-dependence, Munchausen's, Munchausen's by Proxy, and borderline personality disorder.

Michael looked at his watch and saw it was already after 5pm. *We've been at this all day, and he's still only given us the highlight reel.*

Father Harry looked down at a brown leather-bound notebook he'd set on a corner of the front banquet table. "Looks like the last thing that I wanted to cover before we end today's session is more of a philosophical topic. Anyone want to postulate the difference between 'murder' and 'killing?'"

Michael consciously decided to stay out of this conversation, lest he find himself on the losing end of tomorrow's round of *Guess What?*

"Killing is simply the ending of a life," Alpha offered and tried to minimize his French accent, "while murder is the deliberate act of doing so. You can kill someone by accident."

"Murder also requires a victim," Sergio added. "Tragedies kill, but don't create a real victim."

Father Harry nodded to acknowledge both answers. "Is there a Biblical difference in the two?"

"Of course," Thomas blurted out, "otherwise all war'd be mortal sin, and we couldn't subject serial killers to the death penalty."

"Thank you for the transition, Thomas," Harry hesitantly offered, "although I wanna make sure we come back to the original topic in a bit." He stopped as though in search of the right words. "I'm sure you're all familiar with the approved change that Pope Cornelius II and Cardinal Laddeneau recently announced about death penalties. It's caused quite a stir between Catholics of varying ideological beliefs and interpretations of our texts and scriptures. Just for our clarification and dissection of the actual text and its specific words, I'll read it verbatim so we're all starting from the same footing."

He donned small reading glasses, retrieved his notebook, and referred to the pages of its interior. "22-67. *Nations throughout history have used death penalties to punish heinous crimes committed within their jurisdictions. Traditionally, we have conditionally tolerated death penalties carried out by legitimate authorities as an extreme and regrettable necessity to protect common human dignity. However, our deepened understanding now compels us to affirm that death penalties are inadmissible and unnecessary. Humane detention methods commonly exist that protect the dignity of both the populace and the incarcerated. Therefore, it is an inviolable attack on the guilty to deny them every moment of their God-given opportunity to seek Him and His truth.*"

Father Harry looked up and scanned the room as he continued. "So, now, keeping in mind the difference between 'murder' and 'killing,' and the allowed justifications for killing, what does Pope Cornelius' recent death penalty declaration mean?"

Michael and most of the other students glanced around, waiting for one of them to be the first to offer an answer. *Somebody's gotta go first.* "Sir, I think most people read that to mean that all state-sponsored death as criminal punishment is no longer allowed."

"Okay, that's a start, and somewhat specific, right? You brought up several qualifications there: a state, a criminal, and punishment for his crimes. What else?"

Zeb raised his hand and spoke. "It also reaffirms the Catholic belief in the dignity of all human life, which is the core issue around state-sponsored death penalties. It's effectively one man, or group of people, deciding to put another down by majority rule, like an infectious animal."

"That's a good analogy, we can work with that, I think, gentlemen." Father Harry set his notebook down on the front banquet table, removed his reading glass, and slowly paced as he spoke. "So, what change does this make in Church doctrine and dogma?"

Michael wanted to passionately debate this topic, but his opinions and personal experience with violence had routinely been discounted by those that demanded ideology trump human nature. *Best to stay in the background on this one.*

"From a clerical perspective," Z offered, "regardless of my own feelings, I fear for the impact it has on the laity, especially those who support or have personally participated in state-sanctioned death penalties."

Father Harry's face lit up with excitement. "Excellent, Z, excellent. Yes, so, this demands a *lot* of additional inquiry, correct? Does the amended paragraph 22-67 in the Catechism mean, then, that all death penalty killings in years past were mortal sins? If so, doesn't that mean that everyone who carried them out unknowingly added to their original sin, even though death penalties were allowed under narrow exceptions up until now? What if the executioner died between the death he facilitated and the recent revelation, do you think they faced God with that blemish on their soul? If this is in fact, a declaration from God, why now, after several millennia when appropriate and just death penalties were *never* a mortal sin?" Father Harry cleared his throat and waited for a response before he continued.

"For me personally," Thomas loudly offered, "I think this 'new understanding' is just gonna let the worst criminal offenders live out the rest of their unrepentant lives on tax money from the people they wasted their freedom victimizing."

That's the first reasonable thing that asshole's said, Michael thought. *Borderline heretical, but reasonable just the same.*

Father Harry ignored Thomas' inferred denial of the Pope's divine authority and infallibility and let his last questions remain rhetorical. "Can anyone think of an example in His Holy Scriptures where God uses a man, or men, or His children, as tools or instruments to deliver His directed and guided vengeance against His enemies?"

Michael slowly raised his hand and noticed that everyone else in the room did so as well. *There are literally dozens of such examples.*

"Does anything in this change have anything to do with God's wrath or vengeance?"

Alpha shook his head and leaned forward. "No. It only concerns the nation-states and criminals, not God and sinners."

Father Harry nodded his agreement. "So, can we all agree then, that this updated paragraph in the Catechism concerns only those three conditions: a nation, a criminal, and punishment? Well, a fourth concern exists, really. The Church has long held that the execution of a death penalty ultimately deprives the criminal of all further opportunities they would otherwise have to redeem their soul. You see, the state has forced the criminal into an unusual circumstance with the way most carry out death penalties. If the criminal offers a full confession and seeks absolution, that is used against them as evidence of their crimes; if they maintain their false innocence to avoid punishment, they risk meeting God with a stained and blemished soul that may send them to hell for all eternity."

Michael noticed that, to varying degrees of enthusiasm, all the other students nodded in agreement.

"And, so, then," the monsignor continued, "if God calls one of His children to righteous action, to bring violence against evil, against an *unjust aggressor* that threatened another human, maybe many humans, maybe all of humanity; and the unjust aggressor comes to pass, does this amended paragraph 22-67 offer anything about that?"

"No," Michael replied along with several others, adding, "of course not."

"Okay, good." Father Harry put his hands up and looked at everyone seated before him. "Please, focus on this and stay with me now. To tie this back into the bulk of today's discussion on criminal psychology," he paused and resumed a methodic pace at the front of the room. "The defects in the human condition, in the brain, in the body, in the very soul that even medical science and psychology say cannot be treated or rehabilitated; the serial rapist, the pedophile, the criminally insane who see no wrong in denying their fellow humans of their divine dignity. It seems that everyone agrees these few, broken souls, even if they were to realize the error of their ways, confess their sins, and accept Christ into their heart and profess His teachings with their lips; even if they did all that, they can never be rehabilitated and will recommit their sins within hours, minutes, perhaps even *seconds* if their circumstances allowed it. These are the very same *unjust aggressors* that are affected by the change to 22-67, many of them. Very few people descend into the bowels of Death Row without the incurable 'personality disorders' and the criminality that is borne of it. Going back to our fourth concern, about the certainty of the fall of these men into Hell without a sincere confession and absolution. Knowing they are recidivists who *will not* meaningfully repent, can't one argue that we've now only prolonged the collective suffering on earth? Their victims' justice has been lessened, the aggressor's life is shortened and caged, and many will inevitably spend eternity in Hell regardless."

Michael cleared his throat and replied. "To be fair, I believe the intent behind the change was to ensure the sinner, the criminal in this case, had the full length of his natural life to offer confession and seek absolution for his actions."

"I agree," the monsignor responded, "but, if they refuse to seek God's mercy and absolution without significant external pressure, like that provided by a looming death sentence, won't they now just spend additional years in misery and only seek forgiveness at a much later, and unscheduled, unpredictable eleventh hour?"

Michael had to concede the point. "I can't say that isn't accurate."

"Thus, if certain evils cannot be rehabilitated, and men suffering from these afflictions die unexpectedly during a life sentence and never feel the pressure of an imminent deadline to compel them to seek God, haven't we actually condemned their soul to Hell, rather than providing the apparent, intended dignity of confession and absolution?"

Michael leaned back in his chair and considered the monsignor's argument. *An ideological policy that discounts actual human nature.*

"What would you say," Father Harry asked, stopped pacing, and continued speaking to the group at-large. "Could God use specific, select members of His children to separate these infected souls from their mortal shells, perhaps in such a way as to offer them a final absolution before they've had another chance to sully their soul? Perhaps offer their soul its only conceivable chance at eternal salvation?"

The room fell silent, and Michael wanted to ensure he understood the monsignor's question. "Father Harry, are you asking if it would be just for someone to kill another, specifically for the *purpose* of *saving* their soul?"

"In short, yes, as in a case like that of a psychopathic serial killer that's immune to change. He knows, science knows, reasonable people everywhere know it. God knows it. So, with that understanding, I want to postulate an argument that it *is* permissible to work in unorthodox ways to save his soul."

"Like an anti-Hamlet," Z offered in his thick Carolina accent.

"I'm sorry, I don't follow," Harry admitted, frowned, and very slightly shook his head.

"So, Hamlet's the prince of Denmark. Hamlet's uncle murdered his father the king, married his grieving mother, the queen, and Hamlet finds out about all that. He wants to kill his uncle, who's now his stepdad, but when he finally finds him alone, he's knelt down in prayer. Hamlet starts to go through with it, but then figures he'd be doing his murderous uncle a *favor* by killin' him *after* he's absolved his sins and his soul's about as clean as it's ever gonna be. So, he decides to come back later, but, turns out he should've just gone through with it."

"Yes," Harry replied, "I suppose that is a fair analogy."

Michael appreciated the historical, literary reference, but wanted to bring the discussion back to their doctrine. "I think one of the paragraphs that's near 22-67 addresses this topic, depending on the reason for the death."

"I've got the Catechism here," Phillip announced while flipping through the pages of a small hard-cover on the table in front of him. "Let's see. 22-64, this one allows for self-defense even if it results in harm or death of the unjust aggressor. Not really a good fit, unless that condition applies.

"22-65," he continued, "this one deals with, defense and, okay. Got it. Yep, 22-65. '*Those tasked with the defense and care of others have not only a* right *to legitimate use of force, but in fact endure a* grave duty *to do so. Common societal defense requires, when necessary, that unjust aggressors are made harmless. Thus, all in just authority may reasonably use the arms necessary to defend civility and deter aggression."*

Father Harry held a neutral expression and looked around at the small group, as though waiting for a response to the reading. "I offer that the clergy have responsibility for the lives and *eternal* welfare of those around them. If the police are not held accountable to *prevent* crime, neither then can the priest be accountable to *prevent* sin. However, by different means, both are responsible for helping all involved to pick up their mess, ensure the unjust aggressor is 'made harmless,' and productively move forward. Therefore, do you agree that priests may, in fact, have a *grave duty* to act on behalf of their communities and neighbors?"

Damn, Michael thought, *never read those paragraphs in this context, I've always limited its application to cops and the military. As it's written, though, that absolutely applies to* anyone *entrusted or responsible for the defense of a community. Nothing to suggest it wouldn't apply to a priest or duly appointed guardian of the Holy See.*

Father Harry resumed a slow pace at the front of the room. "Given our knowledge of the evils that research scientists and psychologists call 'personality disorders,' well, the worst and most dangerous of them, anyway. Given that, *rehabilitation* is impossible, known recidivism rates are so excessively high, and self-reported recidivism rates among these people is nearly one-hundred percent; when we combine that reality with our understanding of the legitimate right and *grave duty* of those responsible to protect other human dignity and human life, we're left to navigate a *tremendous* moral minefield. Paragraph 22-65 only adds to this, as its second sentence demands, '*that unjust aggressors are made harmless.*'

"Under such conditions," Harry continued, "could a person with such responsibility morally, ethically, or biblically justify allowing a person whose internal evils have caused irreparable harm to the lives and dignity of those around them, could the protector *ever justify* allowing the aggressor another opportunity to predictably and surely repeat his aggression, when he is required to render him harmless?"

Harry opened his arms and held his hands, palms up, just out to his sides as though pleading with them for an answer. "Wouldn't the protector, tasked with such legitimate and grave authority, in that circumstance, wouldn't he be *obligated* to cleave the aggressor's evil from his body, particularly if he were able to absolve the aggressor of his sins in the process? Isn't such a method the only viable and momentary avenue to absolve certain aggressors of their unjust evils and, therefore, allow them their *best* and *only available opportunity* to spend eternity in the *warmth* of God's embrace?"

Gobsmacked by the never-before considered implications debated before him, Michael leaned back in his seat and sought his own intrinsic answer. *I've philosophically agreed with the death penalty my whole life, that a few offenses were so terrible to cost the life of the offender, but I've never looked at it from this narrow perspective.*

Phillip remained focused on his copy of the Catechism and seemed oblivious to the paradigm-shifting debate unfolding around him. "Got another one," he announced. "22-66, won't read the whole thing, it's a long one, but, basically, it allows authority figures to inflict punishment that corresponds to the level of the aggressor's offense. These last few lines seem especially relevant, though. '*Beyond its ability to maintain public safety and ensure human dignity, punitive measures have a therapeutic effect.*' Just above that, it specified that when the aggressor consents to punishment, those measures are *cleansing*. Going on, '*it*,' the punishment, it means here, '*must rehabilitate the psyche and soul of the convicted.*'"

Father Harry still scanned the room, letting them mull over his ethical dilemma. "Punishment has a medicinal purpose," he paraphrased, "especially if that were to include the sacraments traditionally known as Last Rites. I argue that this only adds to the validity of my theory."

Amazed at the revelations presented to him, Michael consciously closed his jaw and hesitantly broke the intense silence that had encapsulated the room. "For me, it seems like someone tasked with that responsibility *could actually* be reticent in their duties if they allowed that very specific, rare aggressor any path *but* immortal absolution and an *immediate* mortal death."

Son of a bitch, Michael thought, *is this why they have us here in the first place?*

TRAINING DAY 4, 2032 HOURS_

RURAL COMPOUND. NIOBRARA COUNTY, WYOMING.

After cleaning and putting away the dinner dishes and leftovers, Michael and his classmates headed downstairs. This seemed to be the only personal time afforded them, and Michael expected to use these few daily hours for prayer, meditation, and letter writing. *The folks got used to a couple letters every week while I was in South America, and I know they'd be disappointed if that changed. Maybe tomorrow, though, I need to spend a little time isolated tonight.* Once in the basement, he flopped down on his bed and found his headphones. *Ironically, Enigma oughta help me meditate.* In his peripheral vision, Michael saw Sergio stuck to his medicine ball routine. *Wonder how long it takes him to wear out one of those balls?*

"That was some left-field shit today," Bartholomew announced as soon as he stepped onto the basement floor. "What'd you guys think about the infomercial philosophy at the end of our Freud lesson?"

"The murder, killing, and avenging-Christ-angel theory," Zeb asked.

Matthias spoke up. "Yeah, but, more like a Saint Michael, I think, a righteous avenger."

"I still don't understand how you worked Hamlet into Catechism philosophy, Z," Bartholomew incredulously offered.

"Not a stretch at all, heck, it's effectively the exact same debate we were having, just that Hamlet *wanted* to send his uncle's soul to hell." Z gave Bart a coy grin. "I don't wanna spoil the rest-a the story for you."

"No chance there, didn't even wanna see the damned movie."

"Which one?"

"There's more than one *Hamlet* movie? Isn't one enough?"

"You might oughta consider readin' a book once in a while," Z countered, "you might just figure out that readin' about the secular enforces your beliefs and faith in the divine."

"I don't think embracing the secular can *possibly* improve my understanding and love for the divine, Z," Bartholomew retorted. "That doesn't even make sense to me. Anyone else feel pretty hot about the garbage philosophy Father Harry tried to ram down our throats today?"

Sergio stopped tossing his medicine ball and, like many of them, turned toward Bartholomew. His apparent animosity about the earlier morality discussion commanded their attention.

"I'd keep it down just a bit," Michael advised, "Pretty sure our ceiling's not soundproof."

"I don't care what they hear," Bartholomew sharply replied. "I think it's terrible they let that guy drag us through that today. How *audacious* does he have to be to sell us on murder?! I mean, it's outrageous that a man of the cloth would advocate the loss of a single human life!"

"Actually, I liked his perspective," Sergio offered. "I feel like a lot of Christians, both Catholics and Protestant, get so wrapped up trying to turn the other cheek that bullies and despots get to ride roughshod over entire countries and regions for decades."

"He wasn't talking about *that,* Jude," Bartholomew responded to Sergio by his pseudonym, "he was talking about *homicide! Murder!* If Father Harry had bothered to let Phillip keep moving through the Catechism, the very next section would've very plainly laid out the prohibitions on his stupid little hypothesis. 'Thou shalt not kill.' It's just that simple."

"It's *not,* actually," Michael countered and tried to keep his blood pressure down. *I don't mind debating differences, but this guy won't rest until he gets us to confirm his misunderstanding.* "So, every cop, every soldier, every parent, *anyone* who defends themselves or someone else from a murderer, and kills the bad guy in the process, they've all committed the same mortal sin? Surely you don't think so!"

"Yes, they have, actually, there is no asterisk in the scripture!"

Michael shook his head and tried to adopt a sympathetic tone. "Even the Catechism paragraphs on intentional homicide are qualified to allow for the existence of a 'proportionate reason,' Bart."

Now Bartholomew shook his head but didn't strive for the same sympathetic inflection. "Without a clear understanding of those specific and narrow reasons, we have no just cause to end the life of another person."

"Well, then we have nothing to talk about," Michael announced and put his hands up to show his surrender, "and I'm happy to agree to disagree." *I've always known Catholics are found all across the philosophical and political spectrum, but his view almost requires a merciless God.* "I suppose I oughta be grateful you're *not* who's gonna judge my soul and sins someday, Bartholomew. Your rules might be a little too absolute for me to live up to."

TRAINING DAY 5, 0728 HOURS_

RURAL COMPOUND. NIOBRARA COUNTY, WYOMING.

MICHAEL hurriedly strode into the converted classroom and found his usual chair, sat down at the plastic banquet table, and glanced at his watch. *Dammit. Five minutes early might still be ten minutes late, but John's schedule isn't ever gonna let me show up 'on time.' Maybe I can shave a few minutes somewhere without being a selfish, raging asshole to everyone else that's gotta get to the same place by the same time.*

The classroom's back door opened, and Michael turned to see Alpha and Father Harry walking inside. *Looks like more ethics and moral theory,* Michael thought.

"Good morning, gentlemen," Harry greeted them as Alpha sat down at his place at the front banquet table. "I'd like to start off the day with a little more discussion, in hopes of engaging your deductive reasoning as well as John and his associates are engaging your physical being. It's a tall order," he smiled, "but I feel that we're more than up to the task. We're going to begin our dialogue with the topic of *scandal.* Does anyone wish to offer an *example* of something that might be called a scandal?"

Phillip half-raised his hand and spoke only after Father Harry acknowledged him. "Wouldn't any organized crime qualify?"

"Yes, that's a good, broad example that encompasses much of the worst human conduct in our societies' criminal codes. What else?"

"Convincing someone to turn away from God," Alpha offered in his French accent.

"That's a great example," Harry responded, "and I think it's one of the most heinous offenses that our society so greatly underestimates. We think *nothing* of commercial marketing campaigns that encourage our entire culture to serve our selfish, internal needs, sleep in on the weekends, spend the holy days watching millionaires play games that don't matter, eat and drink to excess, and, all the while, persecuting Christians for their beliefs. A quarterback is chastised and ridiculed for kneeling in silence to express his gratitude to God, while hundreds of others are celebrated for kneeling in protest. Everyone involved in that entire campaign, that entire conspiratorial effort, has actually engaged in scandal against God and His people. Please turn in your copies of the Catechism to 22-84, and I'd like someone to read aloud, please."

"*Scandal*," Z quickly offered, his Carolina accent seemingly subdued, "*is individual or collective efforts that entice another to evil. He who tempts his neighbor damages virtue, morality, and honor, the result of which may be his neighbor's spiritual death. If committed by deliberate action or omission, this constitutes a* grave offense."

"Thank you, 'Z,' is it," Father Harry asked.

"Yes, sir, much easier on the ear than 'Zealot.'"

"I can appreciate that," Harry replied and smiled. "Someone else, 22-85?"

"22-85," Thomas loudly read, "*Scandal is worsened if those who cause or endorse it are in positions of authority over the scandalized. This abuse by authority compelled our Lord to swear that those who encourage sin would be better off drowning themselves. Scandal constitutes a grave offense if committed by those responsible for the instruction of those around them. In this regard, Christ equated the Pharisees and scribes to wolves in sheep's clothing.*"

"Thank you, Thomas," Harry responded. "Next?"

Michael cleared his throat and read aloud. "22-86. *Scandal may also begin by legislation, business practices, and social institutions. This includes those who support and create laws or societal constructs that detract from common morality, defame or disrupt religious worship, or generally obstruct practical obedience to Christian principles and the Commandments.*"

"That, to me," Harry offered, "is among the most powerful sections on this topic. The portion that addresses social conditions that make Christian life difficult is taken from a writing by Pope Pius XII. He said those words back in 1941, at a time when the world saw a particular persecution of religion, specifically Judaism, and I think he foresaw something of the current assault on our morals and values as mean-spirited, cruel, and homophobic. One more, who wants to offer it for us?"

"22-87," Sergio began, "*Those guilty of abusing their authority so as to lead others to sin commit scandal. They will answer for the sum of the encouraged evil that results.*"

Father Harry stood before the class with his hands clasped in front of his waist and a slight smile on his face. *Now the debate and dialogue begin,* Michael thought. He scanned the trainees before him as though considering how to commence with the mental exercise.

"Now that we know more of scandal, and the potential offenses that one risks in engaging in such activity, let's consider a few scenarios that may, or may not, risk eternal consequence. First, let's consider to whom this applies. Is anyone above the commission of this offense?"

"Of course not," Michael quickly offered, "all humanity is bound to avoid and refute this conduct."

"So, a cardinal who calls for you to violate the teachings? He commits the offense?"

"Yes," several voices answered.

"If he's engaging in intentional conduct," Michael added, "*then* he's committed the offense."

Harry smirked. "I would be hard-pressed to say that such a man could not understand what he's doing in this regard, but I suppose I have to agree with you, Andrew. What if the cardinal is acting on behalf of *his* superiors, instead of his own volition? If he disagrees with an edict, but follows through on teaching and enforcing it, anyway?"

Several seconds passed as the trainees individually considered the question.

"I don't think it matters *why* he does it," Matthias offered, "so long as he understands that what's he's doing is wrong."

Father Harry shrugged. "Does it not lessen his offense that the idea did not originate with him, or that he only carried it out as part of his position?"

"No," Michael firmly answered, "I would argue that it should actually *increase* the offense *because* a man in his position is obligated to stand up against such forces on behalf of all those below him. The laity relies on his action and integrity to protect them from human interference in the divine actions of our Church."

"We haven't had an official Devil's Advocate in the Church since 1983, but I'm going to play one now," Harry explained. "But, Andrew, aren't you forgetting that the Pope is the divinely appointed head of the Catholic Church, a successor to Saint Peter himself? Aren't we obligated to consider that the understanding His Holiness offers will always be greater and deeper than our own? Isn't it at least *possible* that we're the ones that've gotten it wrong and have been acting in error all these centuries?"

"That logic forces us to believe that today's pope is more enlightened and divinely inspired than all of his predecessors," Michael replied. "I'll concede that *someone* has got to be the most divine and enlightened pope in human history, but I feel it's pretty arrogant for us to advocate that *our* pope, who serves in *our* time is him."

"So, you don't give the head of the papacy more leeway than anyone else? His divine appointment is something of a cornerstone of our faith, Andrew."

"Forgive me if that's what I said," Michael humbly countered, "but what I meant is that even the pope is human. He's sometimes proud, vain, arrogant, and selfish, just like all the rest of us, even if it's only for a fraction of a second and he never takes action on it. He can also be power-hungry, and I don't necessarily mean the current pope, I mean *all mankind*, of which he's just one member. If the pope decrees tomorrow that marriages are no longer valid sacraments, I will follow the scriptures and the Catechism rather than the man."

"So, in light of the recent edict and catechism alterations with regards to the death penalty," Father Harry offered, "are *this* pope and *his* cardinals *right*, or are all the other popes and councils correct? I'm sure you agree it cannot be both."

Michael leaned back in his chair and smiled at his self-created dilemma. *I should've looked ahead and predicted that he'd force someone into an ethical corner.* "I don't disagree with the Church's position that death penalties, in general, are egregious and harmful to human dignity and our efforts to proselytize the incarcerated masses. They're probably the population in greatest need of hearing about God's mercy and love. I think—"

Father Harry shook his head in disapproval and interrupted. "You're qualifying the answer and trying not to actually give one. I want to know, based on what you just said, if *this* pope is *right* or *wrong* to alter the teachings and understanding of *centuries* of popes and cardinals before him?"

"He's wrong," Michael blurted out before he had time to reconsider. "Even though we in the 'civilized' world often forget that secular governments are generally too willing to kill their opponents or detractors, or to make the threshold for death penalties too low. However, I believe there are offenses so grievous that they warrant the forfeiture of your life, and there are defects in the human psyche and spirit that cannot ever be improved or altered. In those few, and rare, circumstances, I believe the best option we have to protect, preserve, and celebrate human dignity and life is to end that of the unjust aggressor. Simply put, Father, dead serial killers don't *ever* claim another victim."

"How is it possible that the pope is wrong, Andrew, and, simultaneously, *infallible* as a cornerstone of our faith?

Michael cleared his throat and wished he'd kept his mouth shut this morning. "I liken the paradox to Saint Aquinas' explanation of demons. I think it's somewhere near Question Sixty-Four, Part Three. He explains how God can even use demons to achieve His objectives, should he choose to do so, much in the same way that I believe he used Pontius Pilot to crucify His own son. So, I can believe in the pope's infallibility, even if he does wrong, because God must have directed him to do it."

Father Harry smirked at Michael before scanning the rest of the trainees. "Well played, Father Andrew, you got yourself out of that quandary very neatly without making heretical allegations that Pope Cornelius II is busy scandalizing all the world around us."

Michael smiled back at the monsignor. "This is not my first barbeque, sir."

"Except, perhaps, that the next logical conclusion I'll ask you to defend is this, *hypothetical,* example, of course. I don't expect you to answer now, but I'm curious to hear your thoughts. Will you, Father Andrew, go along with the infallible pope's scandalous conduct out of your belief that, even when wrong, he's divinely inspired and beyond error; or, will you refuse to aid the pontiff's grave efforts and therefore go against God's will, which surely must be for you to conspire to commit whatever acts His Holiness directs, as, surely, they must all come from God?"

TRAINING DAY 7, 1948 HOURS_

RURAL COMPOUND. NIOBRARA COUNTY, WYOMING.

MICHAEL SAT on top of his bed covers, leaned back against his pillow and headboard, and used the hard, back cover of his Bible to write a letter home to his parents. *Gonna be hard to write a full letter without saying anything about what I'm actually doing. I could tell them about the new monsignor who's delivering mass to us here. As long as I don't say anything to identify him, John shouldn't have a problem with it. Seems like the kinda thing I oughta be excited about. What would pop think of all this, at least, what I* might *be doing here?*

Michael brought his focus back to the letter itself and paraphrased Father Harry's homily for his parents. *I can honestly tell them I'm right where God wants me to be. Right place, right time, right reasons. Easy to tell the truth, it's the lies that are tough, no matter how white their intention.* He grinned as he imagined his parents' reaction to learning that his new monsignor was also his psychiatrist. *Probably oughta leave that part out. If they knew the Church was sending me to regular head-shrink appointments, they'll think I've gone all 'coo-coo for Cocoa Puffs.' They've got enough problems already without me dropping that much truth in their lives.*

Michael looked up from the nearly-blank page, and Bartholomew's perfectly-made bed caught his eye. *That dude is definitely* not *cool enough to go by 'Bart.'* He'd tried to suck everyone into another argument earlier that night, just before everyone headed up for dinner. *I don't think there's any grey area in his brain. Everything's black or white, and nothing's subjective. It's like he just wants affirmation that he's right, the classroom discussions and debates are unjust, and Father Harry's a jackass. That might end up being true about Harry, but it's his job to make us uncomfortable and push us to examine our beliefs and the basis for them. As frustrating as it is to live* with *Bartholomew, it's gotta be ten times worse to live inside his head. He won't last long here, and, likely, not anywhere inside the Church. The human experience is a shitload messier than he can tolerate.*

Michael heard the front, upstairs door open and footsteps approaching the basement stairs. A few seconds and two dozen *thumps* later, Thomas appeared and hurriedly walked over to his bunk. "Hell of a week, huh?"

Michael kept his eyes on the paper and wished he could just start writing *anything* to appear too busy to chat. "Yeah," he distantly offered, hoping his nonverbal cues would tell Thomas he wasn't interested in talking.

"So, while it's just you and me, Andrew," Thomas offered in a more hushed tone, "I think we're the only ones that actually have a chance of graduating. Whadda you *really* think they're gonna have us doing?"

Michael quietly sighed, looked up, and still tried to show his disinterest without directly confronting Thomas. "No idea, but I bet we find out if you're right about us graduating."

"Hey, so, I think all this privacy stuff and not knowing our fellow brothers-in-arms is all bullshit, right? I mean, I'm pretty sure they're training us to be some kinda Holy Roman warriors, right, and every war movie and book you read always shows the characters, well, the *heroes,* anyway, pretty routinely breaking all the stupid little chickenshit rules that the old men, their tired old bosses, are puttin' over 'em. I figure this is all kinda like that, you know, and maybe John's just testin' us out to see how far we're willing to take his bullshit. I mean, what's next, right, we can only chew on the left side of our mouth because Templar Knights had to worry about attacks comin' from their right side? Bullshit, right?"

Perplexed by the prolonged statement, Michael looked at Thomas and tried to predict what he wanted. *Silence,* Michael thought, *right now, I will give him silence, and he'll tell me what he's after.*

Only a few seconds passed between them until Thomas stuck out his right hand to Michael. "I'm Shawn."

Michael incredulously looked at the outstretched hand for a moment and didn't even consider extending his own. *I could play this off and give him a fake name. Let him think he's got a secret alliance and quietly got one over on John, but what'd be the point? I don't have the time and energy to keep up the facade, especially when there's no real payout on it.* "Is that with S-H or S-E?"

Thomas' face scrunched, and Michael knew he didn't understand the reason for the question. "S-H, why?"

"Just wanted to make sure I spell it right for the 'Guess What' card tomorrow."

Thomas withdrew his hand and his face reddened with anger. "You don't, why, whadda you think you know, *Andrew?* I'll tell him you tricked me into givin' that to you!"

"Do what you like," Michael counseled and returned his focus to writing his letter. "John's been clear about integrity. Wonder what he thinks about mutiny?"

"*Mutiny?! I did no such thing!*"

Michael remained calm despite Thomas' growing anger, volume, and decreased distance. "I think conspiring to undermine the leadership is a cornerstone of mutiny." Thomas had now stepped close enough that Michael shifted his focus to the man's hands and chest. "Here's my problem, Thomas. If I keep your *faux pas* between us, John will eventually jump in the middle of me with *both feet* when he finds out about it later. I'm not willing to trade secrets with you, or you'd have my name. *Nobody* gets to hang anything over my head. Those kinda debts earn interest that I don't wanna pay."

"*I won't let you do this, I—*"

Michael looked directly into the man's eyes to ensure Thomas understood he didn't fear him. "*Thomas,*" he firmly and quietly advised, "you misread me. You can't act surprised or angry because you knew the rules and the consequences. So, now, you need to back up, keep your distance from me, and just go about your business for the night." *I will ruin more than your night if you force me to.*

"This isn't over." Thomas retreated to his bunk for a moment before stomping upstairs and out of sight.

Michael watched the top of the stairs until he heard Thomas reach the kitchen door and walk outside. *I still think Bartholomew might be the Judas that John fears, but Thomas could be his insider. He's definitely not an external mole, that'd have to be someone like Sergio that's an ideal student, candidate, and teammate that's here for the long haul. Maybe Thomas just has an authority problem. Maybe he's just an asshole. Priests are people, too, and they come in all flavors of personality, just like everyone else.*

Looking back to the nearly-blank page, Michael tried to focus on finishing the letter.

TRAINING DAY 8, 1230 HOURS_

RURAL COMPOUND. NIOBRARA COUNTY, WYOMING.

AFTER TURNING IN THE "GUESS WHAT" card earlier that morning to report Thomas' violation, Michael had chosen to eat lunch in the relative solitude of the basement while most of his classmates stayed upstairs. *Only Thomas and John know who dropped paper, but I'd just prefer some isolation right now.* He stretched out his aching back and shoulders as he ate. John had followed their morning runs with bodyweight calisthenics, two hours of ground fighting, and more practice on the parkour obstacle course. Thomas had spent a lot of that time suffering through intermittent physical discipline. The only part of the classmate's remediation that had actually given Michael some pleasure happened when the female instructor, "Jane," jogged alongside him while Thomas plodded dozens of laps around the grinder while holding a heavy rubber shotgun up over his head.

"Why's this happening, Thomas," she'd demanded.

"Cause, I'm, a piece, of shit," Thomas had gasped in response.

"That's right, Thomas, you *are* a piece of shit, and we're gonna be out here until your corners are square!"

The last few hours of the morning had been taken up with a classroom introduction to firearms. Michael had struggled to stay awake while John droned on about basic vocabulary, firearms components, elementary firearms physics and mechanics, and, finally, the terminal ballistics of different types of ammunition rounds. *They let Thomas stay for the class, but took him out and smoked him on the grinder again at every break. He oughta be grateful I only told them I knew his name and not how I got it. John'd probably dismiss him. Maybe worse.*

With only a few minutes before class resumed, Michael bounded upstairs and out the front door. As he strode across the few dozen yards of windswept grassland toward their classroom, he continued to work on his aching shoulders. *I'll be sore tomorrow, but a couple dudes are gonna have trouble getting outta bed and upstairs. Z's getting along better than that first day. Good to see he really is catching up quick.*

"You sore, too, Andrew," a familiar voice asked from behind him.

Michael looked back and saw Sergio inconspicuously catching up to him. He slowed his pace slightly and nonchalantly glanced around to see if they were alone. "Yeah, not used to this much ground fighting and core training." *Don't see anyone watching us.*

"That's surprising," his friend coyly and quietly responded. "I figured you for the kinda guy that'd *teach* martial arts in his spare time."

"As long as it's not that watered down Marine Corps bullshit," he practically whispered back.

"Real quick, Mike, I'm good pretending we don't know each other. You think of me as 'Jude,' I'll think of you as 'Andrew,' and we'll play along like we just met."

"Good by me," Michael replied just as they reached the classroom doors and he pulled one open for 'Jude' to enter.

"*What's* 'good by you,' Andrew," John asked from just inside the doorway. "Other than some burpees for being late to class?"

Michael looked at his watch and sighed. They were, technically, not back inside the room *before* 12:30. *I fucking hate burpees,* he thought. "Jude's going for a short jog after class tonight to work out some soreness," Michael flatly replied. "Figured I'd join him, so I invited myself along. You wanna go with us?"

"Huh. I get my miles indoors. Runnin' in this godforsaken wind is bullshit. Hurry up, shitheads, we're waiting on you."

Sergio followed Michael through the doorway and on to their respective seats. Michael saw that Thomas sat in his chair, as well, but still wore his sweat-stained workout clothes. *They must not be done with that dude yet. He's definitely sleeping on the floor tonight.*

"Alright, now that we're all here, let's get on with the program," John announced and took his place at the front of the room. "I'm about the best-goddamned shooter you're ever gonna find, especially with a handgun. I'm pretty alright with a rifle, fairly dead-on with a scoped bolt gun, but, man, a pistol? I will shoot you a smiley face at a hundred yards with no trouble. Despite that, I hate teachin' it, at least the classroom portion of it. Absolutely hate it. So, I found some other asshole that actually enjoys talkin' to people that got no idea what the hell they're doing."

A few students chuckled at John's frankness.

"Y'all think I'm kidding? It tries my patience to no end, and I just wanna cut your damned fingers off every time they land on the trigger before you're up on target. Damn, gettin' worked up just talkin' about it! Anyhow, your instructor's name is Paul, and you're damned lucky to have him teachin' you."

A tall, muscular blonde man in his late forties strode to the front of the room with a brown cardboard box in his arms.

Where did that guy come from, Michael wondered. *He wasn't back there when I walked in a second ago, and I didn't hear the door open. Guy's a white ninja.*

"Good afternoon," Paul offered in a deep tenor voice as he set the box down in the middle of the front table, directly in front of Bartholomew. "This is the part of my presentation where my trainees usually hear a little about who I am, what I've done, and what else I'm trained to do, so you have confidence in my credentials and in the credibility of the information and technology that I'm providing.

"However," he continued and moved back to clear the large dry erase board behind him, "John tells me you all aren't privy to that intel, so, I'll just let the material speak for itself. If you don't like it, per John's instructions and in his words, you can just fuck off. I get paid the same either way."

Michael liked Paul already, and he glanced over to see that Sergio had chuckled along with the instructor, as well. *Jude, gotta get used to calling him Jude.*

Paul passed out solid plastic training guns, affectionately called "red guns" because they were made of one solid, non-moving piece of red plastic shaped to look and feel exactly like a real pistol. "When I set these down on the desk in front of you," Paul loudly exclaimed, "*do, not, touch, them.* I would repeat it, but I wanna see which one of you window-licking retards is gonna get in trouble first. You'll notice, if you look *without touching the damned thing,* that the trigger's dark purple. That's because I've coated it with purple food dye and Vaseline. If you touch that trigger, you'll feel the *icky* and know you *done goofed.* Then, *I'll* know it because you're gonna put your hand up so I can see the pretty stain on your finger.

"In short, the lesson here, people," Paul explained, "is that you gotta keep your *booger hooks* off the God-damned *bang switch.* It's not rocket science, and no matter how tempting it is to finger-fuck my red guns, keep 'em unmolested for now."

John stepped forward to briefly draw their attention. "There'll be hell to pay if anything in my beautiful classroom is purple when you leave here today."

Paul began with the four, standard firearm safety rules, and they spent a mind-numbing thirty minutes writing, reciting, regurgitating, and rewriting those same four rules until everyone professed them from memory: *Treat all weapons as if they are always loaded. Do not point your weapon at anything you're not willing to destroy. Keep your index finger straight along the frame until you're on-target and have decided to fire. Identify your target and know what's behind it at all times.*

Paul led them through the inner workings of semi-auto handguns and revolvers. Only then did he allow them to finally handle the red plastic guns.

Immediately, Michael saw Bartholomew try to subtly wipe a smear of purple Vaseline from his right index finger.

"*Bartholomew,*" John called out from across the room, "*how now, brown cow?!*"

The man froze in place as though he didn't understand John's volume or his question. "I'm sorry, John, I don't—"

"*How, now, brown, cow,*" John firmly asked.

"I, don't—"

"Okay, so you don't know what that means," John surmised, "you ain't never heard that phrase before?"

"No, John, I guess not, I—"

"It serves lots of purposes, but typically informs my students they've run their proverbial ship aground and are in dire need of a life preserver. So, it could mean things, like, '*what the hell are you doing*,' or '*what's important now*,' or, like *right now*, it kinda means, '*if you try to hide that goddamned critical error from my instructor, you'll regret it right quick.*' We're all about integrity here, and I'd rather see you shitheads *struggle*, and *fall*, and *fail*, as often as I can damned well help you do it, but you're gonna be honest about it. Nobody learns shit from standing ovations. People learn best when they're busy pickin' themselves up off the ground. We understand each other, son?"

"Yes, John." Bartholomew held his purple-stained finger up to Paul.

"And, we have a *winner*," Paul exclaimed with the excitement of a daytime game show host. "Tell him what he's won, John!"

The lead instructor mimicked Paul's gameshow inflection. "Well, just for being the *very first asshole* to touch the trigger on his simulated weapon system, Paul, he gets *one timed victory lap* down Mother Mary, along with a *hundred burpee bonus* for tryin' to hide it, and it all starts just as *soon* as class is over!"

Michael stifled his laughter at Bartholomew and his public shaming. He already understood the gravity of the lessons his colleagues had to learn *before* they took possession of real guns and live ammunition.

"Alright, Bartholomew," John asked in his normal voice, "how now, brown cow?"

Michael watched Bartholomew assess what was asked of him, and, as he looked at his own finger, what to do about the purple petroleum jelly.

"You mean, how am I gonna clean this up?"

"They *can* be taught, Paul!" John turned back to his student. "Yeah, shithead, what now? How do you plan to fix that particular problem?"

Bartholomew looked around for anything that offered a reasonable solution but found no such thing. "I'll run back to the house and wash up."

"Eat it."

"What, John?"

"You heard me, Bartholomew. *Eat it.* It's food coloring and petroleum jelly, just like your grannies used for Chapstick. We ain't got time for you to 'wash up' across the yard and downstairs, you clearly gotta hear every word Paul says, and you need one more negative experience to fully ingrain this lesson in your subconscious lizard-brain. Get that shit off your finger so we can carry on." He looked over to Paul. "See? This is why I hate teachin' this shit, there's always one or two that're just plain 'paint-by-numbers' stupid." John glared back at Bartholomew. "Why aren't you done yet?"

Bartholomew jammed his finger deep into his mouth and grimaced like he expected a nauseating taste. He pulled it back out and briefly inspected the smaller and lighter remaining stain.

"Alright, thank God that travesty's over and done with," John observed. "Paul, carry on, please."

Paul spent the next four hours teaching proper center-mass targeting areas, along with how to handle, draw, present, aim, carry, holster, and conceal a firearm. By the time he'd finished, Michael reasonably believed the group could return from a live fire range with no more holes among them.

"Last thoughts for the day," John announced while Paul picked up and cleaned the red guns from each student. "Whenever we talk about firearms, really any weapon system that has the potential to do real, prolonged, and profound harm, we're also obligated to consider and discuss the moral and scriptural limitations of the device.

"In terms of a gun, whether it's a pistol, a rifle, hell, a high-powered pellet gun for all it matters, any of 'em. Whenever you *have* a firearm you're thinkin' about using, or someone *else* has a firearm they're thinkin' about using *on you,* what are the justifications and reasons for morally and ethically pullin' that trigger?"

"In defense of yourself or someone else that's presented with a deadly threat," Sergio offered.

John nodded. "Yep. Do you have to wait for the bad man to start pullin' trigger *before* you're allowed to use deadly force to stop them?"

"No," Michael replied in unison with only about half the class.

"What about an *imminent* deadly threat? One that's foreseeable, but not yet deadly at that instant?"

"Shoot 'em," Michael answered.

"We got one Doc Holliday back there, and no other takers?" John scanned the class and gave a few seconds for additional feedback. "Alright, lemme be more specific. You're in a convenience store bathroom, one way in and out. You have a holstered and concealed gun. A *massive* M-M-A fighter busts through the door and attacks you with punches and kicks? Can you shoot him?"

"Yes," Michael and Sergio both confidently replied.

"More people are killed in the U-S every year with hands and feet than firearms, so sayeth the F-B-I," John explained, "so that tells you that punches and kicks are more statistically lethal than guns. So, *yes,* you shoot that man if you don't have a chance of winning a fistfight to the death.

"What if the same guy busts in the same bathroom, in the same black undersized M-M-A t-shirt, but he just stands in the doorway? He tells you that you're not leaving without a fight, and he's got about two-hundred pounds of 'roid-muscle on you. Do you shoot him?"

"Yes," Michael and Sergio again answered together.

"Right again," John replied. "You don't have to engage in a fight where you have a serious chance of severe injury or death. Now he comes in, same dude, same bullshit t-shirt, but he doesn't say anything. He just stands in the doorway, takes up a fighting stance, and puts both fists up and glares at you." John took up a fighting stance and glanced around the room.

"Bang bang," Sergio quickly offered.

"Shoot him," Michael added, "twice."

"That's all spot on, folks. Guns are not just for dealing with other guns, they are for dealing with all manner of deadly and profound threats." John pointed at Michael and Sergio. "Neither of you get to answer anymore. This one's for the rest-a the group.

"So, let's say you find this guy," John looked off in the distance like he was imaging the perfect hypothetical scenario. "Never mind *how,* but just accept that you *know, for a fact, beyond any reasonable doubt,* this man is a serial rapist. He has assaulted dozens of women, dozens. You see him, recognize him, know who and what he is. Let's even say that you know he only rapes if he has his red banana with him, and you see him headed out of his house with a red bandana. Can you shoot him?"

Nervous silence fell across the room. Michael looked around and tried to assess if any of them would pull the trigger in such an obvious "shoot" scenario.

"Yes...?" Z's upspeak revealed his hesitancy.

John shook his head. "I'm sorry, Z, was that an answer or a question?"

"Yes, shoot," Z more confidently offered.

"That's right. We can use deadly force to prevent reasonably foreseeable and imminent death or profound injury. Now, let's take that back a bit more. Let's say you knew just a little less." John again looked off and formed his hypothetical question. "So, you know all that stuff about him, absolutely *know* it, and you can *prove* it to anyone that asks. But, he's not headed out when you find him. He doesn't have the red bandana on him, he's just eating a T-V dinner in front of a *Magnum, P-I* re-run. Even got his back turned to you. Let's add this, though, that you learned all this through the victim's confession, and you have all the corroborating evidence you need to convict him in court, but you can't go to the cops and you can't violate the Seal of the Confessional. *But* you still know he's a *serial rapist* that's gonna rape *again*, and *again*, and *again*, until he's *stopped*, but you can't tell anyone about him. You're literally the *only person on God's green Earth* who can stop him."

John scanned his audience, waited for an answer, and prodded them further when he received none. "What debt do we owe to all the rest of society, to protect the safety and dignity of humanity, knowin' the kinds of things that we sometimes learn through the course of our service to God? If we know that serial rapist cannot ever be rehabilitated, not in prison, not in free society, and we know he won't stop until someone stops him, and we find ourselves in that position, what moral and ethical obligation do we have to act? Are we not indebted and avowed to care for *all* God's children, even if we're protectin' those infected with evil from themselves? We occasionally identify evil, that through its actions, clearly demonstrates an intrinsic, unavoidable desire to commit horrific acts against all human dignity, to prey on the weak, the vulnerable, and the most precious of our people. When we find them, are we *not* obligated to act in some protective manner?" Only the outside wind was audible while John scanned the room.

Michael understood John required an answer from someone. "I say shoot him, recite his Last Rites like a tobacco auctioneer, and hope for the best."

TRAINING DAY 18, 0745 HOURS_

ABANDONED AIRFIELD. NIOBRARA COUNTY, WYOMING.

MICHAEL STEPPED DOWN from the same school bus that had delivered him to John's camp more than two weeks ago. Unlike most of the past seventeen mornings, they'd been bused out to an old, asphalt airstrip in lieu of sitting in the stable-turned-classroom. *Nice to be out in the open air, even if we'll have to spend all day in the early-spring wind. Maybe we can skip the lectures on theoretical violence and ethical debates in favor of something a little higher-speed.* Michael walked a few steps away from the bus and approached a line of assorted sedans and SUVs. *There's gotta be twenty-five vehicles here! Hell, I don't think most of them are even sold in the U-S!*

"*Thomas, Z!*" John's shout drew everyone's attention and hastened the approach of the two he named. "You two shitheads," he publicly explained as they stood in front of him, "are in my goddamned doghouse! Thomas, you're on the floor tonight, and Z gets the cot. You two'd best learn to start keepin' your mouths shut, 'cause I'm gettin' pretty damned tired of callin' you out for op-sec failures! I won't keep doing it forever, so, keep it up and I'll getcha that bus ticket I promised.

"And this goes for the rest-a you maggots, too," John more loudly addressed the group at-large. "I ain't under no pressure to pass *anyone*, and no one'll bat an eye if I fail *everyone.* I ain't got a quota and I don't work on commission. Clean up your act, square yourself and your mind, and get focused on takin' in *everything* we give you out here! Thomas and Z's gonna lead ya off because they each owe me two-hundred burpees before they join my training today. Rest-a y'all, as a show of solidarity and remorse for everything you've each done to fail to live up to my expectations, y'all each gotta gimme a hundred before you can drive my vehicles."

"Once you do finish with your penance," John loudly continued, "you're gonna get in one of my fine, used grocery getters. These are not flashy, high-performance coupes and supercars like the movies, because that's *not* what you'll have access to, and it's not even likely that you'll have a chance to steal one if ya could. These are the most popular vehicles sold, by volume, in the last decade in North America, Europe, Southeast Asia, and the modernized parts of Africa, both of 'em. Statistically, these are the vehicles to which you will have the most frequent and probable access, so that's what you're gonna learn and be tested on.

"Today's course," John paused for the brief moment required to put in fresh Copenhagen, "is gonna start teachin' you basic emergency vehicle operation and control. In total, you're gonna get four weeks behind the wheel in this program. We're startin' slow today, but those of you that graduate will know how to pick the door locks, hotwire the ignition, diagnose and overcome mechanical problems and equipment failures, and, of course, how to *recon* and *surveil* with a car. And, later on, if you're still around, how vehicles help you *survive, evade, resist, and escape.*"

Did he just tell us we have a SERE evolution at some point, Michael wondered. *No way. John's just screwing with us again.*

"I ain't got time to turn y'all into Hollywood stunt drivers, but we can getcha damned close." John offered a rare wink and smile. "For me, this is one of the best segments of the program, as long as y'all agree to disregard everything you *think you know* about auto mechanics and high-speed vehicle operations. Anybody got anything?"

Sergio half-raised his hand as he spoke. "So, do we have to *pick* between being 'fast' *or* 'furious?' I was kinda hopin' for both!"

A broad smile suddenly covered John's face. "Quit tryin' to stall, you asshole! Everybody get on your faces and start pushin'!"

Michael dropped down to the asphalt in a barely-controlled belly flop and commenced working through the appointed punishment. Most of the class started counting them off together, but Michael knew that wouldn't last.

"ONE!"

There's too much difference...

"TWO!"

...in our fitness levels...

"THREE!"

...to keep this up!"

"Four!"

As Michael maintained a consistent burpee-marathon pace, the other instructors walked over from the parked cars. The only one that Michael didn't trust strode right toward him.

"Double-Time, ladies," he called out.

And, that's why you've got the stupid nickname, Michael thought to himself.

"Everybody that doesn't beat Jude owes me another fifteen at the end," John shouted.

Michael glanced over and saw Sergio maintained his pace, even though the rest of the class would surely pay for it. *I've got one-fifteen, then. They'd add to his total for every one of us that beat him, anyway.*

Michael's nemesis stood in front of him with his hands on his hips. "Get that pace up as long as you can! Even if you only got ten D-Ts in you," he shouted at Michael. "Give us whatever you got! Double-Time, go!" The stocky trainer loudly *clapped* his hands together several times as though that, in some way, helped train or motivate the students before him. "You guys should be going *way* faster'n this! Come on, *Andrew,* at least *act* like you give a shit! I know you can do better'n that, but I *don't know* why you refuse to prove it! Let's go, let's go!"

Michael didn't bother trying to meet his demands today. *It doesn't matter what I do, it won't be fast enough, hard enough, loud enough, or tough enough, so there's no point in passing his arbitrary muster. John hasn't given a shit that no one lives up to Double-Time's demands.* As he leapt up to complete burpee number twenty-three, all of the students had begun counting to themselves. *No one's gonna keep up with Sergio!*

Seven minutes and a few brief stops later, Michael jumped up to complete number one-fifteen. He put his hands up on the back of his head, slowly walked around the outside of the group, and worked to catch his breath.

"About half-a you's already done," John shouted to be heard, "so the slower shitheads're gonna have to listen while you work! The point of our driver training is to make sure you can drive real cars on real roads! No point in supercars and racetracks, cause you won't ever get that in the real world. Whether you find yourself in New York City or *Moga-fuckin'-dishu,* you're gonna be on shitty roads and Jeep trails!"

Michael stopped strolling about as John spoke and Sergio walked up and quietly stood nearby. *That asshole barely broke a sweat.*

"What the hell are Vatican operatives doing in Mogadishu," his friend carefully whispered while John shouted over them.

"He forgot Denver," Michael quietly replied without looking at Sergio, "roads are shit there, too. Don't know what the job is, but I look forward to finding out."

"Get used to this shitty blacktop," John loudly continued, "and you'll be grateful when you get to drive on the good stuff. After this week, we're going out onto the local dirt track to teach you a few things about drifting and counter-steer. As y'all get done with your penance, head over to the cars and get started. We're burnin' daylight, shitheads!"

Michael pulled his hands down off the back of his head and walked to the farthest vehicle, which seemed to be first in line to go out on the "track."

Gonna be a good day, now that that's over, Michael told himself. *Never had a bad day on the track.*

TRAINING DAY 29, 0811 HOURS_

RURAL COMPOUND. NIOBRARA COUNTY, WYOMING.

Michael stood behind his flimsy classroom chair by 8:11 but delayed sitting down until he had to do so. The day had started with the usual run, this time just a 5K to warm up before the trainees raced for time through John's parkour obstacle course. Although he'd given his best effort, Michael continued to fall short of the times his younger and more flexible teammates set. The "mandatory fun" had continued with a half-hour of bodyweight torment on the grinder before John finally released them at 7:15. While he waited John's presumed entry at 8:15, Michael stretched his legs and back. *This flimsy chair's gonna put me in one with wheels before it's all said and done.*

"Good morning, shitheads," their lead instructor proclaimed as he strode through the back door with his standard, large mug of steaming coffee and a frown. "Gonna be a good day today. Some of the best instruction in classroom theory you'll have the whole time you're out here. I'm a little biased because I'm teachin' the goddamned class, but I hope to make most of you fervent believers before the day's out." John set his mug atop the front banquet table and made use of the dry erase board.

"Today's theory," he continued, "is all about long-range shooting. *Precision, rifle, operation,*" he slowly called out as he wrote it in large block letters. "Sniper shit. Whatever you wanna call it. I call it 'good times.' Now, I'm not gonna cover anything we talk about today in incredible detail, today's class is more an overview, the ten-thousand-foot perspective. We'll get right down into the goddamned weeds on some of this stuff in the next few weeks, but, for today, just try to catch onto the concepts." During the next four hours, John covered a wide range of related topics, discussing rifle components, terminology, and associated vocabulary; the physics of a bullet's vector, which included ballistic coefficients, transitional ballistics, yaw, precession, and bullet nutation. The last topics he covered before lunch focused on spin drift, maximum terminal range, and terminal ballistics.

"'Terminal ballistics' is just college-boy, fancy-talk for how bullets make things go *splat*," John explained. "With that beautiful picture in mind, let's break you assholes for lunch. I think there's spaghetti and meatballs in the kitchen. We'll pick it back up in an hour."

Michael and his fellow students all migrated back over to the main house and took their meal together in the kitchen and dining room, as had become their practice three times a day. Once seated, they individually crossed themselves and bowed their heads in solitary prayer. Each lifted their heads as they finished, and only then did they address one another.

"Anybody got any reservations about the class today," Bartholomew asked immediately after he finished praying.

"Only that it was just a survey course," Sergio replied and shrugged his shoulders. "I'm into this kinda thing, so it's interesting to me. I think I can learn a lot from John on this."

"Not concerned about the physics and the theory, Jude," Bartholomew clarified and addressed Sergio by his pseudonym. "I'm talking about the practical reality of just what the hell they're gonna expect us to do with this training."

"Maybe nothing," Matthew injected, "maybe something. I don't have any heartburn over it one way or the other."

"You afraid to make people go *splat*, Bart," Thomas smugly inquired.

"Not in theory, Thomas, but I see a *mountain* of moral difference between shooting a man who tries to murder me with a handgun in self-defense and shooting a man from so far away that he can't even see me."

"I can prob'ly guess how you feel 'bout huntin', then," Z joked, and deliberately emphasized his Carolina accent. "Maybe we gotta go back a couple hundred years and go after big game with knives and runners."

"John's not training us to harvest deer and elk," Bartholomew harshly responded, "he's talking about the basics of setting up a murder."

The group sat and ate in silence for several minutes, and Michael had no reasonable, logical argument that would overcome the emotional conviction that Bart had professed. *Ya can't get there from here, bub.*

Thomas predictably broke their silence with antagonism. "You're not some *pacifist*, are you, Bart? Think that we're limited to huggin' it out with evil?"

"No, I'm just trying to find a path to overcome the murderous applications of today's lesson, and I don't think poking fun at my morality will get me there."

"So, we're not ever gonna get to call you 'Black Bart,' huh?" Thomas bit off a large piece of bread and chewed it with his mouth open. "What about 'Bart the Bitch?'"

"I'll continue to pray for you, Thomas," Bartholomew patiently replied. "Still not sure that you're really a priest."

"It takes all kinds of clowns to put on a decent circus," Thomas replied and savagely devoured a meatball.

Most of the remainder of their meal passed in silence, with each man excusing himself as soon as the opportunity presented itself. John reconvened the class at precisely 1:30 and continued his survey course in long-range shooting theory for the afternoon session: heat wave optics, wind, elevation and relative height adjustments; humidity, heat, and weather considerations; moving target solutions; moving shooter difficulties, such as shooting from an aerial platform; and simultaneous, three-dimensional shooter and target movement.

"The best, most recent, and well-known example I can give you of simultaneous three-dimensional movement is the *Maersk Alabama* rescue. Anyone familiar with that one?"

Sergio quickly raised his hand. "Absolutely, John, the Navy SEALS rescued Captain Phillips from a group of Somali pirates by putting all three of 'em down at once with snipers."

"Damned straight," John acknowledged. "What makes that even more impressive is the detail of what was necessary for it to happen. To skip most of the backstory, the U-S Navy is towing a closed lifeboat with three goddamned Somali pirates and an American hostage, one Captain

Phillips. Y'all mighta seen the movie. So, the dumbass pirates let the Navy tow their boat toward shore. The Navy isn't gonna let 'em go, and they've already promised to kill Captain Phillips if anyone tries to take their vessel. So, the Navy brings in some SEAL snipers and hides 'em on the back of the ship towing the lifeboat. They sit in their hides and wait. For days. Just pissing down their own legs and waiting for the perfect shots. Remember, they gotta take out all three assholes at once to make sure none of 'em get to kill Phillips. So, time passes. Eventually, those dumb-shits all stick their heads up together, which is exactly what the snipers were waiting for. At a moment's notice, three snipers took near-simultaneous shots from the deck of a moving ship, at moving targets, on another moving ship, and they went three-and-oh on the day. Three piece-of-shit pirates all went splat together, and can you imagine what it musta been like to be Captain Phillips at that moment?! One second, he's looking at three skinnies that all want him dead and are using his life and safety as leverage, and the next, he's lookin' at three headless corpses with bloody canoes where their faces used to be! *Holy shit,* that'd get your undivided attention, for sure!"

Most of the group chuckled along with John's understatement, but Bartholomew found no humor in the bad men meeting their deserved and justifiable end.

"Excuse me, John," a voice called out from behind Michael. He turned and saw "Double-Time" standing in the open doorway. "Sorry to interrupt, but the doc needs to see Andrew *posthaste.*"

John looked at Michael and nodded toward the open doorway. "Go make it so."

Michael glanced at his watch and saw it was already 5:13pm.

"Go ahead and pack up your milk crate," John directed. "I keep tellin' the doc you're crazier'n a shithouse coon, so you might be in there long after I cut these assholes loose."

Michael nodded, reluctantly collected and crated his belongings, and headed for the door empty-handed. *I'd much rather keep talking about rifles and ballistics than to have a head shrink try to get my innermost fears and secrets outta me.* After he stepped from the classroom, Double-Time strode immediately in his wake as though he intended to make Michael feel uncomfortable, maybe even threatened.

"Doc's in the usual room in the main house," the instructor gruffly offered, his right leg walking in lockstep immediately behind Michael's left.

Taking a small step right and turning himself counterclockwise, Michael stopped and found himself nearly nose-to-nose with the antagonistic instructor.

"Something I can do for ya, *Andrew*?" The man's pupils expanded, and the corners of his mouth turned up, just slightly. "Cause, I gotta tell you, I really hope there is. I been just waiting for the invite, brother, so, if you wanna throw down right here and settle this, I'm game."

"I just wanted to let you know I'm not gay," Michael dryly responded, hoping to motivate the presumed homophobe to throw the first punch. "The way you been tailgatin' me around, I think you've got the wrong idea."

"Fuck you, *fairy boy*," he hissed through clenched teeth and moved closer until their noses touched.

"See, that's what I'm talkin' about, I'm not interested in you, and, no matter how nice you ask, I'm not gonna let you blow me."

"*Please throw on me*," the trainer ferociously begged, "it'd be good for *both* of us."

"Ready when you are, just so you know there's no tummy-sticks afterwards."

Double-Time kept his nose in contact with Michael's for another few seconds before he stepped back. "You'll get your chance to tango, and I'm gonna take my sweet time fuckin' you up."

Michael grinned. "I'm feelin' pretty good today, so, if *you* want my appointment with the doc, he can help you work through your recurring man-rape fantasies. Might just keep you out of prison."

"Like I said," he countered and strode toward the main house, "I'm gonna take my time with you."

"Don't threaten me with a good time," Michael called out after him. *I don't wanna let him catch me by surprise when he snaps. Love to know what made him set his sights on me.*

Michael followed the adversarial instructor into the house and soon found himself isolated with Father Harry. *This guy might make my brain hurt, but he's pretty unlikely to make me bleed.* "Whaddaya wanna talk about today, doc? Anything specific, or just the usual?"

"This is just our normal, periodic check-in to see how you're adjusting to life here at the facility, how you're interacting with the instructors and the other students. See if, maybe, you're struggling with any moral quandaries over the topics and lessons here, which are not necessarily what most people would associate with mainstream Catholicism, no matter how strongly they're based in the Holy Scripture and the Catechism. So, let's start with the easy one. How're you getting along with everyone here?"

After more than an hour of non-answers, half-truths, and avoided revelations, the head doc finally released Michael. He immediately found his way back to the basement without further confrontation. *Had enough asshole for one day.* As he landed on the basement flooring, Michael exhaled, stepped to his bed, and flopped down on the blanket-covered mattress. After a few moments, he noticed how quiet everyone was and glanced around the room. "Who took all Bart's stuff? You guys shouldn't mess with him, not with the day he's had."

"Not us," Matthias explained, "he took everything himself. Got in an argument with John and quit. He left just a few minutes ago."

Michael sat up on his elbows. "What the hell happened?"

"It went like this," Zeb offered. "He said he couldn't make himself carry or use a rifle. Said something real self-righteous about how it had no Godly, defensive purpose. He tried to get out of the rifle training and stay, but John insisted he had to complete all the courses. Bart refused to have anything to do with the rifles, so John offered him the chance to think about it overnight, but he came down here, packed up his stuff, told us all we were gonna follow John and his mystery program right down into the bowels of Hell, and bounced. Took off outta here before John even had a chance to call that damned bus to come get him."

"*Hmm*, interesting," Michael surmised, "not too hard to see that happening after the questions he had at lunch. Some Christians believe we're supposed to be pacifist sheep and just let the Devil's wolves have their way with us. Too bad. He's a little too black-and-white for me, but I think he means well. Bart was a good man."

"Still *is* a good man," John interrupted as he descended the stairs and brought all the students to a heightened sense of foreboding.

Shit, Michael thought, *he's never come down here like this before.* He sat upright and moved over to the edge of his bed.

John waited to speak until he reached the basement floor and had a chance to survey the room around him. "I just wanted to make sure y'all know and understand that I don't harbor any grudge or ill will against Bartholomew. I appreciate his position and that he had to stick to his own morals and conscience. Doesn't matter that I disagree with him, and it doesn't matter that the Church and I both believe he's misinformed."

John briefly paused before pressing on with his monologue. "He knew he couldn't wake up every morning and look himself in the mirror if he continued with my training program. That's far more important than being here. You gotta live in your skin for however long God wants you on this Earth, but you're only gonna be here for a few more months, and maybe in your selected assignment for only a few years, right? Even if you're as good as I was, eventually, age and aches catch up with you, and you gotta find a way to move on and still find meaning in your work. I admire Bart for knowing and vocalizing his limitations. I know it required bravery on his part, because I'm sure he thought he was going against me, but, in reality, he did exactly what I asked of you all on Day One. If you'll recall, I told you that I didn't want you here one day longer than you wanted to be here. I also said something about not wanting you to ever feel any kinda moral grievance. I don't have the time or desire to work through nonstop philosophy discussions every time we start a new training evolution, so, I'm grateful he pulled himself out. I just wish he would-a waited for the goddamned bus. It's a long walk to town with luggage, boys, and the bus ride's free.

"So, just in case there's anyone else with similar objections that just hasn't had the intestinal fortitude or heartburn required to voice 'em yet," John continued, "here's the deal with the rifles, which, sadly, Bartholomew didn't wanna hear. I've done told y'all this training program feeds a number of specialty positions and assignments within the Holy See hierarchy. Some are clandestine, some are intelligence, some are security related. Some are, well, somethin' else. We don't know what you're each gonna be good at, where you're gonna demonstrate the greatest proficiency, and, therefore, where you're gonna be most useful to God and His Pope. So, knowing that, lemme pose this scenario. Vatican Intelligence gets notified that an ISIS-inspired group is headed to Saint Peter's Square right now with a *Vee-BIED,* a 'vehicle-borne improvised explosive device,' and there's no time to cordon off or evacuate the Square. They get an accurate description of the car, its driver, and its projected route to get into the center of the Square before detonating. Only a few minutes pass until the exact vehicle drives toward the Square, and the driver matches the description you've been given, and he's wearing a black-and-white fishnet patterned *keffiyeh,* and there's an ISIS flag draped over his shoulders. He's driving more'n twice the speed limit, westbound on *Via della Conciliazone,* headed straight toward the east end of the Square, and accelerating.

"Who do you want to try to solve this problem? Do you want a trained sniper to put him down before he gets into the Square, and potentially avoid detonation in the first place? Do you want a Swiss Guard standing by the east entrance to give him a chance to change his mind and surrender, maybe give him some verbal commands in Italian, Arabic, and English, just to cover the bases? Or, do you wanna wait for him to do whatever the hell he's got on his mind, just 'turn the other cheek,' and clean up any debris, victims, and body parts he leaves behind?" John looked around the room, and enough time passed to demonstrate he expected an answer.

"For me personally," Michael offered, "the sniper's by far the best option."

"What about that man's *soul,* Andrew," John unexpectedly challenged him, "don't we have an obligation to show him God's compassion, mercy, and forgiveness in this lifetime, along with the additional moral obligation as Catholic priests to try to absolve his soul of its worldly sins? How is your solution *not* murder?"

Michael cleared his throat and saw most eyes of the room had now fallen upon him. *This is what I get for being the first to speak up.* "The bomber's ideologically driven, John, and he made all his decisions long before he started the car that day. He's speeding toward Saint Peter's to murder all the infidels he can, even though they've done him no harm. Logic is no match for ideology, and he'd never accept confession and atonement no matter who offered it. My only moral obligation, based on his actions, is to protect the innocent from predators, from the suicide bomber, the rapist, the pedophile, all the true evils that can't be rehabbed.

Killing him is my only moral option to stop all the murders he intends to carry out."

"So, you'd murder him?"

"It's not murder, John, it's just a killing," Michael replied. "And I'd happily shoot him right in his goddamned face, maybe twice, just to be sure."

John scanned the room to see how everyone else assessed the scenario before speaking. "That's right, Andrew, it's not murder," he repeated, "it's just a killing. I'd *never* train *anyone* to murder. But, for me and those like me, just as war is a viable political engagement, killing is a viable and sometimes necessary solution to the worst problems of humanity and the greatest evils that walk among us. You show *me* a righteous stack-a bodies, and I'll show *you* a collection of assholes that's truly been *rendered harmless*."

TRAINING DAY 42, 1105 HOURS_

UNIVERSITY OF WYOMING CAMPUS.
LARAMIE, WYOMING.

THE SCHOOL BUS driver individually dropped the trainees off around the outskirts of UW's campus. Because he'd drawn drop-off point "3" out of the black felt cowboy hat, Michael was among the first to dismount the familiar jalopy and proceed toward his objective. He strode south on the Laramie sidewalk about four blocks north of the main university grounds. Michael smirked as he walked past the UWPD station. *Maybe I'll stop in and grab an app if I flunk out today.*

Today's field training required Michael to demonstrate his skills in foot surveillance and counter-surveillance, and, if possible, to beat out the rest of the trainees. John's simple directives had been to find and infiltrate the student union building on campus, lawfully acquire independent proof of the incursion, and provide the location and observation angle on every surveillance camera in the union's public areas.

The hard part is gonna be slipping past the five instructors roaming the area, Michael surmised as he walked onto the college campus. *The* harder *part might be avoiding them without making some paranoid eighteen-year-old feel like they've gotta call the cops. Just like every other trip off the compound, getting ID'd by the cops'll win us a seat on an outbound bus. At least it'd be a shorter trip home from here.*

Dressed in shorts, sneakers, and his favorite Western New Mexico State sweatshirt, Michael did his best to blend in with the younger, student population as he approached his target. *Even though John made the instructors wear their normal 'dad clothes' this time out, I bet we won't get that benefit on the next field exercise. Hell, he might even make us wear the plaid button-downs so it's even harder next time.* Despite their advantages, Michael knew the exercise's requirements had already been set pretty steep for most of the trainees. *I'll be surprised if anyone wins. Pretty sure me and Sergio are the only ones with prior surveillance training, and I don't even have much of a chance on this one. The camera requirement's gonna kill us. It'll take too long to get that much intel from inside the structure.*

As he walked by the Education Building, Michael noticed his whole body was a little sore and fatigued from the morning run and parkour obstacle course races. *And my knees still ache a little from mass. Maybe I could convince John to let Amazon deliver some kneepads. Shouldn't have left those in Columbia, Monsignor Medina probably threw them out as soon as he sent me packing.* The pain reminded him of a conversation he'd overheard that morning between John and Tex, and it brought a smile to Michael's face. *'Our Stepmother of Perpetual Suffering,' that was some funny shit. John's doing a good job making sure our experience in his part-time chapel lives up to the name he gave it.*

The density of the crowds around him increased as he reached Penny's Pasture and the Wyoming Union building came into view about seventy yards ahead and slightly left. Michael looked around and realized he needed a backpack to blend in better. *I've got eight hours to win this before the bus picks me up, though, so there's plenty of time to do it right.* The realization reminded Michael of an expression his father frequently said, and he immediately heard the man's voice in his head: *There's never time to do it right, but there's always time to do it twice.* He smiled again at the facetious work ethic mantra. *Not this time, pop, this one I gotta get right the first time.* Michael looked forward to speaking with his father later that night. *Getting to call home is the second-best part of the days we celebrate mid-week mass.*

Michael followed most of the students around him toward the student union building and tried to conceal himself among them as best he could. *Gotta really start paying attention now, the instructors will probably expect us to beeline to the area. They know we've been trained to start with a wide external assessment before moving inside.* Michael briefly considered that and realized most of the Op-For searching for them would work the building's exterior approaches. *There's only five of them, at most, so, if I can get inside now, only one might be working the interior halls. Their typical goal is to punish and embarrass us as soon as possible, so, they probably put one guy on each side of the building, and one's floating around. If it were me, I'd keep the floater outside for the first hour. If I can get by the external team, I might get the interior cameras mapped before the op-for moves inside.*

Michael slowed his pace just slightly and scanned the crowds and people ahead of him without obviously doing so. *Not exactly what Nietzsche meant by watching the watchers.* His stomach and chest tightened as he moved closer to the objective, despite his logical understanding that he'd taken the best course of action. *What are they capable of, what are they most likely to do,* Michael reminded himself. *Going against my own training and penetrating straight in helps address both considerations.* While gravitating between clusters of students, all of whom seemed to have some kind of device out in front of them, Michael realized he didn't have a phone to replicate their behavior. *I* do *have a wallet, though, that oughta be good enough.* He retrieved his brown leather trifold wallet, held it out in front of him to look consistent with most everyone around him, and also slowly thumbed through its contents as though searching for something. *Won't look so out of place if someone takes notice of me.* Even though his sunglasses and head faced slightly down and to the front, Michael's eyes scanned from his ten-to-two-o'clock positions, searching for the instructors he knew had to be close by.

There. Michael saw a tall black male in a red plaid shirt standing off to his right. He glanced over at the man and recognized him as Big Country. The instructor had placed himself beneath a stand of trees across from the building's main entrance, which concealed his position from three avenues of approach toward the primary doorway. *Good position, he's just facing the other way right now.* Because his greatest risk was in being spotted scanning his environment, Michael kept his face oriented toward the building, slowly thumbed through his wallet for another few steps, and deliberately matched the speed, trajectory, and posture of those closest to him. *Don't do anything to stand out, human brains are designed to subcon-*

sciously see and identify movement and differences before anything else. Match the crowd, match the crowd...

Michael passed through the central doorway, just below large letters that identified the building as "Wyoming Union." Once inside, he quickly worked his way to the right and found a place to stand a few feet inside a large plate-glass window that offered him a view of Big Country. *The bright sunlight outside will keep him from seeing more than a foot or so through the window. He's still looking the other way like he didn't see me.* Relief further washed over Michael as Double-Time walked up and spoke with Big Country. *My timing was divine intervention.* He snickered and watched his Op-For. *Luck is for the weak, and moderation is for cowards.* Michael considered what Double-Time's assignment might be. *He's the best choice for their roamer because he gets the most pleasure from punishment. Hard not to take it personally, especially when he spends so much time and effort making it feel that way. He hasn't picked a fight for a couple weeks, but that could change today.*

While the two instructors spoke, they each maintained watch in opposite directions and neither of them looked at one another. *Most people wouldn't realize what's going on. Americans are hardwired to look at people as we talk to 'em, so that's a substantial tell for someone who* does *know what they're looking at.* Without any normal pleasantries, Double-Time walked away from Big Country's spot under the trees and headed straight toward the doors Michael had just entered. He bulled through the aimless, distracted students around him, which only brought more attention to the man. *He's still searching, but he's reckless and arrogant. If they'd seen me or knew I already entered the building, he'd be moving with a purpose. All he's doing right now is showing his ass.*

Michael risked moving closer to the window, turned his back toward Big Country, and sat on the window's narrow lower ledge. Leaving his sunglasses on, he grabbed an abandoned copy of a thin, student-run newspaper from the floor and opened it. Double-Time immediately entered his peripheral field of view, but Michael refrained from turning toward the man. Based on the doorway's position about twenty yards to his left, Michael estimated at least three dozen people moved around between them. *It helps that I'm seated below the crowds and his line of sight, too.* He caught only brief, intermittent glimpses of his adversary's blue-plaid shirt through the student horde, which revealed his opponent had stopped. *He's scanning, looking for anomalies. If he doesn't know what we're wearing, he's looking for other tells. Safe to assume he's decent at finding people, even if he doesn't give a damn about hiding from us today.*

Michael inhaled a deep, calming breath and tried to keep his stress in check. The potential for winning the field exercise was so remote, and the consequences for finishing last were so minimal that his only real objective was avoiding confrontation with Double-Time for the next seven-and-a-half hours. *Unless we finally have it out, what's the worst outcome? I sleep on a floor until someone else messes up in a day or two? After patrol work, lying to Ecuadoran drug traffickers, and nearly being stabbed in a Bogotá back-alley, the possibility of a bad night's sleep just isn't that exciting.* For the first time in his life, Michael realized how liberating his past traumas were and how effectively they worked to shield him from new stressors and anxieties. *If only I'd been shot at before, then I suppose that wouldn't have the same impact today, either.*

Still wanna keep Double-Time from cornering me, though. What's he capable of, and what's he most likely to do. I don't trust that he'd make it a fair fight, or that he'd have the integrity to give John an honest version of events. I think the extent of his lies would directly correspond to the extent of our injuries. If he got the chance to put a blade on me, I'm sure his version would involve me cutting him first. As Michael considered the admittedly remote possibility that the instructor had such intentions, he continued to see occasional glimpses of the blue-plaid shirt. *He hasn't moved yet. Most humans aren't willing to surveil an area for this long, so he's either paranoid or informed.*

Slowly flipping through the student paper as though bored and waiting for a friend, Michael kept his face down and his sunglass-hidden eyes cast toward the Op-For. *Finally.* The glimpses of blue-plaid moved deeper into the building and farther away to Michael's left. He looked down at his watch and noted the second hand. *I'll give him a minute head-start. He'll be much easier to find in here than me.*

After his desired time lapsed, Michael stood but examined the area where Double-Time had disappeared before moving. *Don't see him.* Blending back into the throngs of students moving about the building's interior, he started down the wide, well-lit corridor. Small, hanging placards projected out from the uppermost portion of the walls to identify school offices, businesses, and resources above their corresponding doorways. *Black Student Association. Cowboy Tech, gotta be an electronics store. WYO Bookstore, ahead on the left. Cowboy Credit Union up on the right. I'd bet most everything in here's got 'cowboy' tied to it somehow, but—*

Dammit! Michael swore at himself for not having anticipated Double-Time's path. His opponent stood inside the bookstore, about fifteen yards ahead and to Michael's left and watched the crowd from just behind a large glass display window. He scanned the crowd around Michael but didn't specifically focus on him. As he reached the credit union entrance about fifteen feet before passing Double-Time's position, Michael veered slightly right, turned his back to his adversary, and strode into the branch as though he belonged there.

Michael nonchalantly pulled the door closed behind him and paused once inside to assess his next action. *Tellers to the right, no one's in line there. Can't kill time waiting my turn. Writing station and blank form table's just ahead, one dude there.* He glanced to his left and saw about five students standing in a single-file line about fifteen feet away. *Don't care what they're here for, that'll allow me to stay a few minutes without drawing attention. Bankers don't like strangers hanging out in their office for some reason.* He stepped behind the last person in line, a petite female with a UW backpack and long blonde ponytail. She stood just tall enough that her head fell just below Michael's chin. *Wow, she's pocket-sized.* Michael stopped and faced slightly toward Double-Time so he could simultaneously watch his Op-For and the line ahead of him.

The petite woman's incredible fragrance struck Michael and reminded him of Catherine. He deeply inhaled the familiar scent and memories of his long-time ex flooded the forefront of his mind. *Same perfume, but I couldn't tell you what it's called anymore.*

"*Sir?*"

Michael looked up at the female voice somewhere ahead and saw six people staring back at him. The middle-aged woman behind the counter had clearly been speaking to him. "Yes," he hesitantly asked.

"Can you take off your sunglasses, please? It's a safety policy in here," she explained and pointed toward a sign near the door he'd just entered. "No hats, no sunglasses, please."

"Of course," Michael apologized and pushed them up onto the top of his head. He blushed at the unexpected attention and made eye contact with the petite blonde, who displayed her annoyance at his obvious error. "Sorry, I'm new here."

She turned back toward the counter and put on headphones.

"I really didn't wanna talk to you, either," Michael quietly offered.

"I think she likes you," a familiar voice softly announced from behind him.

Michael cautiously turned to look around and saw Sergio standing behind him. His face was turned down, and he focused on some papers in his hands. *The dude from the deposit station.* To avoid drawing more attention to himself, Michael turned back around without responding. He saw a stack of pamphlets and forms on a counter to his left, just below a window that looked out to the interior walkway. Michael stepped forward past the blonde, but just enough to reach out and retrieve one of each.

She stepped a little farther ahead and to her right, undoubtedly to create distance from him.

"Like, *really,* likes you," Sergio quietly razzed him.

Michael turned his back toward the teller stations and faced the window. He held the documents like he was reading them and projected his voice toward Sergio and away from the antisocial blonde. "Think he can see through these windows?"

"No, they're one-way, got bank ads on the outside glass."

"How long you been in here?"

"About seven minutes. I ducked in when I saw D-T coming down the hall toward me and didn't think I'd get trapped in here."

"Any idea what this line's for," Michael asked.

"Student I-D cards. They tie 'em to a credit union account. Read the literature four times over at the table. Seems like a good idea, couple nice incentives if you're lookin' for a new bank."

"You're lucky nobody called the cops, suspicious Hispanic man like you hanging out in here."

"You didn't see him," Sergio hesitantly stated.

Michael assumed Sergio referred to a cop but didn't remember seeing one. The blonde moved forward as the line in front of her decreased, and

Michael stepped back behind her. Even at this distance, he heard country music from her headphones. "Who?"

"The cop. At my seven, behind the teller counter. Got here before me."

"Well, which is the frying pan?"

"Yeah. How now, brown cow?"

"Next," the same female employee loudly called out. Michael followed the blonde two steps closer to the ID counter.

"I'd rather get caught by D-T than I-D'd by the cops," Sergio quietly explained. "If the cop thinks I'm suspicious, he'll follow me out, maybe confront me. I can't leave until I'm sure he's not interested in me."

"Next!"

Michael looked ahead and realized he was next in line as the blonde stepped up to the ID counter. "Hang here for a second," he quietly offered.

"Got nowhere else to go."

Michael stopped himself from smiling at his friend's expense and apprehensively strode toward the officer. He realized the cop noticed him just after he stepped away from the ID line and kept watch as he approached. *Gotta do my best impression here, should be easy given how many times I've seen it.* "Excuse me, officer?"

"Yeah, whaddaya need?" His voice carried no warmth or concern, but his inflection did convey the officer's minor annoyance.

Shit, Sergio was worried for nothing. This guy's not in here paying attention to the customers, he's probably hiding out from his boss or trying to pick up one of the tellers. This'll be easy, then, if he agrees to play along. "I hoped you could help us," Michael explained and deliberately turned back to look at the blonde, knowing the officer would likely do the same. "So, my friend over there, well, I guess, we're more like, *classmates,* we just know each other from e-con, so I guess I shouldn't *really* say 'friend,' but—"

"Yeah, the blonde, I see her," the cop impatiently responded. "Whaddaya need?"

"Well, she didn't wanna say anything, but, I saw you over here and thought you might need to help."

"Spit it out."

This is either about to go really well, or really bad, Michael thought, *but not much turning back now.* "So, she mentioned while we were standing over there that she *thinks* she's being followed."

"Why's she think that?"

He knows he's gotta pay attention, but I bet he hears hundreds of unfounded complaints every year that start out just like this. "So, we walked over here from class, and there's a guy, probably a few years older than me, even, in a *blue-plaid shirt,* and he's been behind her the whole time."

The cop looked around the branch. "I don't see anyone that looks like that in here."

"He's not in here, he's in the bookstore window across the walkway. He's just standing there watching the bank doors, like he's waiting for her to come back out, *or something.*"

The cop stared at Michael for several seconds as though assessing the validity of his complaint. *And, accepting that he's gotta go talk to the guy even though it's probably nothing. No cop worth his salt can let a guy stalk a co-ed* and *a bank in the same day.*

"But here's the thing," Michael continued and again glanced back over his shoulder. *Good, she's still at the counter.* "She didn't wanna say anything, and she'd be *super-embarrassed* if it turned out to be nothin', so, can you just go talk to the guy without her knowing that I talked to you?"

"I'll see what I can do. No guarantees, though." The cop lifted a pass-through in the countertop, stepped toward the branch entrance, and stopped just inside the doors. "That guy?"

Michael saw the cop pointed to Double-Time, who arrogantly stood with his arms crossed in the same display window. "Yep, same one." Movement to his right caught Michael's attention. He turned that way and saw the blonde walking toward the exit with her headphones back on. *Gotta sell this.* With the cop on his left, Michael waved toward the woman as though they were, in fact, acquaintances but not quite friends.

She glanced up, saw his gesture, and immediately looked uncomfortable. But she gave him a small wave back as she strode out of the branch and disappeared into the crowds to Michael's left.

Thank God for social pressure, Michael thought. He looked across the walkway and saw D-T emerge from the bookstore just behind the blonde. After a moment's consideration, he also walked to Michael's left, undoubtedly doubling back the way he had first entered the building and unaware of the trap he'd just helped set for himself.

"Want some free advice, pal," the cop asked.

"Sure."

"For what it's worth, I'll go chat with the weird guy and get him I-D'd in case your friend ever needs to report anything later, but I don't think she likes you." He stepped over and opened the door to leave. "Might wanna put your efforts somewhere else. You mind waiting here a minute, in case I need a statement?"

"No problem. Thank you, officer."

The cop turned, entered the wide interior walkway, and directly approached Double-Time. "Hey, blue-plaid! Hold up a minute so we can have a chat." The bank door pulled itself closed, so Michael could see them talking but couldn't hear anything they said.

Sergio stepped up to Michael's right side, and they both watched their opponent stop in disbelief. The cop stepped in front of him and blocked his direct path to the nearest exit.

"We gotta go." Sergio's nervous sense of urgency was clear despite his low volume.

"Yeah, soon as D-T turns away from us."

"Sir?"

Michael looked right and saw the woman behind the ID counter was again addressing him.

"Do you still need help?"

"No, ma'am," he apologized, "sorry, I was in the wrong line. Thank you, though." He nonchalantly glanced back, saw that Double-Time now faced away from them and was engaged in a slightly heated conversation with the cop. Michael gently pushed the door open, calmly stepped into the hallway, and stepped to his right to leave the immediate area.

"We should've talked first, about the I-D counter excuse," Sergio explained at a normal volume given the dense population around them. "I told her the same thing!"

"HEY! STOP!"

Michael and Sergio both stopped and turned back toward the cop's shouts. To his immediate relief, Double-Time was crashing forward through the walkway, away from them with the cop closely pursuing him.

"ADAM-31, GOT ONE RUNNIN' FROM ME!"

Michael grimaced as his unintended consequences unfold. "Now, we *really* gotta get outta here."

"Shit, man," Sergio happily objected, "this just became an easy win! The cops are gonna be looking for white dudes in plaid shirts for the next week, so I bet they end up chasing all the Op-For off, except for Jane. She might get a pass."

"Yeah, 'cept for her. The bad news, though, is they're also gonna be lookin' for me and the blonde. If they catch D-T, they'll damned sure want our statements and I-Ds, even if they don't need it for the criminal charges. That cop's gonna rely on everything I said as his legal basis to stop him."

"Well, let's hope D-T stretched out before he came to work today, cause now he's gotta outrun a Motorola." Sergio looked around the upper walls and ceiling of their immediate area. "No cameras in the hall here. They'll definitely have some in the bookstore, but maybe I can get in the other door and get you a new shirt and hat."

"Where's the other entrance?"

"Back the way I came, just down around the next corner. Got cash?"

"Yeah," Michael replied. "Can't end up on camera buying shit with a debit card when we're trying to stay anonymous."

"Alright," Sergio surmised as they stepped off together. "Let's go get us a win."

"And, maybe, D-T'll get arrested and dismissed in the process."

"Hell, I'll be happy if we can just keep you from the same fate, *mijo!*"

TRAINING DAY 58, 1300 HOURS_

RURAL COMPOUND. NIOBRARA COUNTY, WYOMING.

MICHAEL HAD JUST RETURNED to his detested plastic chair when John strode in through the back door to begin their afternoon class. His eyes briefly stopped on the void where Bartholomew had sat in the front row. *They yanked his chair outta here the same night he quit like he was never here. Nothing John does is a coincidence, and I don't think that is, either. Kinda funny, though, that no one's spread their chairs out to take up the empty space. He was pompous and narrow-minded, but I don't think he's infectious.*

"Afternoon, sorry I couldn't be here this morning to watch your physical labor and struggles, but I had other shit to do. How'd y'all like the run and parkour races this morning?"

"Good, John," Sergio quickly responded for the group, "I think they're starting to catch up to me. Gonna hafta work on my afterburners."

"Even Matthew and Thomas?"

"Yep, even them," Sergio offered.

"Well, shit, that *is* good news," John offered, "starting to get worried the Molasses Brigade was here to stay."

"Molasses Brigade?" Z asked.

"Yeah, they're *thick*, and, *slow*." John's dry response made several of the faster runners chuckle.

"We're working on it, John," Thomas defensively interjected.

"Y'all are gonna qualify for the Parkour World Finals by the time you leave here," John surmised. "There is no greater asset to a man in the field than being able to move swiftly and efficiently over terrain that lesser men cannot. The simple ability to easily scale a six-foot wall can getcha away from most people on earth, but being able to get yourself up the side of a two-story building and into an apartment window on the opposing wall, unseen and without using the interior stairs or elevator, that will do more for you than you can understand right now. How about the ground fighting and Krav, that go okay?"

"Yeah, John," Michael answered, "seems like everyone's getting more proficient."

"Anybody get choked out?"

Phillip reluctantly raised his hand.

"Somebody's always gotta learn the hard way about tappin' out, Phillip, but I bet you don't let that shit happen again."

"No, I don't think I will."

Michael thought about how Double-Time had insisted on repeatedly partnering with him several times during the Brazilian Ju-Jitsu and Krav Maga workouts. *No way I was gonna let that guy get a choke on me. He's rough, but at least he didn't do anything dirty today. Maybe he was more interested in sizing me up. Still not sure how he got away from the U-W cops without getting arrested or I-D'd, but, apparently, God wants him here for some reason. I must* need *a thorn in my side.*

"This afternoon, we're working on an introduction to lock picking. Gonna start with the components, mechanics, and vocabulary. Explain why you shouldn't even bother tryin' to pick a Medeco lock. Safecracking starts later next week after y'all have a chance to work your way through a generic deadbolt."

Michael heard the door open behind him, and he turned to see Jane standing in the doorway.

"Sorry, John, can I borrow one?"

"And," John explained to the group, "each-a y'alls gonna get called out to meet with the shrink. Who's he want first," he asked Jane.

"Andrew."

"Go to it, son, but you oughta make it back without missin' too much. I told him you're makin' progress, and ain't cried yourself to sleep at all this week."

"Thank you for your help," Michael sarcastically responded. He rose and walked with Jane over to the main house. Despite having been at the compound for almost two months, he'd had surprisingly little interaction with her. *Not sure if she's only around part-time, or if John keeps her tucked away in the background. She's the only trainer here that's not been a lead instructor on at least one topic.* "What do you normally teach, Jane?"

She paused when they reached the main house and held the door for him. "Masculine humility." Her smile conveyed an absolute confidence that Michael respected.

"Fair enough." He walked into the house and headed straight back to the usual room. Father Harry was already inside, and Michael tapped lightly on the open door.

"Come in, Andrew," the grandfatherly monsignor and psychologist offered. "Care for anything to drink? Water, coffee, tea?"

"Yes, sir, tea would be great."

"Jane, my dear," he called out and looked over his reading glasses, "would you mind?"

Michael saw her expression briefly revealed her inner angst, but she quickly composed herself. "Nope, not at all." She turned to Michael and curtly questioned him. "*Tea,* you said? *Chamomile,* I imagine?"

"That sounds delightful," Father Harry obliviously interjected on their behalf. "Make it two, please."

"Two chamomile teas, comin' right up," Jane unhappily replied and pulled the door shut behind her.

And with a healthy dose of spit, Michael thought.

"So, Andrew," Father Harry began, "it's been a few weeks since I've checked in with you and your classmates. Even though we regularly see one another at mass, I'm busy wearing a very different hat and caring for a very different part of your being. The psyche and the soul being separate and distinct from one another, of course."

"Just as Saint Thomas Aquinas suggested," Michael replied as he sat in his normal chair close to his evaluator. "So, where do you wanna start today?" *I'm gonna work to keep you in the dark just like I always have, Father Not-Harry.*

"First, how are you getting along here, Andrew?"

"I love it here."

"*Love it here?*" He wrote that down with a deliberate and obvious flair.

Don't think he bought that one, Michael thought. "Yep," he replied. "I firmly believe this is where I'm supposed to be right now, and I'm looking forward to seeing how all the training and effort here is gonna allow me to better and more precisely serve God and His people. In fact, I'm thinkin', if John were to allow it, that I'd come back one day to be an instructor."

"You want to be an instructor? Here? For John?"

"Yes, Father, but, if possible, I know I have to leave, at least for a little while. So, I'd like to go out, maybe for a single mission that no one expects me to complete, except for John, of course, and I do such a great job that I get immediately pulled back into here to train everyone else to do it just like I did that one awesome mission. Whatever it is. Maybe something with planes."

"I see," Harry replied and scribbled something on his paper. "Well, I wouldn't go getting my hopes up *too high* on *any* of that, but it is John's program and I suppose that anything's possible."

"What else you wanna cover, Father?"

"Well, I do have some questions from John, actually, since you brought him up. Do you mind if we go ahead and move on to those?"

"That'd be great, whatever you need to do."

"John told me about everything he knew about the mobile surveillance field exercise at the University of Wyoming. He expressed some genuine surprise and concern that the cops chased one of his instructors from the area and stopped almost all the others. And, he believed, closely related to that, was the surprising success that the students enjoyed. Apparently, you and Jude both managed to win by identifying all the cameras *and* avoiding instructor contact. Another five students identified the majority of the cameras, and all but one actually made it into the building."

"Yessir, it was a good day for the home team, and we're gonna work with Matthias to make sure he shows some substantial improvement on the next one."

The monsignor-psychologist ignored Michael's attempted sidestep and watched him as though awaiting a genuine response. *I've played this game before, Father, and someone should've told you I know how it works. The first one to break the silence always loses.*

"I don't think anyone has *ever* won that exercise before," Harry finally continued, "and there's never been a class with that degree of success. I'll certainly give you that the local campus police officers believing they had reason to target the instructors absolutely worked to the benefit of every student still in the game at that point, but it does certainly seem odd that they would have been alerted to question the activity of a trained intelligence professional as 'suspicious.'"

Father Harry again watched in silence, so Michael gave him nothing but a blank expression. *The guilty and nervous are gonna fill the silence, so, without evidence to the contrary, I'm gonna stay mum until I have no other choice.* Michael watched the monsignor-shrink watch him and considered his old police union rep's facetious advice. *Deny everything. Make counter-accusations. Demand to see their evidence. Ask for my attorney.* He stifled a smile. *Kinda doubt John's program offers much in the way of due process. Part of the reason he's out here in the sticks and I'm talking to 'Father Harry.'*

"So, John had decided to cast it all aside as coincidence and write off the whole incident for all involved. Then, apparently, my understanding is that some new evidence came to light and John's asked me to specifically inquire on his behalf." He lifted the first page of his notebook and seemed to read from the page hidden behind it. "John asks, at least, well, this is with his expletives removed, of course, but he wants to know *what, exactly,* did you, Andrew, have to do with his instructor's altercation with law enforcement at U-W two weeks ago?"

Michael worked to maintain a blank expression despite the pit that immediately formed in his stomach. *Focus on the specific words he used and give him an honest answer. I didn't see an altercation, a* fight, *between them.* "I didn't know one of his instructors was in an altercation with the police."

"There's something else here, scribbled down below the question that I can't quite make out, but it seems like a few of the words are 'video surveillance footage.'" The elderly man looked up at Michael with an inquisitive expression. "Does that mean anything to you, son?"

TRAINING DAY 70. 0715 HOURS_

RURAL COMPOUND. NIOBRARA COUNTY, WYOMING.

MICHAEL KNELT in prayer on his rolled-up towel and participated in Father Harry's morning mass. *And now that the stable-turned-classroom turns into 'Our Stepmother of Perpetual Suffering,' as John named it, for about an hour, anyway.* He grinned to himself just before rising back to his seat when the monsignor ended his prayer. Michael smiled pleasantly at the elderly man and worked to ensure he conveyed no unintended information to him. *I've seen him four times now since he first asked about U-W, and he's specifically offered to hear my confessions every time. John hasn't acted any different toward me, but Father Not-Harry is still suspicious. Strange that the monsignor-shrink is more upset about anything I might have done than John. Maybe there's more to their relationship, or Harry's playing a more significant role than I understand.*

"May Almighty God bless you, in the name of the Father, the Son, and the Holy Spirit."

Michael crossed himself, as did the other trainees. "Amen," they responded in near-unison.

Father Harry spread his arms out toward the small crowd. "This mass is ended. Go forth and glorify the Lord by your life and your good works."

"Thanks be to God," the trainees replied.

"And," Father Harry continued, "I'll be available for confessions, should anyone be in such need of me."

Michael noticed the monsignor glanced at him before walking past the trainees and on toward the house.

"Alright, shitheads," John announced as he moved to the front of the room. "How'd everybody like the distance run today? Fifteen miles, right? Everybody make it back alright? I didn't do a remaining body count on the way in."

"Good times, John," Sergio answered for the group, as had become his habit when John asked about the PT regimen.

"Today's gonna be a little familiar to everyone from the U-W exercise. This time, though, we're not working on foot, unless you have no other choice. I want you primarily working out of vehicles. With ten of you left, we're gonna divide you up into five cars. I only got five anyway that's sold here in the U-S, at least that you assholes can use. Wouldn't make much sense to have you roll around small-town Wyoming in cars imported from Mexico, Europe, and Africa. That shit'd be noticed *right quick*.

"So, today's assignment," John continued, "is gonna have you surveilling your instructors. Each two-man team will get an intel package. The targets do not know who is coming for them, or what you're driving. They do, obviously, know what you shitheads look like, though, so you'd best bear that in mind. Much like when you fail, the instructors will have to answer to me for every one of you that completes your intel assignment without being identified. All they gotta do is be able to tell me what you're wearin' and drivin', and you're done, so they've got an advantage any real-life target shouldn't ever have. Easier for them, harder for you. Trading sweat for blood today, gentlemen, sweat for blood. You will get some location info in the intel packets, maybe some vehicle info, maybe some other intel on your targets. It'll also provide you with a list of intel I want you to collect on your target. Everybody's got the same deadline, which is supper time, 1900 hours tonight.

"Every team's going after a different instructor," John continued, "so, if you see one that ain't your target, leave 'em alone. If you see one of your *classmates*, leave *them* alone. You might accidentally tip off their target to their presence. Ignore 'em. The instructors are gonna report to me when they think they've spotted the surveillance team assigned to them, and, if they're right, you're done. You fail today. If they're wrong, then we'll all just carry on like nothin' happened. Questions, comments, concerns?"

"What is the goal, once we find our target," Matthias asked.

"That'll be in your intel packet," John reiterated, "and everybody's got something different. Anyone else?" John looked around the room and understood the silence as adult-speak for "no questions."

"A few final thoughts before you head out. You will mostly be engaged in stationary surveillance today. In general, this offers the same problems you faced with the mobile surveillance exercise, but you now have the added difficulty of tryin' to look non-threatening while sittin' in a car with another dude. I'll leave it up to each team to decide how to overcome that. In certain cities and places around the world, that can help get you mistaken for a cop. The plus-side to it is that most people won't mess with a cop. The downside is the ones that *will* are gonna have a lot more guns and friends than you'll have. Hell, in most places you'll work, you'll be lucky to have a damned Buck knife. The trouble here, of course, is that there's only fifteen-hundred-and-some-odd souls in the Lusk, Wyoming, metropolis. You can expect they all grew up with *every* cop that works in this entire county, so, if someone thinks you look suspicious and kinda cop-like, they're gonna call the real cops over to deal with it. And, normal rules of engagement, that gets you bounced. All the rest of the usual R-O-E's apply, as well. If no one's got anything else, y'all oughta get your dumb-asses moving."

"What's the teams, John," Phillip called out.

"Right, thanks," John replied and retrieved a handwritten note from his shirt pocket. "Jude and Matthias. Thomas and Zeb. Andrew and Z. Phillip and Matthew. Alpha and The Baptist. I don't care which of the five cars each team takes, so first-come-first-served in the driveway."

Michael made eye contact with Z and nodded toward the driveway. His partner seemed to understand and hustled along with him out the door. "Wanna have first pick in case there's only one car that doesn't stand out."

"I'm good with it, you wanna drive?"

"Sure, but that means you'll be on foot if we hafta break up."

"No problem," Z replied. "Think it's suspicious that each car's already got a target assigned to it?"

"Maybe. Wanna trade packets with someone else?"

"Yeah, I do. I don't trust it. I think they're lookin' for a crushin' win after U-W."

"Kay." Michael slowed his pace just a bit and let Sergio catch up to him. "Hey, Jude, we're worried the targets might already be looking out for specific cars. Wanna trade packets?"

"I like it," Sergio replied. "A good friend once told me," he flashed a quick, knowing smile at Michael, "if you're not cheatin', you're not tryin."

That was practically our mantra in Ecuador, Michael thought and stymied his own smile. Michael and Z picked an older white Honda Accord and swapped its intel packet with that from Sergio and Matthias' dark blue Dodge Minivan. Z opened their packet and grimaced at Michael.

"Sorry, Andrew, maybe this wasn't such a good idea after all." Z held up the intel packet contents, and Michael saw they now had to follow Double-Time.

"Doesn't matter. Even if he's really got it in for me, he's still gotta earn it. Let's grab some extra gear and see if we can't make this hard on him."

"What're you thinking?"

"Let's talk about it on the walk back to the basement," Michael offered. "Still not sure these cars aren't bugged."

"Paranoid, aren't you? I'd call myself an avid conspiracy theorist, but you may be worse than me."

They stepped from the Accord and, en route back to their quarters, discussed the tools and tactics they thought might help them carry the day. When they finally emerged, Michael wore a bright yellow, long-sleeved, zip-up running shirt and Z wore an orange Baltimore Orioles t-shirt. John poured himself a cup of coffee in the kitchen as they passed through.

"You boys pick up crossin' guard shifts for extra money?"

"Nope, just hiding in plain sight," Michael dead-panned. They continued straight on to the driveway and found theirs was the only car left.

"Everybody else's in a damned hurry to fail," Z offered.

"Can't ever miss fast enough to win." Michael got into the driver's seat and, as soon as they stowed their gear in the rear floorboards, he piloted them toward Lusk and Double-Time. "If this gets done early, you wanna hit the local watering hole for a pint or two?"

"Sounds like a damned fine idea, whether we're mournin' or celebratin.' Long as they got Bud heavy on draft, I'm good."

Fifteen minutes later, Michael passed the Town Limit sign on US Highway 20. His apprehension grew as they entered the small town. *Feels like some kinda ominous consequence, a foreboding presence, maybe? Like I'm about to get everything I deserve for the few minor transgressions since my arrival here.* As planned, he pulled off on the shoulder, and they both removed their high-visibility tops. Each of them had worn a neutral t-shirt beneath.

"Alright," Z enthusiastically offered as Michael merged back onto the road, "it's now 8:45 in the mornin', and our sum-bitch is supposed to be drivin' a 1998 Buick LeSabre, white, Nebraska plates. The intel packet claimed his car had often been seen parked in the vicinity of the Niobrara County Sheriff's Office in the mornings. By chronology, we're to find out where he goes in the mornings."

"So, the intel is that we know where the car is, but not where *he* is."

"That's right," Z confirmed. "What's the name-a that little café across the street?

"The Blue Bonnet?"

"Yeah, I think that's a good place to start. I'd avoid driving by the building if we can."

"Since that's the only two-story building in that part of town," Michael suggested, "I think we oughta drive somewhere around the back and see if that gives us a look up onto the roof."

After Z agreed, Michael drove them two blocks south of The Blue Bonnet's building. His passenger looked at the roof through binoculars but couldn't determine if Double-Time was up there or not. "Looks like there might be some kinda wall up around the edge of the roofline. Ain't no drainage or vent pipes stickin' up like there oughta be. The actual roof's gotta be below what we can see from here, and, from this far back, we oughta be able to see at least a few of the pipes even if it's a flattop. There is an access ladder on the back, though, on the south wall by the back, kitchen door, looks like."

"That could be good to know for later," Michael replied.

"You plannin' on doing some sniper work, Andrew?"

"No, but we've already been in Lusk on a few field trips, and I bet

John sends us back a few more times. Oughta be good to know how to get to the high ground."

"You ready for the drive-by?"

"Yeah, let's go ahead and get that over with. If you're right, Z, and this works, then we'll know the game was rigged to begin with. We just won't know exactly how."

"It's not unusual for me to find myself in the unique position of hopin' I'm wrong."

After several turns, Michael drove their aging white Accord north and passed along the east side of The Blue Bonnet Café. Because that building's only windows and customer entrance were on the north side, neither of them could see if Double-Time was there.

"Even if he *is* in there," Z surmised, "he's sittin' in the far back corner so we can't see him without stickin' our ugly mugs onto the glass, anyhow."

"The real point is to see how this shakes out from here." Michael continued north another eight blocks until he saw a used car dealership, *Western Skies Auto Sales*. He pulled the Accord onto the commercial property and parked next to the office.

Before they exited the sedan, a tall, thin man with a grey, wispy combover, red western shirt, jeans, and worn brown boots stepped out to greet them. He donned a grey felt cowboy hat and put his hand out to Z. "How you boys doing this fine morning," he asked and enthusiastically shook both their hands. "Can I help you get outta that import and into something red, white, and blue today?"

"Well, actually, sir," Michael replied, "we're not lookin' to buy anything today, but I do have a kinda strange request."

"I'm all ears, son." The man's grin concealed any uncertainty or apprehension.

"My wife and I are separated, and—"

"I'm sorry to hear that," he offered with a more sympathetic smile. "Unless, of course, that's a good thing!"

"That's just it, I don't know. I *do* know she's here, in Lusk, and I think she's cheating on me with an old boyfriend."

"Uh-huh," the salesman grimaced, "and just where do you see me fittin' into this?"

"She'll recognize my car, well, really, it's *her* car, so she'll definitely know it if she sees it. I hoped I might be able to rent a car from you for the day."

"You're right, son, that *is* a strange request. I'm not in the rental business, unfortunately, though, so I don't see how I can help you out."

"I'd only need it for a few hours," Michael pressed, "and I don't care which car it is, as long as it's not a white Accord. I'll take the worst car on the lot, the one you know for sure you're not gonna sell today, and I'll give you a hundred bucks for your troubles."

The man looked them both over and met Michael's eye contact. He slowly nodded his head. "Alright, I tell you what. I been divorced three times, never gonna get married again, and I only had one of them good-for-nothings cheat on me. So, I know how ya feel, son. How'd a Ford Ranger strike you boys?"

"That'd be great," Michael replied and shook his hand to solidify the agreement, "can't tell you how much this means to me!"

"Don't thank me yet, this piece of shit's held together with *bailin' wire* and *bubblegum*! Got stuck with it on a trade-in and this damned little truck's worse'n the clap! I just, *cannot*, get rid of it! Step on inside and let's get somethin' down on paper that won't get neither of us in hot water later today, whaddayasay?"

Twenty minutes later, Michael and Z drove back toward The Blue Bonnet to commence their actual surveillance efforts.

TRAINING DAY 70, 1832 HOURS_

RURAL COMPOUND. NIOBRARA COUNTY, WYOMING.

As Michael piloted the aging white Accord down the compound's rough, rutted driveway, he and Z both donned the high-visibility clothing they'd worn on their way into town earlier that day.

"Now we get to see how honest all these training exercises've been," Z surmised as he adjusted the shoulders and collar of his orange Orioles shirt.

"Maybe," Michael countered. "It's possible we went through all this extra trouble for nothing, and he didn't make us until we changed clothes and rented the pick-up."

"Well, even if we lost fair-n-square, I'll be pretty impressed with Double-Time. As arrogant as he is, I think, if he'd made us, he woulda made sure *we* knew about it."

"Yeah, I can agree with that," Michael replied as he pulled the sedan to a stop near the other training vehicles. *All the other teams are already back. We're the last out and last in today. Wonder if we're the only winners?* "Let's go take our lumps."

Z scoffed and laughed at the truth of Michael's assessment. "One way or another, you can rest assured John'll find a way. Can't let us feel too successful, now."

Michael collected his Mountainsmith bag and checked to ensure it still held his small monocular, Multi-Cam baseball hat, and black watch cap. *If I had one of my cowboy hats and a button-down shirt, I could've put a more complete disguise package together.*

Z led their way to the porch and into the main house, where they saw John and the rest of the trainees had gathered to finish the evening meal preparations.

"'Bout time," John announced from his seat at the head of the large wood table. A yellow legal pad sat on the table in front of him, and Michael saw handwriting scrawled across the top page in black ink. "You two must love pushin' deadlines. Supper's just about ready. Grab a can of suds, pull up a seat, and console your sorrows, shitheads."

"Sorrows," Michael asked. "What happened?"

"I'll break the news to you after you're settled, unless you got some need to take your fate standing."

Z looked at Michael, saw his tacit agreement, and spoke for both of them. "I think we'd prefer to hear it now."

"Alright, it's your funeral." John leaned back in his chair and almost looked disappointed in their outcome. "Your target called y'all boys in right about 8:45 this morning. Switching out the intel packets didn't make up for bad tradecraft. You two shitheads got made almost twelve hours ago, but you wasn't even sharp enough to realize it. Where you been, anyway? Decide to skip town and go find some happy ending massage parlor somewhere in the mean streets o' Cheyenne? Maybe ya figured this line of work just isn't for you, so you dropped some job applications at all the Stop-n-Robs and pizza joints ya drove past?"

"No, we were following our target around all day," Michael explained. "Got all the requested info for the intel packet, and, I think, quite a bit more." He set the intel packet on the table and slid it across the smooth surface to John.

"Bullshit," their lead instructor protested. He leaned forward, roughly grabbed the manila envelope, and tore it open. "How'd y'all manage that, he made your car first thing in the morning?"

Michael shrugged. "I dunno, John, I guess that's a good question for him."

"Doesn't matter, anyhow, he called you two in twelve hours ago." He skimmed through the intel packet pages, and his expression darkened further.

"What did he call in," Z hesitantly asked.

"Got it right here," John pulled the yellow legal pad closer and pointed to a line of handwritten text that Michael saw started with 0845. "White accord, driver, long yellow jacket, male passenger orange shirt. It's right there, just like you're wearing now." He pointed to them and their clothing before carelessly dropping the intel packet on the table.

Michael looked at Z, who nodded and quietly took a deep breath. *Let's step off into this and see if we ruin our pants from the top or the bottom.* "Well, that's just it, John," Michael cautiously explained, "we ditched *these* clothes before we got to town and didn't put 'em back on until we started back down the driveway. We wore totally different clothes in town, so, there's no way our target saw us in these shirts." Michael pulled the front of his yellow shirt up a bit to reveal his tan shirt beneath. Z did the same and showed his light gray graphic tee.

John glared at them, and his jaw muscles flexed several times. "Everybody else, clear the room. *Right now, get the hell out.*" He pointed at Michael and Z with his right index finger. "Everybody but these two assholes."

Chairs scuffed across the wood floor as the rest of the trainees scurried away and descended the basement stairs. *Not that it's really gonna matter,* Michael thought, *this still won't be a private conversation for any of us.*

"What the *hell*'re you doing," John demanded as soon as the three of them were hypothetically alone.

Here it goes. "We wore a few layers out this morning so we could change our appearance a few times," Michael explained, "and we made the first change at the city limits off Highway 20. I was just getting too warm in that long-sleeved running jacket."

Z cleared his throat and spoke. "And we also ditched the Accord right after we got to town and rented a green Ford Ranger. We spent the whole day in that, least until we had to get it back at 1700."

John continued to glare at both of them, and Michael assumed he was deciding on a course of action. *We didn't violate the R-O-Es, we didn't get I-D'd by the local cops. All we did was be creative enough to win, and, test the integrity of the exercise.*

"I suppose you both think you're pretty damned smart right now," John slowly surmised. "Think you got one over on us, huh?"

"No, John, not at all," Michael countered, "but, I do think it's odd that the target I-D'd the car we had for only a few minutes, along with clothing descriptions he couldn't have seen."

"That is weird," Z sarcastically injected, "it's like he had some kinda help, but I can't imagine how that coulda happened. Whoever saw us in those clothes *and* that car would-a had to be somewhere between this kitchen and the town limits."

"Almost like someone wants to fail everyone out without giving us a chance to prove or test our capabilities," Michael added and held John's angry glare. "There is another possibility. Maybe this's all a coincidence. Maybe the target saw a white sedan he thought was our Accord with two guys that looked like us, and just happened to also be dressed in yellow and orange—"

"It'd be understandable," Z interrupted, "given the number of construction workers and road crews that come through here—"

"And the oilfield workers," Michael added. "I'd bet most of them probably wear just as much high-visibility clothing as anyone else in the construction industry."

John leaned back in his chair and seemed to consider the position in which they each found themselves. He pulled their intel and activity log closer and intently read through it. "You boys just might be right," he apologetically offered. "Before we go jumpin' to any conclusions, I oughta check with your target and see if there's any way he mighta made the kinda mistake you boys brought up. Ask around and see if there's someone that could-a given him the kinda help that'd be required for him to have *known* what you looked like when you left here this morning. But, I doubt it."

John stood up from the table with their intel packet in his hands. "Hell, now that you boys bring it up, there's gotta be *hundreds* of men riding together through that little town in old, white Honda Accords wearing orange and yellow shirts. I think the better question, at this point, is to find out why he didn't call in *every one* of 'em he saw throughout the whole day. If you'll excuse me, y'all boys can invite your friends back up for supper and I'mma go have a word. See if we can get to the bottom of this."

Michael watched John leave the room and waited until he was gone to look over at Z. When he did, he saw his teammate appeared skeptical.

"Yeah, Z, I feel like you look."

"Whaddaya gonna believe? The words or the probability?"

"I'm gonna believe," Michael offered, "that *whatever* the cause, that it won't happen again, at least not in a way that we can embarrass John like that." He stomped twice on the wood floor just hard enough to signal his classmates sequestered belowdecks.

Sergio led the other trainees back up from the basement, looked around, and smiled at Michael after confirming John was no longer in the room. "You guys are some *stupid* kinda fools, tryin' to prove the deck's stacked like that."

The front door opened without warning and Jane stepped just past the threshold. She kept hold of the door handle as though she didn't intend on straying farther inside. "Andrew, Z, John says both you two assholes have the floor tonight. Where's Zeb?"

"Right here," he replied and stepped toward the instructor.

"You get a cot. John says to stop being a shithead and you'll get a mattress someday. Updated schedule. John says *Mother Mary* starts at 0-400. See you boys dark and early in the morning." Jane stepped back out and started to pull the door closed. "Oh, yeah," she exclaimed and briefly pushed it back open. "John says you know why this is happening. Nighty-night, boys." She disappeared and the door closed and latched.

"Alright," Zeb smiled, "upgrade!"

"No good deed goes unpunished," Michael said to Z and shrugged his shoulders. "Sorry, boys," he loudly announced to the other trainees. "Didn't intend for this to spill over onto all of you." After a few grumbled their acceptance of his apology, Michael turned back to Z. "What're we gonna do now?"

His teammate slowly spoke while absentmindedly staring at the table. "I'mma start by runnin' in my orange Orioles t-shirt tomorrow morning."

Michael nodded at the small act of defiance. "I suppose I'll have to wear my yellow, then. If they're gonna smoke us anyway, may as well make sure they send us down in flames."

With the accelerated schedule looming over them, Michael and the rest of the trainees quickly ate supper, cleaned up the kitchen, and retired to the basement. *It seems like we're finally starting to come together as a team,* Michael thought, *even though we don't know a damned thing about each other.* He noticed the bed Matthias had spent the last week in was tightly made up, and all his gear was gone. "What happened there?"

"Oh, yeah," Sergio replied, "he quit right after we got back today. That exercise really bothered him."

"Really," Michael asked. "What was that bad about it?"

"He just knew what was coming," Alpha facetiously explained in his thick accent, "and he wanted to get outta tomorrow."

Michael chuckled at the ribbing, but Sergio ignored him and continued.

"So, Tex was our target," Sergio explained, "and that dude's pretty sneaky. We were sittin' down the block from this business he's supposed to be in. We saw him go in, and I'm still pretty sure that there wasn't a back door, but, like ten minutes later, he snuck up on the passenger side of the car and put a red gun right in Matthias' face. Scared the *hell* outta that kid."

"So, he quit because a trainer put a fake gun in his face?"

"No, not really," Sergio responded, "he quit because he realized how bad he messed up, and how vulnerable he'd be following real, armed bad guys around by himself. We came back here after the loss, and he packed his shit. John had him on the bus in, like, thirty minutes."

"The man's bunk isn't really even cold yet," Phillip offered, "and I bet they've already pulled his chair outta the classroom. Any evidence of your time here gets erased before you cross the county line." The nine remaining trainees all looked at one another in silence for a long moment and considered Phillip's observation.

"And then, there was nine," John unexpectedly called down as he descended the stairs into the trainees' basement. When he reached the bottom of the stairs, Michael saw his tone and appearance completely concealed the recent dust-up. "Sounds like everybody knows Matthias quit. Just like Bartholomew, I got no hard feelings towards the man. He realized how isolated and vulnerable he'd be, especially if he had to work surveillance by himself. Said he couldn't stomach the idea of putting himself out there to hunt men who might have guns and weapons when he had nothing more than fists and prayers. Told me he felt guilty that he'd put Jude in danger, if there had been actual danger to be in.

"Too bad," John surmised, "but, the harsh reality is the guy barely made it through our defensive tactics training, and there's still a lot of ground left for y'all to cover there before you get to move on. I understand his apprehension. He mighta just saved his own life, and prob'ly, the life of someone else that didn't need killin'. That's just a small taste of one of the assignments our fellas go to. If you got similar considerations, think long and hard about what we're training you to do here."

"What is that, precisely, John," Sergio asked despite knowing he wouldn't get the answer they all sought.

"Whatever God calls you to do. Early start tomorrow, shitheads. Don't be late."

TRAINING DAY 85, 0345 HOURS_

RURAL COMPOUND. NIOBRARA COUNTY, WYOMING.

MICHAEL WORKED to cast the proverbial fog and cobwebs from his mind as he climbed the stairs to the start of another extraordinarily early day. *Even the sun's still in bed,* he surmised and yawned, *so we oughta be, too. Fifth early start since Z and I peed in John's Cheerios two weeks ago. Maybe coincidence, probably not.* He stepped out onto the porch, and the brisk, high-forties temps immediately reminded him that summer came late and short to this part of the world. The porch lights cast only a small amount of light around them, and Michael assumed they had a dimmer switch somewhere. *Still too early for bright light, and I imagine I'm about to need my night vision to go stumbling around in the darkness.*

"Good morning," John announced as the last of the trainees straggled out on to the porch to join him. Steam rose off the top of his coffee mug and reiterated the coolness around them. "Got a local field trip planned for this morning. In the interest of time and efficiency, I'm combining your morning run with a field problem. Y'all are gonna head into town, on foot, at whatever pace seems beneficial to you. That's about thirteen miles, each way."

John, who had no such prescribed regimen this morning, paused and loudly sipped at his coffee. "Then, each o' you's gonna figure out how to get me a copy of yesterday's local paper. There's a paid dispenser right outside the front door 'o The Blue Bonnet. Even if there's no papers to be had, you're gonna *physically touch* that bin. That's the midpoint of the run and no one gets to cheat me on the distance. Standard rules of engagement. No unnecessary violence. No assaulting cops under any circumstance. No police reports. No witnesses. No sins. Just the typical R-O-Es that you're all used to by now, with the additional caveat that no one gets to take any money with 'em. You'll have to round up two quarters somewhere along the way if you wanna pay for your copy of the paper. Otherwise, you'll have to get creative and come up with some alternate means of entry into the bin."

Michael started shivering a bit as they stood still on the porch. *I'm dressed to be moving and working, not standing around doing nothing.* He tried to quietly jog in place to get his core temp back up a few degrees.

"Now, a few points for clarification," John continued after another sip of coffee. "My cadre has assured me that there will be no more than three papers in the bin. They checked it last night and removed all but three, so, there could still be three. But, then again, there could be *none* if the local townsfolk had a late-night hankering for local news and farm equipment ads.

"Second, I will make my way in to have lunch at The Blue Bonnet at 1100 hours. I will return all of the papers y'all *borrow* and deliver to me by that time. If you borrow a paper that doesn't make it back to my porch before the stroke of 1100, you've got stolen property in your hands that you'll have to figure out how to return without committing a sin or addin' your name to the local police blotter. That gives y'all almost seven hours to get that done, so, that seems pretty goddamned generous. Four hours is a *good* marathon time, and you got near double that to get back a winner. Winners are guaranteed a bunk for the next seven nights. Last man back here without a paper's gonna keep Zeb's floorboards warm for him tonight."

John gave his coffee another pronounced and prolonged sip. "Regardless of when y'all get back here, we start the afternoon class promptly at 1300. Got a specialist that's gonna train you numbskulls in *Body Language Interpretation and Emotional Tells.* Vitally important to what some-a y'all might be doing someday. Questions, comments, concerns before y'all get goin'?"

Michael mentally worked his way through the marching orders for a creative solution, shortcut, or stumbling block that offered John and his instructors an opportunity to sabotage the results. *I'll probably find one on a front lawn or sidewalk between here and there, but that's at least Petty Theft and, maybe, Trespassing, depending on where I find it. The bin's the only viable option, assuming there's even papers left inside. That's the easiest way to make sure everyone loses. More likely that there's only one paper left so we waste a bunch of time.*

"Alright, then. Paperboy drops today's copy about 0-700, so I'd get goin' if I were you. It pays to be a winner."

As soon as John finished his recurring send-off statement, Michael strode from the porch. He consciously let his body warm-up while he worked up to his marathon pace. Several of the other trainees ran with greater urgency, and Michael questioned their decision. *There's always another way to solve John's field problems, always a creative solution that's not immediately obvious. What's the angle here, though? Even if there are three papers left in the bin, we're gonna waste a lot of time trying to get in without breaking the bin, without being confronted by a passerby or the deputies, and being gone before the paperboy shows up at 7am. Wait...that's it.*

Michael smiled at his realization and slowed his pace to a stroll. *That's it! This is an easy win! I don't wanna* avoid *the paperboy, I wanna meet him there and ask him for one of yesterday's copies that's gonna be thrown out, anyway!* He looked down at his watch. 0402. *Three hours, almost. I need to keep a slower pace, eleven or twelve minutes a mile, and I'll get there just after 6-30 to make sure I don't miss him. Then, I'll have more gas to hurry back here with the paper.*

During the next few minutes, Michael fell back into last place among his fellow runners and used his wristwatch and the county road's mile markers to pace himself. *Harder than I thought, my body naturally wants to run each mile a couple minutes faster. Hopefully, my legs still feel this fresh on the way back. Once I get my copy from the paperboy, assuming no one else's reached the same conclusion, I won't even need to worry about hauling ass back. Don't gotta be first, just can't be last.*

Michael pressed on into the predawn darkness and watched the sunrise in solitude. He waved at the few vehicles that passed him on the isolated, rural road. *Gotta work to keep from raising suspicion. Doesn't help that nine strangers are running toward town at sun-up. Better'n running around at night, I guess. Maybe they'll think we're some kind of adult fat-camp.*

When he saw Sergio running back toward him, Michael checked his watch, suddenly concerned he'd fallen too far behind his intended pace. 6-0-3, *I better be getting close.* As they met, Sergio slowed and jogged alongside Michael toward town.

"You better pick it up, Mike, you're in last place by at least five or seven minutes."

"Where's your paper?"

"Bin's already empty, must-a been tapped out overnight."

"Assuming there was ever still three in it to begin with. You tell anybody else about that on your way back?"

"Only Z and Phillip, nobody else asked."

"Kay. Is the cafe open?"

"Should be, sign says it opens at six," Sergio replied and ran with Michael in silence for a few dozen yards. "You *tryin'* to be last?"

"No, I've got a plan," Michael replied.

"You say so. I don't give a shit about winning this one as long as I don't lose. No way I'm sleepin' on the floor again if I can help it."

"How much distance is left to the bin?"

Sergio thought for a moment. "About two miles, little more, definitely under three, though. Haven't paid as much attention on the way back."

"Thanks, brother. See you back at the house, then."

"Yeah, good luck, man, hope it works out for ya, whatever it is." Sergio quickly stopped, turned, and ran back toward the compound.

"Me too," Michael said aloud to himself. He rechecked his watch. *I'll get there a little after 6-30, so, as long as the delivery's not too early, I'll have a little rest, maybe even find some water.*

When Michael finally saw The Blue Bonnet Cafe, he again checked his watch. 6:39. He kept his pace, stopping only when he finally reached the bin. *Still empty. Good, delivery's not here yet.* He had passed only Sergio on the run in, despite taking the most direct route. *None of the others are around. Musta went looking for other bins. Surprised they risked having me beat them back. It'll be hard to win this one, but real easy to lose. No way we'll keep pace on an unsupported marathon with no supplies. Still got half of that distance to get back home.*

"Sir?"

Michael turned to the kind, female voice behind him. A young woman in a blue checker-board apron stood in the cafe's open doorway and smiled at him.

"Do you want some water?"

He smiled broadly before replying. "That would be great."

"I'll grab a couple bottles for you."

I love small town hospitality, Michael thought. *Reminds me of Silver City. Nobody's really a stranger there.* Within a few minutes, he'd acquired two bottles of water and confirmation that the paper delivery should be along any minute. At 06:58am, a rusted, early 1980's Chevy truck pulled up in front of the café with a sixteenish-year-old driver behind the wheel. She stepped from the two-toned olive-green and white pickup and retrieved a bundle of papers from the bed.

"Good morning," Michael called out and approached the truck.

"'Morning, sir," the papergirl replied. "If you're looking for today's paper, I just gotta see you drop change in the bin, they don't want me to take cash anymore."

"Well, actually, I was hoping you might have a copy of yesterday's paper."

She tossed the bundle down on the sidewalk next to the bin and grimaced in thought. "Gimme a second, lemme look." The young woman scanned the bed and then moved into the cab. Finding nothing obvious, she leaned down and stuck her arm under the bench seat. "Got *one*, but it's kinda rough."

"Not worried about the condition," Michael replied. "You want anything for it?"

The papergirl handed over a thin, tri-folded paper with grease smeared across the front page. "No, sir, you're helping me clean the truck out by takin' it."

"Thank you, have a great day."

"Yes, sir, you do the same," she replied and resumed her appointed task of restocking the bin.

Michael started off toward the compound but quickly turned around when a question struck him. "Out of curiosity, does this bin usually sell out?"

"No, sir," the teenager laughed. "Not sure I've ever seen one of 'em empty before. There's almost always six-to-ten papers left in the bins, but every one's been dry this morning, though. Must *really* be somethin' in there worth readin' about for a change."

"Thanks, again," Michael replied and started off again. He rolled the paper up tightly and carried it like a relay baton. *Interesting. John or his instructors either set us up to fail or forced us into a creative solution.* He rechecked the time. *I can be back there by 9-30 if I keep a ten-minute pace, with a week of immunity and a few hours to stretch and recuperate before the Body Language Interpretation class.* Michael intentionally leaned forward and increased his cadence to about 150 steps-per-minute. *Time to see if this gamble pays off.*

TRAINING DAY 100, 0300 HOURS_

RURAL COMPOUND. NIOBRARA COUNTY, WYOMING.

BANG BABANG BANG

Michael awoke with a start at the loud sounds of metal striking metal, and something falling down the stairs into the complete darkness of the trainees' basement dormitory. Subsequent, hurried rustling told Michael his equally panicked classmates also worked to get out of their beds. At least one of them fell hard onto the floor somewhere to his right.

BANGBANGBANGBANG

The bright interior lights turned on and stung Michael's eyes, just as a large metal trash can finished crashing down the stairs and John stomped down behind it. He forcefully struck the garbage can's lid with a pipe wrench. Michael finally freed himself from his bedding, stood, and glanced at his watch. *3am. Son of a bitch...*

"Wakey wakey, shitheads! F-N-S-R-F-N!"

"What the hell's that," Sergio asked, probably louder than he realized.

"*Front and center right fuckin' now*," John shouted back downstairs in response.

"There's no 'S' in center," Thomas grumbled.

John scoffed. "The last man up here owes me a *hundred burpees*, along with every asshole that gets up here *after* Thomas! Make damned sure you land up here ready to work!"

Further chaos erupted as the trainees strove to get upstairs. Sergio chucked one of Thomas's running shoes into the shower at the opposite end of the room. Thomas swore and chased after the shoe.

John targeted each student and used them as scapegoats for persecution and discipline, so Michael expected everyone would get a few turns in the barrel. *You don't have to do anything wrong, and it normalizes his ability to turn us on each other with no explanation or cause. Keep his subordinates ready to cannibalize each other on command for no real reason whatsoever.*

Michael's potential empathy for Thomas couldn't overcome the man's zealous pleasure in punishing John's identified targets. Without explicitly working against Thomas, Michael ascended the stairs with three men still behind him, including the intended scapegoat.

"Your mission," John announced before everyone had arrived, "which you have no choice but to accept, is to get into town without being seen and enter the Blue Bonnet. You will take an item from the cafe and bring it back here to me without being caught. I will, of course, return it later when the boys and I go back in there for lunch. So, just like the last field trip for a local paper, you're not stealing, you're just borrowing, for the purposes of better developing the skills necessary to serve God in these intended assignments. Also, you can't come back here until you lay hands on The Blue Bonnet Cafe. Last one here without something to show for his efforts will ride the pine tonight.

"My standard rules of engagement apply," John continued. "Getting caught and arrested gets you kicked out, tellin' the cops anything about what you were doing will get you excommunicated if I have my way about it. If I were in your goddamned shoes, I'd sure as hell wanna be headed back outta there by dawn, which gives you almost three hours. It pays to be a winner, gentlemen."

A portion of the group took off running toward town before John even finished the statement. As he left the house and jogged off into the early morning, Michael noticed how bright the night actually was. A harvest moon shone down and lit his familiar path up the driveway and out toward the county road. *If this wasn't mandatory fun, I'd enjoy being out here without perpetual consequence looming over me.*

Although he started off near the middle of the pack on this interrupted marathon, Michael pulled closer to the pack leaders. *Need to be among the first ones to the cafe so I can get in, get out, and get gone before someone spots a half-dozen strangers trying to break into the place. Plus, the breakfast staff probably shows up around five o'clock, so only three, maybe four of us even have a shot at getting there in time without being seen and identified to the local deputies. Pretty clear John wants most of us to fail or abort this one.*

The moral quandary of committing burglary-on-command briefly bothered Michael, but only until he considered his task in light of the intended purpose. *These skills must truly be necessary in these 'special assignments,' and I can see there really isn't another way for John to realistically test and evaluate our command of them. Getting into a place you're not supposed to be, finding the evidence you need inside, and getting away unnoticed isn't just something that criminals and burglars have to be good at. It's clearly something that the good guys have to accomplish, especially if we're going after scum like organized crime, rapists, and terrorists.* He picked up his pace a little further as the notion of finally working in a real counterterrorism unit buoyed his spirits and lifted his feet. *Besides, I've found a creative way to win several field problems, and this one's gotta be no different. Got a couple hours to figure out how to win without committing sin, crimes, or violating the R-O-Es.*

TRAINING DAY 103, 1018 HOURS_

CATTLE KING'S GROCER. LUSK, WYOMING.

From the front passenger seat of a rundown, grey Toyota RAV4 SUV, Michael watched the front doors of the town's one grocer and patiently awaited the return of their target. He chewed on a red plastic straw that had been a vital part of their fast-food breakfast an hour ago. Z lightly drummed on the steering wheel even though no music played in the SUV. Because Michael had driven the last time they teamed up on a field exercise, Z seemed excited to get behind the steering wheel on this one.

"What'd you think-a that 'stop-n-rob' exercise a few days ago," Z asked, "the 'Great Blue Bonnet Burglary Caper?'"

Michael snickered and decided against asking how Z knew "caper." *Nobody says that but cops.* "Yeah, I dunno. Part of me thinks these things are stacked against us, part of me thinks that John's trying to force us to look for creative solutions. Another part thinks they're designed to make us fail." He stared at the grocery entrance and thought about the failed exercise. "I'm just glad no one called the sheriff."

"Can't win 'em all," Z surmised. Silence enveloped the cabin, and he started quietly drumming on the steering wheel again. "How much did *you* get to drive," he absentmindedly asked. "Before here, I mean, *wherever* and *whatever* you did, ya know—"

"Yeah, I gotcha, no details," Michael confirmed his understanding of his teammate's question. "I trust you, Z, I don't think you'd try to weasel personal details to get me thrown down on the floorboards tomorrow night. Not much, I didn't get to drive much at all."

"I miss the shit out've it," Z replied and, grinning, wrung the steering wheel in both his hands.

I bet he raced cars, Michael thought. "Hey, Z, so, whaddaya call it, when you start into a corner, let's say a sweeping left. You start on the *inside,* then steer to the outside, light brakes, and then steer *into* the turn, and—"

"And then stomp the gas," Z finished the question, "that's a *Scandinavian Flick.* Manipulates the car's weight transfer going into the turn and lets you explode through it. Why?"

"No reason," Michael coyly replied, "except I figured you probably raced cars in your former life. I figured you'd know the answer if you did."

"*What*? No, that's somethin' we went over in EVOC *here,* and—"

"No, Z," Michael laughed and chided his colleague, "we didn't *ever* talk about *anything* like a *Swedish flip,* or whatever you called it—"

"The *Scandinavian Flick,* you ass-hole," Z replied with disbelief in his voice. "At least get it right if you're gonna throw it down on a damned ole 'Guess What' card." He shook his head. "I can't believe I fell for that shit."

"That's like, some *ice-racing stuff,* right," Michael asked to continue ribbing the man he considered a friend. "Nobody'd *ever* believe you learned about that at a secret, priest EVOC school, Z!" *I know more about the quality of his character than most people I've ever known in my life, and I can't even know his real name.*

"Well, since you got my manhood in a sling anyway, it's also a great technique for dirt track and rallycross, too, not just ice racing." Z shook his head again, disappointed in himself. "At least, that's *what I hear.*"

"Relax, Z, your secret's safe with me, and my secret is that I know your secret. John'd hang me up just as high if he ever knew that I knew."

"You're not gonna trade me some piece of *your* past, even though you just suckered that outta me?!"

"Naw, that seems like a bad idea," Michael joked, "I trust you, Z, but I don't trust you *that much!*"

"Had to happen eventually," Z offered between chuckles. "Momma always said I's too trustin.' This's just more proof-a that, I suppose."

"Well, bless my heart," Michael offered in a fake Southern accent to further bait him.

"Pound sand, Andrew, I ain't got a *clue* what that means." His smirk confirmed his lie. "You ain't gettin' me twice," Z scoffed. Looking back at the store entrance, he sighed and glanced down at this watch. "Whaddayou think he's doing in there?"

"Hell if I know," Michael replied, "buyin' out the whole store?"

"He's had enough time."

Michael had decided his partner had grown up in North Carolina and guessed he'd probably lived in a rural area and spent a lot of time outdoors. *He knows how to really* drive, *not just to* operate *a vehicle. His work on the abandoned airstrip had made the rest of us look like we'd never sat behind the wheel before. I bet I'm not the only one making up presumed backgrounds for the other trainees. Wonder what they think they might know about me.* Michael knew one of his biggest regrets about eventually leaving John's training program would be losing contact with Z. *I'm sure John'll specifically forbid us from exchanging personal information, and I don't wanna put him in a bad position by offering mine, but I sure as hell hope he passes me his. Maybe I can sneak something into his duffel bag later and hope he decides not to wave it around to John. Pretty sure we've got a lot of program left to survive. Seems like every instructor talks about how they'll be back to teach more in-depth classes later. Maybe this is a four-year-degree program and the graduates all walk away with a Bachelor of Science in Espionage Arts.*

"I can't believe Matthias left after that surveillance exercise," Z offered, as though striking up small talk to pass the time.

Or, Michael thought, *he wants to see if I'm willing to risk an actual, personal conversation. I'll bite.* "Yeah, but, if low-level work like that really scared him, it's probably best that he goes back to his parishioners."

"I didn't feel that way *at all.* The whole thing to me felt like I's gettin' to play adult hide-and-seek, or *Spy-Versus-Spy,* or somethin' really *cool* from when I's growin' up."

"Yeah," Michael agreed and smiled at the analogy. "There's just enough danger to it that it makes you really feel *alive,* right, *energized.* I kinda like it, too."

"You really think that's why Matthias quit?"

"I dunno," Michael replied as he wondered how much to reveal. "Jude seems like a trustworthy guy, and he was with Matthias all day. If he says that's what happened, then I guess I gotta take him at his word."

"Yeah, that's about the long 'n short of it for me, too. There's a couple fellas that might rub me the wrong way if they got the chance, but Jude seems like he's good people."

The best, Michael wanted to say. Silence returned to the cab, and Z again checked his watch. *He's not well-programmed for surveillance work and long-term boredom. Maybe they didn't have ADD medication where he grew up in rural North Carolina.*

"So, I got a theory," Z slowly announced, "about what we're really here to do."

"What's your take?"

"I know I already told you about how I'm into conspiracy theories, and, I guess it's not so much a *theory,* as more a kinda *hope,* that we somehow end up deep inside this secret society that's totally devoted to covertly workin' in the shadows to fight the forces of evil."

Michael smiled and nodded. "I can see the appeal of that. Doing all the rough work that others aren't willing to do."

"*But* only the work that's necessary to promote and preserve human dignity and service to God."

"That's a tall order, Z. Does it come with capes and masks, or do we have to supply our own?"

"Well, like I said, it's more a hope than a real theory. I expect I'm gonna end up workin' some kinda personnel security detail somewhere. I just don't wanna hafta learn a new language to get along with my coworkers."

Michael laughed aloud at how concerned Z sounded. "That's one of the things I'm kinda looking forward to!"

"Not me, man, I'm *terrible* with foreign languages. I took a semester of Spanish in high school, and it actually made my brain hurt."

I could easily become good friends with Z, Michael thought. He considered how the past few months that they'd spent together would generally have already made them friends, if only they knew anything real about one another. *That's not entirely accurate. I've spent enough time with these guys to know who I'd wanna take into a street fight. Jury's still out if I'd want more than* Sergio *for a gunfight, but I'm confident I can trust almost everyone here to step into an arena with me.*

Michael's mind followed a logical tangent back into the recurring topic of what, exactly, it was that John and his staff trained them to do. *Even though John won't explicitly confirm what we're training for, every reasonable indication is that we can expect to spend some time in gunfights and close-quarters work. The only thing that makes clear and definite sense is that the Vatican and the Holy See are training us to work in their Division of Intelligence and Counter-Espionage. All the skills we're picking up only make sense in that kind of work. Security forces don't need to follow people around, and they don't need to sneak into places undetected, or to know about underlying spiritual and psychological motivations for sin and crime. At least, I don't think so, do they?* He chuckled at the realization that his cop experience in small-town New Mexico and priest experience in South America might not give him all the available information on how security and protection details might operate in Europe. *It's fair to think that things might be a little different over there.*

"There he is," Z whispered and nodded his chin toward the grocery store's entrance.

Michael looked at the distant doorway and saw Tex walk out carrying a single brown paper grocery sack under his left arm. *That's not a natural way to carry bagged groceries. Bet cash money he's got a gun concealed on his right side, and he wants to keep that gun hand free.* Tex momentarily nudged his right elbow down against his right hip as he walked. Michael immediately recognized the tactic and saw what few others would. *Yep, he just checked to make sure the gun's still secure and in place. Probably not holstered inside his jeans if he feels like he's gotta check to make sure it's still there. They only recently taught these guys body language interpretation, so I'll have to be careful how I word this to Z so he doesn't realize I've taken several masterclasses on the subject. The only people with that kinda knowledge are cops and crooks. He'll easily assume I wasn't ever a crook.* "Alright, Z, let's see how long we can tail him. We only gotta stay on him for another two hours to call this a win. When he came outta the store, did he move kinda suspiciously to you?"

"Yeah," Z confidently responded. "You know he's got a gun, right?" His partner looked at Michael as though assessing his reaction to the information. "Right hip, probably an outside-the-waist holster, if I's a bettin' man," he added, with a knowing expression on his face.

Michael grinned at the revelation. *Looks like Sergio and I aren't the only ones with prior training.*

TRAINING DAY 105, 0600 HOURS_

RURAL COMPOUND. NIOBRARA COUNTY, WYOMING.

As promised the night before, John trudged down the basement steps at the same time they'd typically have been forming up outside for the morning run. "Glad to see you're all up and about," he announced as he looked around at his students. "Also, glad to see y'all took me serious and didn't put on your P-T gear this morning. Like I explained last night, we got a different kinda field problem today, and you'll probably end up getting your P-T in other ways before the day's out, so, no need to feel cheated if you're missin' the morning run." Most everyone chuckled along with him.

"You've been immersed in more than forty hours of classroom work on mobile surveillance, stationary surveillance, and counter-surveillance," John continued. "You can pick almost any lock made on the face of the Earth, and you can sneak through urban environments like a goddamned ninja. It's time you put all that to the test. There's no run this morning, no grinder, no race. Everyone's got the same mission today, and I didn't intend to put you in direct competition with each other, but, the fact of the matter is that there's only a couple objectives today and a lot more'n two or three of you. So, somebody's sleeping on the floor tonight for sure.

"Today's field trip," John announced and again looked around the room. "You're gonna get to town, don't care how. I'll even let you be seen and interact with the local townsfolk today, all one-thousand-five-hundred-and-fifty-nine of 'em, if you gotta. Go out, have a chat, drink a beer, make a few friends. Have a goddamned ball! But the only way to win today is to steal a badge and bring it back to me without getting caught."

"A badge?" Alpha's still-thick French accent emphasized his disbelief.

Sacre bleu, Michael wanted to shout.

"Yep. I need badges, and the only ones that's got 'em in town is the local sheriff's office and the volunteer fire department, but they're a little harder to find. So, if you've learned the damned lessons as well as we've taught 'em, I expect two or three-a you oughta be able to swipe one and get it back to me in a few hours. Today's mission has a deadline, too. I've pushed this morning's mass back to the afternoon, so y'all got until 1500 to be back here to suffer defeat or claim victory."

"John, they wear 'em on their chest," Zeb objected, "pretty close to their gun! They're not gonna just hand 'em over to the kind and friendly stranger cause we asked for it."

"I'll leave it to you to work out the details," John explained. "That's your problem, not mine. So, just to make sure we're clear, here's the rules. Number one: no violence." He specifically glared at Thomas and maintained focus on the man while he next spoke. "Anyone that assaults a cop or deputy, you will be *gonzo,* and not just from my program." John paused and resumed scanning the rest of the group. "Number two: no getting caught. The judge will not be back on the bench until Monday, two days from now, which means anyone that gets arrested will be photographed, fingerprinted, and booked into jail for the weekend. That will *at least* get you dismissed. Can't stay in the program if you have a criminal record that connects your name, fingerprints, and photograph with this town. You'll still have a job as a priest, *probably,* but you won't continue on with the program. Number three: snitches get stitches, and, if it's ever up to me, excommunicated. We were all a lot better off when betrayal was a mortal sin. Number four: it pays to be a winner."

Michael and the other students all stood in place and didn't automatically rush off at his final words as they'd recently grown accustomed to doing.

"Don't know what you're waiting for, but you shitheads are burnin' daylight."

Several of his teammates started past John and up the stairs, but Michael stood fast and waited until they were alone. "John, you don't care how we get to town?"

"Nope, not all."

"Where's the keys to the old beater outside? I don't feel like walking into town with a buncha grown men like we just got let outta county jail with a one-way bus pass."

John chuckled. "I like your style, Andrew. Have at it. You gonna pick them up?"

"Not a chance. They made their choice." After he secured the keys and the old, abused Chrysler four-door sedan, Michael drove up the long driveway as his classmates ran through the tall, dry grass fields straight toward the county road. *Yep, they look an early morning release from the county lockup.* Passing them by with nothing more than a honk and a wave, Michael continued toward the small town of Lusk, Wyoming. *A few of them might end up with three hots-and-a-cot at the Sheriff's Inn, but at least they won't sleep on the floor tonight.*

When US Highway 20 finally guided him into the two-square-mile town, Michael headed straight to the sheriff's station house, which sat across the street from The Blue Bonnet Cafe. A lone rough, mid-nineties Ford Bronco sat in front of the station with a large Niobrara County Sheriff's Office badge decal emblazoned on each door. *The deputies are probably all at breakfast right about now. Hopefully, the sheriff's too busy to see me.* He parked the equally beat-up Chrysler next to the Bronco and stepped out. As Michael strode by the SUV, he noticed the large badge decals were printed on magnetic backing. *John must already know that, but swiping the sheriff's decals is pretty damned risky.*

Michael sensed he was being watched. He looked around and tried to appear nonchalant about it. *There, on The Blue Bonnet roof.* Seeing no immediate threat, he quickly shifted his gaze away from the man. *If he realizes I saw him, he'll move and I'll just have to find him again. Best to let him think he's got the upper hand, maybe do something about that later.*

Michael strode into the station with all the confidence of a fellow cop. *Like walking into a trusted friend's living room.* A few light, audible *tinks* announced his entry. and Michael shut the door behind him, smiled, and walked deeper into the large room. A receptionist sat on the other side of a wide, waist-high wood counter, along with two cluttered but abandoned desks. Four wood chairs and a small, worn bench occupied the public side of the lobby. *No deputies and no sheriff, but that surveillance camera hanging from the back-corner ceiling's pointed right at me and the front door.* Michael covertly scanned for any other cameras or motion detectors. *No others visible, just the one. Probably all the tech the sheriff can justify spending taxpayer money on, but he's still gotta try to keep up with times.* Michael angled his face away from the camera so it couldn't get a still photo that anyone could use for facial recognition later. *Whatever resources Niobrara County doesn't have handy, the State of Wyoming just might.*

"Good morning, sir, how can I help you," the receptionist asked as she looked up from her computer. An old version of Solitaire displayed on the monitor.

That's a good sign. The quality of life in a community is directly proportional to the number of bored cops and their support staff. Michael cleared his throat. "I'm a cop from New Mexico, just passing through on the way up north. Wanted to see if your folks traded patches? My son collects 'em, so I try to pick up unique patches whenever I'm out of town." Michael's stomach leapt into his throat as he realized he just set his own trap. *I drove up in a car with local Wyoming plates! Anyone who sees it will know the first two digits are assigned to this county! Gotta get outta here before she notices that, and before any of the deputies come back.*

She stood up approached the high counter between them. "The sheriff, well, really, *all* of the boys collect and trade patches, but none of 'em's in right now. They're probably over across the street at the Blue Bonnet if you want to try there. I'd give you one, but I don't know where the sheriff keeps his extras."

"That's alright, ma'am, I don't wanna disturb their breakfast, it's not that important."

"Well, if you wanna leave me your name and address, I can get one sent out to you, but the sheriff's kind of a tightwad, so he might not mail it until he gets one from you." She passed a notepad and pen across the countertop.

"That's great, ma'am, thank you." Michael fought to remain calm as he worked on this new problem. *I can't leave enough info that would allow the sheriff to follow-up on it. Can't give him my name and old department, there's still guys there who know me. Can't write down any of their names, cause they'll deny coming up here if he calls asking about his patch later.* He wrote down the most generic name he could think of, a random phone number, and the biggest law enforcement agency in New Mexico. "What about a 'junior deputy' sticker? Do you all have any of those?" Michael slid the notepad and pen back.

"You know what? I think we have a few layin' around here somewhere. How old did you say your boy is?" She opened a low cabinet on her side of the counter.

"He's nine."

She triumphantly produced a small stack of rubber-banded, metallic badge decals and set it on the counter. "Well, I can sure give you one of these, we don't have many left, but at least you won't go home empty-handed." She removed the top decal from the stack and Michael saw it was a perfect foil replica of the NCSO badge, a seven-pointed star. "I know it's not the patch you were hopin' for, but it's something! Here, let me check one other spot." The receptionist handed the decal across the counter and knelt down to dig through the cabinet.

"Yes, ma'am, that'll do the trick perfectly." *It's the same size as a real badge, and it'd have the same authority if the sheriff granted it. Perfect!* Michael took advantage of the brief opportunity and removed one more decal from the stack and concealed it behind the first one in his hand.

"Yeah, it looks like that's all we've got," she apologized and stood up to again face him. "So, sorry, I can only give you the one today. Not sure when we'll get another order in."

"Thank you, ma'am, that's more than enough."

She picked up the notepad with "his" info on it. "If you wanna leave your address, I can make sure he gets a patch sent off to you. Well, I can *pester* him to do it, I guess, but that's about all I can promise."

"How about this? Can you give me one of *his* cards, and I'll mail him one of my patches when I get home? That way neither of us are waiting around on the other."

"That'll work fine, I suppose." She read his info. "Albuquerque P-D?"

"Yes, ma'am, just over five years."

"You probably know Stu Denny, then?"

Michael's heart sank. "Denny, *hmmm,* what's he do for the force?"

"That's it," she beamed, "he plays guitar on *The Force*! The cover band that's all Albuquerque cops? They play for DARE programs at the local middle schools and such? Well, anyway, he's my brother-in-law, married my sister after she went down there to go to U-N-M years ago. No idea what he does for the P-D, I just know he can kinda be an asshole when he drinks too much, just like the rest of us, right?" The receptionist laughed, and Michael chuckled along with her. "But, bless his heart, he treats her good enough, I guess."

"I'm sorry, ma'am, I'm terrible with names, but I'd probably recognize the face. I haven't been to any of their shows for a while." *Time to go...*

She retrieved a business card from behind the counter and passed it to him. "I'm Peggy," she offered and extended her right hand.

"I'm Adam, Adam Smith."

"That's about the most generic name I've ever heard," she laughed again and released his hand. "I bet you get accused of makin' that up all the time!"

"I do, and it doesn't help that there's *three* of us working for A-P-D. Have a good day, Peggy. Thanks for making my boy's day!"

"You're welcome, Adam. Be safe out there."

"Thank you, ma'am, you as well. Give my best to *your* boys." He calmly retreated to the lot with his donated and stolen decals. When he again saw the Bronco parked there, inspiration struck, and Michael poked his head back in the door. "Hey, Peggy, sorry, just noticed that your badge decals on the Bronco are magnets. Might wanna keep a close eye on those, almost all of ours got stolen by a bunch of transient hobos. They stowed away on freight trains and left town before we could arrest 'em. Could be anywhere by now."

"That's good to know, thank you, Adam. I'll make sure to let the deputies know, too."

Michael returned to the sedan and hustled to get out of the parking lot before Peggy noticed his local license plates or his sudden hurry. He opened the driver's door and glanced at The Blue Bonnet as he slid into the car. *The watcher's still up there. Probably one of the instructors, but I'd sure like to know if it's not.* He backed from the Sheriff's Office parking lot and drove west, the opposite direction of where he needed to go, and considered his options for identifying the watcher. *I should probably start with John, but, if it's some outsider that's learned about us and the program, he could be in the wind by the time that I get out to the compound and John gets back here. What would John do if he were in my shoes?*

TRAINING DAY 105, 0747 HOURS_

THE BLUE BONNET CAFÉ ROOFTOP. LUSK, WYOMING.

FROM BEHIND SOMETHING akin to a parapet wall on top of The Blue Bonnet Cafe's two-story building, Damian Haggamore stepped forward to keep visual contact on the ranch car as long as possible. When it turned north and disappeared from sight, he lifted a handheld pac-set similar to a police radio. "John, you there?" The short and stocky fireplug of a man self-consciously pushed a rolled-up shirt sleeve back down over the Green Beret tattoo on his left forearm. He'd spent the last two hours hidden on the roof of The Blue Bonnet Café to keep watch on the recruits' efforts today. Andrew showed up much sooner than he expected and had gone straight to the Sheriff's Office, which immediately made him suspicious.

"Yeah, go."

"Hey, Andrew just left the Sheriff's Office and drove west. Turned north after a few blocks, probably circling back around the area."

"That didn't take long, whatever it was."

"Nope, sure didn't, John. Worries me that he went straight there, like he mighta been warnin' 'em. Want us to contact him, find out what he was doing in there?" He hadn't trusted Andrew from the first time he saw the man, and that had only intensified after John revealed that Andrew had once been a cop. *Can't trust a cop to do a spy's work. We'd be better off sending in teams of Boy Scouts and A-C-L-U lawyers.*

"Naw, don't worry about Andrew," John replied over the radio. "I figure he'll be the first to realize they're on an impossible mission and call it off. Kinda surprised he even went out. I'll rake him over the coals in person when he gets back. Maybe he's just playin' games with us and wanted to see what kinda surveillance package we'd put together for this."

"You say so, John. He's still my lead candidate for being a snitch. I don't think he's the kinda cop that's gonna work out here. Something's gonna rub him wrong one day, and he'll turn on us."

"Speaking of, *you're* rubbing me wrong right now."

The associate grimaced and stepped farther back from the edge to stay concealed from the street below. "Yeah, but you ain't gonna go run and squeal to nobody about it, though. I might taste my own blood when I piss you off, but I ain't gotta worry about you sinking our whole battleship over some perceived slight."

"Get off the radio, windbag, and stay focused on your goddamned job."

"Copy. Standing by to stand by." He released the talk button and spent several long minutes intently scanning what he could see of the streets to the north and east. *Andrew's gotta come back by here, only a couple streets he could use to get back south without me seeing him from here. Can't wait to prove that prick—*

"Ahem."

He turned around at the startling noise, expecting to find a cafe employee demanding an explanation for his presence on their building. To his further surprise, embarrassment, and anger, he saw Andrew.

The despised trainee stood with his arms crossed over his chest and leaned back against the south side of the parapet wall. "You need a hand with something up here, John? I know we're supposed to call you 'John,' but is there another name you'd rather go by? I mean, *all* four of you can't really be named 'John,' right? Unless that's part of the selection process."

"*Screw you,* Andrew, and get the *hell* off my overwatch!" *How did that shithead get by me, and get up here without me noticing? Shouldn't a-been all Chatty Kathy on the goddamned radio, that's shit's always distracted me!*

"Alright, John, I can do that, but you should pipe down. You've already called attention to yourself, and I thought you should know I saw you up here. Think of it as constructive feedback. Me, personally, I'd rate your work just north of 'terrible,' but I'm not the boss."

"Goddamned right, you're not the boss of anyone!" Now further embarrassed by his own words, he aggressively pressed forward to force Andrew into action. *He can swing on me or jump, but he's going over the side one way or another!*

TRAINING DAY 105, 0813 HOURS_

THE BLUE BONNET CAFÉ ROOFTOP. LUSK, WYOMING.

MICHAEL PUT his hands up in front of his shoulders in a feigned surrender and shook his head. "Sorry, Double, *err, John,* slow your roll, man, I didn't mean to ruffle your feathers." He stepped away from the wall to give himself room to work, just in case Double-Time didn't alter his apparent course of action. *This guy's pissed and embarrassed, but he still oughta know this isn't really a surrender position.*

The trainer kept crossing the roof toward him. "Get the fuck outta here, Andrew, or—"

"Or, *what,* you'll call Big John and tell him your little one-man surveillance team got spotted?"

Now only a few feet away, the instructor telegraphed his intent by drawing back his right fist as he lunged at Michael. "*You piece of shit—*"

Because his hands up were already up and just in front of his shoulders, Michael knew he had a tactical advantage over the trainer. He quickly ducked right and sent out a left jab but struck for speed and didn't follow-through. As soon as he connected with the front of Double-Time's throat, Michael pulled back to minimize the damage; at the same time, he swam his right arm over the man's oncoming left and stepped right, just outside his opponent's direction of travel and intentionally maintained his tremendous advantage. Michael's right arm was already bent with that hand up just over the outside of his opponent's extended left forearm and protecting his own face; he powerfully stepped right again while rotating his torso and forcibly slid his right forearm along his opponent's left until he back-fisted the outside of Double-Time's neck. *There!*

The instructor's legs buckled as soon as Michael struck his brachial plexus nerve motor point. Immediately unconscious and unable to protect himself, Michael wrapped the man in his arms and grabbed onto his clothing as best he could to prevent him from face-planting onto the rooftop. He clutched the man tightly, and quickly sat down, taking his felled opponent with him. Michael fluidly rolled backward onto his buttocks and back to absorb the energy of their collective weight. "Easy, John, no reason to lose any chicklets up here!" Michael briefly laid on his back with the bested instructor on top of him. *Damned glad that part's over with!*

As expected, the man's legs, arms, fingers, and toes had straightened and now slightly seized while his body rebelled against the internal trauma. Michael urgently worked himself out from under the man and stood, knowing damned well he didn't want to be there when Double-Time came to. *May as well go all the way now, not like this guy's gonna rat on me and admit all his mistakes.* Reaching into his opponent's back pocket, Michael retrieved his wallet, opened it, and scrolled through its contents. *Maryland D-L, Damian Haggamore, what the hell kinda name's that? His parents should-a read a Bible or watched a few horror flicks before making that decision. Gym membership, supermarket card, couple credit cards, little bit of cash, two condoms. That's optimistic, that he'd need two in the same night. I thought everyone knew not to keep condoms in their wallet anymore. This asshole's gonna impregnate some poor farmgirl that doesn't know any better.*

"Hhhmmmfff..."

Michael expected Haggamore would soon regain consciousness, although he'd remain pretty useless for another five or ten minutes. *His eggs'll need time to unscramble.* The seizures grew lighter and less frequent, so Michael presumed he'd sustained no serious or long-term injury. *Now that I know he doesn't need a paramedic, I can really drive this point home to make sure he doesn't try to even the score.* He opened the man's mouth to confirm Haggamore hadn't bitten his tongue and still breathed on his own. With his welfare now reasonably assured, Michael shoved the man's wallet between his teeth. He carefully turned Haggamore's head to the side to ensure his airway stayed clear while he recovered. *He's lucky I didn't want to harm him, and I'm lucky our places aren't switched. If* he *were standing over* me *right now*... Michael shook off the thought, rose, and stepped back toward the access ladder.

"Hhuugghhhh...wh...wha..."

Just before he reached the ladder, he saw Haggamore's radio on the roof, likely from being dropped during the brief scuffle. Michael collected the radio and descended to the alley behind The Blue Bonnet Café. He considered taking the radio back to John. *I'd rather that this stayed between me and Haggamore, but if he's gonna go running to daddy later, I want John to hear it from me first.* Michael weighed his options for only a few moments. *Haggamore's too arrogant to say anything. I'll just have to watch out for retaliation. His ego's too big to let this go.*

Michael had run across a lot of Damian Haggamores in his life. He knew the bully would take the first cheap shot he could, even if Michael really got hurt. Stepping across the alley to a large Dumpster, he set Haggamore's pac-set radio on top of the closed plastic lid and turned the volume all the way up. *Gotta give him a fair chance to find it.* Michael snickered and strode back to the beat-up sedan. *What else can I uncover between here and the compound?*

TRAINING DAY 105, 0904 HOURS_

RURAL COMPOUND. NIOBRARA COUNTY, WYOMING.

Michael drove back to the isolated compound, parked the borrowed sedan near the main house, and strode up to the porch where John sat in a rocking chair. The lead instructor rose to his feet and leaned against the front handrail as Michael approached.

"You see your comrades on the way back," he called out.

"Yeah, John, they were still making their way into town."

"Figured you woulda picked a few of 'em up and given 'em a goddamned ride back home."

"You said this isn't a team sport, John, so I flipped 'em off and kept driving," Michael explained as he reached the front side of the porch and stood in front of John. "They're big boys, they'll figure it out."

"I think you got some explaining to do."

"How's that," Michael responded. *Dammit, Haggamore ran his mouth.*

"What in the name of Christ Almighty were you doin' at the Sheriff's Office? You got a couple of my guys pretty worked up right now."

"Why? Wasn't the assignment to get a badge? Seemed like the best place to start."

"Eat shit, Andrew, you *know* this's an impossible assignment. The whole thing is set up to make sure any reasonable man sees that and calls 'abort.' The rules of engagement on this are too restrictive to succeed. Hell,

I figured you'd be the first one to realize that, I's pretty damned surprised when you drove off outta here. Kinda disappointed, really."

"Why? Because I got you your badge?"

"Screw off, you ain't got sh—"

Michael produced a badge decal from his front pants pocket.

"That ain't a badge!"

"Sure is. It's the same design and artwork the Sheriff's office uses for their chest badges, patrol car insignias, and cloth shoulder patches. If a badge can be cloth, why can't it be a sticker? Hell, the ones on their Broncos are just damned magnets, and that's enough to make people pull their cars over!"

"I said you had to *steal* a badge to win, Andrew, not *borrow* like I usually specify. Pretty sure there's a distinct 'Thou Shalt Not' about thievin,' so I know you didn't steal that."

kssshhck

"John, you there?" Michael recognized Haggamore's voice and hoped he didn't choose this moment to disclose what had happened to him.

Annoyed, John glared at Michael before he roughly grabbed a pac-set radio from a small table near his rocking chair. "*About goddamned time!* Where the hell've you been?! I been calling you for almost a *half-hour*! We's about to hafta send two assholes to go find you!"

"Yeah, uh, well, I had to move."

"What?"

"Yeah, I, uh, I think I got spotted up there, and had to move to another spot before anyone showed up to investigate."

Michael realized things might go his way. *Haggamore didn't rat me out and he lied about why he didn't answer his radio. At least he was honest that he had, in fact, been spotted up there. Kudos for that, I guess.*

"Where you at now?" John looked back at Michael. "Be with you in a second, soon as I sort out my employee problems." He shook his head but made no effort to improve the privacy of his conversation.

Michael focused on keeping a straight face while his adversary tried to minimize the damage to his credibility.

"I'm, uh, well, you might not like this part, John. The only other tall building in the, uh, area, was the bank."

"Haggamore," John seethed through clenched teeth and showed no concern about using the man's real name, "you'd better not be on top of the fuckin' bank right now! Every rancher and cattlemen in this county uses that farm bank, and they'll happily shoot your dumbass off the roof and call the sheriff for clean-up!"

"Well, I, uh—"

John pushed a red button on the top of the radio and interrupted the man's transmission. "*Get down, right now, right, THE FUCK, now, and immediately come STRAIGHT back here*!"

"Copy."

Michael almost regretted his actions, but Haggamore had been a despicable ass for the last three months.

John took in a deep, calming breath and spit a string of tobacco juice onto the ground. "Good help is so *goddamned hard* to find, Andrew. I mean, how stupid can one man be?"

Michael sensed an opportunity to come clean and deny Haggamore a chance to retaliate. "In that case, John, there's something you should know." *I'm thirty seconds out from getting a gold star or a pink slip...*

"What now? You boinked the sheriff's secretary? You weren't in there long enough to make love, so I know it wasn't consensual."

"No, but I'm the one that spotted Haggamore."

"I shouldn't have used his name, and you'd damned well forget you heard it."

"I already knew it."

John again glared at Michael and his eyes narrowed just before he spoke. "You're gonna tell me everything that led you to that particular piece of information."

Michael took a deep breath before the plunge into whatever fate awaited him. "So, I made him when I drove past The Blue Bonnet to go to the Sheriff's Office. He was standing too close to the front wall along the street, and—"

"No way. I don't believe you. Nobody looks up when they search or scan an area, it's not human nature anymore. *Don't* lie to me, Andrew, or—"

"John, I'm sure you know more about my background than you've let on. It's one of the things we specifically trained on in my last job. We deliberately taught our guys to look up, even when there was nothing above them to look at."

His superior pondered that for a moment. "Alright, I'll accept that until I can prove otherwise. Go on." The man's intense gaze didn't lessen.

"When I came out of the office, I saw he was still up there, so I circled around the neighborhood, doubled back south about a half-mile west of him, and climbed up to the roof to have a, uh, *word*, with him."

"You're just making shit up now, no way he'd let that happen."

"I think the radio had distracted him, but it actually gets worse, John, at least for Haggamore." Now that he had some momentum and John hadn't immediately bounced him off the property, Michael started to enjoy telling his abbreviated version of their interaction. "He got real upset when I surprised him up there, so he rushed me and put my back to the south edge of the roof, so I knocked him out."

"You *swung* on one of my instructors?"

"Not really. He swung on me and lunged, and I didn't wanna go off the roof, so I jabbed his throat, stepped outside, and bitch-slapped his brachial plexus."

"*Bitch*...slapped?"

"Well, sir, I guess 'backhand' is more accurate, but he's such an asshole that I'd prefer to stick with bitch-slap."

"That's when he went down?"

"Yeah, I helped him to the ground, searched his wallet, found his Maryland D-L."

"That a fact?"

"Yessir, it's a fact. He's also got two condoms in his wallet, which makes me think he's either optimistic or he's on the little blue pill."

"What happened next, now that you had him in such a vulnerable position, considering the way he's been tryin' to get you kicked outta here? I assume that's really what this's about, right? Revenge?"

"Not revenge, really, I just wanted him to realize I deserved to be here and that, maybe, he could give me a little credit and lay off me a little bit. So, all I did was leave his wallet jammed between his teeth. It was as much for his own safety as anything else."

"You know the problem you just created for me, and for yourself?"

"I didn't want it to go this way," Michael offered with a less jovial tone, "but, it seems Haggamore couldn't be reasoned with."

John stood up, sighed, and shifted his gaze to the expansive fields behind Michael. "I gotta give you that, I suppose that wasn't a strong point on his resume. Anything else?"

"Well, I took his radio and set it on top of the Dumpster behind the café. Probably why you couldn't get a hold of him for a while."

"Alright. Anything else?"

"Just one more. The car's his, right? The one I drove to town?"

"Are you *shittin'* me?"

"No, it's registered in his name. You might wanna check to make sure this address isn't the same one that's on there."

John slapped both hands down on top of the wood rail and stared at the porch decking. "I'd like to be real goddamned angry with you, Andrew, but, at the same time, I'm glad to know what kinda man I'm workin' with."

"I'm sorry he had to make it go this way, John."

"Wasn't talkin' about *him*, dipshit! I know who and what he is, but he's an expert in his field. I just didn't realize he was also careless. I's talkin' about you, about what kinda man you are. You just might make it outta here, if the other goddamned instructors don't string you up at high noon tomorrow." He looked back up from the porch and met Michael's gaze. "I hope it was all worthwhile for a failed, impossible assignment you were 'sposed to abort."

"I didn't fail, John."

"I'll give you that you technically got a badge, but I already reminded you that my orders were to steal one."

Michael produced the second decal from the same pocket. "Right. That's how I got the second one when she turned away. Didn't wanna lose on a technicality."

John's eyes further narrowed, and Michael recognized his increased displeasure. "Glad you made it back in time for mass, Andrew. Make damned sure you get your ass to confession for this. You'd best start recognizing your goddamned operational limitations if you're gonna succeed here. Get the hell outta my face for a while."

TRAINING DAY 113, 0600 HOURS_

RURAL COMPOUND. NIOBRARA COUNTY, WYOMING.

MICHAEL BOUNDED upstairs to meet everyone out on the porch for the morning run. When he reached the landing next to the kitchen, he saw John sat alone at the table with his ever-present mug of coffee.

"Hold up, Andrew."

Michael slowed and stepped toward the table. "Morning, John, what's going on?"

The lead instructor leaned back in his chair and rested both forearms on the table. His glare conveyed an unknown and imminent reckoning. "Stand fast, we gotta talk."

"Sure, John, what's up?" *Goddammit, what does he know?*

"I make it a rule to never tell any of you why the other candidates fail, quit, or get dismissed, but I think I need you to understand that there's sometimes unintended consequences for your actions.

"Everyone knows that Zeb and Haggamore got dismissed the same day, but I thought you oughta know why Zeb had to go. One of the deputies contacted him in their parking lot and accused him of tryin' to steal a large badge magnet off-a one of their SUVs. Zeb had to give up his real name and date of birth, so that sealed his fate. No paper trails that tie your name to this area, right? Even though I'm sure he was doin' exactly what they accused him of, I started wonderin' how they knew what he was up to. Did a little diggin' and found out someone told the S-O secretary about transients stealing badge magnets. That's a helluva coincidence, right?"

"Seems almost impossible, John." *I won't deny my part, but I'm not gonna just offer up anything he hasn't asked to know, either.*

"That's what I thought. Thing is, like we talked last week, that's an impossible task given the R-O-Es and our morals. If he'd succeeded, he would-a gained, what, a little personal benefit in a training program, and that's even ignoring the petty theft? But that would-a put that deputy and the public at risk if people couldn't recognize that SUV was a cop car. I thought you oughta know, whatever put this in motion, I'm glad to find out now that Zeb didn't have the logical thought process to succeed."

"Good to know." Sensing the end of the conversation, Michael stepped toward the door.

"Oh, one more thing. Keep in mind that everyone failed that exercise, Andrew, even you. Now get the hell oughta here. Y'all got Combat First Aid today, gotta learn how effectively edged weapons lacerate pork."

"Pork?"

"They letcha cut into a simulated forearm made outta P-V-C, pork filets, and plastic wrap to show how deadly edged weapons are. Then you getta jam tampons and combat gauze into simulated bullet holes. All kindsa shit that might come in handy on some bad day."

"Thanks, John," Michael hesitantly offered, "and, I'm sorry."

"I don't want your apologies, Andrew, but I do want you to change your *goddamned* behavior and *think* about what the hell you're doin.' Make tracks."

Michael stepped out onto the porch, collected his morning run assignment from Jane, and hurriedly headed out to his appointed trail. *No coincidence my runtime today is 'almost impossible,' either. Goddammit.*

TRAINING DAY 114, 0730 HOURS_

RURAL COMPOUND. NIOBRARA COUNTY, WYOMING.

MICHAEL OCCUPIED HIS USUAL FLIMSY, plastic chair when John predictably strode through the classroom's back door at 7:30am. *Wonder what kind of retribution John & CO have in mind for me today. It was easier just dealin' with Haggamore, because I only had to worry about one asshole then. Now, I've got five, maybe six, that're gunnin' for me. If they'd just come straight at me, we could get this shit over with. This constant anticipation is goddamned killin' me.*

Instead of walking straight up to the front as he usually did, John stopped in front of the large Matthew and Proverbs scriptures and turned to face the remaining eight students. "Morning, shitheads. Been a while since we brought these up. First time, y'all basically called Matthew the 'good guy traits'..." He slapped each oversized panel as he spoke about them.

smack

"...and Proverbs was the 'bad guy traits.'"

smack

John looked about as though awaiting an epiphany. "Y'all got any new thoughts, ideas, about how these apply to you? To your *calling*, maybe? Perhaps, even to the work we're struggling to teach here?"

Michael grimaced. *I'm still missing the point here.* He focused on the words themselves and tried to read and absorb the verses as though he'd never considered them before. An unexpected correlation struck him, and he had to stifle his laughter.

"You must've got somethin' worth throwin' out there, Andrew," John impatiently offered. "Get to it."

"Well, John, it's not really, what I think you might be looking for," he hesitantly explained.

"Not what I asked. Just answer my goddamned question."

"Right, sorry. Have you ever seen *Pulp Fiction?*"

"The movie?"

"Yeah, it's just that, well, the Proverbs verses kinda strike me now like the Ezekiel 25:17 quote that Jackson's character throws around the whole movie. Maybe our Proverbs verses should've immediately preceded the Ezekiel quote, like they're explaining what the wicked have done, and Ezekiel is following that up with what's gonna happen because of it."

John quizzically looked back at him. *And here comes some consequence,* Michael thought.

The instructor turned to the Proverbs sign, examined the words for several seconds, and nodded his quasi-agreement. "I suppose I can see that. Sure as shit ain't perfect, but that's a damned sight better'n last time, with nothing but 'good' and 'bad' outta y'all intellectual cavemen. Keep ponderin' these scriptures. Rest assured we'll come back to 'em." He stepped to the front of the room to begin his instruction.

"Normally," John explained, "it might make more chronological sense for us to teach you about knife fighting *before* going over combat first aid. However, now that you saw the damage edged weapons create yesterday, I think you'll have more respect and appreciation for the defensive and offensive tactics we're goin' over today. Y'all go ahead and get all the tables and chairs up against the walls, we're gonna need some room to fight and move in here."

Michael stood up, folded the flimsy chair, and helped the other students move their spartan furniture aside.

"Just like everything else," John advised the group as they worked, "today's class is just an introduction to knife fighting, and specifically to *Silat.* And, it's just that, an intro, a beginning. I can't make you competitive knife fighters in the time we got to cover this, but you oughta pick up some defensive skills, a better recognition of what blades can do, how they're used, and how they move in the hands of a competent practitioner. We'll come back to this topic over the next few months, so I just want y'all to leave today with a real goddamned sincere appreciation for how dangerous these tools are. There are skilled knife fighters in the world, but blades don't require skill to kill. Simple gravity makes 'em dangerous.

"If you have some previous experience," John continued, "I hope you take this chance to improve your avoidance and takeaways. That's the kinda skill you'll need if some street urchin ever pulls a knife on you in a dark alley in the slums of South America. You gotta make sure they know right quick they picked the wrong victim." John held eye contact with Michael after his blatant reference to the Bogotá killing.

Michael glanced around the classroom and saw curiosity and confusion from his fellow students. *Asshole!*

The instructor smugly grinned and stayed focused on Michael. "Let's get started. Andrew, step up and be my bad guy." He retrieved a concealed training knife from his back pocket and expertly flipped it around in his right palm. "Promise not to hurt ya, well, *too bad*, anyway."

TRAINING DAY 115, 0303 HOURS_

RURAL COMPOUND. NIOBRARA COUNTY, WYOMING.

THESE ARE the hours of the day I can never decide are 'too late' or 'too early' to be up. Whether it was a college final or a search warrant, I've never slept well knowing I had a major event early the next morning. With only a few hours of fitful rest, Michael looked out the bus window as the tall, moonlit grass fields around him swayed in the ever-present wind. He shifted a large backpack in the seat next to him and below the bus's window and hoped his tightly-packed gear would soon make a decent pillow. *It doesn't have to be 'good,' it's just gotta be 'good enough.'*

As the off-white, repurposed school bus lumbered and swayed up the training compound's long driveway toward the adjacent county road, John stood just behind the driver. Holding on to the two nearest seatbacks to keep himself upright, he addressed his trainees in the predawn darkness. "This field trip's gonna take a few days, and you might be glad to know you'll get outta the wind for most-a that. We're headed up to the mountains so y'all can learn how to survive away from asphalt and Starbucks. If any of you ever find yourself stuck *outside* the urban sprawl, I need ya to understand Mother Nature can't easily kill the well-prepared. The same is *not true* of the arrogant and ill-equipped." He glanced at Michael just long enough to make eye contact.

"Everybody got on the bus together this morning," John continued and briefly held Michael's gaze. "I expect most of you to return in the same manner. Y'all oughta get some rest. We got about five hours to our drop-point. If more-a y'all had had the decency to quit by now, the rest of us coulda taken a comfy car." John paused as a few tired chuckles subsided.

"You shitheads just got instruction in Combat First Aid. We're gonna add additional stress and reality to have you care for wounds and injuries out in the wilderness. Gonna be a good few days to be the hell outta that shit-ass classroom. Hope ya enjoy it, but, frankly, I don't give a damn either way. Father Harry's joining us in a few hours after the sun's up. He's gonna help us celebrate a 'mobile mass' on the way, just to make sure we don't deprive anyone of their dogma. Never had mass *on* a school bus before, but I imagine y'all are resourceful enough to find a way to kneel. Get some shut-eye if ya can, you'll wish ya had before the day's out."

Five hours later, after a fuel and restroom stop bookended Father Harry's modified mass celebration, the bus passed through Dubois, Wyoming, and entered the Teton National Forest. The bus pulled into a deserted campground where Michael and his colleagues disembarked with their respective large-frame backpacks. Without even pausing for a head-count or instructions, John immediately led them into the dense pine forest. Michael turned back and briefly watched the bus drive away from the unidentified site. *Guess we're not getting back on at the same place.* He scanned the group ahead to identify Thomas' position. After John dismissed Haggamore ten days ago, the problem-student remained the only concern Michael had much control over. *I can't limit my interactions with the training staff or John, but I can at least keep Thomas in front of me.*

John spent the morning leading the trainees through overland navigation, waypoint identification, and compass and map work. Michael noticed that only Sergio and Phillip didn't struggle to maintain John's mandated pace. *Maybe we're running late for the Death March?*

John stopped the group for lunch in a clearing that Michael believed was precisely in the dead-center of nowhere, and they all broke out MREs from their packs. *I haven't had to eat one of these since my last lunch with Merci. I hope she's safe, warm, and happy.*

In less than thirty minutes, Michael had eaten, powdered his feet, changed into dry socks, and again donned his own backpack. John led the group through a series of practical exercises to demonstrate proficiency with the morning's topics. Along the way, he pointed out how to improve their wilderness first aid and survival skills, such as never drinking from still waters or downhill from pastures and open rangelands.

By late afternoon, Michael estimated they'd traversed ten-to-twelve miles and John had kept up their blistering pace despite the terrain. They paused briefly at the crest of a small rise to drink water, and Michael noticed a wisp of smoke rising above the trees ahead. *Maybe two, three miles out. Hard to tell distance out here.* "Hey, John," he called out. "Looks like a fire up there."

"Better be," he replied without looking at it for himself. "That's where we're headed, and the Molasses Brigade's got us near *twenty minutes* behind schedule." With less rest than Michael wanted, John led them another hour deeper into the Teton National Forest and stopped at a collection of established tents around a large fire ring. John's four remaining instructors sat around a *popping* campfire in plush, reclining camp chairs. *It looked like everyone else gets to choose between rocks and logs.*

"Place looks good," John congratulated them, "glad y'all made it out here so far ahead of us."

"It's no problem," Tex replied, "but, woulda been easier with *five* of us." He eyed Michael for a brief moment before turning back to the fire and lifting a can of beer.

John ignored the comment and turned around to address the class. "Most students don't make it this far, so y'all oughta pat yourselves on the back tonight. If you don't take your steak 'medium,' you're gonna tonight 'cause that's the only way I grill it. Got some cowboy beans and buttered corn on the cob to go with it. Take a load off until supper's ready. Get some grub, put your feet up, enjoy the cold night air. If you look real hard, you'll find a grip of beers in the cooler by my tent. You're welcome to 'em. You boys could use a night off, and this is about the best I could arrange given the short timeframe we got to work with.

"Just don't let this shit go to your goddamned heads, now," John cautioned. "You're all still worthless to me, and you got a damned long way to go to complete my program. That said, I'll holler when supper's ready."

Michael and the other candidates just looked around at each other in stunned amazement for a moment. *I think we're all afraid to trust it. I feel like the dog in 'To Build a Fire,' and I can't believe the harsh master has benign intentions.* Most of the group strolled together toward the beer cooler as though their safety existed in their numbers. Michael noticed that Sergio stayed behind with him.

"Whaddayou think of all this," his friend quietly asked.

"Don't know," Michael replied, "but I'm pretty suspicious that tomorrow's gonna be somewhere between 'bad' and 'terrible.'"

"Count on it. Those lambs are just following a trail of sweet grass toward the slaughterhouse."

Michael chuckled and considered his options. "Want a beer, anyway?"

"Absolutely. One can isn't gonna throw salt in my game tomorrow."

TRAINING DAY 116, 0402 HOURS_

TETON NATIONAL FOREST, WYOMING.

STARTLED AWAKE by the sound of loud, rapid metal *clangs,* Michael urgently sat up in his sleeping bag and reflexively prepared to defend himself from some unknown threat. He turned on a flashlight he'd placed next to his cot and saw that The Baptist and Z, who shared the three-man tent, had done the same. With no exterior light source, Michael couldn't discern the sound or its source despite having only one suspect in mind.

"The hell is that!" Z exclaimed.

"Alarm clock," Michael grumbled.

"*Wakey, wakey, you sleepy shitheads!*" John's unmistakable voice filled Michael with dread. "*Get out here, F-N-S-R -F-N!*"

"Still ain't no 's' in 'center,'" The Baptist quietly protested as he climbed from his bag.

"And, 'and' doesn't start with an 'n,'" Z added while hurriedly donning his running shoes.

"Anyone wanna tell *him* that," Michael asked, hoping to lighten the impending doom. *They won't try to kill me, and I'll be damned if they drive me to quit.*

"Hell, no," The Baptist quietly replied, "I'm not that smart, but I'm ain't that stupid, either!"

"*Let's go,*" John yelled from somewhere outside their tent. "*You shit-heads are burnin' daylight God ain't even granted you yet! MOVE!*"

The group formed up around John so quickly that Michael assumed everyone had worn their running clothes to bed. *Like we expected early-A-M reindeer games.*

"Good morning, shitheads. Today's training evolution is specifically designed to separate those who want to be here from those that don't, and, for my own personal satisfaction, to punish anyone that had too good a time last night. I was a little sad, angry, *disappointed even,* when I went to my beer cooler last night and found I had too few *cervezas* to offer my dedicated and deserving associates. Since we couldn't relax like we wanted, I'm sure you can imagine that we spent our evening inventing new and creative ways to put your asses through a knothole today. I mean, we added some hurdles to ensure you boys got all the training value possible. That sound P-C enough for ya?

"In addition to the navigation exercise, we're also gonna work on your evasion tactics, your ninja skills. Treat the instructor cadre as armed adversaries. They're the cops, the military, the enforcement you wanna avoid. Our normal R-O-Es apply so you may not harm or assault my cadre, just as you can't ever assault a cop or law enforcement official. Remember *two things* as you navigate today's evolution: one, we're doing all this for *your* benefit, and two, you assholes made us do it. We could-a done the nice little nature hike and *koom-by-yah* singalong I scheduled, but y'all wanted to do this shit instead. Hope you're happy with your choices."

John passed out specific maps to the students, and Michael saw each had a trainee's name at the top. "Matthew, here. Baptist, this one's yours. Phillip, yours. Alpha, here ya go." He continued to pass out maps until only one remained in his hands. "And, last but not least, *Andrew.*" As he handed the paper over, John maintained eye contact with Michael and grinned.

"The point of this mornin's exercise," John explained and returned his focus to the group-at-large, "is to test the navigation and mountaineering skills you learned yesterday. Hope you boys paid attention in the daylight, 'cause this shit gets a lot harder in the dark. Each of you's got a trail map, just like you'd have at home, and no one's got the same route. So, you'd best be alone this morning. If you got a trail buddy, one-a you's dead wrong! There *are* critters out there, and we're the ones stumblin' around uninvited in their home, so watch yourselves. Between the terrain and God's creatures, a few of you just might get the chance to put your knife fighting and combat first aid skills to use today." He looked back at Michael. "Maybe even before sun-up. Hope you boys enjoy your day in the wilderness. Truly God's country out here."

Their trainer looked around the group, who seemed to await his usual announcement. "It pays to be a winner," he finally offered to dismiss them. Instead of their typical, frantic rush to hit the trails and establish an early lead on the competition, Michael and the other students purposefully returned to their tents to gather whatever equipment they might need in the next few hours. Already clad in midweight jogging pants and trail shoes, Michael wanted only to grab his small hiking pack, which held his compass, penlight, KaBar, and headlamp, as well as a few other potential survival necessities. He stepped back into the tent and saw that Z and The Baptist were already inside gathering their things. *Not gonna let 'em win, but I'm still not real eager to run off into the darkness alone this morning.*

"Dammit," The Baptist quietly swore and *thumped* the side of his flashlight, "my light's dead. You guys have any extra double-As?"

"No, I didn't think to bring any extra batteries," Z replied.

"Andrew, please tell me you've got some," The Baptist looked up and pled.

"I don't, sorry. My lights run on triples, and the headlamp runs off some custom size made in China." Michael shook his head and offered a sympathetic look. "You wanna borrow a light long enough to see if anyone else has double-As?"

"No, don't sweat it. I'll see what I can do before everyone takes off." The Baptist moved toward the tent's zippered flap. "Nobody needs to worry about sleeping on the floor when we get back to the house. I'll take care of that for everyone."

I don't know about that, Michael thought to himself. *I bet John and his folks find a way to make sure I learn a few lessons out here.* "Good luck," he offered as The Baptist disappeared into the darkness. Michael rummaged through his small Mountainsmith hiking bag, which was really nothing more than a large fanny pack. His last-minute preparations had slightly lessened his sense of dread, but it still must have been visible to those around him.

Z patted him on the shoulder as he stepped around Michael and departed the tent. "Good luck, brother. Be safe out there."

Michael silently nodded his gratitude. *Even though no one knows for sure, these guys understand that something's up. The training cadre's been in my ass ever since Haggamore got dismissed. Not hard to put together, even if no one here's a real-life detective.*

"Shake a leg, gentlemen," John commanded from somewhere nearby, "get the hell outta my campsite!"

Michael donned his headlamp, turned on its lowest setting, and examined the map assigned to him. His dread immediately increased when he realized it was a poor, partial photocopy of a topographical map. Someone had folded the map over itself before copying it, which made it even more useless. A handwritten message had been scrawled across the bottom in small letters that almost escaped his notice: "Good luck. You'll need it."

Michael committed himself to *surpassing* whatever expectations John and his associates had set for him that day. *I'm not gonna let 'em get the best of me, and maybe I'll have to make another one regret that he tried.*

Before he'd gone to sleep last night, Michael had oriented himself inside the tent and knew the back corner was roughly due north. He aligned the map as best he could and confirmed the direction he was to start this morning's route. Despite any efforts, he'd never regain the obscured, middle section of his directed path. *I'll just have to wing it once I go off-map. Looks like I've got about four, maybe four-and-a-quarter miles before that happens.* Sensing he could no longer delay whatever fate awaited him in the dark, isolated woods, Michael secured his most essential gear in the Mountainsmith bag, zipped it closed, and stepped from the tent. As he slung the bag's single strap over his neck and right trap, Michael recalled how his dad would make fun of it. "It's not a fanny pack," he'd say, "it's an ass bag." The thought brought a brief, needed smile to his face.

John stood nearby and raised his coffee mug toward Michael as he stepped off into the night. "Have fun out there," he offered and grinned.

"I intend to, John," Michael retorted. "I hope your boys do the same."

John sipped heartily from his coffee mug and grinned wider. "I'm sure they will."

Michael started walking northwest and tightened the bag's shoulder strap until it was snug enough that he could easily run with it. He soon found a game trail, which matched the approximate location and direction of travel he needed to go. Michael also saw a spattering of light along the same trail ahead of him. *Can't be that many established paths out here, so they probably started us off in the same direction. The sun won't be up for a while, and I need landmarks and waypoints to stay on track. No reason to hurry up and get lost in the darkness.* Stepping off the trail, Michael hiked about two dozen yards straight uphill, shut off his headlamp, and retrieved a small penlight from his bag. He'd owned the light since he worked patrol in Silver City and had long ago covered its lens in red permanent marker. *Not so harmful to my night vision or so obvious and bright to anyone scurrying around in the dark to find me.* Holding the light close to his map, Michael tried to estimate the time and distance until he had to change direction or leave the game trail. *The map shows me staying about mid-hill for another mile or two, and then turning south when the mountainside cuts away to the north.*

crck-snap

Michael shut off the dim red light and kept his feet in place. Without even shifting his weight, he turned his head toward the sound, which he assumed was one of their instructors stalking their group. He estimated the breaking twig couldn't have been more than twenty or thirty feet behind him, and, probably, downhill between him and the trail. Whatever had caused the sound must have also stopped in place, for Michael heard absolutely nothing. *Definitely a human. Animals are gonna just keep moving along, they aren't bothered by their own noise. So, now we wait to see which of us grows impatient first.* Michael knew that humans were the most restless and impatient predators on Earth. *Prey animals will stand still and stare at an area for ten, fifteen minutes before moving on, and most predators will focus on noise for maybe five minutes. People aren't typically willing to spend more than fifteen or twenty seconds looking at what they think is—*

snap

Michael focused on staying still and silent while they passed by. *They'll probably stay close to the trail, but just a few steps above it to keep out of my line of sight, if I were still* on *the trail, anyway.*

The sounds of very slight, occasional rustling and protesting twigs came closer, but still seemed well downhill of him. Only another few seconds passed before a shadow emerged from between the trees five steps below him and moved parallel to the game trail. *Not truly a shadow from sun- or moonlight, but, more of a black hole that's darker than everything else around it.* Michael immediately recognized the shadow's size and gait as Jane. *They must-a picked her because she oughta be the lightest and least visible instructor. Big Country'd sound like a bull in a china shop this time of morning.*

Michael heard murmuring and feared someone else was nearby. He silently inhaled and tried to calm his nerves.

"No, I don't see him," Jane whispered. More indiscernible murmuring.

"Yes, I'm sure I followed him from camp. He must be farther ahead of me."

Michael smirked and nodded at the intel he now had. *They've got radios, and they're targeting me. That gives me a tremendous edge that they don't know about.*

"I'll press up and advise when I re-acquire," she softly spoke while passing by Michael's unseen position in the darkness above her.

He expected to have several minutes alone to consider his course of action. *I can follow her, but that won't really do me any good. I'll either succeed, which embarrasses her and means more punishment for me, or I fail, and she just calls the dogs in on me anyway. I could stay here and wait for daylight so I can see them, but then I'm also easier to see. If I were them, I'd put one guy at a fixed point along the trail to make sure I didn't get past them. Just enough uphill that no one's likely to spot him. If there's a rock outcropping, steep hillside, or cliff, that'd work the best to get out of the line of sight.*

After Michael believed at least two minutes had elapsed since he heard Jane's movement, he quietly retrieved his map and penlight. He searched its topographic lines for the most significant elevation change immediately adjacent to his designated route. *There, that's gotta be it.* He examined the spot just before the copied fold where six topo lines briefly converged into a single line immediately uphill from his appointed path. *Now that I know where they're probably waiting for me, what to do about it?*

Michael shut off the red-lensed light and tacitly squatted down on his haunches to think for a moment. *I could go farther uphill above them. See what they're up to, maybe. Drop back to the trail after I'm clear of the ambush. Don't wanna risk a repeat of that rooftop bullshit, though. They won't be surprised like Haggamore was. That was stupid,* Michael told himself, *and I really don't wanna risk a fight out here in the middle of nowhere. Talk about a rock and a hard place.* Michael stood back up and realized the depth of his gratitude for his Silver City PD trainers. *They taught me to hunt and stalk a lot more than trophy elk.* He *clicked* the red light back on to examine the map once more.

Better idea, Michael thought.

I'll give her another couple minutes to get farther west, and I'll head downhill, cross the valley floor, and stay just inside the tree line on the opposite hillside. The map looks like I'm supposed to turn downhill and cross the valley not long after passing the ambush spot, anyway, so I should be able to find the route again from there. If they don't have thermal, I might have a shot of making my objective without finding out whatever they got planned.

A wry scowl spread across Michael's face as he cautiously worked his way downhill and on to his new path. *I wonder if my screams will echo better from the valley floor than the mountainside. Even though I'd appreciate the help, I'm glad that Sergio won't be around to risk intervening on my behalf. No sense giving up our secret now.*

TRAINING DAY 116, 0515 HOURS_

TETON NATIONAL FOREST, WYOMING.

MICHAEL HAD BEEN NAVIGATING through the unfamiliar forest and mountainsides for the past hour. After crossing the valley, he'd seen occasional, sporadic specks of light on the opposing mountainside. The specks looked like they came from the game trail Michael had abandoned. *My classmates are busy giving away their positions.* While he'd been stopped for a short rest, a flurry of small lights had suddenly come on across the valley. Unable to intervene or help, Michael watched the lights from two trainers pursue one of his colleagues and push them into an ambush. Their training point made, the mountainside again fell into darkness. *Even out here in the wilderness, you've gotta maintain situational awareness. Wonder if everybody's getting that kind of 'teachable moment,' or did they mistake someone for me?*

Michael pressed on and crossed a game trail just as the sky brightened to his east. Keeping himself well inside the tree line, he rechecked his sabotaged map. Once again, his designated route and present location matched. *Back on track. If I get to the map's objective and nothing's there, I can at least find my way back to the camp. And, if that's all packed up and shipped out, I can hike my ass back to Dubois, the last town we drove through.*

From an abundance of caution, Michael cut a small strip of cloth from the top of his right sock. He found a large tree immediately uphill of the game trail and walked around to the backside, where he tied the cloth to the base of a branch just about his eye level. *Anyone following me won't see it, but, if I have to come back this way, it'll confirm this is where I need to veer southeast.* Although grateful the early morning light made his navigation easier, Michael also knew he could now be found much more readily. *Even if there's some sorta reckoning planned today, I'm not gonna make it easy for them.*

Michael ensured his gear was stowed and then tightened the bag's straps just a bit further and walked about ten yards uphill from the trail. *Even though the hard-packed trail's quieter and faster, that's where people expect* other *people to be.* The morning dew helped muffle his footfalls, but also kept his shoes and feet cold and damp.

For another hour, the emerging day brightened and warmed around him. When the mountainside shifted his vector from northwest to west, Michael stopped and retrieved his map. He couldn't see any landmarks or waypoints from inside the tree line, which made him risk moving out onto the well-established trail. As he did so, Michael took in an incredible view of the Tetons. *Gorgeous, right up there with Rocky Mountain National Park.* The range's steep, green-and-grey upheaved peaks rose to meet a clear, bright blue sky. Cold, crisp air blew lightly on his skin just as the sun finally broke over the eastern peaks and cast warm sunlight on his face. Michael closed his eyes and took in a deep breath. He experienced peace, if only for this moment, and Michael allowed himself to enjoy only a few breathing cycles before he opened his eyes and went back to work. *Can't stay vulnerable for long.*

Michael compared the two portions of his map to what he could see around him and decided he was in the right place. *That means downhill from here, while the trail continues west along the mountainside. Looks like the destination is a flat spot, maybe a clearing or meadow.* Scanning across the valley, he identified two successive sets of rock formations as his new waypoints. As he stepped off to follow his assigned route, Michael silently thanked his dad for teaching him land navigation as a kid. *I haven't seen another soul out here since Jane, and the solitude would be unnerving if I didn't know I was in the right place.*

Just before reaching the valley floor, he stopped inside the tree line, knelt, and surveyed the area. *Valleys are known as kill boxes for a reason. The instructor cadre might not take shots at me, but this is where I'm most vulnerable to being found and pursued.* He silently stayed in place for another ten minutes and heard nothing but birds. A quick review of his map confirmed the destination was near the exposed center of the meadow. *Got no choice but the leave the tree line, so I may as well be quick about it.*

Michael stood up and purposefully strode through a semi-circular clearing that opened and joined the valley floor at its far end. As he reached the approximate center, a small, bright reflection from the ground ahead of him caught his attention. Intently looking at the unexpected object, Michael immediately recognized it as one of John's training knives. *Shit!* He stopped and urgently scanned the small clearing for whatever threat he'd missed.

"Drop your bag, Andrew," John's familiar voice boomed from behind him. "That dull-ass butter knife's the only weapon available to you."

Michael turned around to face John and walked backward toward the training blade. *Here comes the consequence.* His lead instructor, now a momentary adversary, stepped from behind a small stand of aspens off to his left. *Of course, he put himself between me and the sunrise, that was stupid of me not to check that more closely.*

"*Drop, the bag, Andrew,*" he again commanded while pressing toward Michael from about twenty yards away. "I *know* you got better tools in there, but that useless trainer's the only one you get access to use this morning!"

Michael reluctantly complied. He unbuckled the bag's shoulder strap and tossed it aside a few yards to the east. *Keep it close, just in case he's right. I might need better tools in a few minutes.*

"How'd you get by the cadre?" John kept walking as he spoke, although he seemed in no particular hurry to start their dance; his only concern seemed to be separating Michael from his blades and lights. "She didn't go far enough uphill from the game trail, did she?"

Michael backed up until he saw the blade in his peripheral vision in front of his feet. He bent down and took his eyes from John only long enough to retrieve the trainer. Expertly flipping it in his palm, Michael ensured the simulated cutting edge extended down his right forearm. "You gotta earn that kinda intel, John."

"You smug son of a bitch, you really think you're hot shit, don't ya?" John pressed forward, but Michael couldn't see a weapon in either of his hands.

His fists are balled up, though, so I can't say they're empty, either. The best knife fighters never show their blade before it's inbound. "No, John, I just don't like seeing how your training scenarios are all rigged for failure." He stopped moving back to keep himself near the middle of the clearing. *Best to stay away from the tree line. John won't be alone out here.* "I figure you're either not as good an operative as you claim to be, so you gotta stack the deck against us, or you're not that good at teaching us to succeed. Either way makes me think you're puttin' us in danger, John."

"*You piece of shit—*" Having closed within a few yards, John lunged with his right hand, and Michael stepped back and set his feet firmly on the ground to block the punch. He batted his left arm up and out to stop John's forearm while simultaneously punching his right fist into the front of John's shoulder to cease all his adversary's forward momentum. Michael succeeded in suppressing the first attack, but, before he could counter, John reflexively dropped down to his right knee, rotated his torso to his left, and swung his right forearm between Michael's arms and laterally across his abdomen.

A hot singe of pain burned across Michael's stomach as John popped back up and stood off to his right side. Michael urgently stepped back and left to create distance and swiped his left hand across his ribs and stomach. *Blood. "WHAT THE FUCK, JOHN?!"*

His adversary revealed the small box-cutter he'd concealed in his right hand and wiped Michael's blood from its blade and onto his pants leg. "*Ooo,* she did getcha a little bit, didn't she?"

Michael stepped back further and briefly looked at the cut, a minor laceration about two inches long and only skin deep. *It won't bleed much, at least not yet.*

"You wanna bitch about rigged scenarios, Andrew? They ain't been rigged *before,* not until this one!"

"*You're a goddamned lunatic*!"

"Whaddaya wanna do, Andrew?" John circled around to flank Michael's right side, which forced Michael to his left and put him in a weaker stance. "This really a fight you wanna stay in?! The smart play is to *run,* ya know! You're younger'n me, and probably a damned sight faster, especially since you're scared and I'm just mad!" He precisely rotated the bright yellow box-cutter in his palm between presenting the blade toward Michael and concealing it back behind his forearm. "Huh?! Whatcha wanna do? You wanna stay in the fight with that stupid-ass butter knife?! I'll cut you to ribbons!"

Michael knew he had no chance to get past John and retrieve his actual knife from the discarded bag, so he let John and his arrogance close the distance between them. *Keep comin', keep comin'!* John finally lunged again when he'd reached about the same range as last time, but now did so with the blade pointed forward toward Michael.

Michael again set his feet and swung his left forearm up and struck the inside of John's wrist to deflect the weapon's momentum. This time, though, he simultaneously stepped *into* John's center, rotated his torso left to push the cutter farther away, and drove his right elbow into and through the instructor's upper sternum. In an instant, he propelled John's shoulders backward behind the man's hips, which pulled his feet up off the ground, and John reflexively dropped the knife as he fell. The instructor crashed down hard onto his shoulder blades in a heap at Michael's feet and immediately struggled to catch his breath.

Expecting the fight to continue, Michael took one step forward but saw John's empty hands reach for his throat as he fought to get air into his collapsed trachea. Stepping back out of the man's reach, Michael saw John's eyes open wide in pain and fear. His legs frantically kicked at the ground to get away from Michael while he struggled to reopen his airway. Filled with anger at the man's apparent betrayal, Michael consciously stopped himself from pursuing John, despite the righteous beating he deserved.

BOOM!

The close gunshot surprised Michael, and he instinctively looked up and stepped toward the threat. From about twenty yards away, Big Country approached him from the tree line with an AR rifle leveled at Michael's chest. Recognizing he had no realistic options to fight, run, or hide at that moment, Michael put his hands up in a feigned surrender position in front of his shoulders and awaited an opportunity to disarm his new adversary.

Big Country nodded toward Michael and stayed focused on his center-mass. *"That's enough, Andrew!"*

"End scenario," John weakly gasped from the ground, now to Michael's right, and coughed several times. *"End, fuckin', scenario!"*

"You good, John?" Big Country asked without taking his eyes off Michael.

"Yeah," he wheezed and coughed several more times while still sitting down. "I'm good."

Big Country lowered the rifle and stepped back but didn't alter his gaze.

What the hell is going on here?! Michael wanted to scream.

"Nice counter," John offered, "but that's a poor tactical, and," *cough,* "strategic choice, son. It also violates the R-O-Es for the exercise, right?"

"You came at me with a goddamned *blade,* John, a *real one*! *You can go fuck your rules at that point!"*

"Calm down, it's just a damned box cutter, and I had it locked on the shortest setting. Wouldn't do nothing but change your priorities, if you'd kept your wits about ya." John paused to cough again and gently massaged the front of his throat as he spoke. "You're missin' the message, Andrew. You knew you couldn't really use force against the trainers. Your best option was always to *run.* Even if you'd been in a *fair* fight, you should've known that you'd probably get injured or killed and *run.* There's no benefit to the choices you made, and you got lucky that you's better'n me, at least this time. There's no shame in a tactical retreat, and you stayed in a fight you shouldn't have survived. Don't *ever* expect to get that lucky again."

"I dunno, looks pretty good from here. I'll bleed a little bit, but you're only alive because you've got more assholes here than I do." Michael nodded at Big Country, who showed no reaction.

"Andrew, you're a smart sum-bitch, but this one's just flat gettin' past you. One of the most important skills you can know in this line of work, is when," *cough,* "you've gotta step back and abort the mission. You say that my training scenario's rigged, but my three decades of experience is here to tell you they're actually set up to help guarantee a single, reasonable outcome. I gotta try to think of everything to control the variables and potential outcomes so that we can train hard *all the time.* This shit ain't easy, you know? How's the cut? You gonna live?"

"It's fine, John, I've had cat scratches worse than this. How's the throat?" *I hope it's goddamned killing you!*

"It's fine," *cough,* "about like a Texas mosquito bite." John worked himself up to his feet.

"What the hell's *wrong* with you, man," Michael protested, still enraged by the altercation. "You couldn't think of *anything* safer than coming at me with a real goddamned blade to get me to turn and run?! Especially after everything that's happened over the last couple weeks, you wanna put me in a position where I think I'm being targeted for payback out here in the *sticks,* and then *wonder* why I don't give you my back?! When I *know* you could have a gunman waiting to put some new holes in me?!" He pointed to Big Country and his rifle as evidence.

"Andrew, listen to me now, son," John pleaded. "*Hear* what I'm tellin' you, *please!* Haggamore needed to go, and he didn't deserve to be here training y'all. I ain't gonna go into the details, but by the time I'm done with him, he won't even be able to work the register at a convenience store. I'm seeing to it that he never works anywhere near this field again. We've been hard on you the last couple weeks 'cause I can't reward the way you handled that, even though he screwed up and was about to get fired, anyway. I'm hard on you because I need you to make some tough internal changes, not because I got any heartburn with you." He pointed his thumb over at Big Country, who still intently watched Michael. "These guys hated that asshole, too, and they wanna see you become a teammate they can trust to go outside the wire with 'em."

Big Country nodded his agreement. *If it's true, that's a massive weight lifted,* Michael thought. *If they really wanted to hurt me, though, this was the time and place to do it.*

John coughed and cleared his throat. "After all the years I've done this, today'll be the first time I've had to reconsider this particular evolution. You won this round against an old man, Andrew, but you used piss-poor strategy and judgment to do it. You can't take every fight head-on. Someday that'll kill you." He pointed to the hillside north of them. "Get your bag and head up to that big stand of aspens. There's food and water up there while everyone else meanders in. Get movin', 'cause some other asshole's gonna roll through here soon, and I gotta figure out how to avoid repeatin' this shit. I don't think my throat can't take being this right twice in one day."

TRAINING DAY 120, 0835 HOURS_

RURAL COMPOUND. NIOBRARA COUNTY, WYOMING.

MICHAEL WIPED dust from his eyelids, adjusted his "windproof" goggles, and returned his focus to his rifle's iron sights and the distant, torso-sized steel target. *Open sights, four-hundred yards. No problem. Just need the gusts to die off a little.*

thmp

ting

"Nice shot, Andrew," John offered as he walked behind Michael and the other students lying next to each other across the designated firing line. "Try to get it off quicker next time, wind or not. That little A-R round's pretty small and fast, so you don't gotta make a big adjustment for it, usually."

"Thanks, John," he replied without taking his eyes from the sights and the same target. *We should've assaulted each other months ago. Guess that's what it takes to finally get along with this guy.*

thmp

ting

thmpthmp

ting

"Too quick on that follow-up, Andrew," John loudly chided him, "you can *never* miss fast enough to win the goddamned gunfight!"

"Thanks, John," Michael responded just the same as he had for his instructor's accolade.

"Andrew," Alpha quietly sought his attention.

"What's up, man?"

"I can't get mine sighted-in right, are you willing to help?"

"I can give it a shot, but Jude's a lot better and faster at that than I am." Michael sat up on his elbows and looked to his left, over Alpha, and called out his friend's pseudonym. "Hey, Jude."

"Heard ya," Sergio responded. "I'm on it." After carefully laying his rifle on his green foam shooting mat, muzzle downrange, he scooted over to his immediate right to help Alpha.

Confident in his rifle's accuracy and precision, Michael watched Sergio quickly work through the fundamentals of adjusting the rifle's front and rear sights. While other students continued to fire sporadic rounds along the rest of the line, Alpha seemed to grasp Sergio's instruction and directives. In only a few minutes, he struck the four-hundred-yard steel on his first effort.

Impressed with Sergio's combat knowledge and his willingness to share it with those around him, Michael returned to his rifle and brought it back up on the same steel target.

thmp thmthmp

ting t-ting

"Guess what," Thomas loudly asked from his foam mat on the other side of Sergio, who responded with a succession of quick shots.

thmpthmpthmp thmp

ting ting

Michael looked at Sergio and Alpha. All three ignored Thomas and returned to their rifles.

"HA, you missed the first two," Thomas exclaimed. "'Guess what,' I said!"

"No, I didn't, you dipshit," Sergio impatiently replied without moving his focus from his distant target, "you can't hear the steel report from four-hundred yards over a rifle firing two feet from you."

thmpthmp thmpthmp

tingting

"*Hey,*" Thomas exclaimed, "*I said, 'guess what?'*"

I hope John hears him and comes down here just to monkey-stomp his dumbass, Michael thought.

"What," Sergio impatiently responded.

"You two assholes are rule breakers, and I can prove it!"

"What're you talkin' about, Thomas," Michael asked, not concerned that John might actually hear him. He sat up on his elbows again and looked over at the sycophant.

Thomas set his rifle down on the mat and leaned up on his elbows to make eye contact with Michael over both Sergio and Alpha. "I've never heard you and Jude talk about these guns," he explained, "so there's no way for you to know about what experience he does or doesn't have, unless of course..." Thomas paused and smugly glanced between the two men. "...you've broken the rules and trusted each other with personal information."

"Eat shit, Thomas, you can't even *pretend* to know that," Sergio replied, having never left his rifle's sights. He released a short barrage that Michael thought he intended to stop the conversation.

thmpthmp thmpthmp thmpthmpthmp

tingtingting

Michael nodded his head in disappointment at Thomas and laid back down on his shooting mat.

"There's always the other option," Thomas announced loudly enough to attract additional attention from Phillip and Matthew, whose mats were just beyond Thomas and Michael. "You two could've known each other from before, and just lied about it for the last four months."

Sergio continued shooting.

thmpthmp thmpthmp thmp

ting

"I overhead Jude mention it on one of our first range days," Michael defensively explained. "You're not as smart as you think you are, Thomas. Don't start makin' shit up now just to take the heat off of you."

"Don't threaten me, Andrew, I heard the instructors were gunnin' for you up in the hills. Bet they'd *love* to know what you've been hiding."

"Hey, Thomas," Sergio asked loudly enough for all five men to hear him, "I'd keep my mouth shut if I were you. *I heard* that you screamed and *pissed* yourself when they ambushed you up there. You don't have enough credibility to make 'em believe in *gravity, pendejo."*

thmpthmp thmpthmp thmpthmpthmp

Sergio's bolt held open after he sent the magazine's last round downrange. A thin wisp of gun smoke wafted up from the open chamber as he turned to his left and glared at Thomas. "Don't you have enough of your own problems without actually trying to draw out more hate and discontent from the rest of us?" He expertly reloaded a full thirty-round magazine and turned back to the steel torsos. Sergio pressed the rifle's beavertail button with his left hand, which slammed the bolt closed and automatically loaded the top round from the magazine. "Mind your own *fuckin'* business," he advised and returned his right eye to the rifle's sights. "You got eyes on the gong, Phillip?"

"The four-hundred," Phillip asked as he bent down to look through the large spotting scope in front of him.

"No," Sergio clarified, "the eight."

Phillip adjusted the scope so he could clearly see the heavy steel circle eight football fields away from their firing line. "Send it."

The five men fell silent. The small round's accuracy dropped off significantly after five hundred yards, especially from their shorter barreled rifles, and Michael calculated the flight time. *At eight hundred, it'll take almost two seconds for the bullet to hit.*

thmp

The suppressed weapon fired, and Michael strained to hear the hit.

"Hit!" Phillip announced before the sound reached them.

gonggggg

"*Who did that?!*" John's shout emanated from the far end of the firing line.

Sergio scoffed and stayed looking through his scope at the distant target. "Like I said, Thomas, don't shit on everyone else to save yourself. You won't like the outcome."

"*Who the fuck decided to put rounds on my gong?!*"

"I did, sir," Sergio announced, and he stood up to accept his punishment.

John stormed up next to Sergio. "Is it bolt-gun day, Jude, and no one told me about it?!"

"No, sir, it's *pew-pew* day!"

"That's right, it's goddamned *pew-pew* day! We're shooting the *little* rifles with the *little* bullet at targets *inside* five-hundred! How many rounds does the Patron Saint of Lost Causes need to harm my favorite steel?"

"Just one, sir, the rifle's dialed in real well right now."

John leaned back away from his student. "Nobody walked that in for you?"

"No, John. No observer, one shot."

"Well, God damn, man, carry on," John replied in apparent disbelief, "if you ain't gonna miss, who the hell am I to say you can't shoot it? Of course, you're gonna sleep on the floor for the night, anyway, so you may as well have at it, son! *Zebulon Floorboard!*"

Michael looked around at the other students, hoping one of them would correct John's error. He looked over to their instructor to see how he responded to the expected silence.

John put his hands on his hips, clearly growing more impatient. "*I said, Zeb—.*" He stopped, looked down, and shook his head. "Goddammit, I yelled at that kid for so long I forgot he left. *Jude!*"

"Yes, John?"

"Congratulations, you're the *new* 'Zebulon Floorboard' until I say different. If I were you, I'd try to make sure one-a these other assholes takes over for you soon. All the rest-a you shitheads," John addressed the group at-large, "quit yer yappin' and go back about your business."

As Sergio laid back down on his shooting mat, Michael considered what Thomas's revelation meant. *If he runs to John with what he thinks he knows, that could well be the end of this thing for me and Sergio. At this point, though, I don't think he'd have any more mercy if I came clean. However it comes to light, we're both out. May as well keep my mouth shut and go with the union rep's advice: deny everything, demand to see the evidence, make counter-accusations, and ask for a lawyer.* He focused his sights on a steel target five hundred yards away. *Never mind. If John finds out we lied this whole time, I probably won't need a lawyer. I'll need another priest.*

TRAINING DAY 125, 0507 HOURS_

RURAL COMPOUND. NIOBRARA COUNTY, WYOMING.

JOHN HAD STARTED their morning PT even earlier than usual and had designated this morning's efforts as a group run. Michael had stopped wondering what might await them on any given day. *John rarely tells us anything more than a few minutes before it happens. Probably a psychology tactic to get us comfortable with a life of surprise and spontaneity. Most priests' existence isn't like that at all.*

Barely four months had passed since Michael had first trudged down *Mother Mary* with his classmates. *Just about sixteen weeks, one college semester, and so much has happened, even though I don't know any more about what I'm doing here and where I'm headed next than I did on Day One. Everything's different, and nothing's changed.*

Michael's thoughts returned to the run, and he noticed Sergio had only a few steps on him at the moment. He'd fought hard to catch up to his friend's fitness levels and, as they started up a slight hill, Michael decided to pass Sergio, if only for a little while. *He's gonna make me earn this!*

Sergio looked over as Michael pulled alongside.

"*GO!*" Michael sprinted as hard as he could up the hill ahead of Sergio. With the element of surprise gone, his leaner friend required only a few seconds to catch him. As they summited the low hill, Sergio had regained the lead and Michael's legs were spent.

Michael breathed deep and slowed his pace just as the old, abandoned horse stables came into view below them. He slowed further in surprise when he saw John standing next to the isolated building. *He's out there waiting for us. What's going on???*

"Hey, shake a leg," Sergio called out to the group behind him, "the boss's out here!"

"What, the hell!" Z replied between gasps, "didn't see anything, on the program, for more, mandatory fun, this mornin'!"

"Party on, Wayne," Phillip offered. "Ain't no fun, like mandatory fun! You can bet, he's not alone."

Sergio increased his pace toward John, so Michael and most of the other trainees did the same. *Wanna finish strong, especially now that we've got an audience.* They soon slowed and stood in front of John, who offered no visible indication of what was to come.

"Take a few to catch your breath," John commanded. "I'm gonna talk to y'all together here once the Molasses Brigade finally rolls in. Not sure which is the cause and which is the effect, but they're *thick and slow*, either way. Anyone that won't run a six-minute mile's just a bitch where I came from."

"Where's that again, John?" Sergio's jovial inflection showed he didn't actually expect to catch the man off-guard.

"That was when I worked for the N-Y-G-B."

"I don't remember that one. New York Garbanzo Brigade, or what?"

"Not Your Goddamned Business," John explained, still as dry as burnt toast. "Far as you're concerned, I spent my whole career there. In fact, Jude," he called out Sergio's pseudonym, "I'm still on their payroll, so stop tryin' to sneak shit outta me."

Thomas and Matthew caught up to the stationary group and now gasped for air while the others stepped aside to make room for them.

"Herd of goddamned elephants, I tell you what," John surmised. "Good thing for most of you assholes no one lets me keep real strict fitness standards here. Whole bunch of you sum-bitches'd be looking for new jobs. You can go be fat Episcopalians for all I care, eat all the ice cream ya want and preach that Catholic-light bullshit. Obese priests make my heart hurt."

Animal noises unexpectedly emanated from the abandoned stables, and John looked back at the building for a few seconds as though he heard them, as well. *Difference is,* Michael realized, *he doesn't look surprised.*

"Now that we're all finally here together," John offered, "we can start with today's lesson." As he spoke, Tex and Jane stepped out of the abandoned structure. Jane held the door open for Tex, who carried out a medium, black plastic storage tub with a bright yellow, plastic lid. He grimaced as he walked toward them. "Y'all boys've learned a lot of new skills since ya been here, and, maybe, a few things you didn't know you picked up along the way."

Tex roughly set the box down on the ground in front of John, and Michael heard metallic *tinks* as he did so. The man looked at John, nodded, and unceremoniously walked back toward Jane and the doorway.

"We've *talked around* the purpose of your training," John continued, "offered a few potential glimpses of what your future with the Church might hold, and it seems to me that all y'alls been fine with that, at least those of you remaining. We lost a couple of your cohorts in the past few months that realized they wasn't up to the *potential* of what they might be someday asked to do. To that end, before you waste any more time here, and I waste any more time bestowing the hard-earned expertise of me and my instructors, I wanna know who's gonna be here for the duration." John paused and examined the men gathered before him.

A renewed and justified apprehension overtook Michael. *He might call this a 'lesson,' but it's clearly something we're gonna hafta demonstrate, instead of understand.* A lump formed in his stomach. *They're gonna make us shoot whatever animals are inside.*

John grimaced slightly, as though himself displeased with the imminent events. "I need to see who among you is ready for the kinda work that we've gotta offer out here on the ranch. Inside this stable's a buncha stalls, used to keep draft horses here, so they ain't tiny. Each of you men gets a stall. In that stall, a single hog awaits you. Each of em's about 150 pounds, and you might not think that's much, but, considering their low center of gravity and generally motivated demeanor, you'll find that's more'n enough to mess you up." John reached down and urgently popped the yellow lid from the black tub, as though ripping a bandage from a nasty wound. Twelve identical unsheathed, black-bladed KaBar knives waited inside.

Oh, my God, Michael thought, *this is gonna be worse than I thought...*

"You're gonna give your hog the easiest and most peaceful transition you can muster. You'll recall from the *Silat* and edged weapons classes that pig skin and tissue is damned close to human flesh, so this could be a warm-up for whatever work may potentially lay beyond my property. A *gut-check,* if you will, to ensure that you have the intestinal fortitude for what God *may,* or *may not,* eventually put before you.

"Couple things y'all need to know first," John explained as he retrieved a single KaBar from the bin. "The hogs in there's already been condemned to death. We got 'em rounded up after the neighbor's place went tits up last week. The commodities market turned on him, and now he's bankrupt. He couldn't sell the hogs and couldn't afford to pay a butcher to slaughter a buncha animals for meat he couldn't store and freeze. He couldn't afford to keep the farm or keep feedin' 'em. Worst of all, he also didn't have the spine to do what was *necessary* and *owed* to them hogs, so that chickenshit just abandoned 'em. Left 'em penned up to starve or dehydrate, or get mauled to death once the coyotes figured out they's not guarded anymore. They would-a suffered a terrible death in those pens, all the while havin' to hear their neighbors and friends meetin' their own terrible fates for days or weeks from now. The end of their lives will be miserable and prolonged if no one steps in to end their suffering and ease their certain and inevitable transition."

John paused and scanned the group. Michael thought he saw genuine concern and sympathy on his face. *Not sure if it's for the animals, for what's about to happen to them, or for us and what we're about to have to do. Maybe both.*

"I may be a lot of things," John explained, "but I can't abide sufferin'. Death is a natural and necessary part of life on this Earth, but sufferin' ain't gotta be. Even though we're commanded by scripture to use God's animal kingdom for our benefit, this wasn't no way to leave a group of sentient beings. Even those pigs got a soul, and emotions, fears, and pain. What they *don't got,* unfortunately for them, is another way to pay for their own room and board. So, it's been left to us to do right by them. When I found out what my neighbor had done, I thought this'd be an excellent training opportunity for y'all to demonstrate the value of our continued investment in you.

"Just like everything else we do here," he continued, "this is all voluntary. You can leave at any time, includin' right now. If you wanna get a free bus ride instead, that's no problem. If you wanna stay, though, you're gonna stay in there until the work is done, however long it takes and whatever that means. Burning daylight. Pick a blade, pick a pig, and get to work. Given the training you've all had, you should require no further instruction, so, we're all just waiting around on you people."

For a moment, they all stood in place and looked at the tub of large, fixed-blade weapons before them. *I can't argue with John's explanation of the necessity of killing these pigs, and I'm sure he does want to see that we'll justifiably take a life.* This had little in common with his back-alley fights in Silver City, or his killing of the would-be Columbian murderer. *I didn't have time to think about defending myself in Bogotá, even though I intentionally created that circumstance. I reacted to a threat in that instant. These hogs didn't do anything to me. They're just the unfortunate focus of an ordered mercy killing.* As soon as Sergio stepped forward and retrieved his knife of choice, Michael and the remaining trainees did the same.

The large black knife felt abnormally heavy as Michael followed Sergio past Jane and through the stable door. *Probably an equal mix of reality and dread weighing down my hand.* He stepped toward the middle of the dark building, and the smell of animal feces struck his nostrils. *Similar to the classroom, wide middle corridor with six stalls on opposing sides.* Crushed hay and alfalfa lay strewn across the central, hard-packed dirt floor, and it seemed like no one had been inside the building in years, maybe decades.

Tex, Big Country, and The Mouse all stood together near the middle of the interior walkway. Michael saw they examined the trainees as they entered. *Looking for signs of weakness,* Michael thought, *or a lack of resolve.* He saw something behind him caught Big Country's attention, and he nudged Tex. Michael turned around to see what was happening and realized that Thomas urgently strode toward the farthest stall, the KaBar held up and out in front of his body like the caricature of a stabbing suspect.

What a nonstop shit-show, Michael thought, and put the nuisance trainee out of his mind. He chose a stall on the other side of the building from where Thomas would soon be at work and purposefully walked toward it. *May as well get this over with, it's only gonna get worse in here after everyone else starts.* As he reached the stall, he opted to climb over the five-foot-wall, rather than open the gate and risk the hog bolting out past him. A faded and rusted, hand-painted metal sign hung from the wall immediately next to the stall's entrance, and "Chrissy" could still be read on its surface.

Michael climbed the wall and eyed his hog, which had backed itself into the far corner, away from the gate. His eyes, airway, and lungs stung slightly as he lowered himself down into the pen, likely from high levels of ammonia that now also assaulted his senses.

The other hogs began protesting, and the large animal now facing Michael shifted his eyes and head in response. Squeals, snorts, frightened shouts, and angry grunts erupted all around. The hog sniffed the air and backed more tightly into the corner. As Michael cautiously stepped toward his hog in a wrestler's stance with the KaBar up in his right hand, he heard banging from inside the adjacent stall to his left. *They're fighting back, trying to escape, struggling to survive. Poor fucking animals. God make my hands swift and merciful.*

"I'm truly sorry, pig," Michael anxiously uttered, "neither of us wants this, but we both want you to get mauled to death by coyotes even less." As he crossed the center of the stall and veered to his left, Michael thought the hog likely weighed a lot more than one-fifty. *Thing's bigger on all fours than I am!* Suddenly, the animal loudly squealed as it rushed straight at his legs. Michael reflexively sidestepped left, the direction he was already going, and quickly slashed at the hog's right shoulder as it ran past. Pulling the blade back up and ready as fast as he could, Michael saw the cut had injured the animal. It furiously shrieked in pain, protest, and fear as its shoulder joint collapsed beneath the animal's weight. Sensing his opportunity and moral obligation to end its suffering, Michael rushed over, heavily straddled the hog's shoulders, and mercifully dispatched the animal.

The horrific sounds of fear, anger, and death continued unabated all around them, and Michael ignored the desperate, appalling chaos as best he could. Despite his own emotions at that moment, Michael calmly stroked the top of the felled pig's head and did his best to offer some minor comfort to it. *Even animals raised for slaughter shouldn't ever suffer.* As life rapidly drained from the animal beneath him, Michael prayed.

Thank you, Father, for using me to end this animal's certain and terrible suffering. I pray that you take away his pain and fear. I pray that you ease and hasten its transition into whatever awaits its soul.

The animal shuddered once more beneath him and then lay still. Michael bent down and couldn't hear any breathing. *Nothing more that I can do for him.* He stood, breathed deeply, and tried to shake off some of the adrenaline coursing through his veins. As he stumbled to the stall door, shouts and squeals continued all around him but seemed to have lessened for the moment.

Desperate to leave, Michael tossed the stall door open. Tex saw him emerge and purposefully stepped over to the stall to inspect his work. Michael stood outside, hunched over with his hands on his knees and his eyes on the ground just in front of his feet. He didn't watch the instructor or his inspection. *I don't ever wanna see the inside of that stall again.* Tex emerged after only a few seconds, gave a slight nod of approval, and shouted over to John. "Looks like we got a winner."

"Send him out," John urgently shouted back.

Michael stood upright and briefly looked around the stable. A few of his peers sat fearfully "treed" on top of their stalls. Several others frantically ran around inside theirs. *They went in expecting 'Wilbur' from 'Charlotte's Web' and got 'Napoleon' from 'Animal Farm' instead.* The sounds of chaos and suffering escalated as Michael walked alone toward the exit. Misery and terror reigned.

Michael kept his focus on the door in front of him. The soundtrack was terrible enough without any further visual aids. Jane still held the door open. Their eyes briefly met as he passed, and Michael saw sorrow and regret on her face. He turned away, stared straight ahead, and hurriedly strode to the hill he'd descended to get there. *Breathe,* he told himself, *just breathe.*

As his adrenaline subsided, an unexpected mix of nausea and outrage welled up inside Michael, both toward the man who'd given the order and everyone who had followed it.

"Drop your knife back in the bucket and get outta here," John shouted after him from the doorway. "You ain't gotta hear this shit anymore."

Michael looked down at his bloody right hand and realized he still held onto the sticky KaBar. He stepped to the black bucket, carelessly dropped the disgusting knife, and continued toward the hill while his emotions escalated. Motion to his left drew Michael's attention to the back corner of the stable.

Big Country looked back at him, pointed to the ground at his feet, and shouted at Michael. "Get over here and get cleaned up! You're covered in that shit!"

Michael ignored the reasonable command and started jogging uphill, away from the chaos. He covered only a few dozen steps before the nausea overcame him. Doubling-over, he expelled vomit on the hard-packed earth and scrub brush beside the running trail and collapsed to his knees. Michael gasped for air and struggled to process what he'd just done, what he'd just witnessed. The sounds emanating from the stable continued to lessen, but the abject terror behind him hadn't yet ended. *This is not what I thought it would be. Why the fuck are we here?*

TRAINING DAY 126, 0542 HOURS_

RURAL COMPOUND. NIOBRARA COUNTY, WYOMING.

MICHAEL HAD ALREADY BEEN awake for an hour. *May as well get dressed. John gave us most of yesterday off for prayer and reflection on our killing, so there's no way he's gonna tolerate anyone being late this morning.* He rose from his bunk and looked at the two new empties, their bedding made up and pulled tight across the mattresses. *Can't blame Matthew or The Baptist for their decision. It was easier for me to kill a man than that pig yesterday. At least they realized it and quit* before *the first cut. Would've been even worse to leave the hogs injured and suffering while someone else stepped in to finish the work.*

Most of the other trainees were up and about, and no one spoke to each other. *Not many words traded in the last twenty-four.* As he trudged upstairs to form up for their morning workout, Michael winced at the sight of a gallon-sized Ziploc bag of raw bacon on the kitchen countertop next to the stove. *Looks like one gut-check wasn't enough for John.*

The lead instructor stood on the porch and awaited them, predictably, with a steaming mug of coffee. When Thomas finally emerged as the sixth and last trainee, he wore a Cheshire-Cat grin. *That asshole was giddy all day yesterday,* Michael thought, *he's been acting like some kinda serial killer.*

John cleared his throat and finally greeted them. "Good morning, shitheads. Rough day yesterday. We lost two good men who couldn't muster the gumption you six showed, and they've chosen to return to their respective dioceses to seek other opportunities therein. The good news out of their departure is that they realized their personal limitations *before* human lives were at risk. The bad news, at least for me and my associates, is that there's still two hogs that gotta be put down. But that's my problem, and y'all can rest assured that I'm not about to make it yours.

"For your part," John continued, "I hope you boys got all you needed from the hours of prayer and meditation. We're back at it today, and I wanna make sure y'all got all the negativity worked outta ya before we stick you back in the classroom and expect you to focus on new material. So, today's a group run. Y'all're gonna run Indian Races down *Mother Mary.* Single file, and I want Sergio in front and Thomas at the back. Lead runner sets the pace. Last man sprints past the group. Next man in last place sprints to the front when he sees the new leader settle in and set the pace. Lather, rinse, repeat for five miles. Meet back here. Go to it."

The group jogged off together in silence, and Michael ended up just in front of Thomas. As the group put distance between them and John, Thomas tried to strike up conversations with his classmates. *It's like yesterday was* fun *for him,* Michael thought. Everyone else remained quiet and generally ignored Thomas. After Michael completed his fourth sprint and settled into a moderate run pace at the front, Thomas again sought a dialogue between heavy breaths.

"How'd your kill go, Andrew? I heard you, were first out, you done that before, or what?"

"Leave it alone, Thomas," Michael cautioned.

"Seriously," he pressed, "how'd you kill it, *so quick?*"

Michael ignored him and increased his pace to punish Thomas, at least until Phillip passed him in a few moments.

"Soft spot, for the stupid farm animals, huh? It's possible, that I'm the *only one here,* that's *man enough,* to do what's necessary. All you guys, all been actin', like a buncha *bitches—*"

Before he could finish his statement, Michael stopped, spun around, and launched a backhanded, left hammer fist at him with all the force and rage he could muster. The surprise strike caught Thomas defenseless, landed solidly against the right side of his upper neck and jaw, and immediately knocked him out. Gravity pulled him into a pile down on the hard-packed trail. Sergio had to leap to the side to avoid stepping on him.

"*SHUT UP!*" Michael took a fighting stance over Thomas as his opponent lightly seized on the ground and a dark, wet stain ran down his light grey running pants. Sergio quickly wrapped his arms around Michael and pushed him away from Thomas. The other three trainees gathered around their felled colleague as Michael spit toward him.

"Hey, man," Sergio offered, "it's over, man, it's over. He's down, and he won't be gettin' back up. It's over, calm down."

Michael put his hands up to show his "surrender," and his friend let him go. Thomas' body relaxed for a moment, and Phillip checked his vitals.

"Still breathing, still got a pulse."

"He's lucky that's all he got," Z surmised, "asshole's a damned maniac. I think he *liked* yesterday."

"That was a long time coming," Alpha scoffed in his French accent, "I'm just grateful for a few moments of silence from the man-child."

"Question is," Sergio pondered, "is he gonna shut the hell up and get a whole lot better, or is he gonna hold a grudge and get about ten times worse?"

"We don't all need to hang back and help him get to the house," Phillip announced. "I don't think Andrew oughta be here when he wakes up, just in case he wants to even the score. Why don't you guys take off and I'll walk him back after he comes to?"

"You sure?" Michael asked. *Dammit, I reacted with emotion, and now everyone else is gonna pay for my actions.* "He's my responsibility, and it's my fault this happened."

"No," Phillip countered, "I'm just surprised it took this long. If he wakes up angry, you shouldn't be alone with him. Odds are real good that he won't know what happened."

"Wouldn't be a lie to say that he fell and hit his head on the trail," Sergio suggested. "Anyone disagree?"

Michael glanced around the group and saw everyone nodding in agreement.

"Take off," Phillip directed. "I got him, and I'll do my best to catch up if John wants me to." He knelt down next to Thomas now that his body had stopped its micro seizures.

"Thanks, Phillip" Michael offered, "I owe you."

"Yeah, well, you can take care of him if I ever knock him out, how 'bout that?"

Michael smirked at the facetious offer. "Fair enough."

Z looked at his watch and started back down the trail. "Let's hustle, boys, we gotta make up time now."

Michael and the remaining runners fell in behind Z and continued their appointed trail race. *I should feel remorse for hitting Thomas, but I'm only really sorry about affecting everyone else.*

TRAINING DAY 126, 0709 HOURS_

RURAL COMPOUND. NIOBRARA COUNTY, WYOMING.

After the five-mile Indian Race, John repeatedly had the trainees alternate between ten-burpee sets and sprints up the long driveway. Thirty minutes later, he released them for showers and breakfast. Michael had stopped in to check on Thomas, who sat with Father Harry in his office and apparently had no memory of what actually happened. *It's for the best,* Michael thought. *Easier if he doesn't have a grudge.*

He headed downstairs, stripped, and strode to the showers. Phillip and Sergio were already soaping up under the water. Z, still in his running clothes, sans shoes, stood doubled-over in the back corner and dry-heaved over the wet tile floor.

"Way to hang in there, Z," Michael offered. "I thought you got everything up out there on the driveway, though."

"Me, too," he replied between heaves and shook his head. "Stomach's got other ideas."

Michael started one of the showerheads and stood under the already-hot water. *Just what I needed. I don't have the strength to be upset about anything right now.* The morning PT session had sapped most all his energy, and he assumed that had been John's exact intention. *Best way to work out psychological stress and let your biochemistry normalize. Should've done this on my own yesterday, but now I'm glad I didn't. We'd* still *be listening to Thomas' bullshit.*

As water cascaded down his face and body, Michael reflected on how much tougher the pig killing had been. *A lot worse than I expected, and it was nothing like harvesting wild game, or Bogotá. Helluva lot different than shooting an animal from a few hundred yards or defending your own life. I couldn't ever do that again, not in the same way.*

"Nice without Thomas down here," Sergio offered as he entered the shower, "y'all are nice and quiet."

"*Sshhhh,*" Michael replied. "You're ruining it." After he'd cleaned up and dressed, Michael plodded upstairs, and every step pained his legs. *Tomorrow's gonna hurt even more.* He waddled through the kitchen and into the adjoining dining room, where John sat alone at the head of the table. A variety of breakfast foods sat on the table ready for consumption. *Not cooking for ourselves today.* Several serving plates in the middle brimmed with fried bacon and ham steaks. His stomach turned at the sight, but Michael forced himself into his appointed seat. John nodded to acknowledge his presence, but neither of them forced the other into a conversation.

Within a few minutes, four of the five other trainees had joined them, and John offered a prayer before they ate. "Dear Heavenly Father, bless this food to thy use and service. Bless the hands that prepared it. May it help us to serve thy purpose and answer thy calling. Bless the animals that sacrificed themselves for us. We thank you for trading their lives yesterday so that we may eat, be nourished, and serve you today. Amen."

Michael offered the same half-hearted *amen* as his compatriots. As the men passed plates and served food to each other, only John took hearty portions of anything. He alone touched the plates of pork.

"We ain't got much time this morning before mass," John announced, "so I want y'all to carry on while I talk. One of the problems with society today, 'civilization' as we arrogantly call it, is that we don't drink from the skulls of our vanquished enemies anymore. For most-a you, this ham and bacon is pretty damned close to that." He paused and enthusiastically bit into a floppy piece of barely-cooked bacon. "Not all brown and crispy like that bullshit you get at the diners, right?"

Michael looked away and focused on his small portion of scrambled eggs and fruit. *I think we're all struggling with what happened yesterday, with what we did...what we* had *to do...well, what we* chose *to do. Like John keeps saying, everything here's voluntary.*

"Good news is, you boys stocked the freezer for the winter, so long as no one wants anything but pork. For the rest-a the time you're here, you assholes are gonna share in my elevated cholesterol, so plan on eating some kinda hog three squares a day until the cows come home. Maybe we'll give y'all a pass at slaughtering *them*, too." He looked around the group for a few moments as though he expected a more jovial response to his ribbing.

When he received none, John cleared his throat, set down the bacon, and wiped his hands on a paper napkin. He adopted a more somber tone. "Turns out that killin', even somethin' as benign as a farm animal raised for slaughter and human consumption, ain't no easy chore. Every sentient being has at least a *flicker* of a soul inside 'em, something that can be personified and, on some level, equates 'em to us, even if only in the basest of our shared emotions. Happiness, pleasure, fear, pain. If you feel like shit this mornin', like a guilty, murderous sum-bitch who's done wrong, that's good. I *want* you to feel that way *this* morning. That's your conscience makin' you examine your actions and justify what ya did. That'll give you pause every time you're faced with the choice of takin' another life, no matter how big or small.

"The reason you feel like you done wrong," John continued, "it's that you doubt killin' your hog was necessary. You think it didn't need to happen, despite everything I told you. You can trust that I exhausted all available options to keep those animals alive before we penned 'em up over there. They *had to die,* one way or another. With their fate sealed, I knew their lives could serve a purpose and give me a reliable litmus test of your character, to show me you're not *eager* to kill.

"If you *didn't* take action yesterday, I assure you, they woulda met a horrific end, much worse than what little suffering they endured at our hands. Yours *and* mine. Despite how y'all feel today, you saved those animals from untold misery and terror. You won't ever be content with how it happened, but you can rest assured that y'all done a merciful thing yesterday. Mercy can be tough, it's very rarely the easy or comfortable path. I'm grateful you all had the intestinal fortitude to *be* merciful, even though you knew it would be miserable for you.

"Now that that's done, though," John offered, "I want you to consider how you handled yourself. If you helped 'Piglet' pass quickly and easily, you should remember that that's how they're all supposed to go. If God ever calls you to end the life of an animal, or even that of another human, you're not in the torture and suffering business. It's possible you might find yourself called into the vengeance business, but there's a helluva lot a God-damned difference between the two. If you fucked up yesterday and caused needless suffering, I want you to remember that, too. Square yourself, and don't let that shit happen again. Seek forgiveness and precision or express some gratitude and humbly ask for a repeat performance if it's forced on you. Consider your past, but don't let it prevent you from fulfilling your appointed tasks today. Now, get fed, police the kitchen, and get to Mass on time. Don't keep the Monsignor waiting, he's got a schedule to keep, too."

Although somewhat relieved by John's reassurances, Michael wasn't yet ready to partake of their harvest. *At least I can eat the eggs and fruit now.*

"One other thing," John called out before biting back into his slice of bacon and pointing it at Michael. "You. Thomas ain't quite ready to put food on his stomach after the run this morning, and I'm sure you can imagine why that might be. From now on, you switch chairs with Jude and sit next to Thomas. You're both on the floor tonight, too, and you're both gonna stay there until I say otherwise. Neither one of you shitheads gets the luxury of my cots, and it'll be a while before you do. It's not up to you to discipline my students, so you can add a hundred burpees to every workout until I say different. Think about that the next time you wanna knock somebody out, even if they got it comin'. Vengeance is *mine,* says the Lord."

TRAINING DAY 126, 2034 HOURS_

RURAL COMPOUND. NIOBRARA COUNTY, WYOMING.

With a glass of cold beer in-hand, Michael sat on the front porch with Sergio and Z and watched the evening sun set on the western horizon. Michael realized he hadn't seen Thomas since dinner. *I've got no desire to interact with that snake, but I'd prefer to know where he is.*

"Glad John doesn't expect us to hide out in the basement every night," Z announced and sipped at his suds. "Tired of smellin' that much man all the time. Pretty sure somebody shits in there every hour of every day."

Sergio lifted his glass in a mock toast. "I'm glad he hasn't actually *made us* eat bacon yet. My stomach's gonna need another day or two for that."

Michael chuckled and hoisted his pint in agreement. Movement from his right caught his eye, and he looked to see John storming toward them. "Look alive, boys," he quietly offered to the other two, "some kinda consequence inbound."

John pointed at them. *"You three! Grab all Thomas' shit and get it out here, right the fuck now!"*

Michael and both cohorts urgently hopped up to comply with the unexpected directive and purposefully strode to the basement. "Whaddayou think's going on," Michael asked.

"No idea," Z replied," but it sure ain't good."

"Well, maybe not good for Thomas," Sergio offered as they reached Thomas' bunk and collected his belongings.

Phillip and Alpha curiously watched them. Phillip lowered a novel he'd already read twice since their arrival. "What's up?"

"No idea," Michael replied. "John just told us to grab Thomas' stuff."

Alpha pulled his headphones off, and French rap music played quietly for a moment. "Any idea what he did?"

"None," Michael replied. "I think we got everything," he offered to Z and Sergio. They grabbed both of Thomas' duffel bags, which overflowed from their careless packing efforts.

"I bet he took off," Alpha proclaimed. "Tried leaving for town."

"I bet John never tells us," Michael replied as he led the other two back upstairs. He held the front door, and Sergio and Z dropped Thomas' property on the porch at John's feet. "Anything else, John?"

"Not unless you know somethin' about givin' frontal lobotomies, 'cause that asshole's gonna need one to get his goddamned head right. Y'all take your suds back inside and tell the others that we're gonna have a 'family meeting' upstairs in about fifteen minutes."

Michael complied with the request and ensured everyone soon awaited John's return. As they sat around the dining table in uncomfortable silence, Thomas' vacant seat and his unknown fate weighed heavily on Michael's heart. The five trainees spoke very little during the half-hour that passed before John strode back inside the house. He paused in front of their group, and Michael saw blood smeared across the front of his shirt and pants, none of which had been there before.

"Thomas ain't gonna be around no more," John flatly called out.

What the hell, Michael thought and leaned back away from John.

The instructor glanced down at his clothes and looked as though he'd just realized their concern. "Calm *down,* that's *pig* blood, that asshole's still upright and vertical, but I bet he wishes we'd reconsidered." He checked his hands and forearms for stray blood before placing his hands on his hips and slowly pacing near the foot of the table.

"After dinner," John explained, his voice tense and angry, "one of my associates saw Thomas take off down *Mother Mary* on his own, so he followed him. He went back to the hog stalls and tried to kill another one. Thomas'd already stabbed the damned thing before the instructor could stop him, so we had to put it down after we got Thomas under control. I knew he wouldn't make the final cut, but I had no idea he'd go this far off the goddamned rails."

John stopped pacing and looked at the remaining trainees. "Thomas claimed that my speech at breakfast made him realize he wasn't *satisfied* with how he did yesterday. He decided the solution was to go back, pick one-a the hogs that Matthew and The Baptist refused to put down, and make himself *proud* of his second kill. Wanted to do a *better job* this time, he said. *Goddamned psychopath!* I ain't even got the words to express my *outrage* at that man, and I wouldn't usually *ever* tell y'all what becomes of your classmates, but I'm at a loss, boys.

"How did this shit happen," John asked. "At what point did it seem like I *wanted* y'all to be the kinda men that'll kill for the act of killin' itself? You and me, we might be called to use lethal force to defend ourselves or God's children, but killin' in the face of *any* other option is *murder,* plain and simple! That's exactly what Thomas set about doin' tonight, and I'll wager my bottom-dollar right now that he never woulda stopped with farm animals, either."

John looked around the group for several seconds. "I think y'all oughta call it a night. Ask God to grant Thomas the help he needs and forgive us if we did anything to contribute to it."

Everyone else stood and left the table as John directed, but Michael stayed in place.

"Somethin' on your mind, Andrew," John asked as soon as they were alone.

"If you have a couple minutes."

In exasperation, John looked down at his blood-stained pants. "My night has taken an *unexpected turn*, ya might say, but I'll assume it can't really wait."

Michael nodded his understanding. "What are we doing here, John? What're you training us to do that yesterday had to happen, even if it *was* necessary for the pigs? I think we deserve to know more, especially after this."

"You *know* what we're doing here, even though I've never spelled it out for you," John impatiently countered. "That what you need? Do I gotta *hold your hand* and help you *sound out* all the *big* words, or can you admit that you figured it out all on your own and you're okay with it?"

"I suppose I—"

"Here's the thing you need to understand, Andrew. I don't want robots, and I can't have psychos that just wanna kill. We're here to be God's precision instruments that He uses for a *finite* and *rare* purpose. Now, I understand you've *been* a couple places and *done* a couple things, right?"

Michael quizzically looked at the man and tried to assess the underlying basis of his question. *How much does he really know about me?* "Yeah," he hesitantly responded and slowly nodded his head, "what difference does that make?"

"I need men that *intrinsically*, in their *hearts* and in their *minds,* that firmly understand the difference between murder and killing, and they're comfortable with makin' *merciful* decisions when necessary. You know much about huntin' snakes, Andrew?"

"Not really," Michael replied, unsure about the correlation.

"That's one-a my favorite prey. Hate those sons-a-bitches, but, what's nice about huntin' 'em is that they'll always do what you want, so long as you bait 'em right. They'll only strike at a threat if they can't outrun it, but, if they're hungry, they'll go after prey without a second thought. So, whenever you wanna draw a snake outta hidin', you make it think there's an easy meal to be had. Turns out the world's fulla snakes. I don't want *snakes* on my team, Andrew, I need snake *hunters.* You should keep your shit packed, by the way. Real good chance you ain't gonna be here that much longer."

"*Why?* What'd I screw up, John," Michael demanded, now upset at the idea that he deserved Thomas' unknown fate. "I did *everything* you wanted, I put up with *your* miserable ass and your bullshit-psychology antics, and now I'm gettin' *shipped out?! Just like that?!*"

John put his hands atop the chair opposite Michael and leaned forward. When he spoke, his lower, deliberate tone helped keep their conversation private. "That's what happens *after* you pass the goddamned program. At this point, I don't see anyone else washin' out, so you just gotta learn everything you can and keep your focus."

Michael leaned back in his chair and realized how off-guard John's kindness had found him. "Thanks, John, I—"

"One thing you need to be aware of. Even though I believe very firmly in the work my graduates are called to complete for God and His children, you're still overseen by men. Any one of 'em can be fallible, arrogant, and self-serving, even if they wake up in a red cassock or a papal tiara."

John paused, briefly glanced behind him, and spoke just above a whisper. "We're all just *gravediggers* in this cemetery, right? We're the ones out there, in all manner of weather, doing the ugly work that no one else wants or is willin' to do. We get our hands dirty because *someone* has to, and we're willin' and able. It's in the D-N-A of *who* and *what* we are. We run into danger because those around us *can't* or *won't*, because we can't *sit by* and watch what happens when danger comes callin' on those around us.

"Trouble with gravediggers, though, Andrew, is they know where all the bodies are buried. Eventually, the boss decides he needs a *new* gravedigger with a shorter memory. I wish it wasn't so, but I've seen it time and again, regardless of what you call the organization, what it calls itself, whatever its bullshit acronym is. Pick any letters of the alphabet you want, as long as it's run by people, the suits'll eventually come downstairs lookin' for the diggers."

Michael struggled to process John's unexpected candor. "Why do you do it then, John, if you're so certain it's gonna end the same way every time?"

"*Somebody's* gotta do it, and goddammit, I *love* the work. It's what I was meant to do with this life. I can live with everything I've done, gladly answer for all of it someday without hesitation. It's the things I *failed* to do, the times I let fear get the best of me, those are the things I'm afraid to be judged on. Keep that in mind as you're out there diggin' holes, Andrew. Make sure you're not diggin' one for yourself."

TRAINING DAY 180, 0728 HOURS_

RURAL COMPOUND. NIOBRARA COUNTY,
WYOMING.

MICHAEL SAT in his detested plastic chair and flipped through hundreds of pages of notes he'd taken since his first day in John's classroom. *It's unbelievable what we've covered. Gotta be getting close to that B-S in Espionage Arts.* In the two months that had passed since the pig slaughter, their training coursework had become much more narrowly focused and detailed. *It's almost like they're training us to be cops, or anti-cops, but continually re-emphasizing that we're never to act without fulfilling our moral and Biblical obligations. John & CO covered a ton of material during the first few months, but since then we've just been digging deeper into the same recurring subjects and further improving our skills. The only new topics have all been pretty high-speed, low-drag material that almost no one gets to learn.* He flipped through the thick notebook's tabbed sections and scanned the titles: Recognizing Homemade Improvised Explosive Devices, Dynamic Building Entry Tactics, Shortcomings of Modern Forensic Science, Police Procedures and Investigation Methods, Interrogation Techniques, Border Crossing Processes and Weaknesses, Crime Scene Processing, Evidence Collection, Basic Computer Forensics.

Michael smirked as he read his favorite course title: Spontaneous Vehicle Acquisition. *'Grand Theft Auto' would be a more accurate title. Screwdrivers are still the way to go, it's just not as easy to hotwire a car as*

Hollywood makes it look. They're transforming us all into competent and dangerous professionals. Professional 'what' is still T-B-D...

John expectedly crossed the back threshold at just the appointed time and addressed his five remaining students while still en route to the front of the room. "Before we get started with today's *mystery class,* there's somethin' I wanted to make absolutely clear from yesterday's Use of Force class. Y'all can just relax for a few minutes and listen, don't worry about taking notes."

He didn't start out by calling us 'shitheads,' Michael thought. *Is that good or bad?*

"Go ahead and take yourself to your goddamned *happy place,"* John announced, "if you got one, anyway." He set a stack of papers on one of the long banquet tables and looked back at the students.

"We agreed that we're all morally and legally obligated to use *only* the force that's *reasonably necessary* to achieve a just outcome, and it's gotta be proportionate to the offense of the man we're tryin' to subdue. Now, I think we're all pretty damned clear on using force against a *bad* man doing *bad* things. Not gonna rehash that. But, what about the civilian, an interloper, that steps in on the bad man's behalf? How much force you wanna use against *them*?'

Weird. We beat this to death *yesterday,* Michael thought. "They're just doing what they think is right, and we can't explain who we are or what we're doing, so, for me, I wouldn't do anything more than threaten them, if that."

"Alright," John replied. "What about security guards?"

"I would look at them as just another civilian," Alpha explained, "a bystander."

John shrugged. "Okay, but what if they work—"

BOOM!!

Reacting purely on instinct, Michael stood and turned around to face the unknown danger behind him. Adrenaline both sped up his actions and dramatically slowed his perception of time as his brain fought to take in and process all the information available to him. In those slow moments that followed, a tall man in a black ski mask and long-sleeved flannel shirt stood just outside the broken wooden door to the classroom. Splintered pieces of wood from the door cast into the room and fell onto the concrete floor as the suspect dropped a large, black-rubber door ram onto the ground. As Michael rushed toward the door, the suspect retrieved a concealed semiauto pistol from his front waistband and pointed it into the room. Michael began calculating his odds of success and survival, given the weapon and the distance he had to cover to get to it.

A second suspect, this one shorter and also clad in flannel and a black ski mask, stepped in front of the first suspect and leveled a shotgun at Michael's advancing torso. *He's smiling at me!*

Michael knew the shotgun changed the entire dynamic of the fight. With no realistic chance in a head-on confrontation, he moved left toward the nearest stall in search of cover. *I'm too far away, I'll never get there before he shreds my chest!* Michael almost made it to the stalls when he heard Suspect Two expertly rack the shotgun.

chkchk

No weapon, no cover, Michael thought. *I'm dead out here!*

"STOP!! GET DOWN, GET DOWN!!

Despite his internal rage, Michael rationally knew that any noncompliance at that moment was potential suicide. He begrudgingly did as they commanded. He also glanced back and saw his classmates doing the same. John, still at the front of the room, defiantly stood his ground.

"WHO THE FUCK ARE YOU AND WHAT THE HELL DO YOU—"

"HEADS DOWN OR THE OLD MAN DIES!" The second suspect, the shorter one, stepped farther into the room and pointed the shotgun at John. *"EYES CLOSED, HEADS DOWN, EYES CLOSED, HEADS DOWN!! DO IT OR I'LL KILL HIM WHERE HE STANDS!!"*

"You God-damned cowards," John railed on but made no effort to advance. Michael saw him put his hands all the way up above his head. *"Do as he says, boys, don't get yourselves killed over me! Do as I say and do it now! Faces down, eyes closed, hands on the back of your heads!"*

Michael had never been so helpless, enraged, and frustrated in his life, but he did as John ordered. There was no reasonable second option. *I know what's coming, and there's nothing I can do to stop it!*

"How the hell did you find me, you God-damned weas—"

BOOM!! chkchk BOOM!!

The deafening shotgun blasts came in quick succession as the killer proficiently worked his pump action. Even though Michael expected to hear them, he flinched and turned around in terror as John fell back onto the concrete floor. Keeping his head and face close to the ground, Michael turned back to the door and saw both men back out and run off to his right, toward the driveway. *"They're gone,"* he called out to his teammates and scrambled forward toward the door. *"Somebody check on John!"*

Determined to see something that would help find John's killers, Michael just barely exposed himself to look at the driveway with only his left eye. *What the fuck, they're walking and laughing, and there's no getaway car!*

"End scenario, end scenario," John unexpectedly called out.

Michael turned back as John rose up and stood where he'd just fallen. *"Calm the hell down, I'm okay! This was a* training exercise! *Everybody get back to their seats, right now!"*

Anger replaced all his other emotions as Michael's adrenaline subsided. He walked back to his overturned chair but didn't sit down yet. *Better be a goddamned good reason for this!*

"This is important," John slowly explained and brushed dirt off his lower back and the seat of his jeans. "No one else gets to talk but me until I say otherwise. Raise your hand if you actually *saw* the shots. And I don't mean *witnessed them,* I very specifically mean *saw them.* If you *saw* the muzzle flashes, I need to know right now."

Michael looked around and saw no one raised their hand.

"Thank you all for doing as I asked, even though I'm sure you wanted to do otherwise." John cleared his throat and continued. "Right now, before anyone says anything, you're all gonna sit down and write out a detailed witness statement about everything you *saw, heard, thought, and felt* during the attack. Write it like you alone are responsible for givin' cops every last detail they might need to find my killers. You have thirty minutes. And, Alpha, I'm sorry if this creates a problem for you, but you gotta do it in English. Nobody else here *polly-voos.* Go."

Michael exhaled and tried to let his understanding allay his anger. *He wants to show how unreliable eyewitness testimony can be. I get the goddamned point, but they went a little overboard here!* He set about writing his statements just as soon as his hands stopped shaking, and he finished his last sentence right after John called 'time.'

John spent little more than five minutes reviewing all their statements, apparently skimming them for high points and key details. "Came out about like I expected," he announced and dropped the papers on the banquet table. "Some of y'all heard one shot, some two, one heard three. The number of bad men differed; their clothing differed. One said they were both black, even, in reality, they were white and wore ski masks.

"Most of you got pretty close to what they said, but nobody got exact quotes. It does seem, though, that you all had the intelligence to understand and do what I said. If you hadn't, we'd probably have to get your eyes checked to make sure you didn't have any damage from the flash or powder. Unlikely, but I'd prefer to be safe when we can."

Alpha spoke up, and Michael saw he was still upset. "John, what is the purpose and meaning of this, this *bullshit, man*?!"

"In my experience, Alpha, I can talk for hours about how terrible eyewitness testimony is. I can show you all manner of data, video footage from surveillance cameras and murder trials, but it'll never have the same effect. Instead of spending several days trying to get my point through your heads, we're gonna spend less than an hour on the topic and be done with it. The takeaway for *all* of you here today is that *none* of you got it right. No one had the actual events, as they *really* happened from front to back. I think we can agree that you oughta fare better than the average civilian, and you still failed.

"Our brains are wired for survival, not for providing testimony," John explained. "When humans are placed under tremendous and unexpected stress, their truth becomes even more subjective than normal. So, if you find yourself working in investigations, intelligence, anything that might require you to interview, interrogate, or rely on an eyewitness, you'd better make *damned sure* you never act without first corroborating their statements. I don't care what any court says about *relevance* or *admissibility,* we really only care about *accuracy.* If a witness tells you the sky is blue, you'd better open a window and check, no matter who they are.

"Remember that *truth* is relative, subjective, and personal. Eyewitnesses can absolutely *believe* everything they're tellin' you and still be *just, plain, wrong.* They're usually not lying, but their truth isn't consistent with objective facts and evidence. They simply didn't see it from the right physical or mental perspective. Any further questions on the matter?"

Michael reluctantly saw John's point. *Despite how bad the experience of the drill was in that moment, it's hard to overstate its training value. Trading potential trauma for truly internalized understanding.* "So, John," he asked, "was the initial discussion just a set-up for that?"

"Well, yes and no, but thanks for the transition," John replied. "We did cover that pretty heavily yesterday, but I got new reason to make sure we cover it again today. If, someday, in the course of carrying out your duties, you're confronted by law enforcement and they tell you that you're not free to go, you can't leave. Doesn't matter what the *country* is or what the *legal standards* are, you're *detained* or *arrested,* I don't care which. My point is simply *this:* you *will not,* under *any circumstance,* use force against *any* cop of *any* country. They won't have the same concerns about you, especially because you probably won't be able to explain yourself. It all comes back to Day One Op-sec, right? So, again, you *will, not, ever,* assault, stab, shoot, harm, or ruffle the bad haircut of anyone that's raised their right hand and swore an oath to risk their own safety for others. Please try like hell to get away, but you won't use force to do so.

"Worse comes to worst," John surmised, "maybe God changed plans without givin' you advance notice, and now He needs you to serve in a prison mission. ¿*Preguntas?*"

Gotta be a real problem, Michael thought. *Intel officers of all nations eventually have to run into traffic cops or investigators.*

"Moving on," John concluded, "lemme explain how that's tied into today's training exercise. Y'all might recall those two men with flannel and guns that y'all let murder me a little bit ago? Turns out, they're *still outside,* and I expect they might have a couple more friends with 'em by now. Anyone ever heard-a '*SERE School*?'"

No way this is about to happen, Michael hoped. *They're putting us through prisoner of war training?! I thought he was just screwing with us that day on the driving track!* He glanced around and saw a few reluctant, raised hands. Sergio made eye contact with him, and Michael saw in his friend the overwhelming apprehension he felt.

"Good," John smirked and replied. "Just like the big boy version in the military, the name-a the game is in the title: *Survival, Evasion, Resistance, and Escape.* We never know what God's gonna put before us on any given day, and I prefer training that reflects our reality. So, y'all know everything you need to survive, evade, resist, and escape for the next couple days, ya just gotta figure out how to put it all together. This'll be the longest and most profound field exercise in my program, so you can rest assured that this is the *worst shit* I can put you through.

"The R-O-Es for today. No one leaves my property, 'cept by bus or body bag. Your Op-For are all cops in the third-world nation of *Johnislava,* hence their shitty flannel uniforms and piss-poor manners. Recall that you may not, under any circumstance, use force against L-E-Os, not even ones from shitholes like *Johnislava.* At no time can you reveal your professional affiliation with the Vatican or the Holy See. You may reveal you're Catholic, if you choose, that you're men of faith and God, if you choose, but you *will not* identify yourself as a priest, no matter what they do. Questions?"

Stunned and overwhelmed, Michael nervously chuckled to himself, leaned back in his flimsy seat, and tried to predict what was about to happen. *How now, brown cow?*

John mischievously smiled and nodded. "Fair enough." He briefly looked at his watch and then back up at the students. "8-18. Let the games begin." Letting out a loud whistle that Michael assumed would begin their misery, John calmly stepped backward to the front wall with his hands already back up above his head. "Y'all might wanna know that you're about to be captured by federal police and held prisoner for being potential spies. If I'm in *your* shoes right now," he chuckled, "I'd wanna decide just what the *fuck* I'm gonna do when they *bust* that door open again."

TRAINING DAY 181, 2038 HOURS_

RURAL COMPOUND. NIOBRARA COUNTY.

THE LATE SUMMER sun was just setting as Michael plodded back toward the main house. He didn't believe he'd ever been so mentally and physically exhausted in his life. *John was right. We should've had a better plan before they came back through the door.* The permanent wind had been reduced to a pleasant breeze with only the slightest cool edge to it; for the first time since his arrival, Michael felt grateful for it.

Despite the intensity of the events and his memories of the last thirty-six hours, Michael's only concern at that moment was that he didn't fail the assignment. He expected to perform better the next time *Johnislava* authorities detained him for questioning, but, for tonight, Michael's fatigue prevented any further productivity. *I don't even give a shit that I haven't really eaten today. All I want is a shower and bed. Even the shower's getting to be optional.*

He turned the corner of the house and saw John sitting alone on the front porch. *Just about the last conversation I wanna have right now.* A large bucket full of iced beers sat on the deck just a few feet in front of him, and John currently held one such brown bottle in his outstretched hand.

"Evening, Andrew," the lead instructor offered when he saw Michael's approach. "Good to see you back. Heard you mighta earned a couple of these." After Michael accepted the suds, John leaned forward, grabbed another bottle from the ice bucket, and opened one for himself.

Michael drank the top half in one gulp. *Best beer I've ever had...*

"Grab a seat, rest for a spell. Got a buncha three-two beers for tonight, so it's basically bottled water, anyway. Figured that might come in handy after your last thirty-six."

"Thanks," Michael weakly replied, "good to *be* seen, I guess." He sat in an empty chair next to John and held the glass bottle to the side of his neck for a moment before draining it. *Even the ice water running off the bottle's luxurious. Hell, could be worse. There's no death-metal guitar loop cranked up to eleven out here. That alone makes this better than my accommodations last night.*

Michael saw an empty beer box on the porch and gently tossed his empty into it and retrieved another from the ice bucket. "This one can go down a lot slower." The short, stubby glass bottle perfectly cooled his hand. He started to lift it but realized the bottle cap remained in place.

"I suppose you want an opener now," John joked. He retrieved one from his back pocket and expertly freed Michael's libation. "If you give a mouse a cookie, right?"

Michael only nodded to express his gratitude, upended the bottle, and sipped at its neck. *John just gave up some personal intel. I'll hafta think about that tomorrow when I can form a complete thought.*

"I expect you're wore out," John offered and leaned back in his chair. "For most-a y'all, I figure what you just went through is likely gonna be one-a the hardest experiences of your lives. I got the bucket of beers out here, and there's plenty of grub in the kitchen, if you're hungry yet. Don't think that you got some kinda obligation to sit out here and listen to me lecture you about how ya did, or what I want you to take away from all this. That's all for another day. For now, I just want you to get whatever you think you need to put a little bit of light in your evening to make up for all the darkness you've just gone through."

"I appreciate that, John." Michael wanted to take the instructor at his word, but the last six months had mostly taught him to suspiciously examine everything that happened around him. *I should be grateful for his unusual kindness, but it's the words and actions of other people that I can trust the least, followed by my own.* He looked at the beautiful, refreshing beer in his hand. "Last time you gave me a cold beer, I got woke up by a trash can lid at 0-400, got stalked through the darkness, and my lead instructor lacerated my stomach. Any such plans for tomorrow?"

"Not that I know of," John dryly replied. "Shit can change at a moment's notice, though."

Michael took another gulp, careful not to overdo his celebration. "I suppose it's an all-pork buffet in there, as well?"

John laughed aloud and sipped from his beer. "No, not at all, but I'll keep that in mind for next time. Would've been a good chance to get rid of some of it, mosta y'all would probably eat roadkill about now."

Michael grew more attentive and much of his fatigue drained away for the moment. *Did he just give up more intel? He can't count on another hog farmer to abandon his animals during a future training class. Did he lie to us about the hog's fate then to force us into the decision he wanted, or is he joking with me now?*

"Jane's done playin' 'the good cop,' so she's got mashed potatoes with garlic and butter, ribeyes, and roasted green beans on the stove whenever you're ready."

Michael's stomach growled as he thought about the meal that awaited him just inside the house. *Guess I'm hungrier than I thought. When was the last time I ate? Breakfast, yesterday? No, I got half a bologna sandwich last night.* "Yeah, it seemed like there wasn't much need for a 'good cop' in there. Her role didn't last very long."

"Well, in all fairness, Andrew, we didn't figure she was the best way to get to you," John offered. "All the Op-For in this exercise stuck to the tactics that morally flexible cops in the third-world'd use. We use the same principles here as the military's SERE School, but you won't ever face those kinda interrogation tactics. That pretty much makes this a 'SERE-Light,' or, maybe more accurately, a '*SERE-like Experience.*' Calling your last thirty-six hours a 'SERE School' is kinda like callin' the *Pirates of the Caribbean* ride at Disneyland a Navy SEAL BUD/S course. For the most part, cops across the world are there to uphold the law, even if it's a corrupt law. They're not there to torture or kill you, and they're not gonna pull your fingernails out if you don't tell 'em what they think they wanna know."

And there's the trainer I've grown to expect, Michael thought. *Every hurdle and accomplishment have to be minimized. Screw it, it's time to eat.* Michael stood up, stiffly walked to the bucket, and retrieved a third beer. "Anyone else inside yet? No way I'm the first one out."

John didn't respond to the question at all. *Did he even hear me,* Michael thought.

"You wasn't the first one out," John explained. "Ain't no one else inside."

Oh, shit, did someone quit over this? "What happened?"

"Z's gone." John's emotionless statement revealed nothing about the cause or fault for the unexpected outcome.

"What happened to Z, John?"

The instructor met his gaze and glared back at him. *"He's, gone."*

"Why?" Michael heard the anger in his voice and didn't care if John heard it, as well.

"Because, *I said so,* Andrew," John curtly explained, "and I'm gonna give you some slack here because-a the rough times you *think* you had recently. All that matters is that he didn't make it and he's been sent back home, wherever the hell that is."

"But, John, what'd he—"

"Why the *fuck* does it matter," John growled and set his jaw. "I don't owe you or anyone else a single goddamned *word* of explanation for anything I do around here! This program is *my ship* and I run it as I *damned well please!* I don't answer to anybody but God Himself, and that includes you and any other asshole that thinks they got an opinion about it! Z was no different than you, or any other shithead here! You stay until I say you can't, and when I say you go, that's it! He's gone, and you're welcome to join him any time you want! Just say the word and I'll have that bus back en route!" John finally broke eye contact with Michael, gulped his beer, and stared off toward the sunset. "Go get some supper and get outta my sight before I decide you need a second effort at your last training evolution."

Screw you, Michael thought. He took the beers into the house but bypassed the kitchen and everything Jane had prepared. Michael barely noticed the pain in his legs as he descended the stairs to confirm John's statement. There was now an empty, tightly-made bed where Z had last slept. All his friend's personal belongings were gone.

TRAINING DAY 200, 0841 HOURS_

RURAL COMPOUND. NIOBRARA COUNTY, WYOMING.

MICHAEL and his flimsy white plastic chair had been moved up to the classroom's front banquet table. The four remaining trainees now easily fit at one row of tables, so the second had mysteriously disappeared with Z almost three weeks ago. The small group had already celebrated mass with Father Harry that morning, so Michael sat and uncomfortably waited for the first class to begin. *We've gotta be close to getting outta here. How long can this training program be?*

Michael heard the door open behind him. *Well, John's goons did such a poor job of repairing the broken door and frame that I can't actually hear it open or close anymore. I only know it's open when the wind noise increases.* He looked back as Sergio walked in, and Michael consciously reminded himself to use his friend's pseudonym. "Hey, Jude." *Can't be too careful.*

"Good morning. The one day I made *huevos rancheros* for everyone is also the one day you skipped breakfast. Kinda hard not to take it personal, ya know?"

Michael smiled at his friend's facetious assessment. "Sorry, man, I'm sure they were great. Just wanted some time to think."

"Something bothering you?"

"Nothing specific," Michael lied. "Just a general funk right now." *I wanna know what happened to Z and I wanna be done with this goddamned training.*

"I'll *quietly* pray for you then."

Michael smiled at his friend's sincerity. "I'm already better now that you're here. Everyone else's gonna be back any second."

"See, it's that *Mexican Magic*, Andrew," Sergio joked, "my people bring great food and happiness everywhere we go."

Increased wind noise announced another arrival, and Michael saw Phillip and Alpha walk in just ahead of Father Harry, who had traded his clerical garbs for casual clothes. *Looks like today's gonna be another ethics discussion, then.*

"Good morning, all," Harry called out. "I'd love to finally know what happened to the door, but John's been mum about it, and I don't want to risk putting you in an awkward position." He stopped in front of the banquet table and invited them to sit. "Let's open today's class with prayer, shall we?" He paused so the students could bow their heads. "Heavenly Father, I pray for your guidance, that we would *all* better understand and accept your divine mysteries, especially those that are beyond our comprehension. I pray that more of your eternal and infinite wisdom be bestowed and instilled in these men. I pray that you watch over us on our path of service to you and your people. Amen."

"Amen," Michael quietly offered along with his classmates.

"This morning, gentlemen, we're gonna start with an examination of Euthanasia, Suicide, and Scandal. *Euthanasia,* as defined in 22-76 and 77 of the Catechism means bringing an intentional end to the lives of handicapped, sick, or the dying, regardless of motive. God finds it morally unacceptable, the same as any other murder, even if it's intended to eliminate suffering. We are not to end life for convenience, with no more concern or anguish than we'd exercise in putting an animal down.

"The next paragraph addresses the ability to legitimately discontinue medical treatments provided that it's done to avoid over-zealous efforts, rather than to hasten death. Now, 22-79, this one is where I want to start our discussion with the previous paragraphs in mind. Andrew, can you start the reading there?"

"*In circumstances wherein a person faces imminent death,*" Michael offered, "*the treatments usually administered to the ill shall not be morally severed. Continued or new administration of painkillers is permissible, provided its purpose is limited to the reduction of suffering. Even if such treatments may hasten their demise, remedies that respect human dignity are admissible if not enacted to intentionally bring about death. Continued or new methods of palliative care are encouraged to lessen suffering."*

"What is 'palliative care,'" Harry asked.

"Generally," Phillip replied, "it's various medical treatments designed to improve quality of life for terminal patients. Pain medications, other things that help with appetite for chemo patients, that sorta thing."

"So, it includes treatments *other* than medications," Father Harry asked, "perhaps things designed to relieve or reduce the physical and mental stress of an illness?"

"Yes," Phillip replied, "it states palliative *care*, so, not just medications."

Harry nodded and briefly searched for any dissension among the students. "I agree. Medical treatments are the first things that we think of, but we must also care for the psyche and the spirit of the afflicted. Is there anything in these sections that limits the qualifying palliative treatments available for use?"

"Only treatments designed to end life," Sergio surmised. "Seems like everything else is on the table, unless it conflicts with another section of the Catechism or the Scriptures."

Father Harry nodded again. "Keep that in mind as we move on to Suicide. I'm sure we all accept it as a grave and mortal sin." He opened his copy of the Catechism for reference. "22-80 explains that we are mere stewards of our lives and that God has entrusted them to us, on *loan*, rather than granting us *ownership*.

"22-81," he continued, "explains how the act violates our love of self, as well as the societal ties with all those around us. It also declares that the act undermines and corrupts our love and gratitude for the gift God's given us.

"22-82, this one is especially important," Father Harry paused and brought his text up a little closer to read it aloud. "*Those who commit suicide to encourage others to follow their example take on the grave offense of scandal.*" He glanced around at the four students to emphasize that statement's significance and then continued reading. "*Cooperating in suicide contradicts morality and risks scandal. Severe psychological ailments and certain diminished mental coping capacities such as terminal illness, suffering, or torture, can reduce one's personal responsibility for the act of committing suicide.*" Father Harry looked over his text at the four students. "So, even though God sees suicide as a grave moral offense, He loves us so that He's willing to consider the reasons for the action in our judgment.

"This next section, 22-83," the monsignor/psychologist explained, "is among my favorites because I believe it affirmatively demonstrates God's limitless mercy to those who would receive him." He resumed reading from the text. "*The faithful should refrain from concern or mourning for the eternal salvation of those who commit suicide. Through mysteries understood only by God, He offers them an opportunity for Reconciliation through his endless love and mercy. The Church beseeches God to grant eternal salvation to all who have taken their own lives.*"

Closing his text for the moment, he continued. "So, let's think of someone afflicted with a terrible, incurable psychological disturbance. Their psyche and spirit, their very soul, are so damaged that they suffer with no hope of recovery or remedy. They're otherwise in excellent *physical* health that would easily allow them to live several more decades, but they cannot endure the psychological pain and anguish forced upon them. They act to end their own life. What does God say about this matter?"

This is where he baits us with a softball question and forces us into an unexpected position, Michael thought. He answered only after a prolonged silence from his classmates. "Father, the reading seems to make it clear that God takes their reasoning into account and accordingly reduces that person's responsibility for their conduct."

"I agree, *but*," Harry quickly replied and held up a finger to draw their attention, "what might that logically mean for someone *else* who knew all that same information and reasoning. Maybe they even aid or participate in the act, or merely didn't attempt to stop the suicide itself. What might that mean for them?"

So that's where his real point was headed, Michael realized. "There's nothing that directly suggests God lessens that third-party responsibility, but, logically, I would infer that it's possible he might. Certainly, no one involved is off the hook. I suppose it might come down to the reasoning for the suicide and the third-party's involvement in it."

"Does anyone contend that it's a grave or mortal sin, under the circumstances I've outlined?"

Michael saw that no one did.

Father Harry smiled and continued. "Let's take this a step further and give you more information. What if the party's grave disturbance that's ruining his life is that he is a psychopath, specifically, a *serial killer?* He knows absolutely, with no doubt whatsoever, that trading his life and whatever resulting sin he incurs will save the lives and suffering of others. He's willing to respect the dignity of his fellow man and save *innumerable* lives by *ending his own.*"

Father Harry allowed his hypothetical scenario to breath for only a moment before he continued. "What about the serial rapist? The pedophile that knows they can never be cured, never say no, never stop the evil that they do? What if *they* choose to die instead of taking more victims, and thereby remove the evil and suffering that they brought to the earth?"

Father Harry broadly grinned, like he was pleased with himself. "Surely, God looks much more kindly upon those desperate, suffering souls, and judges them with far greater mercy and benevolence than a heartbroken lover who ends their life over a sinful affair. For even as the greatest evils bring misery and suffering to those around them, the perpetrator themselves is *absolutely* and *perpetually* accosted by their own terrors. How much suffering could have been avoided had monsters like Jeffrey Dahmer chosen to take his own life *before* his first murder? Certainly, the resulting indignities and suffering could have been prevented from touching *many hundreds* of lives."

"I would think," Alpha injected, "to answer the next, obvious question about the third party's knowledge or participation, in your circumstance, I believe God would greatly reduce the responsibility of that man, as well."

"I agree," Father Harry beamed, his point driven home. "I completely agree."

TRAINING DAY 200, 1300 HOURS_

RURAL COMPOUND. NIOBRARA COUNTY, WYOMING.

MICHAEL RETURNED from his lunch break and found Jane standing at the front of the classroom. *We're either getting another dose of CBRNE or she's here to impart her previously-asserted expertise in Masculine Humility. Maybe both.* Michael had had some training in Chemical-Biological-Radiation-Nuclear-Explosives operations while he worked for the Silver City Police Department, but Jane knew the subjects better than anyone he'd ever met. *She also taught Burglary Alarm Manipulation. Every group needs a science nerd, and she's definitely John's.*

"Good afternoon," Jane offered, and the four remaining trainees all responded in kind. "If there's no questions from the last CBRNE class, today's featured topic is chemical issues. Toxins, poisons, tranquilizers, street drugs, overdose symptoms and quantities. I'm basically gonna spend four hours making sure you never again touch unknown liquids, especially in a public venue or a target location.

"If you recall from my radiation class, your bodies have natural immuno-proteins that travel around the body and kill off rad-damaged cells. Unless you get a massive dose that overwhelms the body, you're gonna stay operational and probably live for a long time. If it does cause you problems, most'll show up as cancers decades later. So, too much rad today is *usually* a problem for tomorrow. *Time, distance,* and *shielding* will let you complete the mission. Remember that?"

"Yes, ma'am," Michael offered. Even though they weren't supposed to be formal with the instructors, he wouldn't speak to Jane like they were friends.

"Well, that's the first bad news of today's class: you have *no such mechanism* to defeat chemical poisoning or toxicity. Your liver, kidneys, and lymph nodes can try to filter bad shit outta your blood, but it's not the same thing. You might've heard the expression, '*the solution to pollution is dissolution?*' You've only got so much blood, tissue, and interstitial fluid to dissolve chemical compounds, so we're pretty easy to overwhelm. Chemicals will kill you much faster and more efficiently than just about everything else in the CBRNE world. You don't have to be close to the tanker of chlorine gas when it spills, you just have to be close *enough.* Or *downwind.* Or *downhill.* Explosions, generally, are only devastating for the people next to the device. Chemicals are more dangerous at greater distances than anything that goes *boom.*"

Jane wrote "80,000" in large numbers on the dry erase board at the front of the room. "As an example, let's look at one aspect of the atom bomb detonations in Japan in 1945. The detonation vaporized those closest to the point of impact. The shockwaves, both out and back, killed a few more. Radiation poisoning added to the body count for a short while, and cancer did the same for decades. The upper estimates for the total, combined death toll from those devices is 250,000.

"However, the International Atomic Energy Agency studied the survivors of those detonations up until the early 2000's. At that time," she pointed up at the board, "there were still more than *eighty-thousand cancer-free survivors* of those blasts. Each got a *massive* dose of radiation, all at once, but their bodies dealt with the damage, and they lived normal, healthy lives medically unaffected by 1945. Our bodies have no such ability to effectively defeat chemical toxicity.

"So, the Airport Police in Vancouver, B.C.," she continued, "recently intercepted about two-hundred grams of carfentanil, an elephant tranquilizer that's currently replacing heroin on the street drug circuit. Two-hundred grams. Less than a quarter-pound, less than four ounces by weight. But that's enough drug to *kill ten, million, people.* The population of New York City," she snapped her fingers, "gone. Radiation required two explosive devices and decades to put down a quarter-million lives. Chemistry needs a few *ounces* and about *four minutes* to stack forty-times the bodies. Pretty tremendous difference in lethality, gentlemen." Jane scanned the trainees for their response, and Michael knew she'd secured their attention.

"So, while you're soon busy doing *unknown things* in *unknown parts*," Jane offered and flashed a telling smile, "I'd like to instill a healthy fear of overdose and toxicity, and make sure you can identify the warning signs that you've been chemically comprised. Let's begin."

Michael sat and listened to the next four hours of Jane's instruction, which included street drug awareness and identification, overdose symptoms, prescription medication abuse and overdose, and toxins and poisons used by secular governments against the Enemies of their State. *Kinda funny,* Michael thought, *the double-edged sword of information is that someone can always use it for unintended purposes. Probably not a coincidence, though, that we discussed God's view on assisted suicide and opioid overdose limits on the same day.*

When her training session finished, Jane said goodnight and left the room, as she'd typically done, but didn't dismiss them back to the main house. As she strode to the back door, John and Father Harry entered, exchanged knowing glances with Jane, and continued to the front of the room. *Here comes trouble,* Michael thought.

"Good evening, shitheads," John gruffly greeted them. "I'm as excited to see you right now as I'm certain you are to see me. Turns out, your day ain't over yet, so gimme your full-and-undivided.

"We're startin' the next phase of the program," John explained, "and you'll soon know what your respective assignments are gonna be. In the meantime, we're sending ya off tonight to parts unknown to await further instructions. Over the comin' weeks, y'all are goin' out on individual field problems, training scenarios all set in different cities. Under the watchful eye of the rest of my training staff, who're all unknown to you, you'll complete assignments in unfamiliar environments around unfamiliar people. Each one becomes more complex and demanding than the last. This'll be the final phase of your training before you're ready to be promoted up for whatever work God has in store for you.

"So, for right now," John continued, with his hands on his hips, "I want you to study all the class notes you want. Memorize everything you can, because as soon as we're done here tonight, you're gonna step to the back of the room and run every scrap of paper through a shredder while we watch. Then, you're gonna dump your little desktop milk crate and its contents into a burn bag that won't survive the night. Take nothing but your clothes from this room.

John glanced down at his watch. "It's 18:14. You boys got two hours to study and get your shit destroyed. Flights leave before midnight, and ya won't be back for a while. Some of you may *never* come back, but that's up to you. Everything's voluntary, and it pays to be a winner, gentlemen. Get to it."

TRAINING DAY 220, 0804 HRS_

RURAL COMPOUND. NIOBRARA COUNTY, WYOMING.

It's almost like I never left, Michael thought as he knelt on his worn towel while Father Harry delivered mass. *Everything's the same, if everything wasn't so different. After playing spy games all over the country for three weeks, my reward for success is to come back to this shithole. It's like "90 Minutes in Heaven." I've seen what waits on the other side and I don't wanna be here anymore. If my assignment's gonna be anything like the last twenty days, I'm about to walk into the greatest job God ever made.*

At the end of the service, Father Harry made an unusual addition to the celebration. "Let us conclude with Saint Michael's prayer," he offered and bowed his head. Michael did the same, and, from memory, recited the prayer aloud with his colleagues. "Amen."

After Father Harry concluded the mass, Michael ritualistically offered comfort and well wishes to those around him, which included John, who'd joined them fifteen minutes prior.

"Andrew," John called out, "Father Harry and I gotta meet with you. All the rest-a you, make yourselves comfortable and don't go nowhere. We'll be back for each-a you soon enough."

Michael followed Father Harry and John to the same bedroom that Harry had used for their recurring psych evals. An equal mix of apprehension and excitement filled Michael as he sat in his usual seat. *It's not useful for me to be here anymore. I wanna go relive the last three weeks, over and over again, but with real targets and real purpose.*

John sat on the couch opposite Michael and close to Father Harry. "First off," he announced, "*relax. You're done. You made it.* You're moving on with us, and we have a place for you to serve God and His people in an exceptionally rare manner. Most of my graduates take assignments in intelligence, analysis, diplomatic services and security, or close-protection for the Holy See's dignitaries and distinguished guests. Very few get the chance being offered to you right now."

"Some of the other guys," John patiently explained, "they're goin' to those other roles, but you've been invited to join a highly specialized organization that operates under the oversight and guidance of the Holy See Intelligence Services. You're a man of very useful and rare skills, and I've never seen anyone that could be so creative and still stay in-bounds, at least in terms of your ethics, obligations, and vows. Even with your early disregard for what I believed were tacit and *known* boundaries, I'd like to see you in this position. I'd like to know that you're standing watch and helping keep the wolves at bay for one more night. The thought brings me comfort, and, at my age, I'm in desperate need of it."

"I'm humbled and flattered," Michael stammered and took control of himself. "But, what's the assignment?"

"We're gonna get there in baby steps," John explained, "just in case you decide along the way it's not for you. Reason for that, the organization you'd work in, it doesn't *officially* exist. Not on any document; not on any budget request or on any email server. It can only be found in the very shadows where Satan and his demons live and breathe. Your oversight would be limited to the few like yourself, the ones unafraid to do the ugly work necessary to protect God's people from the evils that walk among us, hidin' in plain sight. Op-Sec is exceptionally important here, and almost *no one* in the Church is 'need to know.'"

"As part of this organization," John continued, "you will take our centuries-old spiritual war directly to the demons that infect God's children. You will use everything we taught you, along with your investigations experience from before, and you'll work in solitude to combat the greatest threats mankind's ever known. Every morning, you'll recite Laud in anticipation of making tangible accomplishments that day, followed each night with Compline and the intrinsic satisfaction of havin' actually stopped evil. The world will be a measurably better place because of your sacrifices, and all mankind will enjoy an ever-improving relationship and understanding of God and His mysteries, even though no one'll ever know the debt they owe you.

"Now, for the bad news," John offered and leaned forward with his elbows on his knees. "I'm the one that's in charge of the operations, so you ain't gettin' ridda me by takin' this assignment. If anything, we're gonna get to know each other a helluva lot better'n we do now. I'm recommending you for this posting with some reservations, though, Andrew. Think of this as a probationary period. The tests are over, and there's nothing else that you need to worry about passing, you only need to worry about staying in-bounds and not failing, if that makes sense."

Michael leaned forward and matched John's posture and body language. *Helps convey sincerity.* "I understand the reservations, John, and I have a much better grasp now of what my role and place are. I appreciate any opportunity to do the tough work that God requires of me."

"I'm glad you feel that way. When I was asked to start up this program, the deal I struck was that I'd stay in charge of the operations, personnel, and ongoing training. I didn't wanna train y'all up, polish you to a high shine, and then hand you off to some *jack-wagon* that didn't know *shit* from *shy-nola.* So, even if you don't like me, you gotta be able to trust me. I said on Day One that I'm not your daddy, your uncle, or your friend. I can be a mentor, but, mostly, I'm your boss, your trainer, and I'm the one that's responsible for everything you *do* and everything you *fail* to do. So, I have the final and last word on how long you're here and what you're assigned to do. We clear? Any concerns so far?"

Michael slightly shook his head. "No, none." *I don't need time to decide, if he'd just tell me what I'd actually be doing. This might be everything I've wanted and feared.* "It's all, really, *incredible,* John. I'm interested, but I still don't actually know what I'm committing to."

Father Harry and John looked at one another. Harry nodded as though showing John his agreement.

Or giving him permission, Michael thought.

"If you're gonna make me sound out the big words for ya," John facetiously paraphrased an earlier statement, "then I'm offering you an assignment as an *absolver*, and it's exactly what it sounds like. The veterinarian's office has that one guy that's got the gumption and intestinal fortitude to humanely put down all the animals that's too sick to carry on. The pope and the Holy See? They've got absolvers. When they asked for my opinion, you're the first one I recommended.

"If you wanna think about it," John continued, "I understand, but I'll need an answer in the next couple hours, and not a minute longer. This opportunity won't ring twice, and you can *only* get there from *here,* where you are right now."

Michael had fantasized about working for the Catholic equivalent of the CIA but, now unexpectedly found himself squeamish with the secrecy John described. "I'd still be working for the Church, for the Holy See, though, right?"

"The Church?" John rhetorically asked. "That's just one part of the Holy See, Andrew, and most-a them don't know what's what. It's not fair to say that we work for 'the Church,' because that implies common knowledge and acceptance of what *we* know must be done. It's more accurate to say that you're gonna be working *with* the Church, with its most enlightened members that God's entrusted with a deeper understanding of His mysteries. You'll be takin' advantage of its hierarchy, global reach, and resources, but, no, the local friar ain't gonna ever know you exist or what you do. Op-Sec, right?"

Father Harry leaned forward and interjected. "We're headed toward the End Times, Andrew, we all know it and feel it, deep in our souls. Could be tomorrow, more likely a few years, perhaps even a few generations away. The more time we have to prepare, the more effective our work can be. If you were to start eliminating the devil's spawn from this Earth today, and you had a few years, decades, maybe a generation or two to continue that work in various forms, how much *difference* could you make on behalf of God's people? How much good work could we accomplish with dozens of 'Andrews,' or a whole covert army of apostolic 'demon snipers' in this spiritual campaign? That's what you've got the opportunity to do, if you want it. Starting right now."

If God's put this in front of me, Michael thought, *then it must be my purpose to take it on.* "I'll do it. When do I leave?"

John smiled and knocked twice on the coffee table between them. "Good on ya. Now, with that settled, let's get into some details. Logistically, much of *what* we do and *how* we do it is heavily compartmentalized to protect all of us from hell-inspired betrayal and outsiders. Basically, what you need to understand to do your job is that our intelligence apparatus collects information from all over the globe. Priests, monsignors, nuns, all the cooperating members of the clergy are critical sources of new intel for us. When they learn of particularly heinous sin, they pass that info along. Analysts and desk-nerds help run that down until we identify a single source, an especially flawed human soul. After it's determined all other options have failed, or *will fail,* because they're beyond God's other methods of rehabilitation, we recommend a 'final absolution.'

"Despite the confidence we have in our collection and analysis methods," John continued, "we still demand that the individual absolver begins by corroborating the existence and severity of the alleged sins. There can be no other way. We must have that final safety valve to ensure we don't send God a soul we could've otherwise fixed."

"You and the few like you," Father Harry interjected, "you are the greatest weapons God has given us in the very real-life combat against Satan and his armies. You will make swift and immediate impact on the safety and welfare of God's children and dwindle the numbers of souls saturated with evil. I'm proud that you've been accepted to this clandestine program, Andrew, and I know that God will do great things through you."

"Thank you, Father."

"The most important aspect, especially for your long-term success," Father Harry offered, "is to always remember your very specific distinctions from a 'murderer' or a 'killer.' You're an *absolver,* and there's an insurmountable moral divide between those three. You will investigate accusations from victims who have come forward with *no hope* of direct intervention. They want to be heard, guided, and counseled by our clergy, not avenged. John will only send you on assignments that involve a few, narrow areas of human failings that cannot be altered, changed, or rehabilitated, the rare and absolutely true evils: the pedophiles, rapists, mass murderers, serial killers, and the like. No one else will ever have reason to fear you darkening their doorstep, even if they somehow knew of your existence. All other sins and crime fall to secular courts and confessional booths. They're not our domain or our purpose."

Father Harry cleared his throat and continued. "Once assigned a target, you will search for objective, independent evidence that corroborates or dismisses the allegations, all of which will be rooted directly in scriptures and the Catechism. You will either find the evidence and move toward a final absolution, or you won't. In that case, John will ensure that no further action is taken against that target without new or additional information. They've, in effect, been acquitted without even knowing they've been accused."

John leaned forward and excitedly added his thoughts. "The folks you're gonna be called to *serve,* because that's really what we're doin', is *helpin' them* receive a one-time chance at eternal salvation. Absolving these folks of their sin, cleansing their souls, by itself, anyway, is about as effective as washin' an ashtray. They gonna be tarnished in another few minutes, and they'll never stay clean long enough to matter. That's where you come in."

John cleared his throat and continued. "One of the most important op-sec considerations to this whole thing, this *absolution* and *last rites*, is that you will only ever engage and reveal yourself to the accused *after* you have found irrefutable evidence that absolutely corroborates their alleged sins. Cops and detectives, investigators, they can walk up to anyone at any time and ask questions about alleged actions. It doesn't matter because everyone knows *who* the police are and *what* they're about. No one outside this room can *ever* know about you, about what you do, and the important role you play for God and to His children."

"In the course of your assigned tasks," Father Harry offered, "no one but the subject of your inquiry can ever learn of your role. Should anyone *not* in dire need of immediate and righteous absolution know about you, you have failed and put all our work and effort at risk. You will have exposed the entire program and God's work to the world. Despite the problem such a revelation would cause, you cannot *ever* become a murderer, and that is exactly what would be required to keep our secrets at that moment. We are *not* murderers, and never will be."

"However," John redirected the conversation, "when you *do* find corroborating evidence, the truly important work will begin. You'll need to get the target alone, incapacitate them, and keep 'em isolated with the evidence for the remainder of the ritual. You'll interrogate them and give 'em a chance to come clean and meet God with an open heart and a pure soul. Hear their confession and contrition. Absolve them of their sins, anoint them, and then, *relieve their soul* of its mortal shell. Pray that God accepts their soul into his divine and perfect kingdom of heaven, in spite of the eternal damnation they otherwise deserved, if not for your actions."

Michael sat awestruck. *Is this real? Can I really do this?* He considered all the training and skills he'd acquired over the last two decades in light of the tasks laid before him. *Now it all makes sense, why John made us succeed in* all *the training topics. Son of a bitch. Even the benign classes like Ethics were preparing me for this assignment. Some of the others should've been giveaways. Not many people but dog catchers need to know how to use tranquilizer guns.* Michael smiled and sat up a little straighter without realizing he'd done so.

"By absolving them of their sins and immediately killing their *mortal* body," Father Harry reiterated, "you're giving their *immortal* soul its one and only chance to *ever* enter the Kingdom of God and spend eternity in the warmth of God's love. The only other path available to them is the eternal fire and damnation of Hell. You alone can spare them from that. Despite the evil that Satan has infected them with, God *wants* them to be cleansed, to be absolved, and join Him in Heaven, just as the prodigal son. He has appointed you to that sacred task."

John leaned back on the couch before he spoke. "You also gotta ensure they understand their sins will be revealed to the world after their departure. For their absolution to stick, the remorse in their heart must be genuine. They hafta understand the pain and suffering they've inflicted on others will not go unknown on Earth. They *must* know their victims will get help, and that their sins and crimes will be identified. That is your opportunity to identify additional victims no one else knows about. Who else have they harmed that's in need-a help or recovery? Who else needs to understand God loves and cares about them, and that the crimes and sin committed against them were borne from evil, *not* of an unjust, uncaring, or unloving God?"

Father Harry nodded his agreement. "Every absolution has the potential to bring love, forgiveness, and closure to scores of other lives, and help restore the dignity God always intended them to have. Then, only after they've decided how to spend their eternity, you will end their mortal life. You will sever the tie between their mind, body, and spirit and, in the process, you'll immediately ensure the safety of dozens, maybe hundreds, of unknown and future victims from the indignity of the unjust aggressor."

In affirmative response, Michael somberly combined and paraphrased a few Catechism sections. "The defense of the common good *requires us* to render the unjust aggressor *harmless.* Once accepted, their punishment defends the public and revives their soul. I see no better way to fulfill those holy obligations, Father."

Both men look relieved, and John nodded before he spoke. "How do you feel about your pseudonym?"

Michael shrugged. "Haven't really thought about it. I guess it's nice being named after the first apostle, but I don't have the weight or pressure of living up to Saint Peter or Paul, I suppose."

"Good, cause you're keepin' it," John replied. "It's just a matter of time until someone like you ends up on the evening news tryin' to work out a deal to avoid prosecution in exchange for tellin' the whole world about this rogue band of killer priests 'the Church' has gallivanting all over the world. As much as we talk about God bringin' you into his prison mission, not everyone has the gumption to stay that particular course. Nice thing for us, though, *Andrew,"* he offered and spread his arms out wide in disbelief, "is who'd ever believe this shit is real, anyway, right? I mean, we have the perfect cover story to do everything necessary to save mankind. But so help me God, if you do try to offer up your comrades to save yourself, I hope I get sent to the same shithole so I can get just a few minutes alone with you. Can't abide a traitor, especially one that's sworn an oath to God and His servants. Keep that in mind if you ever find yourself in a dark hole desperately seeking Earthly salvation."

Michael confidently held eye contact with his instructor and dismissed the necessity of his dark warning. *Can't take this asshole's behavior personally.* "Not an issue, John. Everything happens for a reason, even incarceration."

"You ever offered last rites before," John pointedly asked.

"Just the one time," Michael replied, "and it wasn't strictly on-script."

John grimaced in reaction to the admission. "Spend the time necessary to ensure you've got the ritual down pat. That's the most important part of the whole thing. Takin' a life without absolvin' its soul is no better'n a killin', and might even be a *murder*, no matter how much society benefits from the absence of the departed."

TRAINING DAY 220, 1135 HOURS_

RURAL COMPOUND. NIOBRARA COUNTY, WYOMING.

ONLY A FEW HOURS after learning the nature of his assignment, Michael again sat at the far right side of the classroom's banquet table. The other three candidates, now all graduates, sat to his left. John stood before them with only some handwritten notes and his reading glasses. No one else from the instructor cadre was present. Michael shared in his classmates' jovial mood, just like every other graduation he'd experienced. This one, though, had been sprung on them, which made it seem more electric than all those scheduled well in advance with a specific date, time, and location. Given all the struggles and hardships they'd endured during the past seven months, Michael thought they'd earned a bit of frivolity. *Reindeer games, I think John'd call them.*

John cleared his throat to draw their attention, which ended all conversation in the room. "First off, gentlemen, I am exceptionally proud of all that you've accomplished here in a very short time. I figure your experience here at my vacation Bible study was different from anything you imagined, but I also hope it turned out to be everything you dreamed. Some of you came to the table with relevant experience, and you weren't big enough assholes to keep that to yourself, even though I first demanded that you not treat this as a team-sport environment. There's a lot of background information that I gotta share before we start shippin' you off, and there's a lot more that you'll never be privy to, unless you someday find yourself takin' this over from me. That gives me a lotta goddamned heartburn now, just thinkin' that one of you could try to fill my size elevens, but, shit, that's life and I can't keep this up forever.

"The first thing that I need to do, now that I've given you all your goddamned pat on the back, is to remind you that your skillset is fairly limited. The key to your success and longevity will be to realize your own limitations. Regardless of the assignment for which you've been chosen, you're not a buncha Mossad, C-I-A, or F-S-B operatives. You're not the Navy SEALs, or Combat Application Group, or whatever Delta's callin' themselves these days. You don't have their same depth and breadth of training. Not tryin' to demean or lessen the significance of the holy work you'll be doing, but no one's spendin' their all-day-every-day chasin' you. We've imparted you with the skills to protect God's children and pursue evil, but none-a y'all are gonna have spec-ops folks huntin' you in the night, so we didn't bother trainin' you up to that capacity. It's an important point, and I want y'all to stick to the skills we taught you, and the way that we taught you to operate. If you leave here and promptly go off the reservation, you're gonna be dead or imprisoned before you know it. You're a buncha badasses, I'll give you that, but ain't none of you shitheads in here that's James Bond, Master Chief, or Jason fuckin' Bourne.

"Now," John continued, "one thing I don't mind sharing at this point is that my program is the first of its kind, and you're my first graduating class, if you wanna call it that. There is not another group of men like you on the face of the Earth, at least not yet, but gimme another year and I'll probably change that. There's plenty with your training, many of them's got far superior skills because of the particular prey that they're after or that's chasin' them. They're not goin' after the gutter urchins that you are, they're going after, well, men like you who've chosen to play for the wrong team. So, congratulations on being the first. You're goin' out to do critical work and I'll sleep much better at night when I got a lot more-a you out there."

Alpha half-raised his hand and nodded at John. "One question, please, John. I understand we may have different roles and assignments, but, what are we? I mean, what do we call ourselves, as graduates of your training?"

"Nothin'," John frowned and replied. "You call yourselves *nothin'*."

"Like, we're the Nothing Squad?"

John put his hands on his hips and shook his head. "No, there isn't a name, official or *otherwise*, for you all, and there never will be." He began pacing around the front of the room as he spoke, obviously worked up by the topic. "What's 'O-G-A' mean to you, Andrew?"

"Uhh, 'Other Governmental Agency?'"

"Yep. What about you, Jude?"

With John singling Sergio out, Michael inferred that he was the only one with a military background. *Wonder what Alpha and Phillip did to get here, then...*

"John, that's just another acronym for C-I-A."

"Goddamned right," John confirmed. "Their stupid-ass spooks run all over the world identifying themselves as O-G-A, but they're doing C-I-A shit, and everyone knows they're C-I-A! They ruined it by giving themselves a *name*, that's all it took was just a goddamned name, even though it's bullshit! As soon as you assholes start callin' yourselves somethin', some reporter's gonna start stickin' their nose around Saint Peter's Square askin' about 'The Order,' or 'The Vengeance Brigade,' or whatever stupid-ass name you millennials came up with! So, no, there's no name, never gonna be a name. If I don't give you somethin' to repeat to other priests, or girlfriends, or boyfriends, or bartenders, or anyone else you wanna impress with just how goddamned cool you are, you got less chance to violate the op-sec! Jesus! You got me all worked up!" John paced a bit more but came to rest near the middle of the banquet table again. "That clear enough for you, Alpha?"

"Yessir, we're nothing, but I did kinda like that one, 'The Vengeance Brigade,'" Alpha joked, "do you mind if we, just *between us*—"

"Screw you and your goddamned jokes. Moving on," John replied and glanced back at his notes. "You probably noticed you're keeping your pseudonyms. That won't change. I've beat op-sec and compartmentalization to death, so, no more on that. When somethin' goes sideways one day, and rest assured that it will, you'll all be grateful for the anonymity.

"Next, we need to talk about technical logistics," John continued. "In the modern era, it's better for us to go high-tech than low, so you're all gettin' a smartphone today that continuously runs a V-P-N in the background and a VOIP phone number. Never communicate with your chain of command by anything else.

"Related to the tech bullshit," John sighed, "is that your constant V-P-N allows us to do shit like set up Estonian bank accounts for each of you, in your pseudonyms, of course. That's where you'll get paid and access your own money, as well as an operational expense account, all without ever settin' foot in a bank or having to explain your assets to the I-R-S." John glanced over at Alpha and grimaced. "Or whatever their equivalent is in, *well,* wherever the hell you're from." He grimaced at his narrowly-avoided op-sec error.

"What about our current bank accounts and direct deposits," Phillip asked. "If we give those up, won't someone, somewhere, maybe realize we've gone off the payroll at our respective archdiocese?"

"You're probably gonna take this as the good news that it is, but you'll have to keep those accounts and paychecks for that very reason, so, the Estonia money will be additional, supplemental income."

Michael leaned back and put his hand up to draw their trainer's attention. "How much, *supplemental income,* are we talkin' about, John? Not that I'm greedy, or have to have the money, but, you know, I thought, while we were on the topic—"

"A hundred kay."

Michael nearly fell over in the flimsy chair. "Like, wow, a hundred, thousand. Like, a onetime payment, you mean, right?"

"Nope. Every year. The Church is gonna pay you a hundred thousand dollars every year that you continue in your assignments, and forty thousand dollars every year after you're done."

I can pay for mom's treatments in cash after just a few years, Michael thought. A lump formed in his throat and his eyes welled with tears. Michael swallowed hard to fight them back.

"I argued for more," John explained, "given how marketable the skills and training you have are, but the higher-ups already thought that was highway robbery. They wanted you to keep that priestly pittance and take on all this risk and trouble for the glorification of God. I finally got 'em to realize you boys might need some other motivation to stay in their employ and keep all this to yourselves one day. It was the best-goddamned compromise I could work out, so I hope that's enough."

"Damn, John, I don't think any of us expected that, and, honestly," Sergio offered, "I really don't think it's gonna be necessary—"

"It is, and you will, someday," John explained. "Trust me on this. There will be points in this shitty job that you're gonna need new and different motivations to keep on goin'. Right now, you're all jazzed and lit up cause you feel like you accomplished somethin'. You're idealists. In a year, you'll need to find new meaning in this work. In five years, you'll stay for the paycheck and the retirement that'll let you get away from most all the people you've ever met. A decade from now, you'll be goddamned lucky to be upright and vertical, and won't give a shit about any of it. Trust me, gentlemen, it sounds like a lot of money because y'all took vows of poverty, and I encourage you to continue to live like that as long as you can. There'll come a day when you're gonna need every dollar you can drum up to escape with your sanity and, maybe, just maybe, find some peace before you leave this world. Give the rest to whatever charity's gonna help you sleep at night.

"I did the same work for a long time," John explained, "much longer than most, and the only difference between me and you is that I worked for a secular government, and I never knew much of the reason for the work itself. I was just as ideologically devoted to my master and my purpose as you are to yours. I got a target and a timeframe, and I came through, time and again. You've got the benefit of knowing why you're doing what you're doing, but it's still the same job. So, while I hope y'all enjoy a different outcome, I expect you'll eventually walk down the same roads me and all my asshole compatriots did. For that reason, I made sure you had some sorta parachute ready when you decide you need it. Nobody ever did that for me or my friends, and I wasn't gonna help put this program together without providin' some assurances."

The room fell silent for a moment, as all of them considered the gravity of John's words.

"One hundred thousand U-S, every year," Alpha slowly announced. "I might end up with my own Pope-mobile golf cart." Even John chuckled.

"Don't blow it all in one brothel, boys," their instructor advised. "We mighta hid it from the alphabet group 'I-R-S,' but you oughta look into puttin' it into 'E-T-F,' my friends. It'll let you do a lot more good one day when your conscience needs it." John looked down at his notes. "Back to business on the V-P-N thing. We gotta assume every communication other than snail mail and face-to-face is recorded, logged, and searchable. If anyone can put your face and your data at the scene of an investigation, that's when shit goes south for us. Proximity and facial recognition lead to your actual identity, which becomes The Nightly News with Tom Brokaw, and Most Wanted fliers in every goddamned post office in the civilized world."

Sergio smirked as he ribbed their trainer. "I think Brokaw's off the air, John."

"Yeah," Michael added, "I think he left in, like, 2004, something like that."

John looked between the two in frustration. "I just said that whole goddamned thing, all that relevant need-to-know intel, and all you bastards care about is that I haven't watched N-B-C since Brokaw left? You stupid sons-uh-bitches all got chips on your shoulders now that you passed, and think it's time to poke back at Old Man John, now, right?" All four men chuckled at their trainer as he continued his feigned tirade. "Got news for you, I'm gonna send all-a you shitheads back to day one, week one, and see who's still around six months from *now*! I bet I only turn around about twice, and there won't be anybody left standin' but me!"

"See, John, now I'm confused," Michael jokingly offered. "Do you wanna recycle us and make us drop out, or do you wanna fight us right here, I'm very unclear."

John pretended to lunge toward Michael, then dropped his facade and laughed at his own mistake. "I think I hate you most, Andrew, you're just the goddamned worst, and I'm lookin' forward to not seeing your ugly mug around here anymore." He cleared his throat, adopted a more somber tone, and scanned the room for the very few seconds required to bring them all back to the business at hand. "Pressin' on. For each of your assignments, you'll get an intel packet. Sometimes, it might be with a church official, but, mostly, it'll be waiting for you on the plane. It's gonna be—"

Phillip raised his hand as he spoke, and Michael saw genuine confusion on his face. "Sorry, John, I apologize, there's a plane? What plane? Like Delta planes?"

"Phillip, you might not be smart enough for this shit after all. How the hell did you think you were gonna get delivered to the assignments? Carrier pigeon?"

"Actually, Phillip," Sergio joined in, "the African Swallow's the original overseas freight delivery service."

"But nothing bigger than coconuts, I think," Michael added.

"Team effort, right," Sergio replied, "they each grab a side?"

"You assholes done?" John either didn't understand the reference or chose to ignore its humor. "Yes, Phillip, 'there's planes.' Which is actually a decent tangent into another critical part of this. The intel packet will be in a diplomatic 'Eyes Only' pouch that only you will know the combination to. The contents'll be a mix of open-source intel, like local currency, local news, areas of concern or instability in the region. Local customs, especially of the reigning bishop and churches, any known areas of sanctuary. Finally, it'll have the identity and location of your contact at a local church or cathedral as well as operational details and intel analysis of your target."

"John, one more question," Sergio asked. "How do we get access to a diplomatic pouch?"

"That's what I've gotta discuss next, if you'd exercise some goddamned patience. Man, I tell you, ever since y'all found out that you've successfully negotiated my training program, you're like a buncha goddamned high school kids on the last day of school! I swear to God, y'all's tryin' my patience today." He sighed, grimaced, and scanned the small group. "This is probably just gonna make things worse, but the reason y'all get access to a diplomatic pouch is that you'll be traveling with diplomatic immunity, so—"

"*Diplo-matic ee-mun-i-teee!*" Michael impersonated his favorite *Lethal Weapon* villain. All but John laughed along with him.

"That's it," the instructor called out and waved his arms, "y'all need some goddamned miles to get this shit outta your system! Get the hell outta here, and don't come back without five more on your chit!"

Still laughing and enjoying their moment of accomplishment, Sergio repeated the impersonation but also held his hand up to mimic displaying his credentials. "Diplo—"

"*Goddammit,*" John exclaimed. "Make it an hour, and you'd best have a shitload of miles under your belts by then!"

Despite the inconvenient punishment, Michael and his colleagues smiled at their new status but didn't dare further antagonize John. They hurried out of the classroom, ran back out onto the trails, and picked up their collective pace to get out of earshot as soon as possible.

"We far enough yet?" Sergio asked the group.

Still running forward, Michael looked back and determined they were now at least three-hundred yards away from the closest structure. "Yeah, go ahead!" The group slowed but continued jogging, and all eyes fell onto Sergio as he brought his "credentials" back up.

"DIPLO-MATIC EE-MUN-I-TEEEEE!"

TUESDAY, 1835 HOURS_

SOUTHBOUND I-25. LONGMONT, COLORADO.

Michael had only a vague idea of what to expect from the coming days. He sat in the front passenger seat of a black Lincoln Towncar behind dark-tinted windows while John drove and Father Harry kept watch on him from the back seat. *Odd.*

Michael replayed the morning's events in his mind, looking for some additional kernel of intel he'd missed as it had happened. John and Father Harry had met again with him upstairs after the graduates had returned from their disciplinary run. They'd provided him with clothing similar to John's associates' uniform: green plaid button-down shirt, boot-cut Wrangler jeans, and brown packer-style cowboy boots, all of it in his correct sizes. He'd initially been told nothing more than to be ready to leave immediately after the None prayers, and that he needed only bring himself and keep the trip entirely confidential. Sergio had been called upstairs very soon after that but hadn't returned. As his friend's personal items remained in place, Michael assumed he'd gotten similar orders with a more immediate departure. *Eight months after I started all this, and we're finally operational.*

John exited the freeway at its intersection with Colorado Highway 66 and continued west. After they eventually turned south on 75th Street, he saw a sign for an airport and assumed that was their destination. John proved his inference correct when he entered the airport complex and parked the dark sedan next to a large, closed hangar. *And where from there?*

"Go ahead and grab your bag. We're meetin' your plane inside," John explained and nodded toward the adjacent hangar.

Michael complied without responding. After retrieving his borrowed black nylon duffel bag and the contents John packed for him, Michael followed his instructor into the large hangar while Father Harry stayed a few steps behind him. *Are they looking at their positions as a dignitary protection detail to keep me from harm, or is this a prisoner escort to my court appearance? Getting hard to tell the difference.*

John led them through a pedestrian door just a few feet away from their sedan and held it for Michael and Father Harry. As Michael stepped into the hangar, he saw it was completely dark inside. The ambient autumn light from the open door only allowed him to see that the few square feet of space around him offered no trip hazards. Father Harry stopped and stood in place, so Michael did the same. *He seems to know what's going on, so I'll play along for now.* John then closed and locked the door behind them. *Definitely feels like a prisoner escort now.*

click

As soon as Michael heard the light switch, powerful overhead LEDs at the hangar's tall ceiling bathed the space in near-daylight. Michael realized he stood on the right side of a shiny Learjet that faced out toward the secure, wide hangar door. *Looks like the same jet that brought me home from Columbia, just without the Seal of the Holy See on its tail. Surely, it's a charter, how many of these can the Church possibly own?*

Two uniformed men, apparently the pilot and co-pilot, emerged from the far side of the plane to greet them. *Were they just sitting inside a dark aircraft?*

"Evening, boys," John called out, "we'll be with ya in a few minutes." Both men waved to acknowledge their implied directive, and quietly disappeared back around the front of the plane.

"All this private charter flight is going to ruin commercial travel for you," Father Harry offered and smiled.

"This is your first assignment as an absolver, Andrew," John explained, "and this one's a helluva lot more critical than most. You understand how imperative our op-sec and compartmentalization are, so I'm not gonna say any more about that. What I *am* gonna say is that you're flyin' to Midland, Texas, to pay a visit to Father Bullard at Saint Paul's Church in Pecos, another town to the east along I-20. You gotta meet him before midnight tonight. Once you land, there's a rented pick-up waiting for you in the airport parking lot. The keys are in the plane, and you'll find cash in the truck's ashtray to pay the parking fees. Questions?"

Thousands, Michael thought. "Nothing critical, John."

"I know you'll figure out what needs to be done over there. You'll have to carry out the Vesper prayers on the flight over. Father," John called out to Harry, "can you lead us in Saint Michael's prayer to send this young man off to battle?"

"Of course," the monsignor replied. All three men knelt down on the floor and bowed their heads.

Michael dropped his duffel on the cement floor next to his right knee. He closed his eyes and inhaled deeply.

"Saint Michael the Archangel, defend us in battle," Father Harry beseeched, "be our defense against the wickedness and snares of the devil. May God rebuke him, we humbly pray; and do you, O prince of the heavenly host, by the power of God, thrust into hell Satan and the other evil spirits who prowl about the world for the ruin of souls. Amen."

Michael exhaled and rose with his superiors. "Anything else before I go?"

"Just remember that it pays to be a winner," John replied and shook Michael's hand.

Meeting his trainers' eye contact, Michael saw a number of emotions in John's gaze. He wondered how much their occasionally-adversarial relationship affected whatever was going through the man's mind at that moment.

"Peace be with you," Father Harry offered as Michael and John released each other's grip.

"And with your spirit," Michael replied. Father Harry didn't offer his hand, so Michael retrieved his bag instead and confidently strode toward the other side of the waiting plane. Just as he stepped around the nose, he looked back and saw John intently watching him. *No telling what that man's thinking at any given moment.*

Michael stepped up to the hatch and boarded the eight-passenger jet.

He hunched over just slightly to walk inside and realized the passenger compartment was again empty. Glancing into the cockpit, he made eye contact with the co-pilot, who rose from his seat and came out to greet him.

"Good evening, Father. We'll be underway to Cincinnati in just a moment."

Michael stopped in surprise. "Cincinnati?"

"Yes," he nodded his head, "at least initially. The flight plan will be changed en route, Father, but not until we leave Denver Center."

"I'm sorry, what's 'Denver Center?'"

"Sorry, pilot jargon. Most people think air traffic control towers handle all the in-flight radar monitoring and flight plans, but really, it's the Centers. Towers just handle the landings and take-offs. So, we'll start out with Denver and transition to Kansas City Center, and that's when we'll file the change to our flight plan. We understand that privacy is of the utmost importance for you."

"Yes, it is," Michael confirmed with relief in his voice. "Thank you for your discretion."

"Certainly, Father. Can I get you anything to make you more comfortable before we taxi?"

"No, I'm fine, thank you." Michael looked at the eight plush, tan leather seats and considered where to sit. *Normally, I'd always go Doc Holliday and sit with my back to a wall, but that'd look awfully paranoid and antisocial for a run-of-the-mill priest, especially one who's in a hurry. No, the front row is better. I can probably trust that John and the flight crew don't have an elaborate scheme to murder me at thirty-thousand-feet.* The co-pilot first closed the hatch and then the cockpit door, and left Michael sitting alone in the opulent cabin.

Michael spied a black plastic Pelican case next to his seat as they began taxiing. A quick, further glance revealed "Eyes Only – Diplomatic Pouch" written in both English and Italian on its top surface. He waited until the plane was airborne and slowing its steep takeoff ascent before he retrieved the case, which was slightly smaller than a standard messenger bag. The combination locks opened when he input the code John had prescribed, "2270." Its thick, protected lid opened to reveal a single manila envelope that held only two items: a set of Chevy keys and matching remote key fob, and a Post-it note with "F 3 9" written on it. *Guess the Chevy's parked at F39,* he surmised. *Hope that makes more sense in Midland than it does right now.* Michael placed the keyring in his pocket, and the note and envelope went into his duffel bag. He locked the Pelican case back and replaced it next to his seat. *No idea who collects and distributes the cases, and I bet John makes sure I never do.*

Content he wouldn't acquire any further intel on the plane, Michael submersed himself in meditation. He recited a Vespers prayer and sought the guidance, strength, and resolve he assumed would be necessary in the next few days. As he opened his eyes and exhaled his metaphorical stress, the plane gently banked right, and the in-cabin speakers came on.

"Father, we're turning south and are now en route to Midland International Air and Space Port in Texas, as requested."

"Thank you," Michael loudly replied, unsure if they could hear him or not. He glanced out the windows and saw mostly clear skies all around them. *Looks like an excellent evening for flying.* Settling back into his seat, Michael stayed internally focused until the announcement of their imminent landing in Midland.

After a short taxi, the plane stopped next to a small hangar, and the cabin's interior lights came on. The co-pilot stepped from the cockpit and opened the exterior hatch. The pilot emerged to greet Michael as he shouldered the strap of his duffel bag.

"Father, it's been a pleasure having you aboard. We look forward to serving you again one day. Peace be with you."

"And with your spirit," Michael replied and stepped toward the doorway. He stopped there for a moment while the co-pilot made some adjustment to the stairs. A small, subdued image caught Michael's eye on the left side of the doorway. Michael looked at it more closely but tried not to indicate he did so. There, embossed in the leather trim around the doorway, was the Seal of the Holy See.

This wasn't just a charter flight, Michael realized, *this is another Vatican plane. The final confirmation I needed that I'm really where I'm supposed to be.* Unlike the Learjet that had brought him back from Bogotá, this one hadn't displayed anything related to the Holy See on its exterior. *I wonder what the reason could be for that...*

"All set, Father," the co-pilot announced, "sorry for the delay."

"It's no trouble, at all. Everything happens for a reason," Michael explained and glanced at the seal once more before stepping off the plane. "Thank you for your help. Peace be with you."

"And with your spirit, Father."

As soon as he passed into the small terminal, Michael worked to blend in with the clusters of passengers from the regularly scheduled commercial flights. *Now I just have to look and act like everyone else around me. The first time that I leave a conversation with 'Peace be with you,' though, I'm gonna be remembered forever.* To ensure no one followed him, he made stops at several vendors and two restrooms before doubling back through a portion of the terminal. Satisfied with his op-sec, Michael walked out of the terminal and proceeded to the front parking lot to search for an "F 3 9."

Just as he hoped, stall F-39 held a green late-model Chevy truck, and his new fob unlocked its doors. *Oughta blend in pretty well where I'm headed. A lot better than a hybrid Prius, although that would definitely be a less-expected chariot for God's vengeance.* Michael entered the truck, dropped his duffel on the passenger seat, and turned the ignition over. A quick check confirmed the ashtray did, in fact, hold five $20-bills, along with a parking receipt that showed the truck had been there for only a few hours. *Someone else nearby's got a second set of keys, then. Not sure what that means, if anything.* Backing the truck from the stall, Michael proceeded toward the airport exit and the uncertainty of his first operational assignment.

TUESDAY, 2304 HOURS_

ST PAUL'S CHURCH. ODESSA, TEXAS.

Michael pulled the pickup truck into the empty, asphalt lot. His headlights cast across the front and side of the darkened building and the large sign that confirmed its identity as Saint Paul's Catholic Church. *Looks like the place. Now to see if Father Bullard's still up.* He considered stopping near the handicapped spaces at the front entrance but decided that's what a neophyte would do. Instead, he drove his truck around to the back until he identified the rectory. *This's where I need to be.*

As Michael parked, a short, portly priest in a black cassock exited the rectory and walked into the headlight beams. *Gotta be Bullard.* The priest deliberately strode toward Michael's truck, so he turned off the ignition and stepped out to meet him.

"I'm sorry," the priest offered as he approached Michael. "It's terribly late, is it possible for us to speak with you tomorrow?"

"It's urgent, Father," Michael replied. "Is Father Bullard in this evening?"

"I'm Father Bullard." The man stopped several feet from Michael and stood in the beam of the truck's automatic headlights, which hadn't yet turned themselves off.

"I'm Father Andrew," Michael explained. "I need to hear your confession." He watched the pear-shaped priest and searched for any discernible reaction to the beginning of the code phrase. A few seconds passed, and Michael feared something had changed.

"I can't imagine what I would need to confess."

"I can't either," Michael cautiously offered. "I won't know until you tell me. I'm here to offer absolution." *That's the whole phrase, Father Bullard, it's up to you now.* The priest looked Michael up and down with curiosity painted across his face.

"Come inside, we'll see what we can get figured out." Bullard nonchalantly turned and led Michael into the rectory and the private living quarters of the clergy assigned to Saint Paul's.

Once inside, Michael found exactly what he expected: simple, well-worn furnishings, threadbare cushions, and a single, wooden INRE cross hanging on the wall of the only common living area.

"Can I get you something," Bullard asked. "I expect you've traveled long and far to get here."

Not sure if that's an honest assumption or he's trying to bait me into giving up intel. No telling how much these guys are gonna report back to John. "No, thank you, Father, it wasn't a long or far trip, actually, just late."

"I understand. We should start, then."

He seems to understand my inflection, Michael thought. *Wonder how this will go, given that this is the first time for both of us? Maybe Bullard doesn't even really know what I'm here to do.*

Bullard crossed himself as he sat down next to Michael. "Bless me, Father, for I have sinned. It has been three days since my last confession." He paused a moment before speaking freely to Michael. "Father Andrew, I must confess that I have anger in my heart," Bullard began and retrieved a sealed manila folder that had been hidden beneath the small dining table. He offered it to Michael and leaned back in his rickety wood chair, which *creaked* in protest.

Michael accepted the envelope and began his inspection by checking the seals. *Both ends are still glued shut. Red wax seals, just over an inch in diameter, both in place over the sealed flaps.* He retrieved a small penlight and carefully examined the detail within each seal. *Shows the Seal of the Holy See on top and, just below that, an 'X,' the symbol used for the Apostle Andrew following his crucifixion on a transverse cross in Greece. Shows it's been sent from the Holy See to me and verifies the envelope's origin and intended recipient.* Michael removed a small folding knife from his pants pocket and carefully cut into the hardened wax. *There it is, just as John said it would be.* He turned the small blade sideways and cautiously leveraged a small piece of parchment paper from the wax. Once freed, Michael carefully read the series of small, type-printed numbers on it: 2270-75.2284-7.2268.2295. *Those are the same sections of the Catechism Miller's alleged to have violated. The folder's contents are authentic.*

"Go ahead, Father Bullard."

"I've recently wished for wrath and vengeance to come for a specific man."

Ask with a genuine heart, and ye shall receive, Michael thought. "I'm listening, go on." He retrieved and examined the documents contained within the envelope while Father Bullard explained in detail how the confession of a sixteen-year-old girl had made him angry enough to kill. He *hated* the man responsible for the anonymous girl's suffering and hoped he encountered the same pain and injury he'd caused the world around him. The man, whom Bullard identified as Jordan Miller, had coerced the girl into completing a late-term abortion that she deeply regretted. Throughout the girl's interactions with Miller, she learned and inferred that he operated a for-profit abortion clinic that actually paid young and naive women for their babies' tissue.

"Do you any longer have such hatred in your heart," Michael asked.

"No, Father Andrew, I do not. I've prayed about this for weeks now, and God saw fit to unburden my heart of its anguish, but, still, I held so much animosity and anger for so long against a man I've never met."

"While I'm grateful that God has already helped remedy your heart, I ask that you recite one Our Father, one Hail Mary, and one Glory Be as penance. Are you ready to read the Act of Contrition?"

In response, Father Bullard lowered his head and recited the lines from memory. When he finished and looked up, Michael recited the Prayer of Absolution to the penitent. "God, the Father of Mercies," Michael began, "through the death and resurrection of his Son has reconciled the world to himself and sent the Holy Spirit among us for the forgiveness of sins; through the ministry of the Church may God give you pardon and peace, and I absolve you from your sins in the name of the Father, and of the Son, and of the Holy Spirit. Amen."

After concluding the sacrament, Michael collected the documents, bid Bullard farewell, and departed Saint Paul's. *I've still got a long night of reading and plotting ahead of me. If I fail to plan, I will have, in effect, planned to fail. I have no such option tomorrow.*

WEDNESDAY, 0527 HOURS_

JACK RABBIT TRAILS MOTOR LODGE.
PECOS, TEXAS.

MICHAEL WOKE several minutes before his alarm and stretched in bed. After retrieving his cell phone from the adjacent nightstand, he logged into its VPN and checked for new emails and messages. Finding none, he put the device back into airplane mode, deactivated its digital alarm, and turned on the bedside lamp. He hadn't slept that well, and it reminded him from his days as a cop that he never slept well the night before an op. *Nothing to do but overcompensate with caffeine. Better living through chemistry, as they say.*

Michael stiffly rose from bed and meandered over to the room's small table and the carry-on duffel bag he'd placed there. He withdrew a bottle of cold-brew coffee he'd purchased at the Midland Airport the previous night. *Didn't wanna count on the motel coffee this morning.* As he drank the strong liquid, Michael surveyed the room to ensure he had everything he needed. *I only want to leave here once today and never come back again. Every additional trip risks creating more witnesses who can help investigators try to find me later.*

Despite the negative reviews and low-star rating on every site that cared about such things, Michael had stayed there for the anonymity it offered him and, more importantly, it was the only motel in the area with rooms that included a wood-burning fireplace. *Almost seems like the owners oughta be complicit in whatever happens here, considering they're renting rooms for cash, collecting no personal information, and using the in-room fireplaces as part of their ad campaign. I'm not the first anonymous, unregistered guest that's destroyed evidence in here.*

Michael examined the ratty chair next to the small table and decided against using it for his morning meditation and Laud prayers. Stepping over to the bed, he pulled back the worn bedspread and sat on the sheet-covered end of the lumpy mattress. *The sheets get changed and washed much more often than the bedspread. I'd bet that thing hasn't seen soap and bleach since Bush was in office. The first one.*

Bowing his head, Michael meditated to prepare himself to celebrate the mysteries of the Liturgy of the Hours. In just over sixty minutes, he'd recited Laud and set about his remaining tasks.

Michael re-read the documents and intelligence files from the packet Father Bullard had passed to him last night and drank a second bottle of cold-brew. The first page showed the Catechism violations alleged against his target: *Abortion 2270-75, Scandal 2284-7, Intentional Homicide 2268, Human Experimentation 2295.*

The second identified his specific target as Jordan Y. Miller and showed a color copy of his Texas driver's license. *White male, brown over hazel, six-feet-tall, two-ten. Lives near Mentone, a wide spot in the road thirty minutes north of Pecos. Photo on the D-L looks reasonably fit. Might not be competing for the CrossFit title, but he can probably handle himself. Address on the D-L is a P-O box in Pecos. Must wanna keep his business out of the Mentone Post Office.*

The following pages summarized raw intelligence and analytical research on Jordan Miller and his business operations:

"MILLER is the sole owner of Lifelong Solutions, LLC, which offers on-demand abortion services to female patients in several locations around the western US: Las Vegas, Los Angeles, Miami. The company is headquartered in Midland, but it utilizes a shared office space with a common receptionist, no medical facilities, and no on-site records. MILLER performs procedures mostly on weekends, Fri-Mon, and flies out of Midland airport on Thurs and returns home late Monday nights.

"MILLER has twice been investigated by TEXAS RANGERS and LOCAL LEOs, but all criminal charges have so far been dropped WITH PREJUDICE after victims recant their statements at trial. Current investi-

gation into MILLER's suspected witness tampering have gone cold and are no longer active investigations.

"MILLER's for-profit business offers inexpensive, and sometimes free, abortions to patients who authorize MILLER to use and sell discarded human tissue from their aborted babies for medical research. MILLER's patients allege he advocates abortion as birth control, minimizes any potential benefits of adoption, disproportionately counsels young women on the health risks and potential death that may result from full-term pregnancy, as well as emphasizing difficulties of financial care for child and self. MILLER's patients also allege he gives referral fees to his patients who send other girls to his clinic, as well as discounted pricing on subsequent abortions. Several patients alleged they personally knew several women had been paid for their late-term fetuses when MILLER thought they might go forward with birth and adoption, despite the late-stage of their pregnancies.

"Following the dismissal of both cases, patients and former staff members allege MILLER's conduct worsened. Emboldened by the lack of criminal accountability, he began more aggressively marketing his services in publications intended for middle- and high school audiences. Informants are concerned that his current actions will increase abortion-on-demand rates and popularity among the vulnerable teen population; they also offer fears that MILLER will attempt to work around parental consent requirements.

"MILLER has created a subsequent revenue stream by collecting and selling the aborted tissues to medical research facilities around the world. He has regular flights from Midland International Airport & Space Port to three branch offices, as well as nations known to allow and foster such research. MILLER tends to keep a consistent and reliable schedule, leaving his residence at approximately 1630 hours on Wednesday and returning only after 2130 hours. MILLER departs again, normally for his field offices and scheduled abortion appointments, on Thursday morning at approximately 0700."

The last paragraph caused Michael to pause. *I expected to surveil the guy for a few days to find out about his movement. Detailed scheduling information like this only comes from a few sources, and there's no way it came up in a confession.* He read over the last few sentences again, which only further raised his suspicions. *That kinda intel's what we used to get from informants, snitches. And other cops. That could mean John's either already had someone on the ground working this investigation, or they got an insider. Why would someone from Miller's life or office wanna give intel to the Catholic church, though? They'd be looking to trade intel for things only the cops and prosecutors can offer: jail time, reduce their own sentences, eliminate their competitors, or cold, hard cash.* Michael pondered that reality for a few moments, unsure what, if anything, he should do about his inferences. *The most reasonable answer is another man on the ground. It's not enough to delay my efforts, especially if it's true that I only have this narrow window to act before Miller endangers more lives this weekend. Just have to keep a vigilant watch on everything happening around me.* Michael resigned himself to his previous intended course of action and returned to the intel packet.

"One former employee advised prosecutors in both cases that MILLER kept a portable, blue one-terabyte hard drive with all his actual patient and financial records. She insisted MILLER kept only 'sterilized' records at his office, which was twice searched by LEOs.

"MILLER lives on acreage located northwest of Mentone, Texas, on the east bank of Pecos River, west of Loving County Road 100. Overhead satellite map included. MILLER drives a white 2018 four-door Ford truck with general-issue Texas license plates. DMV registration records included."

Michael read through all the attached raw intelligence data again, which showed Miller had millions of dollars at his disposal, mostly in offshore bank accounts in non-extradition nations that also didn't share financial information with the US government or IRS. *This guy's becoming wealthy by selling off the bodies of murdered babies!*

Michael considered what he knew about Miller's schedule and the compressed timeline under which he'd been forced to work. *If I could delay until he left on Thursday, I might have three or four days to find all his secrets. If I wait that long, I'm almost certainly sentencing more unborns to death. Based on the apparent rigidity of his schedule, his neighbors are likely pretty aware of when he's there and when he's not. Can't just park in the driveway and assume no one's gonna call the sheriff. If anything, that'll only guarantee Miller or the local law come calling. Nope, I've gotta go now, and I've gotta find a concealed approach to his house, even though it's out in the flat-ass middle of nowhere.*

Michael read the license plate and tried to associate it with other, personal info to help him easily recall it after he burned the intel packet. *The three leading letters are CAM, pretty easy to use 'camshaft,' as that helps propel the truck. What about the numbers, though? July 9th is mom's birthday, easy enough. What about the '21,' the last two digits?* He required only a few moments to recall a connection between his mother's birthday and '21.' *Mom was twenty-one when she and dad got married. Easy enough.*

Michael set the intel packet aside and dressed in jeans, work boots, and a bright, 'safety yellow' t-shirt with a local oil company logo on it. *Between the local airport vendors and Wal-Mart, I can get everything I need to blend in wherever I go. This has to be about the closest thing to a 'benign stranger' uniform in this part of the world. Booming oil fields constantly bring in new workers from all over the world, so I'd kinda be surprised if people even look twice at newcomers anymore.*

Michael skimmed over each page of the intel packet once more, just to ensure he'd committed all the necessary details to memory. Confident he no longer needed the physical copies, Michael gathered up all the paperwork related to his assignment and searched through the motel room three times to ensure he left none of it behind. *Only one thing left to do before I take the truck out for breakfast, real coffee, and surveillance.* In the absence of nearby banks or private mailbox companies that offered cash-pay shredding services, Michael's operational security had called for a wood-burning fireplace, and it had come time to make use of it.

Michael expertly stacked kindling inside the fireplace and ensured the flue was open. He hand-shredded every paper from the intel packet and placed much of the shredded debris among and between the pieces of kindling. *This time of year, it won't be terribly odd that the fireplace is being used. The added op-sec was definitely worth the extra ten bucks the motel charged me for three pieces of shitty firewood and a few handfuls of kindling.* After lighting the papers with a disposable Bic, Michael gently blew at the bottom of the pile to push the emerging flames onto adjacent fuels. It took only seconds to catch, and he added the remaining papers one at a time to avoid smothering the small fire. *I'll have to burn the hardwood chunks to make sure all the papers are reduced to ash. Not a shred can survive to be found later.* Michael deliberately positioned the three larger chunks atop the growing flames, which immediately licked at the new, dry fuel. With each piece only slightly bigger than his forearm, Michael knew the fire needed little time to consume them and incinerate his documents.

May as well make use of this 'operational pause.' No holy man's ever regretted offering too much prayer. Michael retrieved a small, black nylon bifold wallet from his duffel bag and the rough, laminated prayer card he kept inside it. His father had given him the card at his police academy graduation, and Michael had carried it every day since. Despite knowing this version of the prayer by heart, he preferred reading it aloud from the card. *I think the background image of Saint Michael brings some additional comfort and confidence.*

As the small fire grew behind him and fully engulfed the three hardwood chunks and the few remaining paper scraps, Michael knelt and read aloud his copy of *A Policeman's Prayer to Saint Michael.* "Saint Michael, Heaven's glorious Commissioner of Police, who once so neatly and successfully cleared God's promises of all its undesirables, look with kindly and professional eye on your earthly force..."

WEDNESDAY, 1548 HOURS_

COUNTY ROAD 100. LOVING COUNTY, TEXAS.

After spending the previous seven hours familiarizing himself with the area around Miller's property, gathering on-the-ground intel, and covering his green pickup truck with a fine, light-brown layer of powdered West Texas dust, Michael parked in an isolated temporary dirt parking lot just north of the small town of Mentone, Texas. He'd found the remote field office for *West Texas Wildcatting,* a local oil field start-up, earlier that morning. The company had placed a conex trailer at the intersection of two rural highways and set temporary chain-link-and-barbed-wire fencing around it. The company's oil field workers parked their own vehicles *outside* the fence during their shifts, in front of the mobile office building, and kept the company's expensive work vehicles *inside* the fence during the rare times they weren't in use. *Parked vehicles don't make any money,* Michael thought, *so they're probably only stored here when they're down for service. There shouldn't be another shift change for a few hours, so, until then, the odds of someone taking enough interest to confront me is pretty slim.*

Michael had already preplanned his lies, just in case someone did come out to question the unfamiliar driver parked near the employee vehicles. *As long as they don't actually have a dude named 'Mitchell Tanner' workin' for 'em, then I can pass the whole thing off as a miscommunication and leave without creating a scene. Divorces have to be common enough among these guys that they'll understand a colleague would wanna sign the papers without having to take time off to go back home, wherever that is.*

Having positioned his truck to both blend into the vehicles already parked in the lot and give himself the best available view of Loving County Road 100, Michael estimated Jordan Miller should drive within twenty-five or thirty yards when he passed by. *If he sticks to his routine, Miller should leave his house, just to my west, and drive out eastbound on the dirt access road that connects with L-C-R 100 just about a hundred yards north of here. His only option, other than off-roading through the scrub brush, is to turn south and drive right past me. Glad that Texas requires front license plates, that's gonna make it a lot easier to identify Miller's rig.*

Michael had driven that same route several hours ago, which had confirmed his earlier assumption from the overhead satellite photos. *I can drive past his place and look for other vehicles, people, and animals. All the tire tracks at the end of the road look like the locals routinely park there to access the river behind Miller's house. As long as I look the part, I can leave my truck there without raising anyone's suspicions. My new waders and fishing pole are gonna give me a great alibi to walk upstream and enter Miller's property with the sun at my back. If he hadn't bought waterfront property, I'd have a much harder time getting into his place without being noticed. Who's gonna question a fisherman going up to a stranger's house to get help for chest pains?*

Michael saw an eastbound dust trail rising from the access road about thirty seconds before the truck came into view. *Whatever's coming this way's moving pretty quick. Probably the norm out here, no reason to slow down and enjoy the scenery.* A white Ford truck emerged from behind the scrub brush and slowed before intersecting the county road. Michael raised his binoculars as it turned south toward him and confirmed the black-and-white Texas license plate on its front bumper. *It's the right truck. Windows are too dark to see inside, but Miller oughta be inside his own rig, given the intel on his routine. I'm just gonna have to trust it.*

Michael stayed in the parking lot as Miller's truck accelerated south past him. A black cloud of diesel exhaust and engine noise showed the man was in a hurry. *Miller's place is two-point-three miles away. No time like the present.* He started his truck, shifted into drive, and headed toward his objective. *With any luck, I'll be inside Miller's place in about forty-five minutes.*

Sticking to his plan, Michael parked, donned his waders, and stumbled northwest along the east bank of the Pecos River with a shiny new fishing pole. Just to be more convincing, should anyone have spotted him, he occasionally cast his line into the murky water. *There's nothing swimming in here that's gonna bite on this massive lure in middle of the afternoon.* He chuckled at the small problem that actually catching something would present. *I'd raise suspicion just by tossing it back. Not a lot of catch-and-release fisherman around here.*

By the time he finally entered Miller's property from the riverbank and approached an unusual landmark that he'd identified from overhead photos, a little more than an hour had passed. *I'm already behind schedule, but at least I know I'm headed to the right house.* Although he hadn't been able to specifically identify the small structure from satellite photos, he now saw it was a shaded gazebo with a large, portable barbeque grill and picnic table beneath it. Michael looked back west toward the river and understood why Miller had built it there. *It's the best and greenest view of anywhere around here. He's making do with what he has. Still not sure why a guy with his assets and paradigm would wanna live out here, though. If the locals knew how he makes his living, they'd likely see it as dirty money and refuse to even sell the guy a cup of coffee. Probably why the local sheriff prefers the rattlesnake problem in his rural county to the lawyer problems in the cities.* Michael continued on toward the house, careful to try to keep his behavior consistent with his fictional distress.

Still about fifty yards to go. Didn't consider how slow I'd be hiking around in these damned rubber waders, or how dense the riverside brush was. He plodded through the short, evergreen hardwoods and worked to keep his cover story intact. *If someone is home, I wanna look like I might actually be in distress, but I don't wanna over-sell it. Chest pain comes in all varieties, and I'll have to convince 'em to let me walk away before any emergency medical services arrive. The medics won't care about checking my I-D, but, out here, the fastest and closest responder's definitely gonna be a Sheriff's Deputy.*

Michael paid as much attention to the house as he did to avoiding trip hazards with the clumsy, oversized waders. *Don't see any movement, don't hear any dogs. It's too early for many lights to be on, so that doesn't mean there's no one inside.* Michael took a deep, calming breath and focused on keeping his cover story believable. *Don't need to worry about entry yet, just focus on the first step and making sure no one's home.*

Michael walked up onto the covered back patio and knocked loudly on the sliding glass door there. "*Hello,*" he called out, trying to sound frantic and harmless. "*Anyone home?! I need help!*" Waiting only a few seconds with no response, he pounded on the glass again, only louder. *Someone afraid they're having a heart attack wouldn't be polite or patient. "Hello?! Please help! Call an ambulance, please!!"* Michael dropped his fishing pole on the porch, cupped his hands around his face, and pressed against the glass door to get a clear view inside. *No one's visible, nothing's moving.* He stood still, held his breath for a few moments, and concentrated on listening for sounds or movement coming from the home. *Nothing.* Michael glanced at his watch and saw he had only about four hours left to find corroborating evidence and prepare for Miller's absolution. *If I even find anything,* he reminded himself, *it's certainly possible there's more than one Jordan Miller in this world and I've got the wrong one. That might actually make more sense at this point.*

Continuing on with his entry plan, Michael checked the sliding door. *Unlocked. Probably not that unusual out here.* He pushed the door open and listened intently for any indication of an alarm system. *Nothing. "Hello?! Please, I was fishing and I'm having chest pain! Please, help, I think I'm having a heart attack! Hello?! Can someone help me?!"* Nothing greeted him but the repetitious, exact *ticking* of a nearby wall clock.

Now more confident that Miller had left the residence, Michael stepped inside. *Still have to make sure it's empty before I start. Just a quick protective sweep of the interior and I can get to work after I know I'm alone.*

WEDNESDAY, 2132 HOURS_

MILLER RESIDENCE. LOVING COUNTY, TEXAS.

MICHAEL STOPPED and stood in the middle of Jordan Miller's living room. Frantic and out of time, he forced himself to breathe and focus. *Where is it? Where haven't I looked? Where haven't I searched?* Michael deliberately looked at the furniture in the room and tried to confirm to himself that he had completed a detailed search of each nook and cranny. *I know I've checked everywhere in here. I'm already more than thirty minutes behind schedule. On to the next room.*

Michael moved through the rest of the residence as his growing apprehension and sense of failure dominated his emotions. *I know it's possible that the hard drive was never here. Maybe the information and intel were bad. Maybe this is the wrong Jordan Miller.* He went through the home office again and quickly searched for hiding places. *This drive's not the kinda thing someone'd ever just leave laying around, or even keep in the regular desk drawers. Those secrets are gonna stay locked away.*

Still without evidence in-hand, Michael left the office and moved back into the bedroom. *Gotta move fast, he's gonna be home anytime now, and I won't have much warning before he opens the front door, especially from the back of the house.* He searched through the master bedroom again for only a few minutes before realizing he had to give up. *I'm outta time, and I've still gotta make sure everything's back where it belongs.*

Starting from the master bedroom and working his way toward the back door and his presumed exit, Michael examined digital photographs he took with his cell phone when he first entered each room. He compared the room's condition and placement of its belongings to reduce the possibility that Miller would realize someone had been inside his home. Michael also ensured that he left the home's interior lights in the same condition he found them. *If he's got this consistent a routine, he probably doesn't leave lights on by accident. That kinda dedication to habit is gonna bleed over into all the other aspects of his life.* After convincing himself that he'd returned each room to something close to its original appearance, Michael moved toward the home's main living area.

As he entered the kitchen, Michael saw headlights approaching the residence. *Dammit, I still have two rooms to check.* He quickly strode to a living room window and very slightly pulled the blinds back to look outside. *Yep, the truck's coming here, whether it's Miller or not doesn't matter. Time to go!*

Michael jogged to the back sliding door. Just as he started to pull it open, he saw a thick wood dowel rod leaned against the back of its frame. *The low-tech security system.* He urgently pulled the glass door open, grabbed the rod, and propped it inside the frame against the back of the sliding door. *It isn't how he left it, but I might need to slow him down if he sees me.* Michael stepped out the door just as he heard a truck door slam closed in front of the house. *Not the time to panic, stay calm. Slow is smooth, smooth is fast.* He cautiously pulled the door closed to ensure the rod held against the back of the frame and fell onto the frame's track as the door closed.

thuck

As soon as the rod fell onto the metal tracks as he'd hoped, Michael pulled the door closed the final few inches. He quietly retrieved his fishing pole from the porch and stepped backward away from the sliding door. *I don't want Miller to get a look at my face, but, if he does see me, I need to know to start talking. Or running. Or fake a heart attack. Remember the pain would radiate down the right arm...wait...no...the left! Right?!* Through the glass slider, Michael watched Miller step through his front door. His target absentmindedly walked into the house and tossed his keys onto a small table nearby. *He doesn't suspect anything...yet...* Although grateful for the early autumn sunset and the complete darkness that could soon conceal him, he also feared it would slow his retreat while his vision adjusted from the home's bright interior lights.

Michael cautiously turned around at the end of the porch and purposefully stepped west through the darkness. He tried to land his feet near the base of the low scrub bushes he passed to conceal and limit the footprints he left behind. *I still have to get away, and it might take me another half-hour to get back to the truck and drive past Miller's home. Can't leave a buncha prints that make him suspicious if he looks around out here. Be patient, be efficient. A few extra* seconds *right now might save me from spending* years *in prison. If he realizes someone's been in his house, he might be willing to confront me as I'm driving away from the river and the back of his property. That also might give the local sheriff's deputy time to show up and investigate. I should've left an hour ago! I just couldn't accept defeat, and now I might really pay for it! Dumbshit! I knew success could also be finding nothing, but I took this first assignment too personally! My own ego got in the way, and things might go real sideways because of it! Shortest clandestine career in Holy See history! I'll have to remind myself later to laugh that at least no one would know about it.*

Michael finally reached the gazebo. He moved with greater urgency now that he had fifty yards between him and Miller's back door. With the fishing pole still in his right hand, he ran as fast as the awkward waders allowed. *Another forty yards to the bank, and then I'll have to slow down again. If anyone wanted to fish this section of the river, they'd get here about dusk and stay for a while, probably sitting in lawn chairs on the bank, drinking Lonestar and Shiner Bock in the dark.* He breathed deep and encouraged himself to stay calm. *Slow is smooth, smooth is fast,* Michael reminded himself as he reached the steep riverbank. *Gotta be convincing again.*

Moonlight reflected off the dark river as he stepped down to its lapping water line. Casting his line downstream, he used the ambient light to scan the area for anyone that might notice his presence and departure. *Now I'm the hunted, and anyone pursuing me's not gonna have the same threshold for violence. Even though I went there with the intent of killing Miller's mortal body, I had to try to leave without a trace without the right evidence. If he thinks I trespassed in his home, he might be willing to kill me with or without evidence.* Michael knew he'd have laughed at the irony if it didn't threaten to end his life. *It'd be terrible if I ended up killing Miller in self-defense after I just passed on an opportunity to kill him over unsubstantiated allegations. But, if God wants to call him home tonight, it's not too late for Him to still use me as a tool to make that happen. With God, all things are possible.*

THURSDAY, 2145 HOURS_

DENVER INTERNATIONAL AIRPORT.
DENVER, COLORADO.

MICHAEL SAT in the front passenger seat of Sergio's rental car. His friend drove around DIA's exterior loop at just under the ever-changing speed limits, and Michael swept his hand over the sedan's interior trim and compartments. *Gotta make sure we're clean.*

"Tellin' you, *mijo,* there's no way even John could plant somethin' in here," Sergio chided. "When I saw you on the train to the terminal, I made this rental car reservation just before it stopped. No way anyone could know what car we'd be getting into. Still, we can't circle the airport forever without having the cops take notice, and I got a few things I wanna talk about before we get back up to John's compound."

"I know we're probably safe in here," Michael absentmindedly replied. "If I'm gonna get booted from the program, I want it to be for the right reasons."

"*Not* because we've been keepin' this secret from John the whole time?"

"Dammit," Michael swore and glared at his friend, who only smiled back. "That's exactly what I'm talking about! No point in worrying about it now." He shut the glove compartment and tried to settle his mind.

"So, you wanna talk about it?"

Michael scowled. "Which 'what?' The training program, the fact that you and I have known each other for years? Our assignments?"

"Yeah, the last one, mostly. Pretty sure everything else is old news."

Michael nodded his head and accepted the potential consequences. *At least we'll get to share a ride* back *to the airport if John does somehow get wind of this.* "First, they wouldn't tell me what assignments anyone else got."

"Nope, me neither," Sergio agreed, "they made me an *absolver.*" He looked at Michael with an air of confidence and pride.

"Same here," Michael explained. "You think we're all absolvers?"

"No idea. It's hard to know what's real and what John's made up to backstop their operational security. They might also recruit for security and intel positions at Vatican City, but, then again, maybe not."

"Nobody knows but John."

"Oh, there's someone else that knows," Sergio proclaimed. "John's definitely not the top of this food chain, so there's for-sure another guy givin' him marching orders."

Michael slowly offered his own opinion. "I think it's Father Harry."

"*The monsignor-shrink?* Really?"

"Well, there was this moment," Michael offered, "when they were telling me about the position and explaining what I'd be doing—"

"Without *actually explaining* what you'd be doing," Sergio finished the sentence.

"Yeah, that. Anyway, I kept pressing them for more details, and, just before John said the word 'absolver,' he looked over to the monsignor. Father Harry looked back at him, and, it looked to me, like he gave John *permission* to continue."

"Huh. I didn't get that impression at all when they talked to me. They could've worked the kinks outta their delivery by then, you *did* go first."

"So," Michael cautiously paused and considered whether to ask what he wanted to know. *Best to proceed slowly and offer something up before I get the whole question out.* "You, *uh,* just get back from an assignment, too?"

Sergio smirked at his disclosure. "Yep. You too, then, huh?"

"Yeah," Michael nodded and briefly looked out at the moonlit landscape along the freeway. "Didn't go like I hoped, though."

"Mine, either. I didn't find anything, no evidence at all."

"Are you serious, Sergio? I didn't find a *scrap,* man, not even a *hint* of what I was looking for!"

"No way, you were a cop! I figured you would-a had all that searching-shit down pat!"

"I thought so, too, but I don't think there was anything to be found." Michael looked out at the light traffic around them. *None of the nearby cars have been with us long. We're not being followed...yet...*

"When I was searchin' through my target's place, Mike, I *really* wished you'd been there to help. He's supposed to be a pedophile with a taste for young boys, so I damned sure wanted to find the evidence and follow through on it. The intel packet said I was to search his computer for digital photos, so, I go into the guy's home-office, and it took me like, maybe, two minutes to find where he'd written down his username and password. Who does that?"

"Right," Michael agreed with his suspicions. "Nobody."

"Yeah, so I search the computer on his desk anyway. Nothing. Search through the iPad. Nothing. There was supposed to be *hundreds* of files, pics, messages. Nothing. Not a single porn pic, even legal stuff. I put everything back and got out before he came home. I was worried because I didn't know if they're just gonna let this one go for now, or if someone else is gonna have to go in and try to clean up after me."

Michael checked the side-view mirror for anyone that paid them too much attention. "Same thing for me. Different crime, but I was supposed to find a hard drive with all the evidence on it. Nothing. So, now it kinda looks like there wasn't anything to find in the first place."

"Think that's a coincidence," Sergio asked. "I don't believe much in coincidence, especially not when John's involved. He tries too hard to manage the potential outcomes."

"I agree. Now comes the hard part."

"How's that?"

"Going back and pretending we don't know we struck out. Makes me think that everyone struck out, and I'm gonna have a hard time believing anyone that says otherwise."

"Hell, we did a good job so far. Far as I know, Thomas was the only one that ever caught on to us."

Michael recalled that moment out on the rifle range and deeply exhaled. "That was one of the most terrifying moments of my life!"

"That was even worse than when those damned rebels came into the church, back in Ecuador, remember that? They wanted to string you up as a C-I-A agent!"

"You never told me that, Sergio! You just said they wanted me to leave because they didn't trust white guys!"

"Well, that was true," Sergio defensively replied, "I just didn't give you all the details about why they didn't trust you or how they wanted to go about it."

"Man, I knew something wasn't right. I never could understand the fast-talkers, man."

"Turns out they were kinda on to something, right?"

Michael chuckled at the realization. "Yeah, I guess so, they were just about four years too soon."

"Anything you've been holding out on me?"

"Not intentionally, but there is this one thing, I guess," Michael explained. "I kinda killed a guy in Bogotá a few months back."

"*WHAT?! Are you serious?* You *gotta* tell me this one and start from the beginning."

"We don't have that much time. I'll make it quick, because you still gotta return the rental car so we can go grab the cars John's goons stashed in the long-term lots for us. If we leave his cars at the airport and both show up together in a rental, he'll have a goddamned coronary!" Michael spent fifteen minutes giving Sergio his best summation of the killing and its immediate aftermath. Sergio managed to turn only one circuit around the airport in that time.

"Damn, man, that's a helluva story," Sergio proclaimed. "Anything else you're holdin' onto?"

"I think John has small kids at home, or, maybe, he *recently* had small kids at home."

"Why's that?"

"He made a reference to a kid's book one time, and it's not one that he would've read as a kid, it's too new."

"What's the book?"

"*If You Give a Mouse a Cookie.*"

"How do *you* know about that?"

"My cousins' kids all read it," Michael explained. "Not that old." He rechecked the side-view mirror for tails. "What if we're not the problem, and it's *the program* that's a failure?"

"Like, you mean the intel's bad?"

"Maybe. Hard for me to believe we'd *both* strike out, unless the intel network's a dud and the info's worthless, or this was another one of John's field problems."

"Bet we find out in the morning, but I will add one more potential explanation, at least from John's perspective."

"What's that," Michael asked.

"We're the worst and dumbest shitheads to ever walk on God's green earth."

"Guess what," Michael called out in his best impression of John's voice.

"I dunno, John, what?" Sergio chuckled as he replied.

"I found out Andrew's about the biggest goddamned piece of shit, just as I always thought! And his friend, *Jude,* well, that bullshit's just Mexican-talk for 'Judas!'"

"*How now, brown cow?!*"

"Man, I wanted to laugh so bad the first time he said that, Sergio! My mom used to say that all the time, but she was usually talking about herself in the third person, you know, like she's the brown cow that can't figure out what to do next."

"Who do you think we really work for?"

Sergio's unexpected question caught Michael off-guard. *I assume Sergio did that on purpose to try to get a genuine reaction.* Michael shrugged. "Dunno. I'd say John, but he's just a manager, and not even a middle manager, I don't think. Pretty sure he takes his orders from the guy who takes them from the guy who...you get the idea. This thing has to go pretty far up the ladder."

"Way above my pay grade, anyway, *mijo.* I'm just a lowly Mexican-American priest that's never been paid to think in his whole life."

Michael ignored his friend's intellectual self-deprecation. "I do wonder how far this goes up the Church hierarchy, ya know?"

"Well, like I said, I think we go pretty close to the top, if not all the way to the white cassock. I'm sure they've got this compartmentalized and insulated enough to protect His Holiness from blowback, but it's not like we're working for some Charles Manson cult."

"Probably time to drop this off, Sergio. If John has trackers on our cars, he's gonna wonder why they haven't started moving yet."

"Yeah, just lemme run something by you. I know we're not supposed to call this anything, right, not give the organization a name, or what-not."

"Right," Michael replied, "but you think you've got a winner?"

"Check it out. *Wrath, Incorporated.* Whaddaya think?"

"Wrath, Inc. *Ira Incorporatus,* in our revered Latin. I think I like it, Serge, it's got some legs."

"*Oooo, yeah, Ira Incorporatus!* We've always made a good team, *mijo.* The two-man demon-wrecking crew of *Ira Incorporatus.*"

"Yeah, I dunno now, *Wrath, Inc.,* does have a nice ring to it," Michael offered. "The Latin just sounds more official. Now we just need a corporate logo, Sergio, think we can work that out over the next couple days? You used to draw, didn't you?"

'That *was* a lifetime ago, Mike, but I'll see what I can come up with."

"Something subtle, you know, so we can hide it in plain sight."

"Just like the old days in Ecuador, right? *Quaere veniam, noli potestam.*"

"Yep," Michael agreed, "just like that. Seek grace, not opportunity."

"Definitely sounds better than what we originally intended."

"*Ask forgiveness, not permission,*" Michael recalled. "It's always easier to just go out and do the right things, at the right times, for the right reasons, and worry about all the permissions and politics later."

"Might be why the rebels wanted to kill you, you know that, right?"

"Fair enough. There is safety in permission."

"I haven't had a chance to ask for the last seven months, man, how's your folks doing?"

Michael's mother returned to his thoughts and compelled a much more somber mood. *What would she think of all this?* Michael cleared his throat. "They're good enough, I guess. My dad semi-retired a couple years ago. He quit working full-time so he can take care of my mom. She got diagnosed with an aggressive form of M-S."

"I'm sorry to hear that, Mike! Is there anything that can be done for her?"

"Not really. We're in a kind of holding pattern. The current treatments are slowing the progression, but the only real hope she's got is for new medical advances. There are some promising advances in stem cell therapy, but the cost is too high right now, and the F-D-A hasn't yet approved the treatments here in the States."

"Where would she have to go?"

"Europe," Michael explained, "and she'd need to take about a quarter-million dollars with her."

Sergio whistled and took an exit to again drive them back around the airport perimeter. "I'll pray for them. If I get an unexpected inheritance from a rich uncle I never knew about, though, you're all on the first flight out."

"Thanks, Sergio, I appreciate that. Maybe we should pray for rich uncles."

"I think it's fine as long as you pray for *someone else* to have one."

"You mind dropping me first? Help make it look like we didn't just do this. If our G-P-S trackers light up at the same time, John'll be suspicious."

"Seems legit, where's your drop-car?"

"East economy, row R-R." Michael wondered how tomorrow would go, given what he now knew about Sergio's experience. *We either failed to find evidence that actually exists, or we succeeded by not taking action without evidence, or, worst-case, we exposed real problems with John's program and its intel sources and analysis. And I've gotta play dumb about Sergio's shut-out. John's reaction will tell me everything I need to know.*

FRIDAY, 0733 HOURS_

RURAL COMPOUND. NIOBRARA COUNTY, WYOMING.

"This damned chair," Michael murmured beneath his breath, "swear to God this is gonna be the next thing I kill." Once again seated with his three remaining trainees in their converted classroom, Father Harry delivered their mass celebration. *Hope we never meet here like this again. I thought I'd* already *left for the last time, but this place is threatening to become a bad yo-yo.* As the monsignor delivered a monotone homily, the wind gusted and howled behind him. *So tired of the goddamned wind up here. I'm always gettin' sandblasted, or sunbaked, or windblown. If John keeps us here all winter, this place'll become my Catholic Siberia, after all.* He knelt down in front of the chair and ensured his now-ragged prayer towel was placed beneath his kneecaps. *This is almost as cozy as that piece-of-shit chair.*

After Father Harry concluded the small service, the four students moved the two remaining banquet tables back to create a single row and waited a turn to confess their recent sins. Michael, seated closest to the stall that the monsignor had only recently turned into a makeshift booth, stepped over when Father Harry indicated he was ready and waiting. *No way this guy's getting anything but the Bull Durham speech. 'Glad to be here, part of a great team effort, no 'I' in team.' The works.*

Michael confessed his trespass into Jordan Miller's life, along with his guilt for not finding the evidence that would have allowed him to prevent harm from visiting the man's future victims.

"I understand the remorse that's in your heart, son," Father Harry offered, "but you needn't worry about any of this as a sin. You took reasonable action to protect the victims and their dignity, and it isn't *your* responsibility to find all the alleged evidence. If it's there to be found, and it's God's will that you do so, it will be. Clearly, God didn't mean for you to find anything, maybe just not find it at this time. Just as Saint Thomas Aquinas wrote in *Summa Theologica,* it's entirely possible for God to use the demons among us for His will, as well. Miller might be innocent of the alleged sins, or God might still have a purpose for him. Neither of those possibilities is within your control, so you needn't take on that guilt and remorse for something you didn't do. Do you understand, son?"

"Yes, Monsignor, I understand. Thank you." *There's no way I'm gonna confess my apprehensions about John to him. 'Father Harry' can claim to be an objective counselor, but he's just as anonymous and vested in this program as John.* Deciding that his confessed sins weren't legitimate, Father Harry let him off without any required contrition.

"Peace be with you."

"And with your spirit, Father." Michael stepped from the "booth" and strode back to the banquet table. He motioned to Phillip, who rose and marched over to take his turn. After returning to his uncomfortable seat, Michael leaned forward and sat in silent prayer while he awaited the conclusion of their confessional time.

Almost an hour passed before Sergio returned to the table, which signified the close of their morning services. Father Harry departed the classroom and, as Michael expected, soon returned with John.

"Congratulations, gentlemen," their lead instructor announced. Michael thought he heard actual joy in the man's voice. "You've just enjoyed your last mass here at 'Our Stepmother of Perpetual Suffering.'"

"You feelin' alright, John," Sergio asked.

"It's a great day. We got sunshine, light breezes, and winter's still weeks away, boys. It's taken me and the staff here only two-hundred-twenty-four days, two hours, and about eighteen minutes to transition you four from absolute shitheads to respectable, just, and Godly warriors.

Rome wasn't built in a day, and I guess we can't expect the same of constructing men, either."

"John, that's almost a compliment," Phillip surmised. "I might even take it that way if I didn't know you better."

"Don't get too excited and start pissin' your panties yet, we still got work to do today."

"Told you, Jude," Michael announced across the table.

"Wanna go double-or-nothin' on what it is," his old friend asked.

"Alright," John impatiently announced, "two warriors and two shitheads, but I'll take what I can get at this point."

Michael saw that John and Father Harry both practically beamed. *Maybe that means we're almost out of here for-real. They both look like they just passed the program themselves, but I don't remember ever seeing 'em out running the trails with us.*

"First thing," John announced, "is that I wanna congratulate and thank all y'all for the strong work you did in the last couple days. From what I and a few select others can tell, everything went off without a hitch. Everybody's got a successful operation under their belts, and it looks like Father Harry and me's done all we can do for you here."

And that seals it, Michael thought. *That had to have been a training exercise. We're all back to the compound at about the same time, and I'd bet the other two didn't find shit for evidence, either. Just knowing that Sergio and I both struck out, John oughta be asking us a million questions about our tactics and procedures to make sure we held up our end. No way that was a legit investigation. How could they have stopped us from going through a Final Absolution, though, if we thought we* had *found corroborating evidence?* Michael quickly contemplated his reality. *How now brown cow?* He smirked at himself and the answer he knew was in front of him. *I have to find a way to put more blind faith in John and his program. I won't be effective if I question every detail and directive. John works to tightly control the outcomes, so he* must *have had something in place to keep us from murdering someone who didn't have it coming.*

"Second, before we meet with each of you again, I wanna ask you to indulge me in one final philosophy discussion. Then, and only then, do you get to leave my precious and sacred compound, so make it good." John strode back over to the Matthew and Proverbs verses that hung from the interior wall to the left of the trainees. "Y'all been walkin' in here most every day for the last seven, damned near eight months, seeing these hangin' here every time you did so. I asked you on your second day here, now two-hundred-and-twenty-two days ago, to keep them in mind as you moved through my training program and its curriculum. I hoped you might find new meaning in these words.

"So, after *all* this time," John continued, "here we are together for the *last* time, and I'm hopin' at least one-a you's got something for me besides pop culture bullshit." He crossed his arms over his chest and stood as though he intended for them all to remain there until he got the answer he wanted.

Alpha half-raised his hand and John motioned for him to proceed. "It seems to me now," he began in his heavy French accent, "that the first of the Beatitudes deals with our victims, or, I mean, the victims we're trying to help."

"I gotcha, Alpha," John agreed. "Carry on."

"So, the victims, they're uh, the poor, they mourn for themselves, for the crimes and injuries that their assailants have put upon them. They are the meek, for they did not take action, uh, on their own, and they sought counsel and guidance rather than the vengeance they deserve. They, of course, hunger and thirst for righteousness, in our context, for the wrongs against them to be right. I think the second half, though, I believe that they deal with us."

"How's that," John asked.

"So, our purpose," Alpha continued, "our calling here, providing the final absolution to evil. God is showing them his mercy, through us, by offering their only conceivable chance at eternal redemption, despite the horrible things they have done. We are the ones who are acting of pure heart, without selfish motivation or anger or malice, even though we will surely despise the actions that those men, and some women, have done. We still, despite that we can say they deserve to spend eternity in hell, we offer them instead the kingdom of heaven.

"We are, naturally, the peacemakers," Alpha explained, "for we help ensure the future peace of God's children from the actions of the evil ones.

Ultimately, if we are found, discovered, or betrayed, I expect we will then *become* the persecuted, for I cannot see that the secular government of any nation will understand or excuse our righteous actions. If that is to be, then we, the ones targeted for serving God in this manner, will enjoy our time in the kingdom of heaven."

John looked around the room, his arms still crossed. "Good, Alpha, I like it. Anybody else?"

Michael nodded when John met his gaze and offered his assessment. "Adding on to Alpha's thoughts, I kinda now think the Proverbs verses deal with the evils we're going out to absolve. The scoundrel, the villain, that's obviously our 'bad guy,' but the sins we're called to offer for final absolution are laid out there. He's spilled innocent blood, he's arrogant to think he can victimize God's children without consequence, that he can escape the vengeance of God's wrath. His heart plots ways to commit these acts and not answer for them, long before he goes through with them, right? He's rushing to commit his acts of evil, bearing false witness against God and against his own victims. The more important part, for me, though, is in verse fifteen, which I think is *definitely* us."

"Oh, yeah?" John asked and stepped around to read that specific line.

"A-ffirm. We will fulfill God's word and become the disaster that immediately overtakes evil and destroy it without remedy."

"I like the way you two think," John offered as he uncrossed his arms and nodded approval to both of them.

"So, between the two series of verses," Sergio added, "we've got the most basic underlying foundations of our very existence and purpose. Each section requires the other for completion and context."

"Father Harry, it looks like your job is done here," John proudly announced. "These boys are all my problem. At least for now."

"It has been a pleasure working with all of you," the monsignor offered. "I bid you farewell, and I'll be praying for each of you. Peace be with you."

"And with your spirit," the four men responded.

"Phillip," John called out. "Meet us in the main house upstairs. All the rest of you can head down to the basement, gather all your stuff, and wait your turn. Keep our operational security needs in mind as you're saying your goodbyes, gentlemen. Unless God wills it otherwise, this is the last time you'll ever see each other."

The lead instructor somberly looked around at the group. Michael saw purpose in his eyes and expression. "Playtime's over, gentlemen. You *all* got important work to do now."

MONDAY, 0814 HOURS_

PIAZZA DEL RISORGIMENTO. ROME, ITALY.

AN OFFICIAL HOLY See-owned Learjet had delivered Michael to Ciampino–G. B. Pastine International Airport more than four hours ago, but he'd had to devote time to his morning prayers, allow the priests at his destination to do the same, and ensure his operational security hadn't been compromised. After leaving the *Ottaviano* metro stop four-hundred yards away, Michael walked through the *Piazza del Risorgimento* in the shadow of Vatican City. He'd been riding Rome's subway system for the past two hours to ensure that no one had followed or expressed an interest in him. *Never thought I'd be doing my own 'heat runs' when I worked as a cop, yet here I am. How things have changed...*

After he entered the perpetually busy square and hid himself among its crowds, Michael turned left and strode toward his destination: *Santi Michele e Magno,* The Church of Saint Michael and Magnus. A sense of excitement and history about the city and its relationship with his faith put him in awe, despite concerns about his present assignment.

Michael had never been to Rome or Vatican City before, but he had traveled extensively in college, and his time as a South American priest had contributed to his comfort in unfamiliar surroundings. Although it wasn't the intended destination of his business trip, the church he needed to call upon stood at *Borgo Santo Spirito, 21/41*, just a few buildings east of Saint Peter's Square. As he walked through Rome's vibrant and frenzied morning traffic, Michael couldn't help but feel a sense of familiarity, of comfort. *Home. This is where my heart is.*

As Michael walked south on *Via del Porta Angelica,* the amazingly tall block wall that separated Vatican City from Rome stood just across the narrow street. Another priest exited a small cafe at the intersection with *Borgo Vittorio.* He smiled pleasantly at Michael and nodded in recognition. Not of Michael or his person, but of the black cassock and collarino that Michael wore. *This has got to be one of the only places in the world where working priests see* other *priests they don't know personally.*

"Bonjourno, Padre," the young Italian priest called out.

"Bonjourno," Michael replied in heavily accented Italian. He'd taken a few semesters in college and had used some of his flight time over the Atlantic to brush up on vocabulary and phrases. *That's one of the great things about the Italians,* he thought, *they love the language so much they even appreciate you trying to use it.* "Come sta il caffè lì dentro?" *How's the coffee in there?*

"È il migliore fuori dal Vaticano." *It's the best outside the Vatican.*

"Il migliore a Roma?" *The best in Rome?*

"No, il migliore del mondo esterno, lo prometto." *No, the best in the outside world, I promise.*

The younger priest held the café door open, accurately assuming Michael would act on such a strong recommendation.

"Grazie," Michael offered as he stepped inside. "La pace sia con te."

"E con il tuo spirito." The younger priest turned and walked toward the Vatican City entrance, just a few blocks south of the café on the west side of the street.

Michael stood for a moment and watched him walk away. *How great it must be to work in the Vatican, especially at such a young age. Amazing opportunities await that man. It's entirely possible I just got coffee advice from a future pope.* He looked at his watch and saw he still had time before his intended arrival. As he stepped up to the counter to order his *doppio Americano,* Michael noticed a stack of laminated Vatican maps for sale. He grabbed one and paid for both items, even when the clerk tried to insist priests can't buy coffee in their café. The argument only settled when Michael left cash and a generous tip on the counter and walked to a table near the front glass that allowed him to watch the street outside. *May as well practice good tradecraft and be alert for any carabinieri out on patrol this morning.* He unfolded the map and quickly found his destination. Using that as his epicenter, he circled out from the church in search of new intelligence, information he hadn't yet gleaned from his hasty research since learning of this assignment. *Wait, that can't be right...*

Michael's first impulse was to ask the clerk for help to ensure his translation was accurate, but that carried too much risk. *She's already gonna remember the priest who refused free coffee, if only for a little while. If I go up there and ask her to confirm there's a Russian business next to my church, and something about that site makes the news, that'll for sure be the first thing she thinks about.* Instead of drawing more attention to himself, Michael chose to solve his problem like an adult: he googled it. *Dammit, the business next door to the church is La Cucina Della Russia. The Russian Kitchen. I may be paranoid, but anything Russian means cameras, security officers, people paid to pay attention and remember anomalies. Especially across the street from Saint Peter's and the Vatican.* He exhaled and thought about his options. *Just gonna have to be as anonymous as possible. Can't put on a hat, especially a tourist hat with my garbs, that'll stand out to the next few hundred people I pass and make memories for all of them, probably more than a couple photos, too. Bet your ass they'll end up on social media with a searchable hashtag to make sure the authorities can have a face to go with their hunt. Nope, just gotta be nonchalant and hope the business owners aren't being paid to turn over info to the Kremlin, and that they didn't opt for the unlimited data storage plan on their security system's D-V-R.*

Michael realized he had to leave, right then, to allow time to walk the extra dozen blocks to approach the church from the east, away from the entrance to The Russian Kitchen. *Any security staff worth its salt is gonna have that whole area covered, but I'm much better off if I can avoid walking right past their front door.*

When he finally walked west on *Borgo Santo Spirito*, Michael recognized the front of the church well before he arrived there. In addition to the familiar rooftop architecture, Michael had done extensive research on the church during his overseas flight. *I should've done more checking on the neighbors. Let that be a lesson to me.* He'd learned the church had been dedicated to both Saint Michael and Bishop Saint Magnus of Anagni, and that it was granted to Rome's Dutch community in 1689. *The Church of the Frisians, if I remember right. The priests who serve there are almost guaranteed to be descended from the Dutch or imported directly from the Netherlands, even if the name I got is some kinda pseudonym.*

Michael strode confidently through the narrow walkway that led from *Borgo Santi Spirito* to the front of the church. The front exterior wall was painted in light cream and tan, and contrasted nicely with the surrounding rust-orange walls. A Dutch flag hung over the stairs that led to the entrance. *Seems legit.* Michael entered the church and its familiar smells, sounds, and relative darkness comforted him. A priest slowly strolled behind the last row of pews near him.

"*Scusami,*" Michael offered in Italian.

"*Si, padre,*" the priest asked.

"*Parli inglese?*"

"How can I help you, Father," he asked with a distinct Dutch accent.

"Thank you, Father," Michael replied. "I'm hoping to speak with Father Levi."

"That's me, I'm Levi DeVries."

"I'm Father Andrew. I need to hear your confession." Much like he'd done in Texas, he watched the priest for his reaction. The man showed none and responded immediately.

"I can't imagine what I would need to confess."

"I can't either," Michael cautiously offered. "I won't know until you tell me. I'm here to offer absolution." *How now brown cow?*

"Perhaps I *am* in need of absolution, Father Andrew. Will you follow me, please?"

Michael breathed a sigh of relief. *Thank God he knew I was coming. John's intel network is batting a thousand, but I'm still holding out judgment on the rest of his operation.* He fell into step just behind Father Levi and to his left.

"Have you been to *Kerk van de Friezen* before, Father Andrew?" DeVries spoke in a hushed tone as he led Michael toward the back of the church and past sparse groups of tourists and parishioners.

"No, this is my first time."

"The Dutch, also called the *Friezen,* or *Frisians,*" he explained, "we began worshipping on this site more than a thousand years ago, and this i the Netherlands' national church. The current building, although it's since been renovated, was among the only ones not lost in this area to the construction of the Basilica. In addition to other artifacts permanently housed here, we're temporarily hosting two important relics: a stone from Christ's dedication at the Temple, and another stone upon which Abraham bound his son, Isaac."

"That's incredible," Michael offered. "It must be amazing to work among so much history every day."

"It is," DeVries replied as he slowed and cast a glance at two teen tourists that exceeded his idea of respectful volume. Both lowered their voices. "And, it is not, at times. A double-edged sword, as I suspect you might say?"

"I might, yes."

"If you'll follow me, we maintain a private area in the rectory. It will be less public there."

Once they reached the priests' private living quarters, DeVries led Michael to a small anteroom and closed the door behind them. He retrieved a familiar manila envelope from beneath the cushions of a chair and handed it over.

Michael accepted the envelope and confirmed the expected wax seals were in place and authentic. His pocketknife and another minute freed the concealed parchment paper. He read the same numbers he expected to see there: 2356.2284-5,7.2290-1.

"Go ahead, Father."

"Bless me, Father, for I have sinned," DeVries began. "It has been one day since my last confession."

Michael listened to all the details that Father Levi DeVries could provide about his new target, Pietro Isadore. The man was alleged to be a serial rapist who kept personal trophies, such as locks of hair, barrettes, and IDs, and blackmailed and extorted his victims afterward. *If the priest and this intel packet are accurate,* Michael thought, *this man desperately needs to realize the error of his ways. God willing, he'll not take another victim in this lifetime.*

MONDAY, 2237 HOURS_

VIA DEL COLOSSEO, 43. ROME, ITALY.

RAIN POURED down through the nighttime darkness and thudded hard against the van's roof and windshield. Michael had parked in the small lot just after ten pm, and he'd been fortunate enough to find a spot that allowed him to easily surveil the only entrance to *Via del Cardello, 17*. Despite his preferred tradecraft, he'd faced his small, rented Fiat van toward the target doorway, which allowed the Coliseum to fill his rear- and side-view mirrors. *Even through the rain, it's beautifully lit at night.*

As with the rest of the ancient city, this area hadn't been designed with cars in mind, and the generations of its recent inhabitants hadn't ever seen fit to forcibly inject such conveniences. The "lot" in which he'd parked had space only for about ten small cars, and the Italian "street" Michael watched in wait for the target was little more than an American alley. *A one SmartCar alley,* he corrected himself, *certainly not a one Cadillac alley. It's no wonder the cops have to drive such small cars here. They'd be better off on motorcycles with sidecars for the arrestee.*

The cobblestone street before him glistened beneath a small, under-powered streetlight that stood between him and the target. Few cars had passed by since his arrival, despite his proximity to the Coliseum and the relatively early hour. Especially in Italy's dense metropolitan areas, many of the restaurants would still be busy. *The lack of traffic oughta make my job much easier. There is no immediate crowd for Pietro Isadore to hide behind.*

Michael maintained an intent watch over the front entrance to the mustard yellow apartment building. Perhaps two dozen yards stood between them, but his small binoculars easily erased that distance. The autumn sun had long ago set over Rome, and Michael occasionally struggled to see clearly through the heavy rainfall on the poorly lit residential street. He wanted to use the van's wipers to momentarily clear the glass but knew doing so would risk being spotted. *No one can know I'm in here, it's too odd a behavior for this neighborhood at this hour. People remember 'odd.'* Having left both front windows open just slightly, he hoped the cooling night air would keep the van's interior glass from fogging. Unavoidable, cold droplets pelted the right side of his face, neck, and shoulder, and dampened the right sleeve of his dark blue, one-piece worker's uniform.

Michael inhaled a deep calming breath, which smelled of the rain and the intoxicating aroma of a nearby café. After silently reaffirming his need for continued patience, he turned the radio volume up just enough to hear the replay of the Pope's homily from yesterday's celebration and remembrance of Saint Simon and Saint Jude. *Luckily, I found a station broadcasting an English translation.* Although fluent in Spanish, his Italian wouldn't have done justice to the Pope's holy words.

"*Or to put it in complete context, Jesus sought to explain to all people the true will of God. He conveyed the righteousness that all must exhibit if they are to repent and ultimately enter His Kingdom. And so, the theme of the Sermon from the Mount is the righteous standard of conduct of God's Kingdom.*"

The seasonal rain continued falling hard and heavy on the Italian capital city despite earlier weather reports that it would be short-lived. Michael glanced at a Doppler radar app on his phone that showed no obvious, predictable end. *This decidedly works to my advantage, as uncomfortable as it is. Better to drown out the sounds of confession and absolution when and if it comes to that.* He glanced at his new smartwatch to check the time and noticed the date displayed on the background. *It's dad's birthday today. Wonder how he's doing. I should have time to call after this with the eight-hour time difference. Gotta put that away for now and focus on the task at hand.* Michael returned his attention to the apartment building.

"The sermon begins with the Beatitudes, which tell us the character of the virtuous people of God, those who have a place in His kingdom and can expect the full blessings of His love. In total, they describe the perfect Christian disciple but do not reveal how to become so. Christ, of course, provides that to us at a later time."

He should be along any time now, Michael thought.

Beneath an overhead light above the apartment building's entrance, a man emerged and stood in place, apparently seeking brief protection from the downpour. Michael lifted his binoculars to confirm the man's identity. *Buonasera, Pietro.* He'd just had time to identify his target before he pulled his rain jacket hood up over his head. Stepping out into the deluge, Isadore hurriedly walked uphill, away from Michael and his van. *Abnormal evening wear for Rome, unless you're going to the gym. No one works out in jeans, though, especially not wet jeans. He's probably on the hunt for a new victim. Hopefully nothing more than reconnaissance tonight.*

As Michael intently watched Isadore trudge away, he recited Saint Michael's prayer. "O Glorious Prince of the Heavenly hosts, Saint Michael the Archangel, defend us in battle..." Isadore slowly disappeared from sight as he continued the recitation. By either fate or subconscious timing, Michael saw his target turn right at the top of the small hill just as he closed his prayer. "Amen."

Michael slipped from the driver's seat and into the rain himself. He retrieved a toolbelt and a small red toolbox from the van's rear cargo area and urgently approached the apartment building's entrance. *Gotta work fast to find the evidence. Isadore might only be out long enough for a smoke and an espresso, and I wanna uncover his secrets and get set up before he comes back.* Michael momentarily paused at the covered doorway, reached up with his right hand and touched the plain wood cross pendant concealed beneath his zipped-up worker's suit. *God willing, I'll soon know if this man's the monster he's alleged to be. With evidence to leave behind for the police, I can protect all human dignity from his future sins tonight and still walk away with a clear conscience.* He quickly and slightly crossed himself with his right hand and stepped to a lighted security keypad on the wall to the right of the doorway. Michael quickly punched in the four-digit code from the intel packet.

bzzzzt thunk

The magnetic lock buzzed and released the door, and Michael pulled it open, careful not to appear too nervous or surprised that his code had worked. He saw a poorly lit hallway awaited him, and a small sign at the far end revealed the elevator's location. Michael stepped inside and pulled the door shut behind him. The same radio program he'd been listening to in the van lightly echoed toward him from an unknown apartment nearby.

"When Jesus tells us, 'blessed are they,' He is describing their inner joy and peace for being aligned with God, as well as praising their character and pledging divine rewards for it."

Michael smiled at this small, but welcome, confirmation of the righteousness of his task. Confident and just, he strode toward the expectedly-small elevator intent on determining the impending fate of one, Pietro Isadore.

MONDAY, 2251 HOURS_

ISADORE RESIDENCE. ROME, ITALY.

MICHAEL HAD ONLY REQUIRED a few seconds to pick the old locks on Pietro Isadore's apartment door. *The internal components are so sloppy that I bet a Honda key would've opened it.* He confidently opened the door, as though he belonged there, stepped inside the apartment, and quietly closed it behind him. *No alarm noises, that's good.* Michael tacitly flipped the old deadbolt closed and saw a small, brass security chain hanging on the inside of the doorframe near his eye level. *Ironic that Isadore's got a rape chain on his own door. I guess he's the kinda guy that'd know how important those are.* He quickly examined the doorframe for telltale magnetic alarm sensors but found none.

Turning around, Michael stood still and just listened to the apartment for a moment. *If I'm mistaken and he* is *home, I'll have to convince him that the landlord sent me to fix an emergency plumbing problem and I'm in the wrong apartment. I know just enough Italian to portray myself as a Spanish immigrant, as long as no one speaks more Spanish than I do.*

A long, door-less hallway led to the other rooms and prevented him from seeing much else from the doorway. *I have to be careful walking around in this old building so the downstairs neighbors don't hear me. One call to Isadore to complain about his noise would ruin everything.* Michael heard no movement, no sounds from inside the apartment, and saw nothing to indicate Isadore and the police would be alerted to his presence. He proceeded through the rest of the dwelling and kept his large toolbox in hand, just in case he had to be more convincing. *This short scan for people might save me a lot of time if Isadore keeps his trophies out on display.* The overall glance throughout the interior confirmed he was alone in the small one-bedroom apartment but didn't reveal any obvious, corroborating evidence. *Dirtbags that do what Isadore's accused of aren't gonna keep all that under lock and key in a wall or subfloor, they're gonna keep it accessible where they can easily and privately relive the conquests. I'll start with the bedroom. Probably good that I don't have a blacklight handy.*

Michael quietly strode to the apartment's small bedroom and paused to decide where to begin searching in earnest. There was no closet, but a tall armoire stood on the wall opposite the door. A traditional double-bed with a metal frame, head-, and footboard stood centered against the wall to Michael's right. A long, low dresser that matched the armoire stood against the wall to his left. Above the dresser was a large canvas painting. Michael stepped to his right, alongside the bed, to better examine the painting. At first, it appeared to be a slightly abstract nude of a woman lying in bed, as seen from the perspective of her headboard. Upon closer inspection, Michael realized the void between her legs was a man apparently performing oral sex on her. *Hmm, so he's a romantic. I'm gonna start there.*

Michael set his toolbox down near the doorway and moved over to the bottom left corner of the painting. Lifting it just slightly away from the wall, he wanted to first identify how it had been hung. A small, folded piece of paper fell from behind the painting and landed on the dresser. Setting the canvas back against the wall, Michael briefly inspected the paper and found it was blank. *He probably thinks it's a security measure. If he sets it between the wall and the painting and comes home later to find it on the ground, he'll suspect that someone might've seen what he's hiding behind it. A little silly, though, given his alleged sins and crimes. If someone's interested enough to break in, he'd be dead or in handcuffs before he ever sees the misplaced paper. Maybe this'll be more like cop work than I thought. We didn't often catch the smart ones there, either.*

Michael dropped the paper back down to the dresser and again tried to confirm how the painting was hung. The first thing that caught his eye however, when he looked behind it, was a Polaroid photograph tacked to the wall and concealed just behind the corner he'd lifted. *Can't see th image clearly, but that's exactly the kinda thing I'm looking for.* He glanced farther up the wall. *Single wire near the middle, looks like.* Michael stepped around to the front of the dresser, which was deep enough to allow him to barely grasp and lift both bottom edges of the painting. He carefully slid the canvas up the wall several inches to avoid damaging anything hidden behind it. Once confident he'd freed it from its hooks, Michael picked the painting up, turned around, and placed it gently on the bed behind him. Before turning back to the wall, he momentarily steeled himself for what he feared and expected to find there.

As soon as Michael turned around, dozens of instant-photo images of naked women stared back at him and turned Michael's stomach, even though he hadn't yet taken in any of their details. *The forest is terrible enough, examining the trees will be insufferable. Still, it must be done.* Stepping closer to the images, Michael methodically began with the bottom left, the first one he'd noticed, and worked his way around Isadore's collection as a horrible clock. All the depicted women appeared very intoxicated, and some seemed unconscious. None smiled at him or seemed aware of their actions or current engagements. *No one looks like an active, willing participant.*

Every photographed woman was a brunette, under thirty, and most appeared college-age, at best. *I'm sure there's no shortage of residents and visitors in that age bracket willing to put themselves at risk of meeting Isadore, but none of them deserved or asked to be violated like this. There have to be twenty-five or thirty victims here, and I'm sure he didn't have the guts to start collecting and keeping pictures until he'd already been at this a while. It's still possible this was all consensual, so without the chance to speak with these women, I need more evidence to move forward. There can be* no doubt, *none whatsoever.*

Michael opened the top right dresser drawer, the one farthest from the door, and another small, folded piece of paper dropped onto the floor at his feet. *Jackpot, just like an "X" on a treasure map.* Confident he searched in the right place, Michael cautiously pulled the drawer open. *I might have to put everything back as I found it, even though I'll probably be posing all this for the cops to find in a few days when Isadore's neighbors report the stench.*

Once the drawer fully opened, Michael found another part of

Isadore's trophy collection. Driver's licenses, credit cards, passports. Removed body piercings. Necklaces. A few locks of brown hair held together with clear tape. Distinct, elaborate hair barrettes. *Lock and barrettes, just as the victim said he'd taken from her. This is another time it'd be nice if I could have the victim's name. Seeing her D-L in here would corroborate this beyond all reasonable doubt.*

Michael set that drawer on the dresser and moved to the next one. *Another folded paper.* He found an internal tray that appeared to contain Isadore's supplies: a large tube of personal lubricant and an economy size box of Magnum condoms. Michael frowned. *I doubt it, Isadore.* After lifting the tray, Michael found the last of what he needed: four brown bottles, each about four ounces in volume and two sets of pliers. *That's gonna be his intoxicant. Probably GHB.* The pliers, one large adjustable set and a small pair of needle-nose, were probably for removing the women's intimate body jewelry. *Probably.*

Michael took a deep breath to quell his rage and tried to focus on what he needed to do next. He knew law enforcement would eventually have to try to connect the women from the photographs with the identification documents. *That's not my purpose here, though. I can ensure they're offered counseling and help, but I only need their names and addresses for that.* He started to return to the IDs to photograph them for follow-up, but then decided better of it. *This'll take too long, given the sheer number of documented victims he's assaulted. I have to be ready* before *he comes back. The photos can be done* after *Isadore's been subdued.*

Michael unzipped his overalls and retrieved a holstered tranquilizer gun concealed at his right hip. He checked to ensure its powerful, anesthetic darts were loaded. Having confirmed it was ready to fire, he placed it upon the dresser close to the hallway and pointing toward the front door. *Can't risk an accidental discharge. Now Isadore can come home whenever he's ready. I've got a whole different kinda double-shot with his name on it.*

Michael looked back up at the photos, and tremendous sorrow and sympathy overwhelmed him. *Isadore uses these trophies to relive his conquests, revictimizing these women in his mind and in real life, through his alleged extortion and blackmail. Probably sends his demand letter to the address on their license, so not every victim sees them. Gets new pics delivered to an anonymous email account he accesses with a V-P-N. As long as he continues to prey on foreigners, the odds of him being caught are much lower. The cops might eventually arrest him, if victims start coming forward with enough information and evidence, but he's such a prolific predator that I can't wait around for one of his victims to file a report. I'm not the detective assigned to the case, so I don't have to care* how *he's victimizing these women, I only have to care* that *he's doing it.*

As he scanned the images, Michael noticed small, handwritten dates on the bottom right corner of each. *That arrogant prick!* He thought the dates showed some consistency and checked them against the calendar on his phone. *Most of these are Fridays and Mondays. Today's Monday! He's out hunting somewhere, right now!* Michael frantically considered the intel he had on Isadore and the resources available to him at that moment. *I don't know his hunting ground. I don't know where he went, and I can't risk leaving here to try finding him. I can't ping his phone, I can't call the cops and ask for their help. Hell, I don't even have a phone number for him, but I'm sure that's something the cops could find, if I could break the Seal of the Confessional to tell them what I know!* Michael returned to the images on Isadore's wall and urgently scanned their backgrounds, looking for anything that might identify a location. *A hotel, a business, anything. Wait, it's here.* He looked at the bedroom again and compared it to the photos' background, which confirmed that Isadore brought his victims back to his own apartment. *Every one of them up here, they've all been taken in this room!*

Now confident that Isadore would bring any new victim back to Michael, he set about his preparations. *There's little chance that I can stop him from targeting another woman tonight, but I'll be damned if I can't stop him from following through on the abuse.* He retrieved a pair of nitrile medical exam gloves from his pocket and put them on. Donning a second pair helped ensure he'd leave no prints or latent impressions behind. *Should've put these on when I first came in. Rookie mistake. I know better than that. Focus, Michael, the devil is in the details!* He carried his red toolbox to the small living room and set it down next to a sturdy chair he intended to use for Isadore's confession and absolution. He opened the metal box and hurriedly retrieved and set out the tools he hoped to soon require: three syringes of anesthetic antidote, two sets of padded nylon restraints, a thick gym sock, and a balaclava. *Ironically, the balaclava's for*

Isadore, not for me. I'm not worried about my identity, but I am worried about keeping the gym sock in his mouth without duct tape. Any coroner would notice the skin damage and adhesive it leaves behind.

The sudden, unexpected sound of a key fumbling about inside the front deadbolt immediately chilled Michael. He moved over to the entryway wall and glanced around the corner to his left. The door shook slightly as someone on the other side attempted to get it open.

"*Solo un momento, mia bella,*" a male voice offered.

He's not talking to the door, or to himself, is he, Michael wondered. *He's probably not alone.* Michael scanned the apartment for an additional exit and found none. *I'm stuck in here to deal with whoever's about to walk through that door with him. If he met someone tonight who didn't need to be drugged to sleep with him, that's gonna change everything!* From somewhere deep in his mind, Michael heard John's voice yelling at him. *How now, brown cow?!* Just then, the apartment's front door flung open, and Michael's fears instantly became his reality.

MONDAY, 2358 HOURS_

ISADORE RESIDENCE. ROME, ITALY.

As THE FRONT door of Isadore's apartment struck the wall behind it, Michael filled with panic. *The gun's still in the bedroom!* A quick glance across the open end of the hallway confirmed that his anesthetic tranquilizer still sat on the top end of the dresser where he'd last placed it. *Dammit!*

"Ssshhhhh," a male voice drunkenly whispered from the open doorway.

They're never as quiet as they think they are, Michael thought. *How can I get to the bedroom without being seen? If he shouts at this hour, it's all over.* He risked a momentary glance back down the long entryway and saw Isadore walking backward through the doorway. Michael took another look and realized he was carrying a woman inside. She was petite with long brown hair, but he couldn't tell much more about her yet. *Well, not carrying, really, so much as dragging. He's already drugged the victim.* Her legs didn't move to help or protest, and a black high-heeled shoe slipped off her right foot as it slid across the apartment threshold. Her left foot was already bare. *The first one must have gone missing somewhere between here and there.* Knowing his target couldn't see him, didn't expect him, and had likely been drinking, Michael quietly rushed across the back of the entryway and retrieved his tranq gun from the dresser.

"Un momento, bella, e ti farò sentire molto meglio."

Michael didn't fully understand the drunken statement, but he certainly knew "one moment" and Isadore's obvious intent. He stood in wait, just a few feet inside the bedroom doorway, while Isadore struggled to get the woman inside and close the door. *I can't help her yet, not without risking a conversation with the carabinieri.*

Hefting the unconscious woman through the doorway, Isadore kicked at the bottom of the door with his foot until it slammed back closed again. He didn't bother locking it.

He knows she's not going anywhere, and he's not concerned about being interrupted. As many times as he's done this, it's clear the neighbors must think he's some kind of Romeo.

Isadore kept *shhhh'ing* the woman, even though she hadn't made a sound. He again walked backward toward Michael and pulled the woman deeper into his apartment.

Michael didn't feel especially confident she was still breathing. *He just made her the first priority. I care more about her safety than I ever will about his soul.* Waiting as long as he could, he let Isadore get within four feet of him. Michael raised the gun, pointed it at the meaty back of his target's left thigh, and smoothly pressed the trigger. Twice.

schooockschooock

Before Isadore had a chance to react to the first dart, Michael had placed the second at nearly the same point of impact. Even though the dart tips themselves were covered with the same powerful anesthetic they delivered, Michael was surprised when Isadore only slightly *yelped* at their impact. *Supposed to be milder than a bee sting. I never wanna know, and he may never be able to tell me.*

Isadore released the woman from his left hand and tried to inspect the back of his leg, but her awkwardly descending weight tripped him. Michael's target fell onto his buttocks and back with the woman still on top of him, and he hoped Isadore's flailing had driven the darts in farther.

It'll only be a few seconds now, Michael thought as Isadore's resistance quickly lessened. He flopped down onto his back with his arms helplessly out to his sides. Confident the powerful overdose had done its job, Michael stepped over to him. Looking down on the man, Michael briefly saw recognition and wonder in his eyes, just before his pupils relaxed and rolled back in their orbitals. *You're gonna get lucky tonight, Pietro, just not in the way you had planned.*

With his target out of commission, Michael knew he had several minutes to care for the woman before he had to assess Isadore's vitals. *The anesthetic only works so fast because it's a significant overdose. I don't want him to die yet, the absolution requires his conscious participation!* Michael grabbed the woman by her wrists, pulled her up and off Isadore, and, careful not to injure her head, he slid her farther into the apartment. She wore a small black dress and Michael thought her hair and makeup identified her as American. Her smell and appearance confirmed Michael's suspicion that Isadore probably hunted at bars. *That's the easiest place for him to find and target new victims.* Michael leaned down and placed his ear directly over her mouth. The stink of liquor and cigarettes filled his nostrils and he felt only very shallow and slow breathing. Michael checked her carotid pulse. *Also, weak. If he is using G-H-B, there's a fine line between effective and lethal dosing, and that's without the alcohol she's also got on-board.*

Michael briefly contemplated the scenario before him, but he intrinsically knew what he had to do. *She needs a hospital more than he needs salvation. Fuck him.* With that decided, he ran through his logistical options to simultaneously get the girl medical help, get his gear out of the apartment in case he could not return, and leave Isadore and his place set up to portray a guilt-driven suicide. *She's still breathing, but I can't take long. The closest hospital's almost ten minutes away. Two minutes. I'll do everything I can in the next two minutes.*

Michael hurried to his toolbox, retrieved a pad of paper and a pen, and scrawled out a few remorseful words he'd previously translated into Italian: "*mi dispiace. non ho causato molto dolore.*"

"I hope you *are* sorry, Isadore," Michael quietly offered as he worked, 'and, yes, you *have* caused quite a lot of pain. I just hope it's believable :hat you'd say this, just in case you don't get to write one in your own vords. It'd be kinda funny to find out later that you were the last illiterate ·dult left in Italy."

Moving quickly, he set the pen and paper on the floor next to Isadore nd ensured his prints were on both items. Michael then dropped them on the small kitchen table and pulled one of the dining chairs out a bit. *No, he's been drinking.* He instead quietly turned the chair over on the floor.

Michael returned to the bedroom and hurriedly staged it as he thought a remorseful predator might. He exposed all the known secrets but did so without sullying or scattering them. *He'd still care about the trophies, even if they'd cost him his life.*

Lastly, he assessed the vitals of both Isadore and the woman. *Both are still breathing, but Isadore's pulse is down to about fifty-five. He might bottom out before I get back, but I'd rather risk his death than hers. Neither of them has much time.*

Michael carefully retrieved his darts from Isadore's thigh, urgently packed up all his belongings in the toolbox, and ensured the front of his overalls still concealed his cassock and collarino. He prepared to leave the apartment with the victim and, he hoped, all evidence that he'd ever been there. Placing his toolbox by the front door, he kneeled down to lift the young woman. *I need to move fast and work doors and locks, so I've gotta put her up on my left shoulder.* Michael looked over at Isadore and paused just long enough to ensure his chest still rose and fell on its own. Michael's memory inconveniently recalled John's recent assertion that he had to get the absolution ritual right. He clearly saw the instructor's previous grimace and heard his concluding statement: *Takin' a life without absolvin' its soul is no better'n a killin, and might be a murder, no matter how much society benefits from the absence of the departed.*

"Sorry, John," he quietly offered and picked up the girl. "She's the only one that matters right now."

TUESDAY, 0056 HOURS_

VIA DEL COLOSSEO, 43. ROME, ITALY.

JUST AS MICHAEL turned back onto the narrow street just northwest of the Coliseum, the rain had finally slowed to a fine drizzle. Seeing that his same parking stall had remained empty while he drove the woman to a hospital, Michael pulled the van back in and rolled down both front windows. He killed the ignition and intently listened to the outside world. Only the sounds of a sleepy urban neighborhood reached him. *Very little movement around this area at night, but I have to take a few minutes to be sure. Less movement should mean fewer witnesses for the cops, and no Good Samaritans to mistakenly come to Isadore's aid.*

The 'aid' thought made Michael again consider how fortunate he'd been at the hospital. *Thank God that orderly was taking his late-night smoke break just outside the emergency doors when I pulled up. She was barely breathing, and he rushed her inside so fast that he didn't notice me drive off. If I'd been hung up there, I'd have no chance to now prevent Isadore's death. Well, at least his unintentional death. John's gonna flip his shit if I muck up my first righteous assignment.*

Michael understood that he had very little time to get back inside the apartment, and he desperately feared that he may have already failed. Despite that, Michael knew he couldn't risk rushing back into the apartment building before providing himself some assurance that nothing had changed in his absence. *No cops, no medics. If someone had called the authorities while I was gone, they would certainly have been here by now. I have to risk going back up while there's still a chance that Isadore's alive. As much as I despise his behavior, God wants all His children afforded the opportunity to spend eternity at His side.*

Stepping from the rented van, Michael checked that the zipper of his overalls still covered his cassock and collarino. He adjusted his toolbelt and once again retrieved the large metal toolbox. *It's unlikely that I'll get to carry out the absolution I intended, but I can't deny him the opportunity if God allows it.*

Quickly retracing his steps, Michael soon found himself again standing in Pietro Isadore's apartment. The ominous difference this time, though, was Isadore's body lying at the back of the entryway. *Good news is he didn't get up and call for help. Bad news is I might have missed his only opportunity for salvation.*

Michael closed the door behind him and again locked its flimsy deadbolt. Before taking another step, he donned two new pairs of medical exam gloves. Only then did he approach Isadore and, just as he had done earlier for the young woman, held his ear just over the man's open mouth. *No breath.* Checking the man's radial pulse, he found nothing; the carotid pulse was also absent. *Isadore hasn't been dead for very long. His color hasn't changed, and rigor mortis isn't set in.* Michael rose and desperately turned on several nearby light switches to get a better look. Through almost two decades of police and clerical work, he'd seen dozens of lifeless bodies. More than enough to know that Isadore was gone. *He looks like a wax statue, void of an inner light and sentience.*

His heart filled with panic at the apparent failure, and he hurriedly opened the toolbox and retrieved the antidote syringes. Kneeling down next to his target, Michael resolved himself not to fail at securing Isadore's confession. *Gotta plunge the needle through his sternum and into his heart! The cartilage's too thick for 'gentle' and 'moderate!'* Michael uncapped the syringe, gripped it hard in his right fist, and raised it high above his head. Just before hammer-fisting the antidote home, Michael paused and considered the consequences of his imminent actions. *I could make heroic efforts with all three syringes of antidote and C-P-R, but that's almost certain to fail. Even if I get his pulse back, he could have brain damage from the oxygen deprivation. If I start this, I'm gonna leave a lot of forensic evidence that this wasn't a suicide, and there's almost no chance he'll ever breathe on his own again, anyway. How much point is there in condemning myself and risking the whole program, when there's almost no chance at cleansing his soul? I chose to save her, and that cost Isadore his salvation. The medical examiner's already gonna inspect the small bruises on the back of his leg. If Isadore looks like he got his ass kicked, they'll* never *rule this a suicide.*

Michael lowered and recapped the syringe as reason and the forensic realities overpowered his emotions. *Saint Aquinas believed that God can even use demons to achieve and direct His plans for us. If that's true, then it's equally possible that God allowed the girl to be here so Isadore couldn't enjoy the opportunity I came here to present. He could have compelled me to save her so I* couldn't *also save him. There's so much at play that I can never know or control, it'd just be narcissistic for me to take the blame or the credit for the outcome.*

Michael sighed and accepted his circumstances for what they were. *Unfortunate, but, perhaps divinely orchestrated, as well. There's nothing more I can do for him here that I can't do later from an outbound aircraft. Whatever Isadore's current circumstance is, wherever his soul now finds itself, he and his demons got there all on their own. I can plead for God to show His mercy to* both *of us in the coming hours and days, but I can't offer a compelling argument without Isadore's confession and absolution.*

Disappointed, Michael rose and went about destroying or recovering any forensic evidence of his presence in the apartment. He expected the building's air conditioning had already been shut down for the season, so he turned off the unit's heat to conceal the body as long as possible. *That fact alone won't keep Isadore's death from being ruled a suicide, as long as I didn't leave enough other evidence behind to justify a protracted investigation. It's most important that the medical examiners here don't yet test for this anesthetic, but that's out of my hands. Given the evidence of his crimes, I doubt* anyone *will care what really happened to him.*

Michael slowly and deliberately scanned the apartment one last time to ensure he hadn't left anything behind and wiped down every surface he thought he might have touched. He opened Isadore's armoire to ensure no additional evidence remained hidden there, and, to his surprise, saw a set of blue overalls similar to his. *Different sizes, but close enough to be believable.* He removed the disguise and hung it next to Isadore's. After setting the toolbox on the bed next to the painting, Michael removed the capped antidote syringes and secured them in his pocket. *Everything else can be thought to belong to the deceased. The restraints, gag, and balaclava are all new in the packaging and have no prints or D-N-A to offer investigators.* He set the toolbox and its contents in the bottom of the armoire and concealed it under some clothing, just as he thought a predator might.

As Michael retrieved his lock-pick set and strode toward the front doorway, his thoughts turned to regret. *There's no time to wallow in what I've done here and how I failed the primary objective. The woman's health and survival had to come first, and I'll have to ask for God's forgiveness later that Isadore didn't have one final chance at confession and absolution. With what I knew and saw, I'd have been justified in shooting Isadore to protect her, so I can't beat myself up too badly that he didn't survive the overdose.* He quietly turned the front doorknob and pulled it ajar just enough to confirm no one stood in the hallway outside. *I may not get to walk away from this with the clear conscience I'd hoped for, but, at this point, I'll have to be content with getting to walk away at all.* Michael's growing paranoia only allowed him to pause for a few seconds before he stepped into the building's empty, shared hallway with the pick-set in hand.

Please let this sloppy deadbolt lock as easily as it unlocked.

TUESDAY, 0214 HOURS_

VIA DEL CARDELLO, 17. ROME, ITALY.

Dressed in his black cassock and starched white collarino, Michael stepped out from the murder scene and into the apartment building's shared interior hallway. He pulled Pietro Isadore's door closed and nonchalantly looked around him. *No one's here, time to hurry.* Michael fought the intensifying urgency in his gut to flee. Although he wanted to sprint away from the serial rapist's body as far and fast as his legs and lungs could carry him, Michael logically understood this was the most critical phase of his operation. He now had to do *everything* right to avoid leaving a forensic trail that would inspire a homicide investigation and risk his identification. He set about locking Isadore's flimsy deadbolt with his pick-set. *Slow is smooth, smooth is fast.*

click

Michael breathed a sigh of relief when the lock's cylinder easily rolled over. He stepped away from the door and concealed the set in his pocket as he walked. *Stay calm, stay calm. Now is NOT the time to lose my cool. Everything I do, or don't do, for the next two hours will determine if the cops find me, suspect a murder, or simply close this as the suicide it's intended to be.* Michael's thoughts uncontrollably returned to his failure to attempt or secure a confession and absolve the man of his sins. *Whether his soul is at peace or not, at least he's no longer capable of preying upon God's children. I'll have to deal with that later, as there's nothing to be done about it now.*

Michael nonchalantly walked toward the stairwell. *Don't want to take the elevator in case it has a video surveillance feed. The cops might realize the maintenance worker and the priest are the same guy.*

Michael had walked no more than a few steps before a door suddenly opened just ahead of him and to his left. An elderly woman pushed a walker into the hallway and startled when she saw him there. Dressed in a white cotton nightgown, bright yellow crocheted shawl, and slippers, she didn't look like she intended to go very far. Her thick, white hair was up in rollers, and she wore large, black-framed eyeglasses. The thick lenses made her eyes appear comically massive, and Michael hoped he lived to laugh about it later. *While I'm outside of a cell would be better.* The woman displayed the same surprise that Michael felt. She looked past him, to the end of the hallway and the door to Isadore's apartment. Michael smiled at her and tried to conceal his intrinsic terror.

"Father," she hesitantly asked in Italian, "is Pietro dead?"

The terrifying question compelled Michael to calm his runaway emotions. *She can't know that!* He'd preplanned an explanation if found or confronted on his way out of the building, which improved the speed and sincerity of his response. *I just hope my Italian is up to the task.* "Do you know him well, ma'am?" *Gotta watch my verb tense. I'm the only one who knows that Pietro is now past.* He carefully stepped around the woman's walker toward the stairs. Michael glanced up at the green exit sign ahead and felt its siren call.

"He's lived here for years, always bringing those drunk whores back to his bed." She spat on the floor. "He hates God, so, if you're coming from his apartment, I know he *must* be dead."

I can't panic! If she sees me react, she'll know she's right! "We, *uhh,* we must serve whenever we're, *umm,* when we're called, ma'am," Michael struggled to translate his thoughts. Amid her assertions about Pietro's demise, Michael forgot what he intended to say if confronted. His panic increased and he stepped closer to the stairwell door about fifteen feet past her. "Pietro has a, *uhh,* a bad conscience, a lot of guilt. I hope you will pray for him." *I wouldn't normally say so much, but I can't break the Seal of the*

Confessional if Isadore didn't confess. It's more important that I escape and keep the existence of the absolvers a secret.

"I pray for his soul every day, as I'm afraid he's just not right in the head, Father. I don't like how he looks at my granddaughters, but they're too smart and too tough for that little weasel."

I've gotta end this conversation without being rude, Michael thought. *Negative emotions plant stronger memories, and I need to be neutral and forgettable.* "I understand, ma'am." Michael didn't know how else to respond. *I certainly can't validate her concerns or say that she won't have to worry about that again.*

"I'm too old to care what these other people think, but before I go to bed each night, though, I pray that Pietro finally accepts Jesus Christ into his life and prays the sacrament for himself. He tells me that he doesn't even believe in God, Father."

"I think he's seen the error of his ways." The woman's confirmation of his fears about Isadore's faith brought Michael's guilt back to the forefront of his mind. *Tonight'll be a recurring source of confession and prayer for a long time to come.*

"*Mama!*"

The woman startled at the loud male voice and stared back into the apartment toward the unseen man that called for her.

Michael recognized her "hand in the cookie jar" look and seized his opportunity to move closer to the exit while the elderly woman focused on her keeper. *He sounds much younger than her, gotta be her son, or a son-in-law.*

"*What are you doing out there, old woman? You know it's dangerous to go out by yourself at night! What if there's a rapist out there, and he has his way with you?!*"

"*Maybe I would have* my *way with* him," the woman shouted back in protest. "*I leave the door unlocked* every *night so I might get lucky and feel like a woman one last time!*"

Michael had almost reached the exit door. *Please forget about me for another few seconds.*

"*Get back in here, crazy woman! Your mind gets worse every day! Where were you going?*"

"I'm out here talking with the nice priest." She shouted and pointed a finger in Michael's direction but stayed focused on the argument.

Michael quietly opened the green metal door and urgently stepped into the stairwell. He tried to push it shut behind him, but a small wood doorstop held it open several inches. *No time to dig it out.* Michael descended as quickly and quietly as possible while the upstairs conversation closely followed him down.

"He's right here," the woman explained, her voice echoing down the concrete stairwell. *"Where did he go?"*

"Mama, did you take your medicine? Pietro wouldn't talk to a priest unless he was dead."

"That's what I *told him!"*

Michael reached the next flight and slowed his pace a bit now that he couldn't be seen from the landing above. *Slow is smooth, smooth is fast.* Once at the ground level, he carefully pushed the exit door open, oriented himself in the building's main interior hallway, and turned left toward the street. *Even if the cops take her statement seriously, they don't have much time to find me. Another two minutes and I'll be safely away in the van. Another two hours and I'll be safely out of Rome.*

TUESDAY, 0436 HOURS_

CIAMPINO-G. B. PASTINE INTERNATIONAL AIRPORT. ROME, ITALY.

Michael purposefully strode through the private terminal at Rome's secondary airport. His pace showed he was in a hurry but didn't reveal his inner turmoil. *People would definitely remember a priest who looked like he was running from a murder scene. Slow is smooth, smooth is fast.* His previous intel packet had included the known camera locations inside this terminal, so Michael turned his head, adjusted his hair, or rubbed his temples as he passed them. *Anyone casually viewing the footage wouldn't suspect anything but determined investigators would see my intent. They won't care that I'm wearing a cassock, not even in Rome.*

A panel of six large-screen televisions caught his eye. Two of them, tuned to CNN, showed a report entitled "Vatican's Mental Health Crisis?" Michael slowed and then stopped to watch the news segment. One television projected the CNN audio in Italian and one next to it showed closed-captioning in English. The channel replayed a cell phone video clip of a handcuffed man in a black cassock being forced into the back of a police car. As the video showed him thrashing against the officers and yelling to the unknown videographer, the footage stopped on a frame that clearly showed his face. *Thomas.*

Michael stepped closer to the screens, engrossed in the report and filled with apprehension about what it might mean for him and those few like him. He abandoned the video and voraciously read all the captioning:

"...this young man, who identified himself as 'Father Shawn Moore' to The Powerful 99, a global network dedicated to uncovering and investigating abuses of power and vigilante justice."

The video feed continued playing, but CNN producers had added its audio to the report. *"They're training killers, and I used to be one of 'em,"* Thomas frantically shouted at the camera. Michael understood the cops' efforts to subdue the man without striking or harming him, especially in front of the camera. *"They sent us to a private camp, up in Wyoming, twelve of us, just like the Apostles, and they made me go by Thomas, just like the apostle, and they made us steal newspapers and commit burglaries, and the guy in charge, he goes by 'John,' but I know that's not his name because we all had fake names, and we had to keep everything secret, but then I didn't like the way they made me kill the pig, so I went back and tried to kill another one the right way, and they kicked me out before I—"* The cops finally got him shoved into the back seat of their patrol car. As the door shut on Thomas' shouts, the police turned their focus on getting the camera crew back away from their squad car. Thomas continued yelling, but the camera didn't pick up anything else he said.

The report cut to a dark-skinned, Mediterranean-looking female anchor. *"Representatives of this organization claim to CNN they tried to meet with Father Moore to videotape his allegations that the Vatican is currently training and arming a clandestine group trained to kill on command all those who oppose the church and its holy leader.*

"The investigators claim local police and church officials were already on-scene when they arrived to meet with Moore, and that he was soon forcibly handcuffed, arrested, and taken away on what they assert are trumped-up charges of mental instability and being a danger to himself and the public. In their released statement, The Powerful 99 assert that such vilification actions are typical of those that abuse their power and must work to silence the whistleblowers who refuse to go along with the evil ways. Their statement reads in part, 'We must question authority at every level, especially that which has unlimited power, financing, and ideologically devoted followers potentially willing to do anything to protect their own self-interests and world-view.'"

The anchor continued reading from her teleprompter. *"CNN reporters spoke with Bishop Harold Hoffaburr, a public information office for the Archdiocese of Omaha, which oversees Catholic church operations for the parish where Father Moore is employed in the United States. Here is an excerpt from that interview."*

The news report cut to an edited video that showed the man Michael knew as "Father Harry" speaking into a black foam-covered, handheld microphone. *Oh, shit,* Michael thought, *he* is *more involved than he or John let on!*

"While I cannot speak to Father Moore's specific circumstances, out of respect for his privacy, I can tell you that the Catholic church and the Holy See take the mental health of all our clergy and employees very seriously, and Father Moore has lifelong access to all the best available help for whatever care he requires now, and for however long he requires it."

The report cut back to the anchor. *"Back here in Italy, the Vatican has not yet responded to CNN's requests for comments or interviews, but we did recently receive this statement from the Archbishop of Omaha, who oversees Father Moore and his superiors."* A transcript of the statement appeared on the screen, and the female anchor read it aloud for her audience. *"We take our obligations to care for the physical and mental health of our employees and clergy very seriously. Most priests enter seminary at an age in which they remain susceptible to hallucinations and delusions consistent with schizophrenia. While Father Moore has not yet received such a diagnosis, we have long been prepared to accept and care for clergy that fall victim to these terrible types of illnesses. Father Moore, should he eventually require such care, will be allowed to remain with our mental health professionals for as long as he requires it at no expense to him or his family. We view the care of Father Moore and those with similar afflictions as part of our Holy obligation to care for the dignity and lives of all people. We pray for Father Moore's recovery and hope that you will, as well.'*

"And, in current European news," the anchor transitioned to the next story, *"the Greek economy again shows indications of looming trouble..."*

Michael tried to keep his face expressionless as he continued on to his waiting plane. *So that's what becomes of anyone that John and Bishop Harold Hoffaburr identify as traitors. Predictable, but, still good to know. Doesn't matter that he's right, I bet they keep Father Moore zoned out on psych meds until he's no longer a threat. I wonder if they'll bother with moving the compound, now that Moore's obviously discussed it.*

He looked ahead to the doorway required to access the tarmac and his aircraft. A grandfatherly-looking man stood just to the left of the doorway and appeared to be scanning the sparse crowd. The man looked at him, and Michael thought he saw recognition on his face. *Is he looking for me?* Ignoring the man for the moment, he continued on to his assigned exit. The man smiled and half-raised his hand as Michael approached.

"Father Andrew?" He spoke in English, but his heavy Italian accent revealed his native tongue.

"Yes?"

"Sorry to bother you, but I'm told there's been a change of plans in your destination this morning."

"That's rather inconvenient at this late hour." Michael hoped his objection seemed believable and sufficiently spontaneous to anyone who might have overheard them. *Still feels insubordinate to pretend I'm put off by the alleged schedule change. Please God, don't be a plant already, we're just getting this off the ground.*

"Then whom shall I send?" The challenge question rolled naturally off the man's tongue.

"Here I am," Michael calmly replied. "Send me."

The man smiled and revealed a small messenger bag that he had concealed behind his back during their initial contact. He passed the bag to Michael, which had the same diplomatic pouch markings and locks as the bag Michael had received for the Isadore assignment.

"I'm told this has all the instructions you require to continue on your way," the man offered as he stepped closer to Michael to have a more private conversation. Michael had gripped the bag's handle, but the man didn't yet let it go. "Did you happen to see the morning news reports out of Nebraska, in the U-S?"

"I did," Michael replied and tried to keep his suspicion out of his voice.

"What a shame, Father," the man offered and maintained eye contac with Michael.

There isn't sympathy in his eyes, Michael realized, *only caution, at bes*

"It's such a *terrible thing,*" the man offered in a cold and calculate tone, "that a man of God would succumb to such a fate. I hope you unde stand *no one* believes anything he says. If other priests are found to suff from his affliction, you can have confidence that the church will *always* ensure they receive the same lifelong treatment."

"Thank you," Michael calmly replied and considered his response. "It's a tragedy for such a young life ruined. I'm sure he *will* be properly cared for."

"God Bless you, my son. Peace be with you."

"And with your spirit." *Message received,* Michael thought. He accepted the bag when the man released it, tucked it tightly under his left arm, and strode through the doors and out onto the tarmac. *Did he intend to reveal he holds a higher position than me? Thomas's committal may silence him and warn the rest of us, but inconvenient truths are still true.*

Michael walked directly to the waiting aircraft, and the pilot entered the doorway as he approached. He consciously focused on the bag and its potential contents to put Thomas and the messenger's threat out of his mind.

"Good morning, Father. You ready for this short flight to Vienna?"

"Good morning," Michael replied as if he already knew the flight plan, "and, yes, it's been a long time since I've visited Vienna. I'm looking forward to it."

"We'll have you wheels-up in a few minutes, sir."

Michael climbed the short flight of stairs and found the cabin empty, save him and the pilot. He expected the co-pilot was already in the cockpit by now. "Just me?"

"You're my only passenger this morning."

Michael glanced back at the airport gate he'd just exited. *The messenger's nowhere to be seen. Probably walked off as soon as I did.* He brought his attention back to the chipper pilot. "I appreciate any expedience you can offer."

"We'll make it so, Father."

Although his former-cop instincts still directed him to the back row, especially after the unexpected threat, Michael again sat close to the hatch. *I don't appear tactically proficient or paranoid up here.* He placed the diplomatic pouch in a leather-wrapped storage bin next to his seat. *I don't want to risk reviewing it until I'm alone. I can only trust everyone by trusting no one.*

Likely the result of both the early hour and the aircraft's registry, the crew had them underway almost immediately after closing the hatch. With the cockpit and his privacy secured, Michael opened the diplomatic pouch with its recently prescribed combination of "0401." He found a familiar, red-wax-sealed manila envelope inside. *Seal of the Holy See above a transverse cross. Origin and recipient confirmed.* The parchment inside the wax seal displayed the same, single Catechism section, 401, that Michael had received by email. *Contents are authenticated.* Just as the aircraft gained lift and rose into the darkness beneath Rome's low cloud layer, Michael read the packet's only page:

Congratulations, shithead. Glad you made it through this one. Consider it your official admission to the Merry Union of Snakehunters & Gravediggers. Your initial flight plan is for Vienna, but they'll take you anywhere you wanna go. Lemme know where and when you land. Keep your phone on. More work headed your way right quick. Keep section 401 in your prayers. It deals with original sin and the evil inherent in all of us. No rest for the wicked. – John

As the jet steeply climbed through the clear, dark autumn sky, Michael looked out and noticed light cast off the full moon brightly lit the clouds below him. *The world is still a beautiful place, even with us in it. I pray that God uses me to lessen the negative impact we have on each other.* He picked up a telephone cradled in the cabin wall next to his seat.

"Yes, Father, how can I be of assistance," the unseen co-pilot almost immediately asked.

"I've just learned of a change in my travel plans. I'm required to be back in the U-S, in Santa Fe, New Mexico, as soon as possible, please."

"Certainly, we can do that for you. We will need to make one fuel stop somewhere on the East Coast at about sunrise there. Is there a particular location you'd prefer for the layover?"

"No, whatever's most convenient for you."

"Thank you, Father. I'll let you know once it's decided. Do you want the change of flight plan filed immediately?"

"No," Michael replied, "that can wait until we've transitioned to our next center. No need to bother anyone else with this for now." *It's nice to know the proper vocabulary.*

"Very good. We'll make it so."

"Thank you." Michael returned the receiver to its in-wall cradle secured the pouch and its contents, and leaned back in his reclining seat. *'No rest for the wicked,' indeed. In the last day, I became operational, succeeded in protecting an untold number of people, failed at my primary objective, and had a grandfatherly messenger threaten me after I watched a former classmate get put on a psych hold for being honest. It can't always be like this.*

Michael wondered if Sergio and the others were getting the same treatment. *It's possible there's an established list of targets. You don't open a new business without first identifying your customers. No rest for the wicked...* Michael kept turning the misquoted phrase over in his mind, wondering if John had intended to make the error.

His mind predictably returned to Father Moore, *Thomas,* as Michael had known the man. *How far will John and Hoffaburr go to keep our secrets, and theirs? The Vatican's trustees failed in their screening process, and that's put all of this at risk, even if only for a little while. If the program's in jeopardy, then so is everyone involved in it. Somewhere, a scared old man in a red or white cassock is watching CNN and deciding what must be done. Actually, what* others *must do on* his *behalf...*

Even if he could have spoken with Sergio at that moment, Michael expected the jet's interior wasn't a safe place to question their hierarchy. Thomas' public psychiatric committal confirmed that Michael's bosses didn't let perceived threats quietly go by the wayside. *John warned me about accidentally digging my own grave, but given the scandal of this betrayal, what'll he do if that scared old man orders us to dig one for Thomas?*

NOVEMBER 1. 06:32AM LOCAL_
NEW YORK CITY.

CARDINAL PAUL DYLAN already sat behind his oversized Italian mahogany desk despite the early hour. Concealed under the desk from view of anyone but him, a small red light unexpectedly blinked near his right leg, and a smile immediately spread across Dylan's aging face. *He's early. That almost always means good news.* He pressed a small adjacent button that unlocked a private, downstairs access door to his dedicated en-suite elevator. Bishop Harold Hoffaburr soon stepped into his office, which Dylan knew the subordinate someday wanted for his own. *He wants the office and the prestige, but he knows almost nothing about the responsibilities that come with it.*

"I hope you bring good tidings."

"I do," Hoffaburr beamed. "We've had our first successes last night, three of them, actually, and two more are expected today."

"And all is well, they're clean and undetected?"

"It's even better than that. Only one has been reported in local news, and it's already declared a remorseful suicide. 'Driven to take his own life by his heinous crimes,' I think it roughly translates." Hoffaburr turned over a closed manila envelope from his shoulder bag that contained a few printed pages of an online Portuguese news article, along with its English translation. He sat down in his usual chair near the sheer-curtained window. Dylan saw the man looked vindicated by the early success.

"And we expect the other two matters concluded today?"

"That is the expectation, Your Eminence, although it may be necessary for them to delay to ensure their operational security and escape."

"Of course, Harold, I expect perfection, and I understand that takes time and effort well in excess of the recklessness of instant gratification. Which brings me to the matter in Omaha..."

Hoffaburr cleared his throat before he spoke, obviously uncomfortable with the unexpected development. "I assure Your Eminence that it's all been handled and won't again be an issue for anyone involved."

Dylan skimmed over both news articles, even though he didn't read or speak Portuguese. "Good. Make sure it *stays* that way, Harold. You will let me know as soon as you hear about the others?"

"Of course, Your Eminence."

"*Cardinal Dylan?*"

The sound of his desktop intercom speaker interrupted their conversation. Dylan reached over and depressed the 'talk' button as he spoke. "Yes?"

"*Sorry to disturb you so early, sir, but you have a call holding. It's Cardinal Rorke with the Travel Office. He has some details he wishes to share about your upcoming appointment to Vatican City.*"

Dylan looked across his desk at Harold and smiled. He depressed the 'talk' button once again. "Thank you, go ahead and put him through, please."

"It's finally happening, Your Eminence. Just as you anticipated."

"No, Harold," he corrected, "just as *God intends*. It's all coming together just as He intends."

EPILOGUE_

NOVEMBER 1, 1:34PM LOCAL. THOMAS RESIDENCE. SANTA FE, NEW MEXICO.

FATHER MICHAEL THOMAS woke up in his childhood bedroom, thankfully no longer decorated in sports posters. Once fully revived, he slid from the twin bed and knelt on the floor to complete the third part of daily recitations. Out of habit, Michael spoke just above a whisper as he recited Saint Michael's Prayer. As he finished, he smelled brewed coffee and opened his eyes. *Plenty of time left in the afternoon for my None prayers.*

He rose, donned sweatpants and a t-shirt, and put his work cell and a sealed envelope in his pockets before stiffly stumbling toward the kitchen. *Jet-lagged and sore is no way to start the day on a few hours' sleep. Not old enough for these problems yet.* Michael found the coffee pot half-filled and still-brewing. His favorite coffee mug stood waiting next to the machine with a sticky-note that read, "HAPPY BIRTHDAY! WELCOME HOME!" Michael smiled, looked around, and realized he was alone. He stuck the note to the adjacent countertop, filled the mug, and sat on a barstool at the breakfast counter to await his parents' return.

Michael stretched his neck and shoulders, and then retrieved his new cell phone from his pants pocket. *May as well check in while I'm alone. Comms have to come first, so John says.* Michael first checked his personal email account and found two new messages.

Opening the first, he found a short message from Sergio with a JPG attachment: "*Couldn't help myself. Good weekend here, pretty eventful.*

Hope you're having a wicked time on the beach!" Michael chuckled at the coded message and understood Sergio's experience must have been similar to his own, including the strangely worded message from John.

Michael opened the attached photo, which he saw was a simple, very well drawn image of the traditional Catholic cross, which looked like a capital "P" with a small "x" at its center. On second inspection, Michael noticed the "x" had been replaced with two crossed capital "I"s. *Ira Incorporatus!* Just below the pencil-drawn symbol was the acronym "HNBC," which Michael knew was Sergio's reference to John's infamous motto. *I was joking when I asked him to create a subversive 'corporate' logo for us, but Serge hit it outta the park! How now, brown cow?!*

Michael deleted the message from his inbox, and then from the trash folder to remove it from the email server. He opened the second message, from Monsignor Hernandez, and read the short paragraph: "*Rec'd a call for you from a Dr. Renard yesterday. She asked me to convey a specific message to you. Said she regretted that you had to leave the way you did, but she understands you must have had a good reason for it. She prays for your safety and that your paths will one day cross again. She sounds like a woman in love, Michael, like Catherine used to sound when she talked about you. Be careful and graceful with this one."*

Michael sighed and considered what to do. As much as he wanted to save this message, it could only put her in danger if someone with the right motivations ever found it and wanted to get to him. Instead, he ensured it, too, disappeared from the server.

What to do? Best thing would be to put her out of my mind, but that's not gonna just happen overnight. It's been eight months since I last saw her and I still think of her almost every day. I'm married to God and His Church, so there simply cannot be room for another love. I don't know how Protestant ministers balance both.

Heavy footfalls betrayed his father's approach, and Michael smile and stood to greet him. He also nonchalantly locked his phone. Fran Thomas stepped into the kitchen with a broad smile and bright, happ eyes. He remained a poster boy for graceful aging and still ran at least fou miles a day, ate right, and had recently taken up yoga with Michael mother. Michael saw he wore a short-sleeved yellow polo shirt, jeans, an loafers, which had become consistent attire in his last few years.

"Hey, pop! Good morning!" Michael hugged his dad and noticed the man had shrunk a little since he'd last seen him.

"Hell, it's after lunch, you gonna sleep all day?" They released each other and Frank stepped over to fill his own coffee mug.

"I thought about it, but I've decided that eighteen hours was enough rest." Michael facetiously smiled, leaned back against the counter, and sipped his coffee. "I thought you'd be at the office today."

"Your mom gets her treatments on Thursday, so I only go in for a couple hours in the mornings."

"How's she doing?"

"Good. I think it's just a matter of time until she's well on the road to recovery."

"Dad, it's just us. I know you always wanna be positive, but it's okay if you wanna talk about what's really going on. I do get paid to listen, and it turns out I'm pretty good at it."

His father reached over and placed his hand on top of Michael's and squeezed, much tighter than Michael expected. "It's not fair to burden you with my problems, son, that's what Monsignor Hernandez is for. Are you going to help him with mass on Sunday?"

"I don't know if I'll still be here, pop."

"You plannin' on getting called away on an emergency, or something? They gotta rush you to put out a fire at the Vatican, or what?"

Michael chuckled at the unintended truth in his dad's jest. "Something like that. I'm just glad I got to be here for my birthday. That hasn't happened for four, maybe five years?"

"Thanks for reminding me. Your mom and I thought about going down to *El Pinto* for dinner tonight. Our treat for your birthday."

"Speaking of birthday money," Michael offered, "I have something for you." He removed the envelope from his pocket and set it on the counter in front of his dad.

"What's this?"

"It's a small token of my gratitude for all the help and sacrifice you and mom made over the years."

"Whatever it is, I can't accept it."

"Dad," Michael quietly protested, "it's $15,000, and it doesn't even begin to repay you two for everything I've borrowed or used over the last ten or fifteen years."

"I can't take your money, Michael," he exclaimed, clearly flabbergasted at the notion. "You're a *priest,* where did you get that kinda money?!"

"Dad, they *do* pay us, it's just not much. I don't need it for anything, and I thought you and mom could do something better with it."

"No, son, I can't accept it, I won't."

"You're looking at this the wrong way, pop. I'm not *giving* this to you and mom, I'm *investing* it with you. If you use it for mom's medical expenses, I'm getting more time with her. Hell, we *both* are! If you wanted to use this to pay down the house, or pay off the cars, then it's going toward my inheritance. It's not a *gift* or charity, and I already have everything I need. It can only make me more comfortable if it takes care of you and mom."

His father's eyes welled up, and Michael stepped forward into his embrace. "I'm so, so very *proud* of you, son!"

"I know, pop, even though you're still a better man than me."

His father scoffed as they released each other, and both leaned against the kitchen counter. Holding the open envelope with its small stack of currency visible, his father chuckled. "Your mother's never gonna stand for this, you know that, right?"

"Why does she have to know?"

"And just what, exactly, do you propose I say when she finds it someday?"

Michael laughed as if the answer was obvious. "Just tell her you took a night job and went back to playing piano at the brothel." Though he tried, Michael couldn't keep a straight face as that imaginary conversation instantly played out in his head. "She'd understand once you tell her you've been busy making money the hard way, $14-at-a-time!"

"She'd see right through that," his father dryly replied, "she knows how much I hate the smell of nursing homes." His dad briefly smiled at their banter and then changed topics. "Did I tell you that I saw Catherine at the grocery today? She asked about you, just like she always does."

"How's she doing, pop?"

"She's good, still single. Just moved back to town, and I thought it wa very sweet of her to ask about you after all these years."

"I'm a priest, pop, I can't have a wife. Hell, I can't even have a girlfriend. Catherine needs to find someone who can give her what she needs in this life."

"I know, I know, but, I'm sure you can understand, too, that after dating you for all those years in college and while you worked as a cop, it's kinda left her in a tough spot."

"How so?"

"Well, she's in her late twenties, Michael, and there's not a lot of men, even inside the church, who're willing to stay celibate until marriage. Catherine might be the only virgin left in the chapel's singles group."

"That's not my problem, pop, I gave her plenty of chances to leave along the way and go find someone else. She hung around and waited, even after I told her I might not ever marry. It's weird, right, like *almost* as if my subconscious knew this is what I would be doing with my life."

"Yes, Michael, and we're very proud of you, son, it warms my heart every day that my wife and I raised a son with enough character and compassion in his heart to do what you do, and what you did before. I just, you know, as I'm getting older, I'm really starting to like the idea of grandkids, and I think your mother would, too. So, if you ever think you'd done enough and wanted to live a more normal life, we're okay with that. Actually, it'd be really nice to have you back home."

"Pop, where's this coming from? All my life you wanted me to become a doctor or a priest, and now you're telling me it's okay to walk away from this kinda calling?"

"You're my only son, Michael, and there is no prouder moment in my life than when you told us you wanted to join the seminary. I knew I'd raised you right, and that my mistakes as a parent had to be minimal. But you've been gone ever since, and we've been sharing you with the world. Actually, it's more like the world took you away and, maybe once a year or two, you get a few days off for good behavior and come home to see us. You may as well work in Antarctica, or on the moon, for all we ever get to see you. We're getting older, and, even though I try to always look at the positive side of your mother's diagnosis, it's probably not ever gonna get any better. M-S is a life sentence right now, and I know, statistically, she won't live long enough to see a cure. Maybe in *your* lifetime, but almost certainly not in *hers*.

"And, I know how much Catherine meant to you, and probably still does, and it's obvious she's still in love with you. I do think she's holding out hope that you're gonna ride back into town one day, get married, and make a house full of babies."

"Have Jack and Jacqui been hassling you about not having grandkids again?"

"No," his father chuckled, "your aunt and uncle haven't mentioned it, lately." He rolled his eyes. "I'm probably just becoming a selfish old man, but I'd like to get to spend time with my adult son before I die. I'd like to be better acquainted with the man he's become and see him more than a couple days a year. Is that so wrong?"

"No, pop, I can't hold it against you, but I'm doing really important work. My heart's in it, actually maybe now more than ever."

"Oh, really? What do they have you doing now, you were kinda ambiguous about it when we picked you up at the airport."

"I'm gonna be moving around quite a bit, I guess you could say that I'm a *troubleshooter*."

"Troubleshooter? Sounds mysterious, or maybe a little like James Bond!" He again chuckled at his own joke, clearly intending it to be ridiculous and impossible.

Michael's cell phone vibrated on the counter and interrupted their conversation. Seeing John had sent an email, he opened that application. "Sorry, pop, gimme a second. Work."

"Yeah," his dad suspiciously replied, "another church emergency?"

"Maybe." *Not gonna give him the explanation or argument that he wants. He's too curious about my job. Need to figure out a decent cover story that'll be just boring enough that we don't have to talk about it all the time.* He opened the email and found it was a single paragraph:

"*Your urgent assistance is required to aid a parishioner. Meet your transport at Ohkay Owingeh Airport in Española, New Mexico, at 200 hours on Saturday, 03-Nov. You are requested to meet Father Timoth Flanagan at Saint Etheldreda's Church, Holborn, London N6 6BJ, at you earliest opportunity. Time is of the essence. — John.*"

"Not gonna make mass on Sunday, pop. Gotta leave late Saturday evening."

"More troubleshooting, huh? So, what does that mean, exactly, like what kinda Catholic *troubles* are you called to *shoot*?"

Michael kept a straight face while responding. "Whatever they ask me to, pop," he dryly offered, "whatever they ask me to."

The story continues in The Trafficker. Continue reading for a sample, or click here to purchase now.

The Trafficker: https://www.amazon.com/dp/B09C91JZVD/

THE MICHAEL THOMAS SERIES_

The Absolver
The Trafficker
The Bombmaker

THE TRAFFICKER_

The Trafficker
A Michael Thomas Thriller : Book Two

Read on to experience the next riveting story in Gavin Reese's original, pulse-pounding series!

THE TRAFFICKER - PROLOGUE_

Hours after midnight, Michael hurried over the wet Roman cobblestones and onto the narrow residential side street. His quick footfalls echoed harshly in the narrow alley and provided the only sound. *I've gotta get to the body first!* As he rushed back to the scene, a nearby radio replayed Pope Cornelius' familiar homily in English. Michael couldn't place the source.

"...in context, Jesus conveyed the righteousness that all must exhibit if they are to repent and ultimately enter His Kingdom. And so..."

The radio program faded out as Michael reached the target building ind confirmed the address above the exterior doorway. *Via del Cardello,* 7. Four quick presses on the keypad unlocked the door. Michael ran up a earby metal spiral staircase, but it looked different from what he remem-ered. *They were concrete last time.* The radio program played again, and echoed through the apartment building's interior.

"...the Beatitudes tell us the character of the virtuous people of God, ose who have a place in His kingdom. They alone can expect the full lessings of His love..."

Michael reached the second-floor landing just as a doorway opened ead of him on the right. A familiar elderly woman pushed her walker t from the apartment again, her white hair still pinned up in rollers. The oman's eyes remained comically massive, but she didn't wear glasses this ne.

"Father Michael Andrew Thomas," the woman called out and strangely addressed Michael by his clerical title and full birth name. *"Is Pietro dead?"*

Michael grimaced but didn't respond to her unwelcome question. He sprinted toward Pietro Isadore's apartment, where that man's body should await him. When he realized the apartment door was open, Michael's fear escalated into panic. *People will find out, and they'll try to intervene!*

Rushing into the small apartment, Michael saw Isadore, a serial rapist, remained down on the tile floor just where Michael had left him. The radio broadcast returned but boomed as though coming from somewhere inside Isadore's home.

"WHEN JESUS TELLS US, 'BLESSED ARE THEY,' HE DESCRIBES THE INNER PEACE OF ALIGNMENT WITH GOD, AND PLEDGES DIVINE REWARDS FOR HIS LOYAL FOLLOWERS."

Michael rushed to the body, but Isadore was already cold and stiff, a little mummified even. Without explanation, Michael suddenly held a large, oversized syringe in his hands that he somehow knew contained the antidote necessary to revive the man. He raised it up above his head and prepared to plunge it through the dead rapist's sternum to bring him back. *You can't die like this until I'm ready to kill you the right way!* Before he could administer its contents, the syringe melted from his hands and dripped onto the floor, the antidote now useless to save the man's immortal soul.

"Father," the elderly woman again inquired from the doorway behind him, "is Pietro dead?"

"Yes," Michael answered, "and I killed him." *Why did I say that? can't* ever *admit anything!*

Overwhelming terror rose up inside Michael as Isadore's mummy opened its eyes to gaze into his own. *Wait, you're dead,* he wanted to say, *you can't do this!* The serial rapist's pupils glowed bright, fiery red, and Michael struggled to stand up and get away. *My legs are too heavy, they're locked down to the floor!*

Isadore's pain, fear, and misery, his genuine suffering, it all appeared his expression. The man's voice began as a harsh whisper. *"hmmph...you you sent me, TO HELL!"*

Michael snapped awake and shot up in his darkened motel room. Sweat dripped down his face and soaked through his t-shirt, pillowcase, and bedsheets. "*God, dammit,*" he uttered to the otherwise empty room. Against his better judgment, Michael wiped his face on the comforter. *My shirt sleeves are already too wet.* He threw back the damp bedding, stepped over to the adjacent double bed, and laid on his back atop its dry covers.

Michael sighed and considered the recurring nightmare. It had haunted him every few weeks since Pietro Isadore forced his hand almost four months ago. *The paradox of killing monsters to save their souls only works when I can first reconcile their sins. Nothing I've done before or since bothers me, not in the least, but Pietro Isadore's ghost refuses to let me go, or my paranoid psyche refuses to forget* him. *No idea if it's God telling me I messed up, or just my innate Catholic guilt eating away at me. I keep hearing that alcoholics don't dream. There's some real benefit to that. No wonder so many of us priests end up at the bottom of the bottle.*

Michael comforted himself by recalling some of Saint Thomas Aquinas' philosophy. *If God can use demons for good, and to further His plans, then He can absolutely use good people for what seems like evil results. All that matters to me is that the girl Isadore drugged and brought home outlived him. I couldn't save them both, and she survived, untouched by that monster. He was a serial rapist, after all, so I shouldn't bother getting hung up on what his eternity looks like. I wanna believe Isadore alone is responsible for the choices that probably damned him to Hell. I couldn't reconcile his sins and prepare him to meet God, despite that being the very reason for my entry into his life.*

Michael sighed, stretched, and inhaled a deep, calming breath. *We can't take our possessions with us when we die, but we sure as hell take our baggage along for the ride. Isadore packed all that himself, and he did it by choice. He probably got what he deserved, so I've just gotta stop giving a shit about it. I sealed his fate the moment I shot him full of tranquilizer and, now, I fear that my eternity is entwined with his.*

Just as all the other times the distorted memories had visited, Michael knew he wouldn't fall back asleep. *I'm already awake, may as well get started.* He checked his watch, which read 03:00. *Mom always said our guardian angels come to us in the wee hours of the morning. I'm supposed to seriously consider my dreams and epiphanies at these hours. If that's the case, I might be in real trouble.*

He sat up and turned on a dim bedside lamp that sat atop a cheap, built-in nightstand between the room's two undersized beds. The digital clock displayed the date and local time. *February 11, 3:01am.* Just in front of that, a new notepad showed the motel's logo and location. *Niobrara River Inn. Lusk, Wyoming.*

"Burnin' daylight, shithead." Michael smirked at the irony of reciting his boss' phrase. *I wonder how many secret agents have to call their boss by some bullshit pseudonym. No way his name's John. Probably something like 'Ned' that used to get his ass kicked in school.* He rolled his neck to ease the stiffness that hours on a worn mattress and flat pillows had cultivated. *Good thing Isadore woke me up early. I'm running out of time to spy on John and his new crop of recruits. Gotta be in and out before sunrise, at least if I wanna bring my skin back out with me.*

Michael sat in the room's stillness for a moment, and he recalled the recent investigative news reports spurred by public revelations from one of their own. *Father Shawn Moore. I knew him as Thomas then. Now he's become Thomas the Traitor. John told us there would be a Judas among our training group. I didn't believe him then, but it turns out the old man was right.* Michael stared at the narrow beam of light that emanated from his motel room door. The concrete walkway and parking lot outside remained lit all night, but he doubted much crime existed in the area. He took in a deliberate breath and considered his objective for that morning. *If John and his superiors are working to protect us from the outside investigations, they should have new security measures in place at the training compound. That's gotta be part of any reasonable response. If not, the only possible conclusion is that Thomas won't live long enough to testify against us. If John weren't so dedicated to compartmentalizing every aspect of the organization, we could just have a conversation, and I wouldn't have to sneak back onto the property to get some sense of what's going to happen next Instead, I'm out here risking my life to save an asshole priest who shoulc never have been admitted to the clergy to begin with.*

Rising from the bed, Michael stretched his back and shoulders as h waddled across the barren room toward his suitcase. *Even though Thoma is a piece of shit, he doesn't need to be absolved. Yes, he's engaged in scanda against us and our efforts to combat evil, which supports and harbors our spiritual and physical enemies. His betrayal might even be the direct work of the devil, but no one can say that with enough confidence to justify ending the man's life. At this point, whatever's going on with Thomas, however he's being treated, his fate is a cautionary tale for the rest of us. I have to know what that is.* Michael sighed and retrieved this morning's clothing from his suitcase. *As Thomas' condition goes today, so might ours tomorrow if John's minders decide we've stepped too far astray. I have to know how far the scared old men running this show will go to control us and protect themselves. If they ever send killers my way, I'd like to know they're coming.*

THE TRAFFICKER - ONE_

February 11. 04:45am.
Niobrara County, Wyoming.

Surrounded by harsh, gusting winds and pre-dawn darkness, Michael eased his rented Chevy pickup northeast on County Road 15 with all the exterior lights turned off. Its heater struggled to keep the bone-chilling cold outside the four-door cab, so Michael wore a heavy, straw-colored barn coat and flannel-lined pants. His clerical garments offered no protection this morning, so Michael had reverently folded and stowed them away in his suitcase. As the truck crawled toward his objective, he shifted its transmission into Neutral and idled to a stop without touching the brake pedal. Having chugged along in complete darkness since turning north off Bruch Road more than a mile ago, Michael had now taken the truck and its lukewarm interior as far as he dared. *This is close enough to walk in, but far enough to keep any sentries from seeing my approach.* He slipped the transmission into Park, shut off the ignition, and set the parking brake. Everything fell silent but the howling winds, which gusted and swayed the Chevy four-door. *Lucky to be here between storms, so I just have to deal with* old *snow blowing sideways. Only place in the world I've ever been that folks keep bald tires and kerosene in their trunks to make sure they won't freeze to death on the side of the road.*

Keeping his gaze toward the black void to his northwest, Michael subconsciously nudged the inside of his right elbow against the back of his Glock 19. *Still secure and in its holster.* He crossed himself and kept watch where he knew John's training compound to be. Michael planted his feet against the floorboard and away from the truck's brake pedal and the unwanted consequence of its telltale, bright-red LED brake lights.

"God," he offered over the howling winds outside the truck, "please don't make me need Roscoe today. I'd appreciate the chance to keep him holstered right where he is." With the cabin's interior temperature already dropping, Michael grabbed his hiker's sling bag from the passenger seat and ensured its combat medical gear was in place. *Tourniquet, quick-clot, and super-max tampons, just in case I get into real trouble.* While he donned a pair of mid-weight gloves stashed in his coat pockets, Michael reminded himself that they were the best available compromise between the warmth he *needed* and the trigger dexterity he prayed he *didn't*. He inhaled a deep, calming breath, exhaled a portion of his stress, and covered his face and neck in a thick white-and-gray shemagh. *Fuck it. We're doin' it live.*

Having already shut off the interior door-light switch, Michael stepped out into the moonlit darkness and the ever-present eastern Wyoming wind. He zipped up his heavy barn coat until its collar covered the bottom of the shemagh and fell just below his nose. *This bullshit might help the ranchers by keeping the snow off their cattle's grass and feed, but I'd hoped to never feel this constant goddamned wind again.* He pushed the door closed and smirked at his own cautiousness. *Wouldn't matter if I slammed it shut and set the alarm off, no one's close enough to hear it. Not in this wind, and not even if they were standing next to me.*

Michael strode across the dirt road, and his heavy boot treads *crunched* over the frozen surface. He trekked into a tall, dry grass field and, even though he wouldn't see it until he walked most of a mile, he hustled toward the familiar training complex. Sporadic snow had fallen in the area for the last three months, but the low humidity and constant wind had sent most of it on to Nebraska and South Dakota. Only a thin layer of snow-crusted ice broke beneath Michael's boots.

Gotta keep the low hills between me and the structures. Keep an eye on the running trails. Oughta see the flashlights and runners long before the see me. If they're even out in this shit. Depends on whether they pissed John off yesterday. That masochist might have 'em out here doing wind-sprints in banana hammocks if they messed up bad enough. Michael didn't know how John would react to his presence there, but he didn't want to find out. *I'm not sure the potential benefits of being here are worth the risk. Even if I get the answers I'm after, that still won't amount to objective proof that John and his minders won't kill Thomas. Hell, he might already be dead, for all I know or can prove. Nothing out here will ever convince me that I can trust everything John tells me. I'd like to know they're working to protect us without killing Thomas, despite his public betrayal. I'm long on questions and awfully damned short on answers. If things go far enough sideways, maybe me and John can figure this out together. I got the better of him last time, but he'll never underestimate me again.*

As he approached a short hilltop just south of the *Mother Mary* trail he'd spent so much time on, Michael crouched down in what remained of the windswept grass and crawled forward to the low summit to get the best view of the target. Retrieving his binoculars from the sling bag, he lifted them up to his eyes and apprehension filled his insides. *What the hell happened out here?* Michael blinked hard several times to clear his vision, but the structures before him and their condition didn't change. *They look abandoned!* Spending the next half-hour on the windswept hilltop, he repeatedly scanned each visible building, window, doorway, and crawl-pace for any sign of human occupancy. *No movement. No lights. No new rash. No fresh tracks anywhere, not even tire tracks across the driveway. No ne's been here since the last snowfall, maybe even longer.*

After deciding his gloves wouldn't allow him to stay outside much onger, Michael risked a closer look. He dropped the binos back in his bag, ipped it closed, and navigated down the hill toward a back, blind corner f the main house. *It's got the least number of windows for anyone to see e.* Hearing nothing but the wind and the slight crunching beneath his et, Michael pressed onward to the structure. *John should've been up inking coffee a half-hour ago, and his new crop of shitheads oughta be out ffering a distance run on Mother Mary by now. Not a light on in the hole place. They could be out on a field exercise, but even John wouldn't ke them into the mountains this time of year. Nothing to learn up there t hypothermia survival.*

By the time Michael reached the corner, he realized the two windows closest to him were broken. Even the pale moonlight cast enough reflection to reveal the damage. *That can't be right, John never would've let that stand.* Working his way counterclockwise around the house, Michael kept the structure on his left side, which allowed his right hand a better chance of staying free to access his concealed Glock. Each window he passed was shattered at best and missing at worst. Stopping just short of the next corner, Michael peeked at the large, converted stable that had served as their classroom and chapel during the eight months he'd lived at the compound. Dismay overcame him when he realized the now-dilapidated structure barely stood on its own. It listed about twenty degrees to the east, as though it had given in to the ever-present Jetstream years ago. *It's gonna collapse under its own weight! How did all this happen in four months?!*

Michael grew bolder and more confident he'd find no one at the property. He hustled down the long side of the main house as wind gusts propelled hard snow-pebbles up into his face. Squinting his eyes against the assault, he tried not to lose his situational awareness. Just before reaching the front corner and stepping onto the once-revered porch, Michael retrieved a small tactical flashlight from his pants pocket and kept it in his left hand. *Just in case I need to draw or punch on something hidden inside.*

Without slowing more than a step, Michael reached the front door turned the knob, and stepped inside his onetime residence. He shifted lef toward the kitchen to get out of the doorway and cast the flashlight' bright, focused beam around the house's interior. *All the furniture's gone flooring's gone, no appliances. It's been stripped.* Gobsmacked, Michae stood and worked to reconcile what he knew *had been* with what he sa *now was.*

The ceiling's drywall panels had been pulled down, and most of th electrical copper wire was gone. The scene reminded Michael of a fe abandoned homes he'd seen methamphetamine addicts demolish in h former life as a cop. *It's like I'm back in 2007 Silver City again, taki patrol calls about tweekers scrapping wire from construction houses to p for their next fix.* Shining his light downstairs, Michael looked into t basement, which had been partially finished when he last saw it. It w now demoed down to the studs and dirt subfloor. The toilets and massi six-head shower stall was gone. Wind-drifted snow had piled up in the one corner he could see from upstairs. *Had to have blown in through the windows up here, there's not a window downstairs to break.* Michael crept about the rest of the ground level, but it was clear the house hadn't been occupied since he left. *The floor creaks a lot worse than it did before, kinda like somebody loosened the boards on the way out.*

Michael grimaced when he realized all the interior doors had been removed. *They'd be the second-best sources of fingerprints and DNA evidence if a forensics team ever got a warrant to examine the place.* He paused in the front bedroom where he'd spent so much time with "Father Harry" discussing his psychological state and parrying questions about his efforts to best John's training staff. *There's a lot more to that guy than he presented. Still convinced John's taking orders from him, not the other way around.*

Curious about the forensics angle, Michael checked the bathrooms and found all the toilets had been taken out, as well. He stopped near the middle of the structure and heard only the increasing winds blowing through broken windowpanes. *Hell, the house looks like it was abandoned long before I ever lived here. Even the light switches are missing. Only thing left to do here rhymes with 'match and kerosene.'* He considered the Herculean efforts required to have erased the compound's recent history. *Wouldn't surprise me if they got somebody just waiting for that one windless day to torch the place. The typical gusts up here would blow the flames all the way to Nebraska, and that might be the only reason she's not a charred shell yet.* Michael shook his head in disbelief as he looked around the interior again. *It's like we were never here.*

"Somebody went to a lot of trouble in a real short timeframe..." Michael whispered the words in case he wasn't alone. *John's people are either operating from an abundance of caution, or they're concerned something's gonna come from all the news reports. Even if they've taken these kinda precautions to keep the journalists and investigators from corroborating Thomas' assertions, his name and face still need to disappear from the news cycle. If he hadn't first contacted that activist organization, his story would've already lost traction and disappeared. Every time the group demands the Church release Thomas from its psychiatric facility, it just starts the headlines up all over again. They think they're protecting him, but, the longer they keep his name and face in the public's conscience, the more likely John's minders are to take decisive measures. If the 'Powerful 99' don't give up, Thomas might not live to see the summer.* He again looked around and marveled at how well decimated the residence was.

Although he expected to gain nothing from it, Michael moved back toward the stairs. He wanted a closer look inside the basement where he and his fellow Absolvers had lived, if only to confirm their presence had been erased. As he cautiously put weight on the top step, a low warning growl rose from beneath the stairs and halted his descent. Michael reached under his coat and drew his Glock from its holster. His flashlight revealed a few piles of canine feces in the basement. *Coyote, probably, and hopefully,* not *plural.* Realizing he'd been focused only on threats from the apex predator, Michael swore at himself for being so reckless. *Always look for dogshit in the yard! That's a rookie mistake!* A quick scan of the ground floor confirmed he hadn't yet been surrounded, so Michael carefully stepped backward and kept his light and gun sights focused on the top of the stairs. *Time to go.*

Now grateful that he'd elected to bring those specific gloves along, Michael cleared the areas ahead of him and kept a frequent watch on his six. *I hate having the only known-threat area behind me.* He stood just inside the main house's doorway for a long moment, and the coyote downstairs didn't hurry to follow him up. Sensing it shared his desire to be left alone, Michael decided to inspect what remained of the property. *I can't leave here without knowing if they left the door, and there's no chance I'm ever coming out here again.*

He shut off the flashlight and gave his eyes a few moments to adjust back to the darkness, all the while listening intently for the stairs to reveal the animal's ascent toward him. Once Michael's sight had improved, he struck out toward the collapsing stable. During John's course on eyewitness testimony, which had taken place about five months ago in the last few weeks of the covert training program, the instructors had splintered the stable's doorframe. The trainers didn't adequately repair the door or it frame before Michael graduated, and he hoped to find the same evidenc still in place now. Crossing the open area between the house and th condemnable stable, Michael shifted his gaze and the Glock's sigh around him and made sure nothing followed him out of the house. *No other tracks out here but mine. Incredible...*

When he reached the doorway, Michael cast light into the stable to make sure he was alone this time. *Can't check all the interior, but it looks like I've got the only heartbeat out here.* This building had sustained more damage than the main house. Its broken door had finally been removed, and the interior condition convinced Michael he wouldn't find anything to corroborate his presence and purpose there.

Frustrated and confused, Michael stood just inside the doorway and looked back to the west, where the Grinder had once been. *Flagpoles are gone, obstacle course is gone. I can hardly recognize this as the same place.* He shone his flashlight on the doorframe, and his heart leapt, if only for a moment. The shattered wood frame showed a substantial difference in the visible age of the exposed wood. *It was obviously locked and busted open. The interior wood's been exposed to the elements more recently than the rest of the frame, but what the hell does that prove? Nothing. It proves, absolutely, nothing. It doesn't even corroborate my memory of two men in ski masks breaking down the door and fake-murdering John that day. All so he could have us, his students, prove firsthand that eyewitness testimony is unreliable without direct corroboration.* He considered the irony of his visit and ran a gloved hand over the broken frame. *Powerful lesson I'll never forget, and a memory it now seems that no one can ever prove happened. At least I know I'm not insane, though. Without this small proof that I'd lived through John's training program here, I might have to question that I came back to the right place.* Michael pulled his cell phone from an interior coat pocket and snapped a quick photo of the frame damage. *It won't do anything for anyone else, but it does a helluva lot for me.*

Part of Michael appreciated the effort that John's team must have gone through to demo the property and its structures. In only a few months, it appeared that years, maybe decades, had passed without anyone having t foot on the site. *There's nothing here that anyone investigating Thomas' legations could use as proof. I'm sure that's the point: 'Go ahead and try to y something. Take your little, maniacal shreds of evidence public. We'll stroy you anyway, just like we're doing to Thomas.'*

Michael considered how little he knew about his boss and his chain of mmand. *Pretty damned eerie to see they have this much power and ability to manufacture an effective, immediate outcome. I have to keep this place in mind if I ever decide to spill my guts to the New York Post.*

Michael had wanted to leave the property before sunrise, and its condition further encouraged that notion. *The lack of footprints oughta give me some comfort that I'm alone, but all it does is drive home the reality that they're determined and capable, and I have no back-up. No one's gonna come to help, no one's gonna hear me yell. Especially over this howling wind. Just me and the goddamned basement coyote.*

As Michael replaced the phone and zipped his coat back up against the cold, incessant wind, a sharp bark and whimper from the house caught his attention. He pointed the flashlight's blinding beam and his Glock's sights at the porch where the sound had come from. A full-grown, black-and-white Border Collie mix with a mottled chest hesitantly wagged its tail and looked back at him across the open space. Michael lowered his gun and brought the flashlight's beam down below the dog's eyes. Its tail wagged wider, despite its underweight appearance. It whimpered again and barked optimistically at him. Michael whistled back.

wwhhssst

"Come here, boy!"

The dog sprinted over to him and stopped just before running int Michael's knees. After putting his Glock away, he used the flashlight t examine the excited animal and spoke to it like he was a favored child "Are you the mean ol' vicious dog from downstairs, huh? No, you're just good boy!" The collie mix turned circles and whimpered as he looked u at Michael, his tail wagging much faster and wider now. He didn't have collar, which wasn't all that unusual for a ranch dog, but getting lost wa "Who wantsa go get in the warm truck with me, huh, boy?" He rubbed th dog's sides and estimated he was at least ten pounds underweigh *Shouldn't feel his ribs like this. He's been out here for a while.* "Can yo sit?" The dog faced Michael and sat upright. His head tilted to the si like he waited for another command. *Or a treat for being a good bo* "Wanna go for a walk?"

The dog jumped up and led Michael back out into the cold.

"Alright, boy, let's get the hell oughta here." Michael left the stal behind, and the collie mix stepped in behind him on his right side. *Bet h trained to walk in that spot.* As Michael led their way out toward t county road, he veered north toward the property's running trails. Now out in the open, he'd had his fill of surprises for the morning and didn't dare use his flashlight.

The far eastern horizon brightened ever so slightly and winked out stars from the sky to warn him of the impending sunrise. Michael looked back at the dark, lifeless structures. *There's already been three different times I thought I'd finally left this miserable place forever. If nothing else, I'm sure this one's gonna stick. I can't ever again set foot on John's terra firma when it doesn't exist anymore.*

THE TRAFFICKER - TWO_

February 11. 07:49am.
Niobrara County Sheriff's Office. Lusk, Wyoming.

Michael drove his rented truck into the small lot in front of the Sheriff's Office and parked near the front entrance. *Not the best tactic, but it's what* :*ops expect from the typical civilian.* He reached over to the passenger seat ınd pet his new best friend, whom he'd named *Ira,* behind his ears. The log was so tired and warm under his new fleece blanket that he didn't vake up. *I'd sleep pretty hard, too, if my belly was full for the first time in a ouple weeks. Thank God feed stores open early in cattle country.* Michael lanced down to the passenger floorboard, just below Ira, to make sure the og's new water bowl hadn't spilled. *He's already drained most of it. See* ɔ*w he does and maybe give him some more in about an hour.* "Good boy, a." The dog still didn't do more than breathe. "Definitely keeping you, ıd we'll see if the name gets to stay, too."

Ecstatic to have rescued the dog from the abandoned compound, he :pped from the truck, zipped his barn coat back up to seal out the ›wling wind, and pushed the door shut. Michael glanced at The Blue ›nnet Café, which stood across the street and two buildings east of the ıeriff's Office. *At least that's still in place. I'd check myself into a rubber* ›*m if that had changed, too.* Ducking his head away from the wind, he strode into the small cop shop. Small motorcycle "Gremlin" bells chimed from the back of the door, and Michael saw a familiar face behind the counter. *What was her name? Patty, maybe, something with a 'P' for sure.*

"Good morning. How can I help you today, besides the obvious?" She pointed toward a large Thermos of coffee that sat on the lobby's counter just inside the doorway. "I've got hot water for tea, too, if you're the one man in Niobrara that doesn't drink coffee in the morning."

Michael smiled. *Peggy. Her name is Peggy.* "No, thank you, ma'am, this looks like just the God-send I need this morning." He stepped to the Thermos, pulled a Styrofoam cup from an adjacent stack, and poured his morning's third cup of coffee. Heavy steam rolled out of the white cup and dissipated in the air above.

"You look familiar," Peggy offered and walked closer to Michael and the counter. "Have we met somewhere before?"

"No, ma'am, I don't believe we have," Michael lied. "I'm Tom Giles. I'm wondering if you might help answer a couple questions I got about some properties near here."

"Nice to meet you, Mister Giles, I'll be happy to help if I can."

"I help run a program for the Archdiocese of Santa Fe, back in New Mexico, and we take down old barns and use the reclaimed wood to teach job skills to folks in halfway houses. Try to give 'em a new skill, a legi trade, so they can get back on their feet and keep their noses clean. I go sidetracked a little out east of town here, figure there might be a couple places with old barns they might wanna get rid of and donate the material to us." Michael knew rehabilitation programs were not especially wel received in rural communities, but he hoped that a story about one tha provided skills training would be. *If I offered to pay top-dollar for th lumber, I bet she'd have the deed-holders on the phone in nothing flat.*

"Well, bless your heart, that sounds like a, a, well-intended program She grimaced, and skepticism dripped from her voice. "I just don't kno anything about that, though, you'd have to get in touch with the individu property owners to work that kinda thing out."

Good, Michael thought, *she doesn't wanna jump through hoops for m* He glanced at the wall to his left, which displayed a large map of Niobra County. "Maybe if I could point it out to you." Michael stepped over ur he touched the map's epicenter, which was Lusk, the county seat and present location. He followed Highway 20 east until he found Bruch Road, then guided his finger north on County Road 15. "I think it's about right here. There's a place on the west side of the county road that looks like the whole place might be abandoned. Few buildings, a stable, maybe, just about fallin' down. Any idea who owns that?"

Peggy stepped closer to the map but stayed behind the counter. "The only abandoned place out there's the old Ahern spread."

"It's on the west side, a few miles north of the highway?"

"Yessir, only place out there without occupants. Well," Peggy smiled and corrected herself, "there's sure to be coyotes, antelopes, and wind. Maybe some prairie dogs, but that's about it."

"Any chance you'd have contact info for the owners?"

"Mister Giles, the only way anyone's talkin' to Mister Ahern is through a saint or a seance."

"He's passed?"

"Bless his heart, yes, a number of years back. He died in prison, actually, up in Rawlins, in the maximum-security facility there. Killed his wife and her lover, terrible thing, just cut that man to pieces." Peggy shook her head as though chilled. "Anyway, he's been dead for a while now, and left no heirs. The property's been with the state since then, and I guess they haven't gotten around to doing anything with it. Not like it costs 'em anything to let the wind and the coyotes reclaim it."

"That's terrible, ma'am. Must've been a hard thing in such a small town."

"Not really, we figured it was just a matter of time. Can't cheat on a jealous drunk in a town this size, ya know?"

Peggy smiled and then appeared as though she'd just remembered something. "Now that we're talking about it, there was another man that was just in here askin' about that place. I came in a couple hours early this mornin,' cause I gotta drive down to Cheyenne this afternoon, so, anyway, you don't care about that. So, this fella was chattin' with our overnight deputy about that very place. Is there something goin' on with it that I just don't know about?"

Who else is out here digging up bones? Michael tried to conceal his sudden apprehension. "I don't know of anything. I'm just out hunting old wood. Heck of a coincidence, though."

"It sure is. Nobody's cared about that place for two decades and now it's hot real estate."

"Any idea, ma'am, who the other party was?"

"No, I hadn't ever seen him before. Wasn't familiar lookin' like you. I only know he wasn't from around here."

"Any chance he left a name, or anything else?"

"John," she slowly replied and nodded. "Yep, when he left, he shook hands with the deputy and introduced himself as 'John.' Said he was doing some kinda property assessment for the state. Just wanted to know if anyone had expressed interest in the place, like maybe the state hopes they'll be able to sell it soon. Guess he showed up a little too early, right?" Peggy laughed at her own observation.

Michael smiled and tried to chuckle along while keeping his anxiety under control. He retrieved his cell phone and opened a password-protected photo app. After swiping through the first four digital images, Michael settled on the last picture he'd clandestinely snapped the same day he got the device. *There he is. I knew these might come in handy one day.* He zoomed in on the picture, which showed his former lead instructor and current boss seated at the dining table in the main house of their training compound four months ago. *Still amazed the place looked like this.* Michael presented the photo to Peggy. "Any chance this is him?"

She put on her reading glasses and looked at the image. "Well, yes, that *is* him, that's so strange that you two would know each other! I bet there's a heck of a story behind all this, Mister, Mister, I'm sorry, what did you say your name was again?"

Dead Man Walking, was the first one that came to Michael's mind.

Visit https://www.amazon.com/dp/b09c91jzvd to purchase now.

AUTHOR'S NOTE_

I must first thank Mrs. Reese for aiding and abetting in the development of this series. She loves a good conspiracy, and I'm proud this one passed muster and compelled her to question its real-life possibility. After helping set my course on this series, she then had the (dis)pleasure of tolerating my writing schedule and obsession with this story. Thank you, baby. *Mo Anam Cara.*

Tim Flanagan helped ensure this series saw the light of day, and I'm forever grateful for his advocacy and encouragement. Brian Shea, LT Ryan, and the cast and crew at Liquid Mind Media and Liquid Mind Publishing ensured that it found its way into your hands. Editing contributions from Barbara Wright and Valerie Blow significantly improved the quality of this endeavor.

I owe BL a specific debt of gratitude for his expert technical advice. Thank you, good sir, for calling kind and constructive attention to my shortcomings.

Jay Tinsiano, an excellent conspiracy author and friend, provided poignant advice and guidance that helped me craft this series. Thanks for helping me step foot into this incredibly daunting and demanding genre, Jay.

T&L brought their ever-present support, encouragement, criticism, and confidence. This story begins a new adventure, and I'm grateful that your optimism exceeds even mine.

My indefatigable early readers helped develop this idea into a story worth reading. Thank you all for trading time spent with the things that matter to you for time with the things that matter to me.

To my audience and fans, I offer my sincere gratitude. You followed my writing and helped this starry-eyed cop manifest my pipedream. As with all my works, I hope you come out ahead in our trade of time, treasure, and goods. Thank you for your support, encouragement, and kind words. They matter more than I can ever explain.

As mentioned in the Foreword, I've based this fictional series on a strong foundation of reality. After hundreds of hours of research, I've fictionally used many actual places, events, and realities to try to present a *possible,* but still *fictional,* series. For that reason, it will be much easier to identify those elements entirely of my imagination.

First, the secret Absolvers cabal Sergio nicknamed "***Wrath, Incorporated***" is a product of my own imagination, as is its copyrighted logo. The ***Absolvers*** name is also entirely fictional (thanks, Tim!), as is the ***Division of Intelligence and Counter-Espionage, Lifelong Solutions, LLC.,*** and ***The Powerful 99.***

For my scenes and locations, I relied on my travels, experiences, open-source research, Google Earth, and Google Maps. The real-life location that contributed to this book and series also far outnumber the fictional, s the shorter, entirely fictional list is as follows: ***Capilla de San Benedicto*** (*Ecuador*), ***La Iglesia de San Francisco*** (*Bogotá*), ***Rura Training Compound*** (Niobrara County, Wyoming), ***The Blu Bonnet Café*** (Lusk, Wyoming), ***La Cucina della Russia*** (Rom Italy), ***West Texas Wildcatting*** (Loving County, Texas), and the actu locations of the residences of both ***Jordan Miller*** and ***Pietro Isador*** I might have missed one or two entirely fictional elements, but I belie the remainder of the book's locations are, to varying degrees, based reality and are used fictionally.

All characters in this book are entirely figments of my imaginati Any references to actual persons are used fictionally and have been clea identified (e.g., Abraham Lincoln).

I've never worked as an international spy (that's what we all s right?), but I found my thousands of hours of patrol, investigations, and specialized police training incredibly useful in designing John's training program. I've also never been Catholic or a priest, so I partnered with a technical advisor and spent the bulk of my research hours here. I tried not to give away LEO tactics and worked to respectfully include Catholic ritual, paradigm, and dogma. Any errors therein are entirely my own.

I relied most heavily on the following as reference materials: my personal ***Bible***, ***Summa Theologica*** by Thomas Aquinas, ***Catechism of the Catholic Church (Second Edition)***, ***The Real Story of the Catholic Church*** by Steve Weidenkopf, ***Emotional Survival for Law Enforcement*** by Dr. Kevin Gilmartin, and ***Murder for Hire*** by Jack Ballentine. I also read dozens of open-source articles from sites that included ***National Catholic Register***, ***Ask a Catholic***, ***Vatican News***, ***TVTropes.org***, ***US Department of State***, and ***Open Democracy***.

RELEVANT REALITIES_

"The whole concern of [Catholic] doctrine and its teaching must be directed to the love that never ends. Whether something is proposed for belief, for hope or for action, the love of our Lord must always be made ıccessible, so that anyone can see that all the works of perfect Christian irtue spring from love and have no other objective but to arrive at love." –*Roman Catechism, Preface*

A preparation for the final journey. If the sacrament of anointing of the ick is given to all who suffer from serious illness and infirmity, even more ightly is it given to those at the point of departing this life...The Anointing f the Sick completes our conformity to the death and Resurrection of hrist, just as Baptism began it. It completed the holy anointings that ark the whole Christian life: that of Baptism, which sealed the new life us, and that of Confirmation, which strengthened us for the combat of is life. This last anointing fortifies the end of our earthly life like a solid mpart for the final struggles before entering the Father's house." — *1523, ıtechism of the Catholic Church*

is lawful to kill an evildoer in so far as it is directed to the welfare of the ıole community, so that it belongs to him alone who has charge of the nmunity's welfare. Thus it belongs to a physician to cut off a decaying limb, when he has been entrusted with the care of the health of the whole body. Now the care of common good is entrusted to persons of rank having public authority: wherefore they alone, and not private individuals, can lawfully put evildoers to death." — *Saint Thomas Aquinas, Summa Theologica [II-II, Q-64, Art 3]*

CAST OF CHARACTERS_

ABSOLVERS

- Michael Thomas (aka "Andrew"): Priest, Former Police Officer
- Sergio Guzman (aka "Jude"): Priest, Former US Marine
- "Phillip": Priest
- "James Alpheus" (nicknamed "Alpha"): French Priest

CHURCH OFFICIALS AND AFFILIATES_

- His Holiness Pope Cornelius II: Theocratic Head of Holy See and Roman Catholic Church
- Manuel Medina: Monsignor in Bogotá, Columbia, chapel
- Eduardo Hernandez: Monsignor in Santa Fe, New Mexico, chapel
- "John": Spymaster and security forces trainer
- "Matthias": Priest
- "Matthew": Priest
- "James Zebedee" (nicknamed "Zeb"): Priest
- "John the Baptist" (called "The Baptist"): Priest
- "Bartholomew": Priest
- "Thomas": Priest
- "Simon the Zealot" (nicknamed "Z"): Priest
- "Big Country": Security forces trainer
- "The Mouse": Security forces trainer
- "Tex:" Security forces trainer
- "Jane:" Security forces trainer
- Damian Haggamore: Security forces trainer, (AKA "Double-Time")
- Bishop Harold Hoffaburr, Ph.D.: Assistant to Cardinal Dylan

- Cardinal Paul Dylan: Archbishop, Archdiocese of New York
- Father Bullard: Priest at St. Paul's Church, Odessa, Texas
- Father Levi De Vries: Priest at *Santi Michel e Magno*, Rome, Italy

THE REST OF GOD'S CHILDREN_

- Merci Renard: French medical doctor, aid worker
- Peggy Branam: Receptionist, Niobrara Sheriff's Office
- Francis "Frank" Thomas: Michael's father
- Mary Thomas: Michael's mother
- Jordan Miller: Subject of Investigation
- Pietro Isadore: Subject of Investigation
- Jesus Salinas Escobedo: Bogotá parishioner
- Catherine Bustamante: Michael's ex-girlfriend

ABOUT THE AUTHOR_

Gavin answered his call to service by working as a professional cop, spent many weekends and holidays in a cop car of one kind or another, and is honored to have protected and served the public in this manner. His training and experience in areas such as Patrol, Narcotics, Undercover Operations, Counterterrorism, Sex and Human Trafficking, S.W.A.T., and Dark Web Investigations provide an ever-growing queue of ideas and stories for his fact-based fiction. Gavin currently works on advanced academic degrees that he hopes improve the public good.

Gavin's rare free time is devoted to family, travel, martial arts, SCUBA diving, mountaineering, and pursuing the perfect ice cream. Never all in the same day.

A portion of all Gavin's sales is donated to crime victims, as well as charities that serve law enforcement professionals and veterans, their families and heirs, and honor the memory of our Fallen Heroes.

Follow Gavin at gavinreese.com

Made in the USA
Monee, IL
14 May 2023